ON THE RUN

COLIN McLAREN
ON THE RUN

On the Run is a work of fiction. No character has any bearing on any living person. Although, I did take divine inspiration from a few colourful souls I met in my career as a detective.

VICTORY BOOKS
An imprint of Melbourne University Publishing Limited
187 Grattan Street, Carlton, Victoria 3053, Australia
mup-info@unimelb.edu.au
www.mup.com.au

In association with X15 PTY LTD

First published 2009
Reprinted 2009
Text © Colin McLaren and X15 PTY LTD, 2009
Design and typography © Melbourne University Publishing Limited and
X15 PTY LTD, 2009

This book is copyright. Apart from any use permitted under the *Copyright Act 1968* and subsequent amendments, no part may be reproduced, stored in a retrieval system or transmitted by any means or process whatsoever without the prior written permission of the publisher.

Every attempt has been made to locate the copyright holders for material quoted in this book. Any person or organisation that may have been overlooked or misattributed may contact the publisher.

Text design by Phil Campbell
Typeset by Megan Ellis
Printed by Griffin Press, South Australia

National Library of Australia Cataloguing-in-Publication entry:
McLaren, Colin.

On the run / Colin McLaren.

9780522857030 (pbk.)

A823.4

Dedicated to the memory of the talented and once powerfully effective National Crime Authority and its many fine investigators, including Geoffrey Bowen. Their impact on 'nationally significant crime' left a lasting impression.

Many hope the more recently formed Australian Crime Commission, now the obvious adversary to Italian organised crime, can replicate the former glory of the NCA in tackling law enforcement's relentless foe, the *Mafiosi*, before the game is well and truly lost. Forever.

Prologue

A crack of lightning missed the pilot's cockpit by mere inches. Close enough to bounce the fourteen-seater Navajo Chieftain twin-propeller aircraft off course, tossing it contemptuously through the thick clouds. Ziggy gripped his controls as if he were throttling an assassin; he let go just long enough to tap the fuel gauge, reading zero. He held a long squint of his sleep-deprived eyes and gawked again: empty of fuel and still fifty kilometres to fly. And overloaded.

He flicked his head behind him to where all fourteen seats had been removed, turning a passenger aircraft into a cargo hold. Now crammed with hessian bags stuffed with marijuana Buddha sticks, a tonne of contraband worth millions. And somewhere among it all was buried the jewel in this planeload, a hundred kilos of pure cocaine, ripe for the nostrils of the rich and wannabe famous. Nice work if you can get it.

Riding shotgun were three nasty-looking heavyweights from the Calabrian Mafia, the N'Drangheta, and their weapons of choice, Browning 9mm semi-automatic pistols with enough clips and ammunition to tease a Taliban's smile.

Except for a fuel stop half-a-dozen hours earlier, the plane had been in the air for the better part of two days. Hopping over the humid Cape York Peninsula, skipping along the northern Queensland mosquito-coast and jumping each border all the way home to Griffith: the capital of the desert, the capital of drugs and HQ of the Australian Mafia.

Ziggy tapped again, sweating on a correction from his gauge. He must have miscalculated. He snapped a look at Cole in the only other seat on the plane, beside him. He too got the drift, looking at his watch, the fuel gauge and Ziggy's face. Worry and perspiration covered his face. If they landed safely, they'd be legends.

PROLOGUE

The weather was also slowing them down: a minestrone of unseasonable southerly winds, tropical rains, fat clouds and turbulence. How were they to know that, tough as they thought they were, Cole and Ziggy were new to this caper?

Nor were the goons in the back to know that they had been magnificently duped. The Australian Crime Authority was tracking their every move, until the lightning severed the satellite signal an hour earlier, sending the cops into a freefall of guesswork.

In ten minutes the three snoozing toughs in the back would wake to face the business end of the SOG swat machine guns and the start of half a lifetime in another confined space. Prison.

Ziggy dropped one hand from the controls to indicate downwards just as the aircraft wavered precariously, left and right. Time to descend on to the specially prepared landing strip five kilometres out of Griffith. The Godfather, Antonio, lay in wait with his army of whiskered soldiers, and a quarry of trucks, flashing their headlights, calling them home.

Like a 'welcome home' gesture, a fresh shard of lightning grazed the cabin. Followed by another, as Ziggy sliced through the pre-morning. The succession of jolts gave the Italians an early wake-up call; they were getting fidgety, reaching for their Brownings and peeping expectantly through the only gap in the otherwise blackened windows.

'Where we?' yelled the boss of the crew.

'Home!' yelled Cole, leaning his head into a fuselage full of body odour before raising five fingers. The reply failed to gain an acknowledgement as each of the Italians crawled over the minimal air space left, working their way across the contraband to the side exit door ready for the unload.

Ziggy's face was the clearest indication of his panic as the aircraft disappeared into a massive fluffy white cloud that seemed to stretch on forever, blinding him and his navigator. Apart from the rotten luck of the fuel level, Cole was developing a slice of guilts for getting Ziggy on board at the last minute. He'd been quick to raise his hand when the Mafia went looking for a dodgy pilot to help with their importation and here they were, seconds from falling out of the sky. Cole was sure he felt a spluttering cough of a starving engine. Certainly, one way or the other, he was honouring his promise to Antonio to get the drugs home.

Then the nose of the aircraft broke free of the cloud and exposed the twinkling lights of the town below and a smile from the strained face of the pilot. Ziggy snapped Cole one of his customary winks as he eased the craft down to take a line with two pairs of flashing ground lights ahead, one each side of the mulga track. Another run of coughs from the engine came just as the wheels hit the red dirt. They were home, rolling blissfully to a stop.

Ziggy slumped over the controls, breathed deeply and closed his tired eyes. His work was done. The propellers putted to a miserable stop.

'Open door,' came the guttural voice from the angry pack leader. Cole almost fell from the cockpit to comply with the demand but not before whistling up Ziggy's attention and giving him a well-earned thumbs up.

He then sprung the door of the fuselage to free his Mafia mates. Just as the swat team, under the cover of the last of darkness, crawled out of their fox holes and crab-marched across the scrappy terrain. Antonio and his army stood ready for the fast work of unloading. Once southern Italian peasants doing what they knew best: hard, fast yakka, no questions asked … and away.

Antonio strolled over to a stiff-bodied Cole, who was oozing anti-climax, and embraced him, shaking the hand of his great friend.

Then came the roars from behind: 'Police—freeze! Police—freeze!' and the rest was a blur.

The next year

Covert operative Cole Goodwin walked hesitantly into a tidal wave of faces at the Melbourne Supreme Court. Just the sort of thing he didn't need. A courtroom awash with journalists scratching words onto Spirax notepads, and a sea of detectives who had found a half-pressed suit for the day. Most of the gallery were family and friends of the accused, all of them Calabrese Italians. Most minus a suit, and none taking anything more than a mental note.

Each of the Italians Cole knew well, some of them too well. For two years he had eaten with them, sat in their homes and cuddled their kids. For two years he had negotiated and purchased pure cocaine, and truck-loads of marijuana, as well as conspiring to import tonnes of Buddha sticks from New Guinea. Now the game was up; his Italian friends were his enemies. They were all set for the big holiday to the big house.

The too-familiar discomfort of perspiration returned, trickling slowly down Cole's neck. His Armani tie felt like a noose. He squeezed his way through the oppressive stench, into the heat of a full house that defied the air-conditioning. Every seat was taken, except one, which Sandra had reserved for him. The chit-chat stopped as he stood at the end of the long aisle. Completely alone.

He looked for Sandra's mop of dyed blonde hair in a room of brunettes. Once spied, he headed her way, hoping for safety in numbers. He noticed Ziggy, now clean shaven and in his suit, standing against the back wall. He gave his customary wink and chewed his gum as if there were no tomorrow. They nodded a mate's gesture to each other.

Cole felt utterly naked as he shuffled in front of a dozen pairs of knees to get to his pew, watched intently by a dozen pairs of eyes from the duped, now sitting in the dock. The hatred in the air was palpable.

THE NEXT YEAR

His boss from the Anti-Mafia unit of the Australian Crime Authority, Inspector Mack, leant into Sandra and asked, 'What's that cunt doing here?' He paid no attention to Cole's uneasy smile and kept looking straight ahead. They never did like each other.

Sandra ignored Mack's question, and did her best to make sure that her mate was comfortably seated. Cole raised his head tentatively towards the Italian contingent in the public gallery and received three nodded hellos. He smiled momentarily, until a look of such bitterness and betrayal from Antonio had him reduced as low as a Sydney cockroach. Cole turned away to study the wall panelling.

Cole was relieved when the judge's gavel came thundering down, shifting the feast of eyes away from him, and onto business. He tried desperately to ease back into his hard chair.

After the usual legal niceties, the dockside Italians stood; the upper echelon of the Mafia in Australia, and not a smile among them. Cole swore he could hear a melodic drum roll rippling through the painful silence as he awaited their sentencing.

'Guilty, your Honour', 'Guilty, your Honour,' over and over, to a cacophony of angry murmurs in the gallery. A tear welled up on his bottom eyelid, whether from relief or regret, he wasn't sure. From the seat next to him, Sandra reached across and squeezed his knee. He slowly breathed out, a long and deep sigh. They were done, they were dusted. It was over.

The Anti-Mafia unit watched Antonio being dragged from the court, surrounded by a mass of high security. He'd be gone for half a lifetime, twenty years. As he disappeared from life as he had always known it, he flicked back to look at Cole, his face full of malevolence. Clearly, they were no longer great friends.

In no time Inspector Mack was striding commandingly towards the courtroom steps, straightening his tie, and attending his cowlick, as he prepared to face the media. Of course he was, there were brownie points ahead. As the remaining audience battled to clear the courtroom doors, Cole remained frozen to his seat until the anger faded, and the theatre eventually emptied. The tipstaff roused to reclaim his now empty workplace, and headed to the door with a bunch of keys. He stopped for a moment in front of the detective, who was now examining the pattern on the Axminster. He, too, was done.

'End of a long ride, son?' the tipstaff asked amiably. His voice held the soothing tone of a man well acquainted with the gamut of emotions to be found in his domain.

Cole looked up at the aged, yet perfectly attired gentleman in front of him, in his ivy green uniform with its gold buttons.

'You could say that,' he replied.

'But was it a great ride, son?'

'It was a ride, that's all. There was nothing great about it.'

At that moment, Leigh, one of Cole's trusted ACA team members, strode back into the courtroom. Suited up, carrying a shotgun and exuding loads of discipline.

'All clear, mate. Let's get you out of here,' he said, directing a weary Cole towards the non-public lift.

Saying his goodbye, the tipstaff found the right key to perform his last task of the day, locking the door behind them with a thunderous bang.

Downstairs in the basement, Leigh and Cole arrived at the court security muster room, tucked neatly away at the back of the judge's carpark. Leigh checked in his weapon with the uniformed cop, who looked all of twelve years of age. The eager young police officer unracked the shotgun and signed it back into the inventory.

'You can sneak out the laneway exit if you like. There's no media there,' offered the pimply-faced constable.

'Good on you, champer,' replied Leigh. He dropped his signature casually on to the inventory as the boy-cop stared long and hard at Cole.

'You're that undercover guy, aren't you?'

The question was ignored.

'Don't worry about that, champer,' said Leigh, who turned sharply and ushered a pensive Cole through the heavy security door, where they both disappeared onto a busy city footpath.

THE NEXT YEAR

• •

Cole's team in the Anti-Mafia unit had started life a few years earlier as a mere handful of detectives with two things each in common. First, they loved being detectives on the hunt, chasing the bad guys, the badder the better. Second, and probably more importantly, they were all mates. Cole might have been the team boss, but only because he was a detective sergeant. In his opinion, and in that of the other four crew members, they were always equal. That was the key to their success.

He had hand-picked each one of them when he was first assigned to the Anti-Mafia unit. The luxury of selecting his crew personally was a trade-off for working in such a pressure cooker environment. His first choice was Sandra, for her brilliance in gathering evidence. Then his old Homicide Squad mate Leigh, because of his unflinching loyalty and strong arm. Attributes he'd called on often. And, of course, there was Spud, mostly due to Cole's belief that he was the best analyst in the ACA. Last on the team was in fact Cole's real first choice, if the truth be known; Jude, due to her honours in the good-looks department. Cole was the first to admit he was a flawed individual.

If asked separately, each of the crew would give the same answer as to why they were so tight a team. They shared a table. At least once a fortnight they would sit in one of Melbourne's many restaurants, usually Japanese, often at the back table of the Osaka in Russell Street, over sushi and sashimi and a magnum of warm sake. But one day raw fish and rice wine was put on hold for a couple of years. Cole and Jude went undercover, posing as an art dealer and his pretty girlfriend, and infiltrated the Mafia.

Tonight's celebration, therefore, was not only about the gaoling of the worst Italians in the country, it was also a reunion. The team hadn't shared a hangover for a hell of a long time.

'So, what's the bottom line, team?' asked Cole, who sat as contentedly as that boy who pulled the plum out of the pie.

'Twenty gloriously long fuckin' years!' Sandra declared loudly, as the table erupted into laughter.

'I think I'll order another magnum,' said Spud, as he drained the last of the sake. The mood on the table was blissfully happy.

'Why, Spudly-duddly?' queried Sandra. She sneakily popped the last morsel of wasabi-infused tuna into her mouth, and squinted noticeably as the wasabi hit her brain.

'Coz I believe we're empty, Detective,' he retorted as the last drops fell from the bottle neck.

'God, you're accurate, for an analyst,' Leigh said as he inspected the now empty bottle.

'I got it right most of the time for the last few years, didn't I?' Spud replied solemnly.

'You did, buddy, every time, and I thank you. I'd never doubt your word. Cheers to Spudy,' said Cole.

The four tiny ceramic cups with their fragrant contents were lifted into the air and emptied simultaneously down four merry and well-fed gullets. Spud caught the eye of the ridiculously humble Japanese waitress and ordered another bottle as a tray of unagi-smoked eel was laid delicately onto the table.

'Mack wasn't too pleased to see you today, was he?' probed Sandra.

'Is he ever?' Cole asked in a matter-of-fact monotone.

'What is it with youse two, champer?'

'Come on, give. It's okay now, it's all over,' said Spud.

'Bloody nosy detectives. Alright, alright, anything to shut you up. I had an Asian informer once, a good solid contact—he reckoned Mack was bent. Claimed he found Mack's name and home phone number on a piece of paper clipped to an address book inside a house he burgled.'

'Home phone number? Whose house, champer?'

'His boss's.'

'No big deal. What sort of business was his boss in?' asked Spud as he chowed into some marinated kaiso seaweed.

THE NEXT YEAR

'He imported truck-loads of uncut heroin from China,' replied Cole.

'Jesus! What happened to his boss?'

'Found dead in a dumpster as a two-bit drug overdose.'

'And the informer?'

'He decided to run back home to Cambodia. Figured it was safer there than here in Australia.'

'So, who's got the piece of paper?'

Silence spread across the table and pairs of chopsticks froze in mid-air.

'I can answer that,' helped Sandra. 'Cole walked into Mack's office the day he started this taskforce and plonked it down on his desk. So it's ever since that day … that the boss has hated your guts? Why did I never put that together before? Some detective, eh?' Sandra smiled sheepishly at her colleagues.

'And you never worried about that over the last few years, champer?' said Leigh.

'Funnily enough, I didn't. It was all to do with Asians. Not Italians,' said Cole.

The restaurant was now almost empty. The ever-so-polite waitress, dressed in a brilliant red floral kimono, white socks and dainty satin embroidered slippers, shuffled elegantly to the front door. She fumbled through her enormous bunch of keys and locked the front door. Shuffling just as gracefully back to her reception counter, she smiled at her remaining, now quiet guests and busied herself at her till.

'What do you make of Antonio's look today, Cole?' said Leigh, negotiating the last of his sushi.

'Yeah I saw that too, that was fuckin' heavy,' chipped in Sandra.

'A look to kill,' said Spud.

'Hey, pull up, aren't you the accurate one?' said Leigh.

Cole fumbled for a piece of eel, dropping it unceremoniously in his lap. He abandoned his chopsticks altogether.

Spud's comments hung ominously over the table. Their night had ended.

ON THE RUN

• •

While camaraderie, hard work and great achievements were the attributes of this team of detectives, each of the crew, if they were to be honest about their success, would say that it all hinged on thorough investigation. There was no room for second guessing or presumptions. Just like there was no room for chasing rabbits down burrows. The Anti-Mafia unit went out of their way to confirm facts over and over along their investigative path. Spud was the driving force with his analytical brain, feeding information to a thirsty team. Despite their thoroughness, Cole knew that just sometimes a coincidence or hunch was worth listening to. As he sipped his warm sake and fuzzed up his tired brain, such a hunch was gnawing away at him. A hunch he couldn't share with anyone, at least not just yet. He needed a few more sleepless nights and sweaty sheets to work this one through.

• •

Three blocks away, an ageing, portly Italian waiter, wearing a pair of ten-dollar shoes, wash-and-wear slacks and an apron that hadn't seen a cleaner for a while, reached his grubby hand into his trouser pocket. As he got to the front door of the restaurant, he pulled out a set of keys and locked the door, at the same time throwing the security bolts at the top and bottom of the door frame. He turned off the lights, darkening the dining area on Lygon Street first and then killing the bulbs inside his restaurant. He walked towards the rear of the spaghetti bar, stopping halfway at the sight of a single gold dollar coin on the floor. He made quick work of the coin, dropping it safely into his pocket before disappearing into the kitchen. Tucked away in the back of the restaurant, at a table not visible from the street, was the subject of Cole Goodwin's hunch.

Inspector Mack was on his third short black. His face was jowled and he wore a heavy frown. He sat with the expression of a seriously

THE NEXT YEAR

troubled man, staring helplessly at the electronic organiser he had placed beside his coffee cup.

Opposite him sat the only other man in the restaurant. An Italian at least twenty years his senior, and who carried enormous weight in the Italian community as well as in his stretched dinner jacket. The old Godfather, Antonio's uncle, was sipping San Pellegrino mineral water and wrapping up their meeting. He spoke in hushed tones. Inspector Mack nodded obediently, as he had done for most of the night.

• •

Cole parked his car on the street under a magnificent oak tree that had probably been planted when East Melbourne was founded. He stepped out into the moonlight and looked at his poor work, two wheels up onto the gutter. He walked slowly across to his apartment block, pressing the door remote firmly as he glanced back at the flashing of the indicator lights. Two paces further on and he stopped dead in his tracks, listening to the sounds of silence. He was exhausted. His 37-year-old body felt twice that age; he yearned for a holiday on a beach, under a palm tree with a sand bucket and an umbrella drink. The bright city lights were straight ahead of him, at the end of his Victorian street. Possums had the run of the trees. He looked along both sides of the road, observing all the cars. Each one empty. None of the neighbours' lights were on; it was well after midnight. From where he stood, he could see down the side of his apartment complex, and the three levels up. The beautiful building was constructed in an era when security wasn't necessary.

He looked at the maze of plumbing and sewerage pipes leading vertically to his top-floor windows. He stood deep in thoughts best left for daylight hours. He studied the ease of breaking into his building, his car, his world. Fatigue and too much sake made him stop. He climbed the stairs to the top level and strolled down the hallway to the door at number thirteen. The sight of it made him stop again and realise just how vulnerable he really was. He opened the flimsy timber panel door with a single key, turned on a light in his superbly designed apartment and closed the door behind him, locking it tight for the night. Or at least as tight as a 70-year-old door could be locked.

17th April

Leigh pushed heavily on the front door of the Australian Crime Authority building, leaving his sweaty handprint on the logo. Facing him was a receptionist sitting pretty in her crisply pressed protective security uniform. Leigh pulled up his stride, pushed his sunglasses to the top of his head and turned to the security officer.

'My, my, you're new,' he said, presenting his very best cheery smile to cover his hangover.

'And you're old,' she said. He dropped the sunglasses to cover his weary eyes as he ferreted around in his pocket for his identification. The pretty security officer smiled at a now befuddled detective.

'I just meant you're new ... new. I haven't seen you before, champer,' he said presenting his ID.

'I'm surprised you can see anything through those glasses,' she replied before checking his identification against a list of authorised names. Her thick lead pencil scratched right through Leigh's name.

'So you've crossed me out, have you?'

'Well and truly, Detective. Good morning,' she said, hiding behind her smile. Leigh let out a sigh and turned to face the sterile corridor again.

At the end of the corridor, and up a flight of stairs, Leigh met another front door, this time without a pretty girl but with the latest security-code device. He keyed in his PIN and entered. The buzz of the noisy office staff hit him: a dozen or more detectives hard at it, reaching for telephones, arguing about cases, launching into their workday. A few of them acknowledged Leigh, stating the obvious about his hangover. He waved them away and moved towards the back of the office, home to his own team. Sandra was quietly pulling drawing pins out of police mugshots and an assortment of photographs pinned to a cork board. She carefully placed each photograph into a separate folder, matched to an information report, and stamped 'Confidential'.

'Packing up, sweetheart?'

'Trying to. How do we shove three years into cardboard boxes?'

'Who else is in?'

'Everyone.'

Sandra leaned over and pulled off a blown-up photograph of Cole and another of Jude. She stood looking at them. Leigh wandered over and looked at both photographs, as well as a few others of the couple arm in arm in restaurants and walking together in the gardens. Undercover photographs showing a loving couple: all part of their scam. At the height of the covert investigation the two operatives even became 'engaged', inviting their Mafia targets to the celebration to enhance their relationship with the Italian mobsters.

'They *were* the happy couple, weren't they?'

'They were. What a sting.'

'What a sting alright.'

'Suckered the Italians.'

'All the way to gaol,' offered Sandra. She hesitated, looking for a missing photograph. 'There's one missing, the one of Jude and Cole together at their engagement.'

'Maybe Jude souvenired it. Why didn't she join us last night?'

'Real boyfriend troubles.'

'Ah ... so he still thinks Jude and Cole are an item, eh?'

'Wouldn't you, if your gorgeous cop girlfriend went undercover with a hunk of a detective and spent her working hours living the high life?'

Leigh didn't bother answering. He dropped the photographs into a cardboard box and headed off in search of strong coffee. He took the long way around to sticky-beak at who might be in the Inspector's office. Two steps away from Mack's door and there was no need for second guesses.

'I've assessed the risk to you, Sergeant, and there isn't one. And that is the end of it.'

17TH APRIL

'You know damn well there's a risk. No one puts these bastards away without some comeback.'

Inspector Mack raised his voice, 'I'll authorise the purchase of a security door for your home in a week or so. That's all you'll get. The job's over.'

Mack's voice was loud enough for Leigh to hear as he walked past, attempting to merge with the corridor. Cole turned abruptly away from the Inspector and left the room, slamming the door behind him. The rest of the office ground to a halt.

By the time Leigh returned to Sandra's desk, coffee in hand, at least one box was full, and Cole was at his desk reading a movie magazine.

'So, I heard the result of your risk assessment,' said Leigh.

'Yeah, interesting. There is no risk,' Cole answered flatly, turning a page.

'Would you expect anything else? We're yesterday's news.'

For the next half hour, Leigh and Sandra worked quietly, filling the boxes, methodically deconstructing their work of the past years. Cole sat reading an article on how romantic movie star couples first met. Sandra peered over Cole's shoulder every now and again.

'Good girlie story?' she asked teasingly.

Cole looked up briefly, as if about to speak, then went back to one particular story.

'Sweet yarn. Read it some time,' he said finally. He left the magazine open at the article on top of the desk. 'I'll leave it out for you.'

The only other interruption to an otherwise uninspired morning's work came from Spud. He rushed in from the outer office with an armful of print-outs, his shiny forehead rosy with excitement. He clutched the papers tightly to his chest until he reached Sandra's desk, where he released them, leaving them to spew all over the cardboard cartons.

'What the fuck?' said Sandra as she stood with her hands now placed firmly on her heavy hips, blowing loose strands of wayward blonde hair from her face.

By now Spud was an expert at getting the crew's attention. He'd long known that detectives could be conveniently deaf when they wanted to be, and the surest way to gather their attention was to rush at them with an armload of papers and then dump them. Coupled of course with a compulsory look of urgency. The three investigators leaned towards the analyst.

'It's what you said last night.'

'What do you mean what I said last night?' said Cole.

'Mack's phone number on the Asian's sheet of paper,' whispered Spud.

'So?'

'Well, I snuck into work a few hours early this morning and put Mack's home and mobile phone numbers through my NATSCAN system. You know, the one that records the link of every phone number to every job ever done by the Anti-Mafia unit?'

'Cut the lecture and get on with it,' said Leigh.

'Well, Mack's mobile number got one hit,' Spud offered, his smile now stretching from ear to ear.

'To whom, may I ask?' Leigh's sarcasm was lost on Spud who was enjoying their growing interest, and drawing things out just that little bit longer.

'A hooker from Surry Hills in Sydney. Last week.'

'So what? He's having a root while at a conference in Sydney? Come on, Spud, is that all?' said Sandra.

'Maybe,' said Spud, 'but I did the background on the hooker. She works at Fluffy BeGood parlour in Paddington.'

Cole smiled as he looked at Leigh, who couldn't contain himself and burst into laughter. 'Come on, champer … Fluffy BeGood massage parlour, what a name!'

'Does it get any fatter than that?' said Sandra impatiently.

'I mean, who's going to walk into a parlour with that name?' said Leigh, still sniggering.

'Our boss, by the sounds of it,' said Sandra.

17TH APRIL

'Chill, guys. I'm serious. BeGood is owned by a shelf company with three directors, all square-heads.'

'And tell me it's going to get better,' added Sandra, as she began to search through some of Spud's print-outs.

'You're not chillin'.'

Spud dropped his voice just a fraction to deliver his *pièce de résistance*.

'One of the square-heads is also listed at ASIC as the sole director of the Griffith Regional Horticultural Supply company.'

By then Spud had their complete and undivided attention. At that very nanosecond they saw Inspector Mack walking down the corridor towards the kitchen with an empty coffee cup in one hand and his electronic organiser in the other.

'And I just finished a financial search. The horticultural company's biggest account is our now incarcerated leader of the Mafia, Antonio,' completed Spud. He looked as proud as punch as all eyes now focused on the arse end of Mack.

• •

The chef gently spooned the two orange roughie fillets onto the brilliant white china plates and added a Caribbean citrus salad with a sprig of fennel to top off his creation. He took half a step backwards to view his work and looked awfully pleased with himself. He quickly pulled the semi-soiled cloth from his waistband to wipe a minute smear from the lip of one of the plates. Once he turned away from the dish, a toey waiter took possession of the two plates and weaved his way into the restaurant, making a bee-line for a table of two against the massive glass window at the front.

Cole and Jude were seated with smirks on their faces as they shared a bottle of pinot grigio. Jude wore a fine black silk blouse with a plunging neckline that exposed her dainty lace bra. Cole took notice as he pulled the wine bottle from the ice bucket. Jude, catching his gaze, ran her fingers seductively along the line of her cleavage before correcting her blouse.

'You've seen it before.'

'But not a hell of a lot more, unfortunately,' Cole said, offering up a sad puppy look. They both giggled.

The waiter walked into their fun and placed a plate in front of each of his guests, then fussed enthusiastically over the salt and pepper shakers before leaving them.

'So how's the new team treating you?'

'It's okay,' offered Jude, her smile falling away.

'The change will be good.'

'You reckon ... I suppose we couldn't keep working together,' she said.

It had been a week since Jude asked to change crews. A last-ditch effort to try to sort out her private life, now that the undercover operation was over.

'So ... are you going to marry him?' Cole quizzed.

'I don't know.'

'I've heard that before.'

'He's so jealous,' said Jude as she emptied her first glass.

Cole splashed more wine into her glass and then his own.

'Maybe he has reason to be?' Cole offered optimistically as he looked above the bottle, now in mid-air, at Jude.

'You and I never really did anything,' countered Jude.

'Well ... not everything, but only because you're engaged, otherwise we ...'

'Maybe,' said Jude, cutting him off mid-sentence, the smile returning to her face.

They spent a minute glancing cautiously at each other as they pushed their expensive fish around their plates. Neither of them seemed to have an appetite any more. Something was troubling Jude.

'What is it? Is he giving you that much stick, the boyfriend?' said Cole.

17TH APRIL

Jude dropped her knife and fork and leaned on her elbows.

'It's not just him, Cole. It's a whole lot of stuff. I mean, I often wonder what could have happened with you and me.'

Cole reached for his wine.

'Maybe some things are best left hanging,' he said.

'Maybe.'

'Maybe again, Jude. Lots of maybes.'

'And that's my problem, Cole. Lots of maybes.'

The knife and fork got her attention again and she started to eat.

'Spud rang me an hour ago.'

'Bloody Spud. I can only imagine what he's told you.'

'He reckons Mack's bent, and Antonio will fix you up.'

'All Antonio will do for the next twenty years is count the days. Don't worry about him.'

'You are such an idiot, Cole. It's the fucking Mafia. And you screwed them over. They won't forget.'

'*We* screwed them over, remember?'

'Yeah, but I was just your handbag. You bought the drugs. You suckered in Antonio.'

Cole did his best to avoid the rest of the conversation. The waiter busied himself topping up their wines before he moved on to annoy the next table.

'What are you going to do, Cole? Your security's at risk.'

The question was met with silence.

'What are you going to do?'

Cole rinsed the fish from his mouth with pinot grigio, and swallowed.

'I have no fucking idea.'

• •

'Okay, Boss. I understand. But when are the next promotional exams?' Leigh asked Mack as they sat in the tearoom alone. Leigh was tracing circles on the table with his empty coffee cup.

'The sergeant's exams are twice a year. You know that, Detective. Have you done any preparation?' Mack asked, uninterested but stuck with yet another silly question from his subordinate. He only half listened as he flicked through a girlie magazine.

Leigh glanced over Mack's shoulder to the kitchen doorway where Sandra was standing, covertly watching, silently gesturing for Leigh to keep talking.

'So when do you think I should start studying? And could you give me some advice, Boss?'

As these ridiculous questions were being fired at Mack, Spud was hidden in the Inspector's office nervously holding the electronic organiser and keying in possible code-names. 'Dorothy'. Instantly the code-name was rejected. He tried another, 'Collingwood', the boss's football team. No. He placed the organiser back on the desktop and snuck out into the main office area. On the way out he noticed a wad of paper sticking out from the inside pocket of the boss's sports jacket. Sandra walked past the office door and indicated for him to hurry up. He shooed her away. He pulled out a bundle of share certificates from the coat pocket. The top certificate he could read clearly. It was for the purchase of 2000 blue-chip shares in the buyer's name of Wall Street Lady. He quickly returned the papers to the inside pocket, patted down the jacket and stepped from the room.

Only three paces from the office door he was met head on by Inspector Mack, who was on the run from Leigh.

'For Christ's sake, Leigh, if you want to do the bloody promotion exams, just do them. Stop bothering me with these inane questions!'

Mack frowned at Spud, then at his office door, then at Leigh, failing to join the dots. Spud kept walking, heading directly for Sandra's desk. Leigh executed the perfect U-turn and followed behind.

'Yes? No?' asked Sandra expectantly, with both hands working nervously through her mop of hair.

'No,' answered Spud.

The three of them sat in silence, deep in thought.

'How many codes have you tried?' asked Leigh.

'Too many. I'm sick of waiting for him to go to the dunny. I'm sick of his coffee breaks, and I'm sick of your promotion aspirations, Leigh.'

'What could it be?' said Sandra.

'If he really is corrupt, what would a corrupt copper use for a code?' said Spud.

'Especially a cop as warped as Mack,' said Leigh. 'He's odd.'

Spud looked at them. 'I've got an idea. Last chance. Give me one more chance.'

• •

Three hours later Cole parked his squad car in the underground car-park of the ACA building. Jude was in the passenger seat; both were seemingly unable to open the car doors. Cole leaned over to her. He ran his fingers softly over Jude's cheek, then down her neck and across her chest. She let her head drop onto the back of her seat. His fingers disappeared further into her blouse. She closed her eyes and enjoyed the feel of his touch. Quite suddenly, she grabbed his wrist and pulled his hand from her blouse and looked solemnly at him. She buttoned up two of her wayward buttons, leant into Cole and deliberately straightened a few errant whiskers of his large moustache before getting out of the car, and walking purposefully to the lift area.

• •

Cole headed for the stairwell entrance, his usual method of entering the office to avoid the gossip of coming and going with Jude. It was then that he spied Leigh loitering at the fire door to the staircase. There was the sound of a fire engine in the distance. Nothing too unusual there, he thought. What was unusual was what Leigh did next. With the handle of a screwdriver, Leigh quickly and very purposefully smashed the protective glass cover of the fire alarm, and depressed the red fire button. He turned to find Cole watching.

'What the fuck are you doing?' asked Cole, bemused.

'Don't ask. Just follow me.'

The two of them sprinted up the first flight of stairs to the office. Cole grabbed hold of Leigh and said, 'Is there a fire?'

Leigh whispered, 'Just pretend there is and shut up. I've done the three alarms.'

When the door swung open, a wave of staff carrying boxes gushed out.

'Get out,' they said. 'Get out!'

Cole could see smoke oozing from the gap underneath the door of the stationery vault. The sirens were now so loud that it was obvious the brigade had arrived.

Spud was moving quickly, heading straight for the front door, yelling, at every opportunity, 'Get out! There's a fire!'

'Fuck, Spud, give us a hand to grab our boxes,' said Cole as he watched more smoke pour from under the doorway.

All Spud would offer was a 'Shhhh ... don't worry about it,' before he once again yelled, as loudly as he could, 'Fire, quick, get out!'

In no time, the only people left standing in the now sealed office were Spud, Cole and Leigh.

'This better be good,' said Cole.

'Come downstairs with me. Sandra's got the boss down there dealing with the fire brigade. You'll know more later. Just play along.'

Cole reluctantly followed Leigh, leaving Spud alone in a room that was slowly filling with smoke.

• •

17TH APRIL

Spud sprinted into Mack's office and grabbed the organiser, just as he heard the automatic fire-alarm locks snap into place on the security door. He had the luxury of at least five minutes with the Inspector's organiser before the fire-fighters unsealed the door.

He moved quickly with his prize into his own room and a tangle of pre-arranged infra-red jacks and leads hooked up to his laptop computer. Fingers trembling, Spud turned on the organiser. He knew the password was up to twelve digits. He also knew he only had three attempts. Get them wrong, and the organiser would automatically shut off for two hours. Game over.

He had come up with three possible passwords. He went for the easiest first, G-E-C-K-O. Rejected.

Two minutes left.

He went for the harder of his options as the fire brigade officers could be heard forcing their way through a sealed door in the next office. Very quickly he keyed G-R-E-E-D-I-S-G-O-O-D and hit enter.

The menu flashed up.

A screen welcomed him on board. Spud fell back into his chair, almost shocked that he had broken the code. He stared at the illuminated face of the organiser and scrolled down the index, selecting the telephone listings. With the touch of four keys on his laptop keyboard, he set up the command for the spy-ware to beam the telephone database to his computer. His eyes locked onto his wrist watch, knowing the clever technology came at a cost. About thirty seconds. And each second was a tick.

He heard the slow heavy jogging of a group of fire-fighters moving along the outside corridor towards the Anti-Mafia cell security door. Nervously he blew air across the face of his watch, as if to push the second hand faster, until the laptop screen flickered a faint blue colour and formed the words 'task completed'.

Spud pulled the jack from the organiser and ran with it towards Mack's office, turning it off before crashing his shoulder against the door jamb. Miraculously, the organiser landed squarely face up on Mack's desk.

Spud heard the automatic locks retreat from the security door. He threw himself in a passable attempt at a stunt roll across the front of the stationery vault door and lay motionless.

Seconds later, four burly firemen bounded through the office. One stopped immediately in front of Spud and yelled, 'We've got the fire, and one's down. Get an ambulance.'

18th April

Any excuse for a BBQ was the culture in most police environments. Yesterday's fire at the ACA office, although nothing more than a smoke screen, was a good enough excuse for a mid-week soccer game. After all, the office had to be vacated for the day to allow the carpenters and fire-alarm contractors to make good the security doors and to reset the alarms, as well as the health and safety inspector to satisfy himself that the office was adequately clear of the toxic fumes.

The sausages sizzled and wine corks were pulled at the park immediately opposite headquarters. The office had been divided into two teams, Australia versus the rest of the world, six a side. The other fifty or so staff watched, sipping cheap Beaujolais, eating snags and dribbling tomato sauce down their forearms. Inspector Mack sat proudly at the front of the festivities, just far enough away from the rest of the squad. Alongside in a matching garden deckchair sat his pretentious and rarely seen new wife Dorothy, who was the focus of many curious eyes. Dorothy had elegantly draped their own private card table with a white linen cloth to host the lavish picnic basket she had stuffed with chicken legs, lobster claws and a Caesar salad. Topped off with two chilled champagne flutes to which she added a fine drop of Pomeroy. Mack lowered his glass temporarily to blow the starter's whistle. The players jogged onto the field to a hearty round of applause and a few catcalls. Dorothy gently squeezed Mack's arm as he sat down, congratulating him on the well-organised event. Half-a-dozen players dressed in the national green and gold colours took to the field, looking fearfully fit and dangerously threatening. They urged the rest of the world onto the muddy turf.

From behind a fat oak tree, where he had hastily pulled on his soccer shorts to the audible delight of the younger office girls, came a prancing Leigh, Brazilian colours proudly displayed. His arms raised in presumption of victory, announcing over and over, 'Pele, Pele, Pele, Pele!' At each call of his name the bystanders prefaced his cheer with the word 'banana', much to Leigh's disgust. Katherine, the office administrator, was next on the field, wearing the all black uniform of New Zealand, and was clearly interested in keeping up with Leigh's cheekily short shorts. Closely following in his hometown Maltese colours was Spud, dribbling the ball professionally between left and right feet before head-butting it across to Leigh. He was targeting his antics towards the pretty security officer, who seemed more occupied chatting to a younger, tall investigator next to her.

The next round of applause welcomed the Italian pair of the team, Jude and Cole. Both forced, due to recent circumstances, to dress in matching azure Italian colours. The crowd announced a raucous chorus of 'Mafia, Mafia!' The loudest cheer of all was reserved for Sandra, the captain, dressed top to bottom in the colours of the Union Jack. She bounded onto the field calling her team-mates to a pre-game huddle. Mack's second whistle blew and the ball was thrown into the centre as both teams collided in an afternoon of hilarity, poor athleticism and good high jinks.

Across the park, sitting in a car hidden among dozens of other cars, was an unmarked drug unit vehicle. The autumn sunshine silvered the windscreen. Sitting alone behind the steering wheel was the infamous Donny Benjamin, a suspected corrupt investigator, famed for running his own race and his own scams. He turned the ignition and placed the gear in drive, taking one last look into the park. His glance ignored everybody except Cole.

19th April

No need for sunglasses this morning. Leigh was feeling fighting fit, spurred on by his victorious effort of three goals the day before. Before he got to the glass panel reception desk, he checked himself, sucking in the two spare kilos above his belt, and straightening his otherwise firm body. He plastered a dazzling smile across his face, just in time to confront the pretty security officer. The smile instantly dropped away and his belly with it, as he stared hopelessly at the massively built, oily skinned Tongan female who had crammed her vast womanhood into the uniform a few hours earlier and was now squeezed behind the desk. He went through the motions of proving his identity before ascending the stairs and coding himself into the Anti-Mafia unit, shaking his head all the way.

The office wasn't its usual hive of activity this morning—too many ankle injuries being nursed. Most were happy just to sit around and relive plays of the soccer match or talk about the strange fire. Everyone wondered how a wastepaper basket full of cigarette butts found its way into the stationery vault. Or how the wastepaper basket had burst into a ball of flames. But the most intriguing question of the morning was whose stationery vault key was broken and stuck inside the lock, making it impossible to open the door when the fire started. Most of the detectives couldn't give a rat's arse whose or how, preferring the dramatic end to the day.

If everyone was happy about one thing, it was the fact that the fire brigade didn't have to spray their mega tonnes of water everywhere, as once the stationery door had been prised open, all that was left was a smouldering dustbin full of ashes, which included the now burnt receipt for the spare key cut by Spud earlier in the day.

Passing Leigh and on his way out of the office was Inspector Mack, who looked perplexed. He carried his electronic organiser in hand.

'I'll be back in a couple of hours, Leigh. How's that study going?'

'Yeah, yeah, good, Boss, and good again,' Leigh returned as he took his usual chair among his team-mates.

The first thing Leigh noticed was the quiet. Not even a 'Good morning' and definitely no mention of the shenanigans of the day before. Spud was tapping away on his laptop, Cole sat alone, still reading his film magazine, and Sandra was taping up the now full cartons. She peered over Cole's shoulder every now and again at the article he was reading.

'What's got you fascinated, Cole, same story as before?'

'You can read it after Sandra, Leigh. It's a sweet yarn,' Cole repeated as he placed the magazine, folded back to his favourite article, in the top drawer of his desk.

'Help yourself, Sandra,' he said. She nodded politely, continuing her packing.

Suddenly, Spud jumped up and down excitedly, impatiently waving everyone over to him. Mack's phone numbers had been fed into Spud's system and he had a hit. Four pairs of wide eyes were soon staring at an illuminated screen. Spud pointed to a set of telephone numbers. When they remained none the wiser, he singled out one particular number, and more importantly, the subscriber's name. Giovanni Carbone.

'I know that name,' said Leigh.

All too well, in fact, better than his own uncle, or even his own brother. It was the name that was on the very top of their target list during their investigation into the Mafia of the past few years, the name of the only suspect who had escaped prosecution because of his old age. The old Godfather, Antonio's uncle. And now, it was irrefutably linked to another name he knew well: Inspector Mack. Thanks to the clever work of a smart analyst, a Mr Minit key-cutting kiosk, and five minutes of a fire captain's time.

• •

19TH APRIL

Sandra was running horribly late for a meeting that she had instigated. She jogged up the four steps and into the bar. It was 6 p.m., and she pulled her beige tweed coat in tighter around her. Standing at the side of the bar in a quiet corner were her three colleagues: Cole with a whisky sour, Leigh and Spud enjoying their boutique beers. Sandra's long Bombay Sapphire and tonic sat waiting on the polished jarrah bench top, the ice slowly melting. She grabbed the glass.

Spud was finishing a story. 'Wall Street Lady was registered in his wife Dorothy's maiden name, since its inception, two years ago.'

'What value is her share holding?' queried Sandra, slurping her drink.

'Two hundred and seventy-three thousand dollars so far.'

'Not a bad bit of lovely,' said Leigh, using the crooks' slang for money. 'Why don't we tip off the Toeys and get her twisted?'

'And have us all looking over our shoulders for the next ten years?' Cole said, knowing only too well that the internal investigations unit, known as the Toe Cutters, had more leaks than a colander. Cole's world of cops was familiar with the fraternity that existed between high-ranking officers. How they stuck together with their dirty scams, occasionally tossing a sacrificial lamb to the slaughter to appease the media: usually a low-level rookie who'd fucked up. Just enough to keep the threat of a royal commission from the door. Meanwhile the more senior cops, the hierarchy, got away with their fun and games.

'A wife with shares, so ... what are we going to do?' Sandra asked.

'His wife owns a trendy café. They can easily explain the cash to buy shares,' said Cole.

'What if the amount of share purchases was twice that?' Sandra asked.

'Sure ... that's serious lovely for a cop ... but not his wife,' Cole pointed out.

'What can we do, champer?'

'What *have* we done?' chipped in Spud.

Everybody turned to Spud, who realised he was now the centre of attention. His wiry hair started to stand on end, his bald forehead glowed with heat.

'What do you mean, Spud? What have you done?' enquired a worried Leigh.

'Well, we can't just sit around holding our dicks waiting for someone to have a go at Cole or Jude,' said Spud.

'Surely nothing will happen to Jude; she didn't carry the drugs. Only Cole,' replied Leigh. 'So what have you done?'

'I've put the boss's mobile phone off,' Spud answered, stepping back from the other three, as if waiting for trouble.

Sandra reeled back at him before raising her glass, discarding the straw, sculling the remaining contents and slamming it down hard onto the bar.

'You are a dickhead!' she said in a raised voice, enough to grab the barman's attention, of which she made good use by ordering another round of drinks. Leigh broke out in a loud belly laugh, seeing the absurdity of the situation: bugging the boss's phone.

'You need a search warrant, stupid. How did you get that?' asked Cole.

'I didn't. As from today the boss's mobile is off for one week. I've got a mate in the phone-tap unit who's on night shift for seven nights. He's going to monitor it ... covertly.'

The barman interrupted the conversation with a fresh whisky sour, two more Grolsch beers and another tall G&T. Cole's brain ticked away, trying to find a problem with tapping the boss's phone.

'Night shift ... one week,' he echoed, thinking to himself.

'Yep, perfect, isn't it,' Spud said almost bragging.

'What's the bottom line?' Cole asked.

'No one will know,' repeated Spud.

'Anything that can be tracked back to an illegal phone tap?' asked Cole.

'No way, Jose. He'll just have his head phones on and listen and scribble a note for us if anything is dirty.'

The three investigators nodded. It all sounded very simple despite the illegality. They stared at Cole in silence, waiting for their sergeant's

19TH APRIL

acquiescence. It was as if Cole was scanning his brain, reliving every day of the past few years undercover, negotiating drugs, telling lies, ingratiating himself into the Mafia. He realised that his glass was empty, as was his tolerance for a boss he had long suspected of being corrupt. He also realised that if he allowed the illegal phone tap, he was not only breaking the law, he was also crossing the line in a brotherhood of cops that never sold out another.

'Fuck him. Let's bug the prick!'

He placed his hand on the bar top, fingers splayed, something that he had done many times with his crew. Leigh's hand reached over the top of his, as did Spud's and finally Sandra's.

Cole yelled to the barman, 'Another round of drinks, mate!'

• •

It was close to midnight as Leigh drove along Banner Avenue, Griffith, looking for somewhere to idle. Alone, he showed signs of the six-hour drive. His spare hand slowly rubbed the whiskers on his chin. One of those actions men do when they feel weary, and one of those actions that always feels good. His hand moved up into the still well-groomed hair—his best asset, he thought, good hair. He hit the off button on the CD player and the car crept silently along the street, past a length of shops with darkened windows. Not much happened in the main street of Griffith after dark. The real action was inside the packing sheds, at the back of the vast orange groves surrounding the town. Scenes of late nights of wheeling and dealing, before semi-trailers rolled out, laden with hundreds of boxes of juicy fruit and sometimes a few dozen boxes of green vegetable matter that wasn't normally sold in greengrocers.

Leigh wasn't too worried about being alone in town, as his car was registered to a dodgy name. He'd get what he came for and head straight back to Melbourne, just in time to update the morning crew. Just in time to clock on, so the boss would have no idea he'd been, and returned.

He was a little different from most cops, preferring to fly solo. There was good reason for that. The success of his enquiries into criminal activities depended on the women he met and dealt with. Leigh was a ladies' man, an important asset to any team. As long as the detective kept his dick in his pants. And used his charm to gain information. Leigh did just that—most of the time. But he was happy with the way he played the game. Some of his best bed companions had been cute podium dancers, tough barmaids or the occasional good-looking crook's moll. The types who had tired of the ways of their criminal beaus, preferring to sample the grass on the other side of the law enforcement paddock.

His car pulled up a few doors down from the Café Azzurra, a little restaurant owned by Antonio, a place where Cole and Jude had often met and eaten with the Mafia during their infiltration. It was also the workplace of Penny, Antonio's one-time bit-on-the-side, who broke down and took to crying on Leigh's shoulder when the Italians were busted.

He called up Penny's number, then hit 'dial'.

'Hey there, gorgeous, how long before you have five minutes for me?'

He received an answer that settled him into his driver's seat for a spell, and he reached for a cigarette. As he sucked in the deadly fumes he stared at the windows of the upstairs restaurant, long enough to end the relationship with his gasper. A frumpy middle-aged woman, rugged up in a thick woollen overcoat, walked from the building. She strolled off in the opposite direction to a small, sad-looking car, got in and drove off along Banner Avenue.

Less than five minutes later, the lights went out at the restaurant and Penny, a vivacious 25-year-old one-time local beauty queen, locked the front door. Despite a ten-hour shift she still looked immaculate in her white fitted waitress shirt, hipster black slacks and black shoes. She had made an effort in the past few minutes to refresh her make-up and sweep her long brunette hair into a neat ponytail. Once she pulled the keys from the door lock she jogged across the street, throwing a sleek black fur-lined parka over her shoulders as she ran. She looked cautiously up and down the roadway, seeing the town was as deserted as a state school on Christmas Day.

She opened the passenger door and got in. She gave Leigh a friendly kiss on his cheek.

'Hello, gorgeous. You know you can cease with the granny kisses and focus on a wet one whenever you want.'

'Hey, my life's complicated enough, Leigh. Besides, it's a long way to drive, just for a quickie,' she said, tongue in cheek and turning the heater up.

'What if I told you I was secretly of Italian ancestry?'

'Then I'd be convinced you are just a no-good liar.'

'You really are gorgeous, you know.'

'Just a sweet little country girl, Leigh, doin' the best I can.'

A police patrol car turned into the street, cruising at a snail's pace. This gave Leigh the perfect opportunity to lean closely into Penny, who responded with an embrace and a kiss, which held long enough for the patrol car to decide there was no value in interrupting two lovers on such a cold night. When she deemed the police were far enough away, Penny pulled away.

'It's the talk of the town, the gaol sentences,' she said, fingers to lips.

'Sorry, gorgeous.'

Penny shrugged, knowing that twelve sons of Griffith got mostly what they deserved. She paused, as if having trouble finding a starting point.

'There's been anger in town, Leigh.'

'Go on.'

Penny dropped her pretty face into her hands and held the pose for a minute.

'Something's not right. The old boy was at his usual table tonight with other trusted oldies and I heard some stuff.'

'Just do it slowly, babe ... tell me what you remember.'

'They were talking mostly Italian but I could work out he had paid some guy in Melbourne to make it all go away. To make someone go away—I couldn't work it out—but he's got a punk coming in from Calabria in a few days. He's going to make someone go away. And there was something said about 200 000.' Penny stopped there, locked in thought, trying to recall the sequence. 'Yeah, Leigh, 200 000 was said. That must be dollars, yeah?'

Leigh listened to the brave and misguided girl as she told her tale. She repeated herself over and over as witnesses tended to do. Then, once all the details had been vented he enjoyed another granny kiss before it was time to start his engine again. Penny zipped her parka snugly over her lithe body and pulled up the fur-lined hood, tucking some stray hair behind her ears. She quickly jogged down the empty street.

Leigh watched her disappear around the corner, then put the car in gear and headed home, rubbing his spare hand across his whiskers once more, before hitting the on switch to his CD player.

• •

It was a little like a passing parade into the office, with Sandra following Cole, behind Jude, then Spud, who led the way. The four had caught up for an early breakfast around the corner. As soon as they approached their desks, Jude branched off to her newly assigned crew on the other side of the unit. As she walked off, she looked back at Cole a couple of times, poking out her tongue and almost bumping into a neighbouring desk.

Leigh lay sleeping on the floor between two desks, snoring his head off and every now and then making a lip-smacking noise. Sandra playfully flicked a few droplets of water onto his face, causing him to stir madly, thrashing his arms about, until he realised where he was.

Cole offered him a coffee. Leigh kept his voice hushed, and urgent. 'We've got work ahead of us, guys. A Calabrian punk's coming to town.'

24th April

Sandra charged along the international arrivals concourse at Tullamarine Airport. Trailing behind was Leigh, mobile phone glued to his ear. They hadn't counted on so many excited Italian families waiting to greet long-lost relatives. With all the skill of a bull in a china shop, Sandra forged her way through the hordes. At the customs security door, a flash of their ACA identification gained them entry to the sealed customs investigation area. Sandra took a few deep breaths as Leigh finished his call.

'It landed ten minutes ago,' gasped Sandra.

'Slow down, sweetheart, we're here. The rest is up to Spud.'

'And us,' Sandra snapped. 'We've no fucking idea who this punk from Calabria is.'

'No, but we've worked out a short list. It could only be one of four on this jumbo jet.'

Sandra and Leigh were hidden behind the two-way glass in the customs security area, able to watch unobserved. Passengers queued at the immigration desk.

'Is Cole coming?' asked Leigh.

'No. Didn't want to be seen. We'll show him photos of the dude later.'

The customs shift supervisor swaggered confidently across to Sandra, coffee cup in one hand, the other running through the gelled hair of his tired head.

'Here they come,' he said as he took a gulp of his long black, his fourth for the day.

'Can I get you both a coffee?'

'Two cappuccinos,' suggested Leigh.

'It's Nescafé black, or it's Nescafé white.'

'Pass.'

'How many have we got?' queried Sandra.

'A near-full flight, 367 and ten mortadella.'

'What—no salami?' said Leigh.

'The route?' asked Sandra.

'Milano to Hong Kong, Hong Kong to Melbourne.'

'Emirates Air advises there's only four possible males who joined the flight in Milano from Calabria or Sicily. We haven't got any ages though,' added the customs officer, 'but you've got to get lucky with one of them, surely?'

'What if he joined the flight in Hong Kong?' asked Leigh.

'No one knows he's coming into the country, so why would he go to the trouble with all that shifty stuff before he even gets here?' asked the customs officer. 'My staff are watching the stampede and will direct any lone males into your aisle.'

'Good luck, champer.'

'Don't need luck, mate, we do this all fucking day long.'

• •

Spud sat proudly in his customs booth trying to look efficient in his pale blue uniform complete with epaulettes and a pocket full of pens. One after the other, mostly Italian passengers stood to semi-attention in front of him with their schmoozing smiles. A few with a mouthful of gold teeth to complete the look. All of them overtired and in need of a bed.

The first was a university professor travelling alone. Spud gave him an Italian *'Benvenuto'* greeting and stamped him through immediately. A little further along the queue came another lone male, an ageing, very rotund doctor from Costanza in Calabria. Hardly a 'punk', Spud thought, as he quietly stamped his passport and waved him through. Ten passengers on and his arm started to get weary. The customs guys ushered the lone males towards Spud, in between grumpy couples and noisy kids. He faced his third lone male, a

20-year-old Calabrian with iPod earphones and far too much wiggle-jiggle and high-fiving to be seriously considered any threat to the ACA. Or anyone.

Right at the back of the queue, and watching cautiously, was his fourth lone male. Just the sight of him was enough for Spud to want to bet a month's wages on the outcome. He plonked his passport on the desk, a 32-year-old 'farmer' from Plati, the centre of organised crime in southern Italy. Spud knew well this N'Drangheta stronghold in Calabria, a village in the foothills of the remote Aspromonte Mountains, home to hundreds of hidden caves where unfortunate kidnap victims were stashed, awaiting a ransom.

His well-travelled Italian passport revealed far too many visits to Amsterdam, Frankfurt and New York for Spud's liking. No doubt documenting the career history of a very busy Mafia lieutenant.

Spud looked up at the security camera and then back at the passport.

'You are a tourist, sir? Welcome to Australia.'
'*Non parlo Inglese, Signore.*'
'You enjoy travelling, I see.'
'*Scusa, Signore. Non parlo Inglese.*'

The stony-faced 'farmer from Plati' with the physique of a welterweight boxer pulled a brilliant demonstration of a foreign traveller unable to communicate on any official level. Spud took an instant shine to him. He scanned the passport and brought down his stamp.

'I think you'll enjoy Australia, *Signore* Massimo Cattiloco.'

In less time that it took to stow his passport in his back pocket, Spud's hard-nosed Italian suspect had headed off to the baggage claim carousel.

• •

Massimo carried his cheap and well-travelled powder-blue suitcase out into the arrivals lounge. He faced a flood of tearful faces, and moved confidently through the crowd, making a bee-line for the taxi rank. In the queue ahead of him was a heavy-set woman with a mop of dyed blonde hair, a beige tweed coat and a fake Prada overnight bag. Sandra had him covered. All she needed to do was press the call button on her mobile phone, and that would alert the others as to which cab to follow. When Sandra found herself two spots away from a cab door, she quit the line as if she had forgotten something, clicking her fingers and mouthing an annoyed *Fuck* as she stormed off.

Before too long Massimo was in the back of a taxi on his way to the city. Sandra immediately transmitted the rego to Leigh, who was waiting patiently near the freeway entrance.

• •

Half an hour later the taxi was held up at a set of red lights at Flinders Street—peak hour on Friday night. Horns blazed incessantly, a cacophony familiar to any Italian moving through traffic. It seemed to worry the taxi driver more than the passenger.

'Sorry, mate, for slowing you down. There's not long to go.'
'Okay, driver. It's okay.'
'You must be buggered, mate, all the way from Italy.'
'Very tired.'
'You speak good English, mate.'
'Sometimes.'

Within five minutes the taxi was opposite the famed Flinders Street Railway Station. Massimo looked across and up at nine antiquated clock faces over the main entrance, and then down at the crumpled piece of paper in his hand bearing the words, 'Flinders Street *Stazione alle diciotto*'. The main clock, the one that told the actual time, told Massimo he had fifteen minutes to find an Australian version of an Italian espresso before his 6 p.m. rendezvous. He converted the note into a small handful of confetti and let it fall to the floor of the cab. Fumbling through his pocket he came up with a

24TH APRIL

lone hundred dollar note and handed it to the driver as he alighted, opening the door to another chorus of car horns. The taxi crawled forward with the driver now sporting a very pleased look on his face as he tucked the note into his shirt pocket.

Four cars behind Leigh sat in his hire car, mirrored shades and American baseball cap. His keen eye was fixed on Massimo, who was expertly playing the casual tourist as he walked towards the Station. Leigh parked the car in an empty space on the street, and quickly scampered across the road to follow Massimo. As he did, something made him look back at his vehicle, probably the 'Clearway' sign prominently displayed at the nose of his bonnet. He walked on.

For the next fifteen minutes Leigh dogged his target, as they wandered through the busy railway station from platform to platform. He hadn't had so much fun since he was in the surveillance unit years earlier. Up flights of stairs, between news stands and coffee shops. Leigh whispered to himself, 'Come on, Hades, prince of the underworld, you can do better than that.'

He couldn't help but break into a smile at one café where Massimo ordered a short macchiato. To see what was actually presented—a near-full glass of murky brown dishwater, posing as coffee, with a touch of milk. That was the only time Leigh saw a reaction from the Calabrian. Mr Cool-as-a-Cucumber pushed the coffee away, flicked his right hand under his chin to mouth '*Non mi piace*' before moving away from the kiosk and down onto Flinders Street again. The most intriguing observation of this insignificant exchange was that Massimo walked calmly away without even paying for the drink. A very confident man, thought Leigh.

The Calabrian's timing was perfect. Once he stepped onto the street, a late-model white Holden Statesman came seemingly out of nowhere. Despite the hubbub of traffic and pedestrians the Statesman stopped right in front of Massimo. Leigh's target, running strictly to rule, didn't look left, right or behind. He simply opened the rear passenger door and threw himself and his suitcase onto the seat. Leigh stood in the crowd watching the vehicle pull away, before his attention was diverted to the opposite side of the roadway, where his hire car also pulled away, chained to the rear of a tow truck.

• •

Inspector Mack stood alone at his office window, looking down on the crowded street below. His face held the unmistakable look of worry. For ten minutes he had been gnawing at his small fingernail, biting it dangerously close to the quick as he thought his secrets through.

He decided on a walk around the office instead. It was amazing what sort of information could be gleaned moving from desk to desk, from crew to crew, immersing himself in the fascinating reading contained in the various investigative files perched on each detective's desk. He thought no one knew, in fact he was almost certain no one suspected, that every now and again, late at night, he would code himself into the deserted office. And make delicious work of the photocopying machine. Under the guise of legitimate business, he duplicated information reports and secret memos contained in the files left behind on desks. The desks of his hard-working honest detectives.

The garden shed in his cupcake-pretty house in well-to-do Malvern was home to his Sidchrome toolbox, tucked neatly away among the pesticides and snail bait. The perfect place to stash confidential photocopied documents before his secret go-between could broker a buyer for the information. He'd done well these past few years, amassing a battler's fortune, squirrelled away in shares, cash buried among the azaleas and his secret apartment in southern France. A booty that no one knew about except Dorothy.

He had met and married Dorothy only half-a-dozen years ago, after he got his two now adult daughters and his chubby, dull ex-wife off his hands. The last years with the ex had been a difficult juggle, what with the affair with Dorothy, which he had kept quiet from

24TH APRIL

everyone. Not because it was an affair as such, but because she carried the surname of 'Wakelin', a family of bad-arse bank robbers. He had met his little dove on a 5 a.m. police raid. There she'd been, sitting pretty in a bed not nearly grand enough for her, he thought. Wearing nothing more than a cheeky smile. Her gangster husband had fled moments earlier with the lovely, leaving Dorothy to face the music. The rotter never came back home. Neither did the money Mack was chasing.

It was love at first sight for Mack and Dorothy, so he rented her an apartment two streets away from the family home till he could erase his past. Eventually they married in Paris, soon after his divorce. And the rest had been sexual bliss, at least until recent pressures had fallen heavily on him.

Dorothy was more disappointed than Mack at her husband's passing over as the new deputy commissioner three years earlier, and that drove her scorn.

Until this massive social blow, she often saw herself strolling along the roads of fashionable Malvern in her new life as the wife of a deputy commissioner, lunching with the girls, keeping hairdresser appointments in the finest salons and offering up the juiciest gossip to an envious ladies' tennis team.

If Inspector Mack were honest about his entrepreneurial activities of the past few years, he would probably say that his wife enjoyed the risk more than he. She was used to it. He recalled sadly the months after being passed over for high promotion, how depressed his wife had become, and how disheartened he had felt.

Then the dinner invitations had dropped off. As did the sex with Dorothy. That was when he began to suspect that she had strayed. But by then he was almost defeated, lost and completely uninterested in confronting her. Until the day petty greed graduated to outright corruption: when a go-between made an initial approach on behalf of a Romanian drug syndicate.

Donny Benjamin, a less-than-average detective on the drug unit, had his fingers in more pies than a Beechworth baker. He made the simple proposition after a dozen beers one night at the police club. For Mack to photocopy a confidential ACA report on the status of an investigation into Romanian drug dealers in Australia. In exchange for $50 000. An obscene amount of money, Mack thought, for ten minutes' work, and who would even care—everyone hated Romanian drug dealers.

It was a couple of minutes after 5 a.m. when he worked out that the $50 000 would mean $2000 per photocopied page of the 25-page report. It was the very difference, before tax, of the salary package between inspector and deputy commissioner. At that very moment he had his first erection in almost three months. The sensation he experienced at being a complete man again excited him beyond control. He tapped his sleeping wife on the shoulder. Midway through the most driven love-making session they had had for years, just before his orgasm, he stopped to tell the now breathless and elated Dorothy of his willingness to stand by the photocopy machine.

Like the pigeon pair they were always thought to be, Dorothy seized on the plan. The ker-ching of cash registers drowned out the hum of the sadness she had been carrying. Their love-making intensified, taking Mack to a place he hadn't been since he was a young constable. The days when, after emptying the pockets of junkies, Mack would come home late at night to his first wife to make excitable love till the wee hours of the morning. At last, he thought, he now had a second chance at love … and the lovely.

Inspector Mack had learnt much from his youthful days. He was known as a survivor, a very cautious individual, not tempted by silly half-baked scams. Each involvement with Donny was well thought out. Researched over and over to ensure that the risk level was as close to zero as possible.

It was almost time to start taking French lessons. He figured he was only one smart move away from cashing in his chips. One more clever, well-planned scam and he and his beloved Dorothy would be in Provence. The only problem was that the deal required the execution of an undercover cop.

24TH APRIL

Yet for $200 000, less 20 per cent for Donny's brokerage fee, the scam was tempting—tempting enough to give an old Godfather the nod, tempting enough to set a dangerous train in motion.

And Mack accepted the killing of this detective. It had taken him very little time to come to terms with, given who was to be bumped off.

Goodwin he had despised for too long, with his smart-arse ways, excessive achievement and his annoying little manner. Like the time he dropped a piece of paper with Mack's name and home phone number on his desk, and then, without a word, walked out of Mack's office, as if he had delivered some great and powerful message. Yes, he would be glad to see Cole Goodwin disappear.

Who the hell did Goodwin think he was, anyway? Inspector Mack thought. Who?

Mack also knew that there were others who would enjoy the end of Cole. The Calabrian faction of the Mafia, for instance, still reeling from the global embarrassment that came from being so magnificently stung. A clever bit of work by old Cole, he grudgingly admitted.

Cole's removal would solve two substantial problems: restore faith with Italy for the N'Drangheta arm in Australia and speed up his retirement aspirations.

The medieval village of Beaucaire was where his and Dorothy's apartment was located. Nestled above an attractive bistro sporting dainty wrought-iron tables and cane chairs and complete with sun-faded red-and-white candy-stripe awning—his and Dorothy's perfect daily luncheon location on their annual visit to Provence. Not a soul knew of the love nest. All his work colleagues, even his daughters and ex-wife believed that they were staying in a cheap and cheery two-star hotel. They didn't mind playing out the thrifty traveller story, whining about cheap airfares, tiny aircraft seats and shared meals in cafés to stay within the budget. The sort of stories that would appease work colleagues and put a stop to any rumour of an otherwise opulent lifestyle. They did, of course, suffer the economy airfares, but once they landed in Paris, out came the lovely, fistfuls of cash they would take on each trip to ensure a few nights at the Ritz before a very fast train to their gorgeous *pied-à-terre* in Beaucaire. Here Mack and Dorothy lovingly sanded and repainted their splendid French windows, potted geraniums and wisteria to drape their ornate twin balconies and basked in the view of the village as they fussed over a list of antiques to complete the furnishing. They relished their daily handy work, their preparation for early retirement, often to the sounds of Edith Piaf in the background. Such heavenly culture, they thought, until 2.30 each afternoon when they downed tools and washed up the paint brushes to enjoy the grandest long lunches downstairs. Complemented by choice bottles of Bordeaux and followed by playful love-making before a traditional European siesta.

Yes, they loved their second chance at life, and worked hard at keeping Dorothy's past in the past.

Just then Mack found himself standing next to Spud's small office. The door was locked. As he adjusted to the now, he felt certain of the taste of sour cherry lingering on his palate from the 1994 Chateau de Seguin Bordeaux Supérieur, but his annual holiday was still a few months away.

He was sure he could hear voices on the other side of the opaque glass panelling. Was that Spud's voice? He looked around to check that he was alone and pressed his ear to the wall.

• •

Cramped closely together around Spud's tiny desk sat Leigh, Cole, Sandra and Spud himself, chairing the meeting. The light was out and each of the participants whispered.

'He's a piece of work, this punk,' said Spud.

'What does your mate at the Anti-Mafia unit in Naples say in his report?'

'*Commissario* D'Alfonso is his name, Leigh. He's the "Liaison Agent" and a trusted associate.'

24TH APRIL

'What a magnificent name and title, champer.'

'Yeah, anyway, he reckons there's a history of kidnapping, suspected of being involved in murdering a judge, you name it.' Spud read from a confidential email received an hour earlier about Massimo Cattiloco.

'Where's the arse-wipe now?' asked Sandra.

'The Statesman took him straight to Griffith two days ago, and he's holed up at the old boy's house,' said Spud.

'Stuffing pasta in his face?' said Sandra.

'Getting his orders, more like it,' said Spud.

Cole didn't say a word. He was acutely aware that everything being discussed had a hell of a lot to do with him, and he really had nothing to offer other than nervous bewilderment.

• •

Jude pressed the save button on the PC. She eased her numb backside from her poor excuse for an ergonomic chair and headed for the tearoom, weaving between neighbouring desks. As she often did, she took the long way around, just in case Cole was up for a chat. Or better still, a few flirtatious lines. She was a little disappointed to see that his desk was empty, as were his team's chairs, as she marched towards the kitchen.

It was then that she saw Inspector Mack leaning against Spud's office. She was certain his ear was pressed firmly against the glass wall. A pregnant pause hung in the corridor between the two as Mack turned and feigned a silly false cough. And Jude threw out a smile just as silly.

'Boss,' she murmured, with her head down, as if she were trying to say 'I didn't see you'.

'Judith,' came the response, as Inspector Mack continued his spell of coughing, at the same time striding purposefully back towards his own office.

ON THE RUN

As the two of them reached opposite ends of the corridor, they simultaneously glanced back, and shot each other a weak grin before disappearing, Jude to the tea urn, and Mack to the next corridor.

26th April

The music of Pino Danielle played at the perfect background level inside the apartment. The track changed to '*Amici come prima*', Cole's favourite song. Jude topped up both wine glasses from a bottle of 2000 Antinori Sangiovese, before she resumed her main course, a plate of home-made pappardelle with a prawn, white wine and garlic sauce and a side offering of sautéed *spinaci*. Cole slowly worked on his meal, despite the fact that he was a little preoccupied.

'So, out with it—what's ticking away in your head?' asked Jude.

'What makes you think anything would be ticking?'

'Something's on. I can tell,' Jude persisted as she took another mouthful of wine, savouring its quality before she swallowed. She eased her glass onto the table. 'You invite me around for dinner, you show off cooking my favourite meal, you open a big Italian red, and you don't reckon something's ticking?'

'There's nothing,' Cole replied.

'You put on your favourite music, you lay a great table, and you invite me into your beautiful apartment, something you never do. What's cooking?'

'Nothing's cooking.'

'It's as if you re-created a scene where we used to wine and dine with our Mafia mates. So come on, Cole. What … is … cooking?'

Cole ignored Jude, electing instead to get up from his chair and start clearing the table.

'Mack's up your nose, isn't he?'

'Actually, I don't know what Mack's up to,' Cole said.

'And that's what's worrying you?'

'I have no control over stuff, Jude. Don't you see? I don't know what's going on.'

'What do you make of Mack's snooping around Spud's office?'

'Just being himself.'

'Are you sure he couldn't have overheard anything?' asked Jude, a worried tone creeping into her voice.

'I hope not. I don't know any more … It all confuses me,' said Cole.

They gave up on questions and answers, knowing that neither would get very far. Instead they settled in to play the happy couple. Jude washed the dishes and Cole dried. And every now and then as Cole stacked the dishes in the cupboards, he took the opportunity to brush closely against Jude. But Cole was cautious. Despite their obvious affection Cole knew that in an hour or so Jude would be on her way home to the house she shared with her fiancé. While the issue remained unresolved, it would be, tonight, a case of two workmates catching up. One other thing, however, was eating away at Cole. Something that he needed to say to Jude, something that Jude would find confusing. The way things were stacking up inside Cole's head, it had to be said.

He found a suitable pause in their conversation as they sat down on the sofa with an after-dinner vin santo.

'You know I think the world of Sandra, don't you?' Cole began.

'As do I. She's your best detective, right?' Jude replied.

'I trust her, you can lean on her when you want,' he said, watching her inquisitive look as she placed her finger in her glass, dangling it temptingly in her vin santo before sucking it.

'What's that supposed to mean?'

Jude pulled the finger from her mouth.

'Nothing yet, I can't answer that tonight. Save it up for a rainy day.'

Satisfied with his answer, she leant over to Cole and, brushing his hair away from the side of his face, kissed him on the mouth. Cole responded, enjoying the kiss, then broke free, leaving Jude to look at him confusedly again.

• •

26TH APRIL

Spud slept soundly in his bed alongside his lumpy and grumpy wife. His two kids rested peacefully in their corner of the average three-bedroom home in Yarraville. One cat, one dog and a four-door station wagon completed his version of domestic harmony. Unlike the detectives, Spud's work was very much office-bound, tapping away on keyboards, reading flowcharts and linking names to addresses to bank accounts to dodgy investments. On and on it went, until he'd amassed enough information to hand across to the detectives. But he loved his work. Great analysts weren't trained, he believed, they were born. Spud was born for the ACA.

The best thing about being an analyst was that you never had to worry about death threats, paybacks or vendettas instigated by criminals. They never saw you. It was the detectives who kicked in the doors or threw telephone books around interview rooms, instilling hatred and plots of revenge. The analyst goes home each night and tucks himself in bed until the 7 a.m. alarm breaks his slumber and points him towards the office again.

So it was with shock that at 3.50 a.m. this day, Spud sat bolt upright from his sleep, as if jolted by a cattle prod. The telephone had rung. He reached for the handset as his wife raced to the children, who had started to cry on the second ring. It was another five seconds before he worked out which part of the handset to place to his ear, and with a rough attempt at a 'Hello' he listened. What he heard roused him instantly. It was his trusted contact in the phone tapping unit, who had removed his headphones long enough to make a quick call.

'Twenty-four hours,' his contact said.

'And that's it? Nothing else?' asked Spud.

'That's all that was said. Just twenty-four hours.'

'What was the phone number?'

'B115637486KL.'

'What the fuck is that phone number?'

'A public payphone in Griffith. Out the front of the Café Azzurra.'

'What did our guy say?'

'Not a single word. He just hung up.'

'Clever bastard,' said Spud, as the howling from the kids' room became overpowering.

• •

Twenty-four hours later, the streets of East Melbourne were completely silent and as dark as a nun's habit. Leigh and Sandra peeped through a crack in the weathered, locked garage door large enough for them to spy on the driveway and entrance to Cole's apartment. Their view also allowed them to see the windows of the top-floor apartment that had been left deliberately open, with a night light on. To tempt anybody with ill intent.

The detectives had been holed up in their observation post for hours, waiting for the punk to arrive. Leigh's trusted shotgun was one of a number of weapons that leant against the boot of Cole's car. Sandra had no doubt of the ruthless efficiency with which Leigh would tackle the punk, should he rock up. Just in case, she wore an ill-fitting kevlar vest that made her look like the Michelin man. As silly as she looked, she was worried senseless about Cole's safety.

They heard footsteps in the distance. Three, maybe four houses away. Leigh reached over to grab his shotgun, winking at Sandra. The footsteps moved closer to the apartment building, eventually crossing the driveway, allowing Leigh a glimpse at a male silhouetted figure. Sandra took a peek, but the lone figure moved on down the street, and was no longer in sight.

'Fuck,' she whispered.

'Shhh … shhhh … champer,' said Leigh.

The footsteps stopped. They both listened until their concentration almost hurt, hoping for more steps. An eternity seemed to go by, or at least a full minute. And then another. To Leigh's surprise, a full-sized image of a male appeared a metre away from him on the other side of the crack in the garage door. Leigh's left hand reached to cover

26TH APRIL

Sandra's mouth; she nodded understanding. It was obvious that the punk had crept down the side of the neighbouring property to arrive at the rear of the apartment block.

Massimo walked stealthily the dozen paces to the sewerage pipe that ran up the wall to Cole's bathroom. He shimmied up the two levels with extraordinary speed. Once at the sill he made easy work of the open window. The hairs on the back of Leigh's neck rose when he realised that the manoeuvre had all been done in complete silence.

Sandra and Leigh watched Massimo's shadow move from room to room. They could just make out the image of a pistol in the assassin's hand. It took Massimo less than a minute to fully appreciate that the apartment was empty and to memorise the internal layout. No doubt for a return visit. With more confidence than Muhammad Ali, he opened the front door and disappeared, gently closing it behind him. He walked down the flight of stairs to the street, without so much as a glance in any direction. Leigh listened to the steps return the way they had come until they faded away.

• •

Cole stood impatiently outside the front door of the Crumpler designer bag shop in Gertrude Street, Fitzroy. He couldn't stop pacing, sweating on 9 a.m. As he waited, an odd breed of workers and locals hustled by. A mix of Goths, tattooed lesbians, early-morning drunks, funky stick figures and other types that were too cool for real. The passing parade helped take his mind off what had happened six hours earlier at his apartment. Nerves were getting the better of him.

The Mafia game is on, he thought. He looked across to the opposite side of the street where Sandra, seated in her car, didn't help matters by tapping on her watch.

With great relief he heard the front door open and the shop manager stepped aside to welcome him. She had seen his impatience from inside as she went about turning on the lights and preparing the till. Yet she chose to wait till the exact millisecond of 9 a.m. to end her client's anxiety. Cole took it on the chin; he knew that they made fabulously good bags and he also knew that they were in Fitzroy, a suburb full of attitude.

'You're early,' the quirky 20-something said.

'Sorry. I said I'd be back again this morning,' Cole replied.

'Awesome,' was all the girl offered, displaying her tattooed arms and the range of cheap silver rings on each of her fingers. She reached behind her counter to grab the shoulder bag. She did her finest shop-assistant demonstration of the features of the bag, showing off the secret internal pocket of the Bees-Knees, the biggest bag they made. The pocket was at the bottom of the bag, which he hoped would not be located on any cursory baggage search.

'Good to go,' said Cole as he inspected the custom work.

Once they'd sorted out the payment, and Cole got over the desperate need to take the nose ring from the girl's nostril, he jogged across to the waiting car, his bag slung carelessly over his shoulder.

'It's like being on planet Mars,' Sandra said as a seriously drug-affected Goth drifted past the windscreen.

'You get used to it. I lived around here once. It's an acquired taste.'

'You won't make it,' said Sandra, looking at her watch.

'Is your driving that bad?' said Cole, trying to break the mood. Sandra launched the car into the traffic, playing dodgem cars in an attempt to meet their schedule. All Cole could do was hold on with white knuckles.

• •

The new Bees-Knees was stuffed full of clothes, hastily packed on the drive to the airport. Even so, it sat comfortably on Cole's shoulder as he stood under the departure board. It was the four red lights flashing

26TH APRIL

on the Auckland flight that had his and Sandra's attention; otherwise there had been far too much silence since they had parked the car.

'You've got twenty minutes, hon. You'd better go,' Sandra said.

'I guess so,' was all Cole could counter. A lump had come into his throat. He pulled out his mobile phone and handed it to Sandra.

'They'll only trace it,' he said, also handing over his driver's licence and police ID.

'Emails?' Sandra asked.

'Traceable again. No gadgets, just old-fashioned travel.'

'They'll come looking for you once they realise you're missing.'

'That's why I don't need gadgets pointing out where I am.'

'You don't have to go. We could take what we've got to the Toe Cutters,' Sandra made a last-ditch effort to change the mind of a man who was far too set in his ways.

Cole reached over and placed a hand on each of Sandra's shoulders very gently before he said, 'Think about it. We've got a fat lot of zip. One illegal phone tap, entry into an organiser without warrant, a punk who came and went in the night, and we can't even prove that, and a wild hunch by paranoid investigators. We'd be lucky if the Toeys didn't lock us up.'

Sandra nodded as tears welled up and she bit into her bottom lip.

'Make sure Spud doesn't let the boss get into his computer.'

'Yep.'

'You have to hold the team together,' he said, as she nodded with tears now streaming down her cheeks.

'You know I trust you more than anyone,' Cole said solemnly.

'Of course ... thanks,' said Sandra.

'I have no idea when or if I'll be back. I'll sneak back into the country when I feel it's right. I want you to remember one thing, though.'

Sandra stood firm and listened intently, sniffling.

'Don't ask for explanations. Just remember—Ingrid Rossellini. Got that?'

'Yes … but … what?'

'Keep it to yourself, girl, it'll make sense later.'

She shook her head from side to side, bewildered by his comments, then changed the subject.

'Have you got enough of the lovely?'

'Stop playing mother. And I don't need a cut lunch either. I'll contact you when I can.' Cole smiled, dropping both hands away from her shoulders as he glanced at the departure board. He headed for the customs departure hall and disappeared behind the partition, flicking a wave goodbye.

He was on the run.

27th April

The noisy ping that came from the safety-belt warning sign of the aircraft led to a chain reaction of straightening seats and clicking seatbelts. Turbulence was causing an uncomfortable flight. The hostess walked up to the toilet cubicle, gave the door a quick tap and called to its occupant, 'Return to your seat please. Return to your seat please,' before moving on to dispatch a drinks trolley to the rear of the aircraft.

On the other side of the door, Cole braced himself as he tried valiantly to shave. He was beginning to resemble a startled walrus with a moustache full of shaving cream and a miniature hand-basin full of whiskers. He clipped away the end of many years' growth. It would take all of his last three Gillette razors to chop through the defiant stubble and expose skin that hadn't seen sunshine for a decade. What he thought would be short work took ages. He was conscious he'd occupied the toilet too long and figured he'd be unpopular once he flung the door open, despite his fresh new look.

Back in his seat, when the turbulence had abated and two glasses of New Zealand Sauvignon Blanc had taken effect, he delighted in the feel of his naked upper lip. All smooth and shiny, like a baby's bottom. The upside was, he reckoned he looked five years younger. So why the bloody hell did he keep the damn thing on for so long?

• •

Cole ambled down the main street of Auckland with the first sense of relief he had felt in almost a week. While he adored New Zealand, he wasn't too sure if he was far enough away from the strife that lay in Melbourne for his complete comfort. Perhaps well enough away to allow the return of a sleep pattern.

He needed time out. A chance to review all that had gone before him since Antonio had stared him down at the Supreme Court. He couldn't help but wonder what Antonio would be up to now, having heard of last night's failed attempt at revenge. Would he be pacing his ten-square-metre concrete cell? Calling the old Godfather for more plotting and planning, or would he just dismiss last night as a night when Cole wasn't home?

Cole figured the latter proposition was probably more realistic. He also figured he had three or four more nights in front of him before the punk from Calabria reported him missing. He only hoped those same three or four nights' grace would come from Inspector Mack, who tomorrow would get a doctor's certificate claiming a bout of influenza from Detective Sergeant Cole Goodwin in absentia.

It was late in the afternoon when he got to the bottom of the street. He spied a hairdressing salon, the one his hotel concierge had told him about. He stepped inside. Just as the closed sign was turned to face the street, Cole walked out into his new world, with a new haircut, leaving most of his shoulder-length mane on the salon floor.

• •

It was an appealing little town, Russell, on the east coast of the north island of New Zealand, a three-hour bus trip from Auckland. In fact, it could be said to be the perfect fishing village. Not that its throng of yearly visitors would necessarily venture to this neck of the woods just to catch marlin or yellow-finned tuna. It was mostly its natural beauty that attracted. Being the main commercial hub of the Bay of Islands, this little button town was well considered on the tourist trail. And it was just about far enough away from Griffith to allow a man a good night's sleep.

27TH APRIL

When Cole had jumped off the old wooden-hulled ferry at the tiny pier a week earlier, he had spent a good hour taking in the glossy painted weatherboard buildings and shopfronts on the foreshore. He stopped for a coffee to gather his thoughts. It was during this break that Cole realised that New Zealanders had no idea how to make coffee, serving up flat whites in cups the size of cereal bowls, and suggesting they were caffe lattes. He also had a strange sensation that someone was watching him. At the foothill immediately above the village, he saw an open black umbrella in the garden that belonged to a quaint little white house. A tiny 'B&B' sign swung off a post. An older looking man was walking the gardens, a speck in the distance. In less than ten minutes Cole and his Bees-Knees had hiked up the rocky zigzag path that led to the B&B, and he had taken a room.

Inn the Black B&B was run by the elderly yet sprightly and charming retired New York stockbroker, Cary Peterson, and his American wife, Lynette. Best of all, they were running a cash business. He paid for an indefinite stay.

Another thing about Inn the Black was its magnificent view onto Russell, and across the Bay of Islands. It was the most perfect observation post, as well as one of the finest views he had ever seen. He also enjoyed the New Yorker and his wife, ridiculously suntanned, fit and healthy, and full of great anecdotes and stories. Yarns that he would share under the black umbrella overlooking the township every afternoon with a glass or three of Cary's regional pinot noir. The only thing he didn't care too much for was the sombre mood created by the splashes of black throughout the two-room guest house. Lynette had gone overboard: black towels, linen, serviettes, and just about everything else you could buy at the local gift shop that was a darker shade of grey.

Cole shook Cary's hand, using the surname McLaren, a guy he'd once met some years earlier. When the small talk swung to Cole's work, he had no problem in running the art dealer line he had used so successfully with the Mafia. He knew much about art, it was his great hobby, and he could easily bluff his way through even the most in-depth conversation. He soon fell into a routine that very much involved Cary and Lynette. He'd start his morning with a run on the back beach along the beautiful sands gracing the open ocean. Then he'd relax and laze around Lynette's delightful terrace garden enjoying Cary's company with a glass of wine, before the three of them would take an evening stroll around town and dine in one of the many restaurants. He felt completely safe in his new world with his new appearance, and with being seen around town as one of three people.

• •

'What's with the boss? He won't let up,' grumbled Katherine, the administration officer for the ACA. Katherine had one of the dullest jobs in the city of Melbourne, reconciling sick leave notices, annual holidays and pay scales for the fifty-plus staff. She was holding a leave application form in the name of 'Cole Goodwin', for four weeks' leave dated a week earlier, which she had authorised herself, once submitted by Sandra.

'I authorised Cole's leave, but ever since then the boss has been hounding me to find out when he's coming back. What is it? What's Cole done wrong?'

'Beats me,' said Sandra, realising the need to be as cagey as possible. 'All I know is that Cole rang me at the tail end of his flu, asking me to put in a leave form, saying he needed more time off. So I did and you ticked it. What's the big deal?'

'That's what I'm trying to find out,' said Katherine. 'Inspector Mack seems to have something up his arse over it.'

'Wasn't it you, Katherine, who urged him just last month to take some of the leave he has owing? He's got months, hasn't he?'

Katherine began rifling through Cole's personnel file and quickly assessed that he was indeed owed ten weeks' leave, most of which he had accumulated during his undercover work on the Griffith job.

27TH APRIL

'Sure, he's owed heaps of time. He can have this current four weeks, and another four if he wants it, and I don't give a shit! I just wish Mack would leave me alone.'

∙ ∙

Inspector Mack sat heavily on a bentwood chair at the back table of a now familiar empty Italian restaurant in Lygon Street. His idyllic world in Provence had been taken from his mind. He was looking haggard. Alongside him sat his partner in crime, Donny.

'He'll surface soon,' stated Donny, with a look that would have trouble convincing the most naïve.

Silence hung as Donny and Mack swapped glances. They were lost, on a small table. Mack straightened his tie and attempted to sit a little taller in his chair. The old Godfather, a master with generations of listening to nervous bullshit, knew exactly how to play the conversation. He kept his arms folded, his body still and his eyes fixed on Mack. Not a word uttered.

Mack, an equal master of his own game, was starting to regret ever listening to Donny's first proposition, despite his new-found wealth. He was in a game without any dice and he knew there was absolutely no way of ever turning back the clock.

'I think we just have to wait and flush him out. Tell your visitor to wait.'

'And what he fuckin' do, *Commissario*? Pick fruit?' said the old Godfather.

'The second we find him, we'll let you know,' the Inspector offered unconvincingly.

The old Godfather turned to Donny with a look as hot as Calabrese salami. 'We give you $40 000, Donny, start workin'.'

∙ ∙

Leigh stood at the light switches putting on his overcoat and scarf as he closed down the ACA office for the night. It was well after 9 p.m.

'Hang on!' came a yell from a desk on the opposite side of the office.

Leigh, a little on edge these days, was initially startled as he turned to the direction of the voice. He immediately relaxed as he saw Jude tapping away on her PC in the near dark.

'Sorry, champer,' he called out. 'I didn't know anyone else was still here.'

He wandered over to Jude's desk and stared at a girl he had seen become more depressed with each passing day.

'So, what are you still doin' here?'

'What does it look like?' she snapped.

'Sorry just askin', I'll turn the lights back on,' he offered.

'No, stuff it, don't worry. I'll go home, too.'

Jude closed down her computer and pulled her coat and scarf off the rack beside the group of desks.

'You're not handling it well, are you?' asked Leigh, genuinely concerned. He watched Jude struggle with even the most menial task of putting on her scarf and gloves. She gave up on the gloves and threw them angrily on the desktop before kicking her chair a couple of metres away from the desk. She was clearly frustrated.

'Why don't you guys tell me what's going on?'

Leigh ignored the question.

'I mean, youse guys know, don't you ... what's happened to Cole?' she demanded. 'I mean, the last time I saw him, there was this bullshit with a fancy meal, and all that weird shit he said about leaning on Sandra. Then he ups and disappears. What the fuck has happened, Leigh?'

Leigh didn't want to lie so he tried to change the subject instead.

'How's the fiancé?'

Jude looked hard at Leigh for a few seconds before angrily collecting her gloves from the desktop and saying in too loud a voice,

27TH APRIL

'Finished. I moved out last week. But that's not what we're talking about, Detective.'

Leigh kept a stony silence on the subject as he watched Jude storm towards the main security door.

'And how do you know he isn't dead?' she yelled as she walked out into the evening.

• •

The miserable drizzle of rain hadn't put a dampener on the day. Cole, Cary and Lynette wandered onto the jetty. Cole thought the hospitality of the two old codgers so perfect, especially over the past month. It had been a month of peace and quiet, a month to think things through and let sleeping dogs lie. Now it was time to reward his hosts. The least Cole could do was shout them a spot of marlin fishing. All before returning home the following week. He had it all sketched out: he'd fly into Queensland and test the water from there, give his office a quick call—surely the threat would now be dormant. In the interim, it was time to dust off Cary's tackle box.

Cary hadn't stopped talking about getting out into the Pacific blue for a day, swapping the strike chair in the hope of catching a big one. Although he and Lynette had lived the life of Riley for half-a-dozen years on the Bay of Islands, rarely had he been able to venture out. Lynette was very much the homebody and Cary was always by her side. He knew most of the boat owners and had suggested to Cole that he book the craft *Catcher in the Rye*, owned by a good acquaintance who promised mate's rates.

They had the most perfect day, as the Captain took them to his secret reefs and holes, just off Zane Grey Bay. Renowned as the one-time home of the legendary American author, a raconteur who trawled for the open water fish with Hollywood stars, Zane Grey Bay was an idyllic fishing destination.

By 6 p.m. the sun had well and truly gone, as had the energy of the Inn the Black crew. Two of the three said goodbye to their

Captain, and struggled along the jetty with a 56-pound yellow-finned tuna in tow. Then it was off to the fishmongers, who would take their prize, ensure it was smoked overnight, and hand it back in convenient freezer-size packs.

Cole let Lynette and Cary take the lead with the fish. He knew that they would enjoy the attention and accolades of the local crowd gathered along the pier to watch the day's boats come home. And he smiled at Cary's proud face, watching him puff out his chest as he strolled along. Cole stood back to settle with the Captain for the day's fun. He pulled out his wallet. To his amazement, the surly Captain informed him the cost was $2000, and that was with a 50 per cent discount.

How to pay the Captain the $2000 with only half the cash on hand? The rest of his money was squirrelled away in the ceiling of the guests' bathroom. He needed more of the lovely but not without his hosts becoming aware. The Captain was on charter for the next ten days with wealthy Yanks, and wanted payment on the spot. Finally, Cole reached for his MasterCard, tucked away neatly in the back of his wallet. Why not, he thought; he was returning home next week.

• •

A pair of well-worn Nike runners sat propped on top of a desk in a busy drug unit office. Both runners were attached to a pair of feet owned by the lazy detective Donny, who had found himself time for a quiet snooze while his workmates busied themselves around him. On a neighbouring desk a fax machine kicked into life, and spat out a single page. It failed to capture Donny's attention. A pretty young female detective walked past, grabbed the fax and took a quick look. Realising it was not for her, she placed it like a blanket over the docile Donny. He didn't stir.

When he did, he picked up the fax and read the contents. Sent from his dodgy contact, a less-than-honest security officer of the

27TH APRIL

Internal Investigation Unit of the National Bank, the contents were brief, and focused on the movements of an alerted MasterCard.

25th May. Cole Goodwin MasterCard
$2000 'Catcher in the Rye' Fishing Tours,
Russell, New Zealand.

He raced towards the lift with the fax clutched tightly in hand.

• •

Lynette was on her way out to the garden to catch the last of the sun. She had just prepared her second plate of canapés, mostly consisting of smoked tuna with her delicious home-made relish on water crackers, part of their staple diet since their successful outing. Her two boys were busy recounting exaggerated fishing stories while giving a good nudge to a bottle of Cloudy Bay chardonnay.

During the four weeks, Cole's firmness of body had returned. His complexion showed signs of an easier life. He enjoyed the daily repartee that flowed between himself and Cary, whom he saw as a surrogate father figure.

Cole's mind would often drift back to life as it was in Melbourne. He'd lost both his own parents in recent years. His father had died at a far too early age with cancer, and his mother soon after, as is often the way with couples married so long, not surviving a quadruple bypass. Almost weekly, the three of them had sat together discussing everything from artworks by the great masters to the trivial goings on of the neighbourhood. In the five years since their passing, he'd missed their talks, the cosy familiarity of their company, and the sometimes hilarious arguments that would ensue. Of all the acquaintances who had drifted through his life since then, none was more similar to his father than Cary. The two old men would have had a great old time together, he thought, as he sat listening to the warm timbre of Cary's voice.

While his parents, his mother in particular, were saddened at the collapse of Cole's short marriage, their greatest disappointment was that their only son had never given them the grandchildren they so longed for. He was sure that his mother compensated by grandmothering the young ladies that he would bring home for a meal every now and then. He only wished that they had been able to meet Jude.

He did wonder, however, with a slight smile, what his mother might have made of him bringing home a girl betrothed to another. On the other hand he was certain his father would have picked up on the romantic and sexual tension that existed between him and Jude. He snapped back into the moment and thought how he longed to talk with Jude. To be in her company, instead of second-guessing what she was up to, in her job, with her fiancé, and her list of 'maybes'. He wondered how she had handled his disappearing act. However, he kept reminding himself she was spoken for. Jude belonged to the past now; time had helped on that count.

He was grateful to his new mates from Inn the Black, who sensed, in the way only older people can, that skeletons lay in the closet, but were decent enough not to pry, although they were getting a little curious as to when he might go home to his art gallery and his life.

By the time Lynette's canapés had disappeared, Cole was thinking about an afternoon siesta as he raised himself from his seat, leaving Lynette and Cary to watch the afternoon ferry come in. Cary had his eye focused into the telescope he kept beside his chair, and was fixed on the mooring post of the jetty. It was at this time of the year that tourism almost packed up and went home in Russell. The scheduled daily ferry was lucky to deliver a man and his dog. Still Cary chose to spy on them each afternoon and run his humorous commentary.

Cole's last thought as he dropped off was to tell Cary and Lynette about his impending desire to return home. It was then he heard the laughter coming from Lynette. Cary was in fine form, he could hear, recounting the exploits of a mother and father getting off the jetty with a couple of kids, each of them nearly falling into the water,

27TH APRIL

and a silly 'dago'-looking guy on his own with an old powder-blue suitcase, heading purposefully for the Marlborough Hotel. Cary principally objected to the colour of the suitcase.

About to drift off, Cole sat bolt upright. In no time he stood anxiously beside Cary in nothing more than his jockey shorts.

'Where is that guy?' he asked urgently.

Cary was a little taken aback by the forcefulness.

'What's wrong, mate?'

Cole realised the tone of his question was out of kilter with his normal demeanour, and had concerned his hosts. He composed himself and changed tack.

'Sorry, Cary. I just remembered I spoke to a mate on the phone last week and suggested he might come over if he had some time. Maybe that's him? I forgot about it.'

His explanation was delivered perfectly. Of course it was. He was a covert operative and knew how to deliver lines when the pressure was on.

So convincing were his comments, Lynette then offered, 'He's gone into the Marlborough. Do you want him to come up here? We'll ring them, there's a spare bed.'

Cole stood dumbfounded as Lynette got up out of her chair to lean across and pick up the cordless telephone.

'They're on speed dial,' she said helpfully.

'Wait, wait,' Cole pleaded. 'I'd like to surprise him. Just ask your friend at the Marlborough who's checking in but don't alert him.'

'Why?' asked a now very curious Cary as he looked across at Lynette.

'Well, that way, if it is him, we'll surprise him tonight in their dining room, and drag him up here tomorrow,' Cole said with his fingers crossed behind his back.

'Fabulous!' said Lynette. 'What a great idea. I love surprises. I'll go and start fixing his room now, and find something special to wear tonight.'

She got up from the table, carrying the cordless phone, leaving Cary less than convinced, mulling over the change in human behaviour that he had witnessed in the last minute.

Cole quietly retreated to his own guest bathroom. His eyes fixed on the manhole cover, just as Lynette yelled from the kitchen, 'Cole, I spoke to the Marlborough. It's an Italian guy … he "no speaka the English". Is that him? … Cole, where are you? … Cole?'

• •

Lynette was in her laundry, busily ironing the heavy fabric dress she had picked out for the evening. Perry Como crooned from the tape deck perched on the laundry shelf. Lynette nodded her head left and right in time with the music. Cary hadn't moved from the terrace, although the volume of chardonnay in his glass had. It was now all gone. He leant forward, looking through his telescope to the bosun, who had unravelled the mooring rope of the ferry to commence the return journey across the bay. The V8 diesel engine churned the surface of the water as the Captain slowly eased the ferry from the dock. Cary checked the focus ring on the telescope and looked again. He saw his guest of one month sprinting from the flower shop along the jetty carrying his fully laden Bees-Knees shoulder bag, just in time to jump the last metre and land safely, if not dangerously, on the very end of the ferry platform.

Lynette walked out into the garden carrying an elegant black silk shirt.

'Shall I iron your shirt for dinner tonight, darling?'

Cary replied with a frown on his face, 'I don't think we'll be eating out tonight, sweetheart.'

29th May

The backstreet internet café tucked between the technical bookshop and the art supply store behind Auckland University was packed to the rafters. Students fought over computers to check their emails and Facebook entries before classes resumed for the afternoon. Cole found himself squeezed between a geeky Japanese kid of about nineteen and a pretty Indian girl wearing her iPod earphones as she tapped her slim elegant fingers on her keyboard.

It took no time to create a new email account on Yahoo. Cole put in Ingrid Rossellini's last details. In less time than it took to drink the small bottle of fruit juice beside him he had created a 35-year-old woman from San Francisco. It made him realise how easy it was to be a terrorist these days. Communicating with others around the world. Or, worse still, a paedophile, cruising the planet for unsuspecting victims. Madness. How much harder it was to be a detective in the globalised world.

But he had other uses for Ingrid. He was on the move again, and would need to speak to Sandra somehow. No doubt she had worried herself into a pink fit.

He was tempted to check his own personal email address on a different server, but he stopped himself. He knew from investigations within the ACA that a tag could be placed on email addresses. While such a ploy required the authority from those at the highest levels, he had no doubt that Inspector Mack would have set those wheels in motion.

After securing his Yahoo account, Cole went online to Air New Zealand to check the flight schedules for Auckland to Buenos Aires.

He had to make his next move. When he woke in the backpackers' dormitory that morning, to the sound of half-a-dozen snoring

20-year-olds, he realised that he could neither stay in New Zealand nor head back to the east coast of Australia. It was time to get smart.

• •

The doorbell at Inn the Black was pressed for the second time, with a long pause in between. Cary sat in his usual position in his garden, his trusty telescope within reach. A lone ant was making its way up Cary's left forearm, his head rested back on an embroidered black cushion and his eyes were shut, as if he was taking it easy for the afternoon. His chin was whiskered and he wore the same clothes as the day before. A narrow, long-bladed knife was embedded in the centre of his chest.

The doorbell rang again. Lynette lay slumped on the laundry floor, awkwardly wedged between the washing machine and the door. The ironing table had upended itself in the struggle, and collapsed over her legs. She had suffered a massive laceration to the throat. The laundry door, which acted as a side exit to the white wooden house, was wide open. A set of footsteps could be heard coming from the front door, along the side path, towards the laundry. The proprietor of the Bloomin' Russell flower shop walked smartly down the side footpath in her white sneakers, white linen slacks and sailor jacket.

'Lynette!' she called out, in a voice that indicated familiarity.

She approached the door carrying a magnificent spray of Aurelian lilies with a little card attached that read, 'Sorry to treat you that way, you were both such fun, Cole.'

The gift shop lady had no hesitation, on seeing the laundry door open, in walking straight in with another call of 'Lynette, honey.'

The sound of her initial scream, one of four in total, would pierce the air across Russell, ensuring all siestas were put to an end that afternoon.

• •

29TH MAY

Almost twelve hours later, just after 4 a.m., Cole stood at the New Zealand Airlines ticketing counter at Auckland International Airport. Despite the early hour, there was at least half a planeload of travellers going through the final motions of check-in and seat allocation on the Auckland-to-Buenos Aires flight. Cole was a lone soldier at the ticketing counter, attempting a one-way fare, without a reservation. A procedure he knew he couldn't undertake via email, without offering up his credit card details again.

'I'm sorry, Mr Goodwin. There is nothing my supervisor can do, I've checked. You will have to pay the full fare rate.'

Cole found himself in no position to argue, and counted out $2900. As the counter attendant recounted his bills, Cole glanced around at his fellow passengers. He took particular note of every male, none of whom looked familiar. Although he did notice what he reckoned to be an Italian man, possibly thirty years of age, walk through the lounge wheeling a trolley. His eyes followed the man's path till he and his trolley reached the newspaper stand on the other side of the foreign currency exchange kiosk, which Cole had visited earlier. His initial concern was allayed when he realised that the Italian was merely opening his news stand for the morning. His trolley was full of early edition newspapers.

Fifteen minutes later the grumpy counter assistant, who had obviously suffered from the early morning blues, put on her best smile as she handed the very expensive one-way ticket to Mr Goodwin, as well as a boarding pass. Cole declined the offer of checking in his Bees-Knees, electing to carry it on board. He walked from the counter and took a seat nearby to make a last-minute adjustment to his shoulder bag and check his ticket. The only other lone male in the nest of seats, a suited man, had walked across to the news stand to buy a newspaper. The Italian had now opened for the morning and was snapping the wire from the bundle of newspapers. Cole heard the final call announcement for his flight. By now the check-in lounge was all but empty. The 5 a.m. flight was the only scheduled international departure before dawn.

ON THE RUN

As Cole made a final adjustment to his bag and headed for the luggage X-ray machine, he spied the man in a cheap suit at the kiosk staring at him. He knew that expression—it was the unmistakeable look of a surveillance cop who had been burnt by a target. Both sets of eyes met when they shouldn't have. He stopped dead in his path, seeing the now empty X-ray machine. The only exit door to the opposite direction.

Cole turned back to glance at the suited newspaper reader who was now walking briskly towards the empty ticketing counter. The final call for his flight sounded again over the public address system. Convinced his initial impression was due to paranoia, he placed the Bees-Knees on the X-ray machine. A dozen steps later and Cole and his bag were on the other side, clearing customs, sprinting for the departure gate. The suited man moved quickly through the X-ray machine and customs.

After the $15-an-hour team of airline security guards had seen the last of their passengers through the security regime, they ambled along lazily in a small herd in search of coffee, taking advantage of the hour's lull before the next stampede. One of the security guards broke from the herd momentarily to wander past the ticketing desk; there was a free newspaper on the counter. The security guard picked it up to see on the front page a colour photograph, of Cole standing proud holding a prize catch. The photo accompanied the main story: 'Bed and breakfast slaying. Suspect sought'.

• •

Despite the best efforts of the flight attendant, Cole rejected the breakfast tray, opting for another orange juice, his fourth for the morning. It was his only tell-tale sign of pressure. Otherwise, he was known for his reliably calm demeanour. Still, the suited gent had rattled him and triggered the need for cold drinks. The rattling only increased when he saw the same guy board the aircraft a minute after

29TH MAY

he had. Just as the cabin doors closed and the stewards began their customary pre-flight checks, Cole made it his business to know exactly which seat the nosy male occupied, six rows ahead on the opposite aisle. Apart from one serious glance towards Cole, when stowing away his hand luggage, there had been no other reason to be concerned. Nonetheless, Cole firmly believed that two hard looks from the one person meant that something was not right.

• •

While Cole was rejecting his breakfast, Sandra sat in a pink terry-towelling dressing gown at her breakfast bar, 6000 kilometres to the west. She was alone in her modest Edwardian home in suburban Melbourne, with her bigger than usual bowl of Special K. Alone, apart from the overweight fluffy Persian cat that was pushing for attention. Sandra ignored his protestations and instead topped her cereal with a carefully sliced Fuji apple. The 7 a.m. news on the tiny bench-top television caught her attention. It wasn't so much item one that made her take notice, but the flash of the photo on the next news segment, which caused her spoon to drop into her cereal bowl, splashing milk onto the bench, appeasing the now happy feline. She reached for the phone as the newsreader told of the macabre murder in New Zealand of an American, and his wife, whose life hung by a thread in intensive care.

• •

The morning newspaper was already old news by the time Sandra had charged into the office, with more urgency than to a Boxing Day sale. 'Bad Cop' Cole Goodwin was all over the headlines. During initial enquiries into a lodger named 'Cole', the New Zealand police were told by virtually the entire village of Russell that Cary and

Lynette were often seen dining at night in the restaurants with their long-term guest from Melbourne. Enquiries overnight with their Victorian counterparts had revealed an uncanny resemblance to one of their own, a Detective Sergeant Cole Goodwin, minus the moustache. And, true to form, the late shift duty officer who handled the enquiry had passed the information onto his contact at the daily newspaper, ensuring himself an invitation to the media Christmas party that year, always a lot of fun, and the chance to spy a few celebrities.

Not a desk was without the front-page headline glaring up at Sandra as she strolled past. The room reeked of suspicion. But then she stopped dead, angry at the denigration of her dear friend, one of the finest police she had ever met. Her hands balled into fists and she turned to face the doubting Thomases. She stepped slowly towards them, grabbed a newspaper from the detective closest to her, snatching it clean from the woman's hands, and yelled, 'If you believe this fuckin' crap'—and with that she threw the paper high into the air and let it fall to the floor—'then you believe in the fuckin' Easter bunny.'

She spun around and continued towards her desk, hurling her handbag against the pin board.

'Mack's walking around as if he's won Tattslotto,' said Leigh, his face riddled with stress.

'He couldn't have done it, could he?' chirped Spud, who stood alongside Leigh.

'It won't fuckin' change, Leigh, if you read it all day long,' snapped Sandra, trying to gather her composure. 'And if you ask me that fuckin' stupid question again, Spud, I'll put you on your arse.'

'Okay. I'm sorry,' said Spud, 'but what's he doing over there?'

'Fishing, by the looks of things,' said Sandra, as Jude joined the team, tears running down her cheeks. The four of them sat together in silence.

• •

29TH MAY

His world had changed overnight. Inspector Mack was reading the comics pages of the daily paper, his body swaying rhythmically to the music on the tearoom radio. He ate his fingers of toast and Vegemite with precision.

It was 6.30 a.m. when he first received news of the slaying in New Zealand. He had just dragged himself out of his bed at home after having spent another night impotent and gripped with worry. It was his mate, Donny, who had seen the early news, laughed his head off, and who had told the boss to go find a television. For the next ten minutes, Mack channel surfed until he locked on to a news service that was running the story. When the photo of Cole and the big fish appeared on screen Mack dropped to his knees and crawled closer to get a better look. The fisherman bore an uncanny resemblance to his Detective Sergeant Cole Goodwin, minus the handlebar moustache and head of hair.

His first thought was of the perfectly presented exit door that now opened for him.

Cole Goodwin, a suspected murderer. His name blackened. Something which would be of great use to the Mafia, in time. Mack knew the New Zealand detectives had the perfect case against Cole, in a tiny fishing village that would have no stories to tell about Italians. He bounced back into bed to join Dorothy.

•   •

Like lost sheep, they followed one after the other. Each of the passengers returned their tray to the upright position; seats moved forwards, in readiness for landing. With only fifteen minutes to go before arrival, the suited gent quickly snuck off to the toilet, but not before giving Cole a third hard glance as he passed. That was one too many for Cole who just as quickly unsnapped his seat belt and made a bee-line for the toilet, brushing aside the unnecessary roll of the eyes of the stewardess staring at him.

'Stomach cramps,' was all he could muster.

The hostess nodded sympathetically. Once at the engaged toilet door, Cole stopped to look around. The closest passengers were occupied with their hand luggage and their cat grooming before landing. He tapped on the engaged door, whispering 'Steward, open the door, sir.'

He watched the red door indicator glide to green and the door open to expose a man with a mouthful of toothpaste looking at him. Cole forced his way into the toilet cubicle, snibbing the door behind.

'Take your fourth look, fuck-head. What's your problem?'

'What?' was all the man offered as he almost swallowed his toothbrush.

'Why all the looks? Are you a dog?'

'What?'

'Since Auckland.'

'I saw a picture on the front page of the paper. Some bloke and a fish. Some old couple in Russell,' stammered the trembling businessman.

It all fell into place that one split second. All that was left for him to do was to summon the cleverest answer he could deliver.

'Who's Russell?'

'It's a little town on the Bay of Islands.'

'Mate, I just flew in from Sydney at 3 a.m. to connect to Buenos Aires. What are you fuckin' talking about?'

The businessman spat out the last of his toothpaste into the basin. 'I'm so sorry, just a silly mistake, I'm sorry, mate.'

'I'm not too sure what you are talking about, but I get it. A mistake is a mistake.'

They left the cubicle together much to the bemusement of an elderly Maori lady seated in the aisle seat closest to the cubicle, who gave them both a stern look. One that Cole didn't bother about.

• •

29TH MAY

There was no reason for a headline story on the catch of a big fish. Especially when the catch was only a minnow compared to what was normally caught in the Bay of Islands. All Cole could think of when he returned to his seat was what the businessman had said about the elderly couple in Russell. He did an autopsy on those dozen or so words, trying his darnedest to come up with an interpretation that didn't include some harm having come to Lynette and Cary. He asked for the newspaper, only to be rebuffed and told in a short manner that the flight had left too early for the morning papers. Thank God, otherwise he would have to confront the entire planeload of passengers inside the toilet, he thought stupidly.

All he could come up with was tragedy. Good news didn't make it in to the daily papers. No one was interested in cheery happenings and big fish stories. He feared the worst. And he ached to know what had happened to the Petersons.

• •

Cole's eyes flicked from one face to another to another to another and back again, trying to read them, looking for signs of an alert. He watched for a face pretending to be uninterested. So far so good, as the next person stepped forward from his queue.

He looked back to see passengers with fat suitcases headed his way, but none with a suit. He gave each of the passport control guys another sharp look. He was good at reading faces. Another passenger from his queue stepped forward, and he found himself at the front of the queue. Soon he would know exactly how efficient the New Zealand police department was.

When called, Cole moved forward as if he were being released from a slingshot. He dropped his passport on the desk with the photo page open and his immigration card beside it. The bow-backed official flicked his grubby fingers over the pages of the passport before returning to the photo page, shaking his head.

'*Cis non you, Señor.*'

'*Mio noma* Cole Goodwin, *Señor. Io Australiano,*' confirmed Cole.

'*Non, non, Señor, problema,*' he uttered as he waved for assistance from his next-door *compadre*.

Cole turned back to view the crowd behind him. Towards the back of his queue he saw the tall businessman looking straight ahead. Their eyes met. He was trying desperately to work his way through the unresponsive throng.

The two customs officials put their heads together and looked at Cole and then at the passport and then back at Cole again before both shook their heads. One of them uttered the word, '*Problema*'.

It was then that Cole realised the problem.

'*Si si, Señor, no problema. Io non moustacho, non lungo capello,*' he said as he attempted to explain that he had shaved off his moustache and cut his hair. The pair of customs officers let the explanation sink in before the second one broke into a smile and nodded, and then returned to his desk. The passport stamp hit the page and the official signalled to the next in line.

Half-a-dozen strides to the other side of the booth, and onto Argentinian territory, Cole picked up his pace. The suited man had finally pushed his way to the front of the queue. He was gesturing loudly and pointing frantically towards him. Cole disappeared quickly towards the nearest exit door, leaving four national security guards to jump onto the disruptive businessman, taking him to the ground.

• •

The heavily dented, canary yellow–coloured Fiat taxi pig-rooted to a stop in the main street of Recoleta. Cole freed himself from the nightmarish ride from the airport, paid the driver and walked down the lane alongside the Alvear Palace Hotel. He strode confidently through the side door to the hotel, to the gift shop entrance and the smiling welcome of the shop assistant. At first glance this appeared to be among the finest hotels he had ever visited. It was silly to give it a five- or even six-star rating, as he found it far more opulent. Without fuss, Cole casually selected an Armani long-sleeved T-shirt and took it to the counter, paying in cash. He asked for it to be wrapped and delivered to him at the business centre of the hotel. He left his name on the hotel stationery at the counter. As he started to walk out of the store, he hesitated, returned, and with a smile that would charm any shop assistant, asked if he could leave his shoulder bag with the shirt. To be delivered at the same time, as he had errands to run. The pretty shop assistant was more than obliging to such a pleasant hotel guest.

Cole moved through the lobby of the hotel, and grabbed a copy of the *New York Times* as he went. He tucked it under his arm and headed straight for the bar, where he ordered a whisky sour from the strikingly beautiful barmaid, possibly a mix of Brazilian and Argentinian ancestry. He caught her name, Lola, and her smile. He offered her a 20-peso note for the 12-peso drink and requested it be delivered to the business centre. He left his name on a cocktail napkin.

Cole then moved to the lobby of the hotel and sat with his newspaper. It offered little more than a run of boring stocks and shares stories from New York and political diatribe about the Iraq war. No mention of New Zealand.

Before long he watched the smartly attired porter carrying his Bees-Knees and gift shop purchase up a flight of stairs above the lifts, and into a corridor. Not far behind was an equally smartly attired Lola, with a run of better curves, carrying a tray and whisky sour, headed in the same direction. One more page of newspaper digested, and Cole headed up the same flight of stairs, easily finding the business office and another smiling face. The young man at the desk fell into line as soon as Cole entered the office, giving the same surname as the drink and the T-shirt delivery. The assumption worked. The assistant believed him to be a hotel guest wanting to use the email facility. Cole spent a moment or two complimenting the young man on his professionalism and his obvious ability to gain promotion in the near future. The young man, without hesitation, ushered Cole to a computer by the window.

Half a whisky sour later, Cole was glued to the internet news page of Channel Three in New Zealand. He stared blankly at the breaking story of the day. Now he understood the hard looks from the businessman on the aircraft. He could only wonder what stories he was telling the Argentinian police now. If the newspapers were right, a heartless murderer had just entered their country. As he scrolled through the article, Cole kept reading his name; obviously the detectives had joined the dots. No doubt with the help of Inspector Mack.

And of course there was no mention of any Calabrian punk. The ruthlessly dangerous yet extraordinarily clever man had no doubt slipped the country, flying in an opposite direction to Cole once he failed to solicit anything useful from Cole's Inn the Black mates.

The details of Cary's death were upsetting; the only comfort he drew was the fact that Lynette was still alive, but in a medically induced coma.

The sense of responsibility he felt for them swept over him. He sat staring at the screen for the rest of his whisky sour. He listened to the quiet in the office and fought back tears.

Eventually, semi-composed, Cole dangled his fingers across the keyboard and started typing.

Sandy,

It's been too long, I know. Please don't be angry with me. It's just that since our wedding, I've been so busy, and what with moving into our new home and organising our furnishings, I've been meaning to write for ages. I know you will be upset by what was said, but you must understand me, Sandy. I had nothing to do with the family strife. Please try to keep in touch.

Much love, Ingrid

29TH MAY

Once the message was sent, Cole logged out. He needed to find a safe bed for the night, as the city of Buenos Aires would be on the alert for one Cole Goodwin. He quickly and quietly upended his bag, emptying the contents in a neat stack on top of the office desk. He ran his finger carefully along the inside seam of the bag and lifted the secret flap exposing a wafer thin compartment with just enough room to hide a set of identity papers. He flicked open the Australian passport in the name of Tommy Paul as well as a National Bank MasterCard, an ANZ Visa card and a driver's licence.

It had been a long time since he was Tommy Paul. Four years, he thought, when he was undercover buying cocaine from a very clever nightclub owner in Sydney. He was glad he hadn't surrendered the identity at the end of that job, and more glad that he had started feeding money into the Tommy Paul bank account a few days before he left Melbourne, when the stench from his boss's office had sent him down to the bank.

He stripped his wallet of everything to do with Cole Goodwin and placed them, and his passport, into the hidden compartment. Tommy then walked out of the corporate business office. 'Goodnight, Mr Paul,' said the attendant as he waved him goodbye.

• •

Sandra's despondency seemed to hang around after the news from New Zealand. What was Cole doing? Where was he? Was he okay? Work ran a poor second to her preoccupation. She missed her close friend. She didn't know why she elected to sit at Cole's desk, but somehow sitting in his chair, bossing everyone around, brainstorming ideas, firming up suspects, all seemed to help bring him closer. She feared the crew was losing direction.

Mindlessly fidgeting, she pulled open his desk drawer, and noticed the film magazine that Cole had been reading only days before he had left. She smiled as she picked it up. Cole loved the cinema and all the trivia associated with movie stars. The magazine had been left open at the last page he had read, the story about a couple of old-time stars who fell in love while filming on a European island. Sandra wasn't up to romantic escapism, so she placed it carefully back in the drawer for another time.

Katherine interrupted her musings with the news that Inspector Mack wanted to speak with her immediately in his office. Sandra began to grudgingly pull herself out of the chair. Katherine continued, 'He's got a couple of suits with him, Sandy.'

That comment would normally send a shiver through any detective, but this morning Sandra half-expected to be interviewed so Katherine's news was no real surprise. After all, her close friend and boss was the prime suspect for a murder in New Zealand. All the same she straightened her blouse and skirt, fluffed her mop of hair and composed a suitably solemn expression as she walked to the Inspector's office. As it turned out Sandra knew the suits; both were detective sergeants from the Homicide Squad. One of them had wanted to poach her only a year ago to be a part of his crew. She had declined. Nonetheless, she was glad to see a familiar face; somehow it seemed to make what was to come less arduous. At least, she figured, she had credibility with one of the investigators liaising with the New Zealand team.

The pleasantries completed, Sandra sat down opposite the trio.

'What's your take on this, Sandra?' her friendly detective asked.

His partner busied himself with note taking.

'There's no way, Mick, that he did this. You know that. We all know that. It's just not Cole,' replied Sandra.

'He was due back at work last week. No contact. No explanation. It's looking awfully like it was him, Sandra. His dabs were all over the crime scene.'

Sandra interrupted, 'Of course his prints were there! He was a guest there for weeks.'

'He was the only one at the bed and breakfast,' Mick continued.

'Because it's winter!' snapped Sandra.

'The New Zealand boys have got thirty statements. Nearly the whole God-damned town, Sandra, saying that Cole was hardly ever out of the company of the deceased and his wife.'

'Come on, Mick, what do you think, he'd just sit in his room all day long on his own?' Sandra said.

'So how do you explain the bizarre card he wrote, sent with flowers ... lilies, Sandra?'

'Something out of Hannibal Lecter,' chipped Inspector Mack, who had great trouble looking at Sandra.

'All I know is that he couldn't have done it. There has to be another explanation,' Sandra surmised, sitting firmly back in her seat.

'Then where is he? Why isn't he here to help us?' Mick queried.

'Because he's on the run!' a thoroughly fed-up Sandra yelled as she sat forward and slammed her hand down hard on Mack's desk.

Silence. Her eyes moved tentatively from one detective to the other and finally rested on Mack, who sat utterly composed with the faintest trace of a smile on his face.

31st May

Tommy never actually made it out of the front door of the Alvear Palace Hotel. He stopped, turned his head to the right and left, and marvelled some more at what a truly magnificent establishment it was. He had never stayed in a place as nice, despite his worldly travels. Everything about this splendid-looking building kept pulling at him, dragging him back towards the reception desk, including Lola at the bar, from whom he hoped to receive another smile later in the night. And so, Tommy Paul checked into a mid-priced suite for $1000 a night. It would want to be a fucking good breakfast, he thought.

There was an old saying, well known in covert work, a saying that he had relied on once or twice before when dealing with bad men and worse situations: 'There is nothing more inconspicuous than the conspicuous'. A funny proposition, especially to a wanted man, but in the world of cops and robbers, undercover operatives and Mafia, sometimes being neatly tucked away in the centre of a shit fight was the safest place to be. Most of the time, cops on the hunt ran through dens of iniquity and down the backstreets and laneways, or through the seedy end of town, never thinking to knock on the door of the best hotel in the country.

He felt more comfortable about staying when his check-in clerk told him during their counter small talk that he was knocking off in ten minutes' time and had a two-day break planned with his girlfriend. That would remove from the picture anyone at the hotel who could recall his face at check-in.

• •

Decisions, decisions, decisions. Which decorative glass bottle of ludicrously expensive bath salts to empty into the now full tub?

31ST MAY

Having succumbed to the ruby red bottle, Tommy's fragrant lagoon of a bath presented the perfect haven in which to rest his tired body for a couple of hours. He jumped in and began to soak.

He really was kidding himself. The planned two-hour soak didn't last a quarter of that time as he was continually confronted with the plight that faced poor Lynette. How Cary must have suffered, and what pain Lynette must now be enduring, conscious or not. He tried desperately to think of other things, anything. But his urge to know more hung heavy.

As a compromise, he sat on his king-sized bed with its crisp cotton sheets and luxurious duvet, and flicked through the 38 channels on offer on the giant screen, naïvely hoping that something to do with the New Zealand investigation might be on. But it wasn't. He turned off the TV, lay back on his bed and pondered the brutal reaction of the Mafia family, which had resulted in the death of Cary and shocking injury to his wife. Cole tried to fathom what it was that had angered them so much. His mind drifted back to a time, more than a year earlier, at the height of his infiltration of the Mafia. A conversation he had never forgotten …

He was standing in the winter sun in Griffith, overlooking rolling hills of vineyards and orange trees, eating tasty, simple-flavoured food, with sips of vino di casa, and the sounds of Maria Callas through the outside speakers. Antonio had invited him to his family's country property as a special guest, like so many times before. Cole felt that he was on the edge of being accepted into the Mafia. The sun shone warm on their backs as he allowed Antonio to play host and take him for a stroll through the orange groves. The covert tape recorder hidden down the inner side of his leg was switched on.

Antonio walked with confidence, taking the occasional glance at his fruit trees. He was wearing a pair of Italian Replay jeans, soft calf leather shoes and a brilliant white Versace shirt, pressed to impress. He had the classic look of Italian style, as well as charm. He peeled an orange and handed one to Cole.

'You know the Italian life well.'

'It's the family ways that work for me,' Cole replied, enjoying his fruit.

Antonio stopped walking, threw his peel onto the ground and took a bite of his juicy orange. He looked neither at Cole nor his orange as the sun hit his face and he squinted.

'Don't ever make our road hard, Cole ... ever,' Antonio said, as he shifted his piercing gaze to Cole's face. He finished his orange before wiping his hands on a perfectly clean, white handkerchief. As they wandered back to the farm house he placed his hand on Cole's shoulder and reiterated his final word on the subject, 'Ever, or else we will kill you.'

By the end of the day, both men had reached an understanding.

Antonio made sure that Cole left the farm laden with wine and boxes of oranges. As he walked to his car fresh-faced kids with peppermint smiles held Cole's hand and Antonio opened the driver's door for him, whispering, 'Welcome to our family.'

Sporting his new Armani T-shirt Tommy ventured out into an otherwise fresh early evening to clear his head. He needed the exercise and the distraction. As he walked around the gardens he encountered a sight he had never seen before. Twice daily throughout Recoleta and its wealthy neighbouring suburbs, professional dog walkers would take their socialite charges for their morning and evening walks.

One dog handler, a girl he thought to be no more than twenty years of age and five foot tall, held a handful of diamond- and precious gem–encrusted leads. Each lead collared one of a small army of fourteen dogs ranging in size from the tiniest chihuahua to a rather portly labrador and many sizes and descriptions in between. Each pooch valiantly attempted to outdo the others as they pulled their handler along for the evening walk. The petite girl handler was unceremoniously tugged violently to the right as the group of dogs decided en masse to bound off and greet another group of dogs that had just appeared across the park, pulling her helplessly after them.

Tommy sat on a park bench until well past dusk, watching, until the novelty of his observations fell away. His thoughts pulled him back to New Zealand again and again. His head slumped down into his hands and a lump rose in his throat. Without the slightest hint of self-consciousness he broke down and sobbed, until there were no more. Wiping his cheeks dry as best he could with his pocket tissue, he straightened up and disappeared deeper into the lush gardens. He paced as fast as he could, for over an hour, around and around, till he tired himself out and walked off his heavy mood.

As darkness fell over the city, his appetite stirred, and he decided to see what all the fuss was about with the famed Argentinian steak houses. He admired the beautiful Italianate architecture along the way and settled for a lone table at a restaurant that oozed razor-sharp interior design. He was served the biggest T-bone steak he had ever seen, accompanied by a plate of relishes, chutneys and mustards, and he devoured it with a perfect medium-bodied Malbec.

The growing chill in the night air sent Tommy back to his hotel for nightcap. A stroll in the cocktail lounge had him face to face with a cluster of single female organisms, all sitting alone, all in search of the great invite to a $38 cocktail. Tommy smiled to himself as he thought back to Australia. Leigh would call such divas 'sharp aunties'. Forty-something darlings, lip glossed, hair tousled and teased, and ready for action ... or at least the company of a visiting overseas wallet in need of a special cocktail hour. Seeing the price list, Tommy opted for a Quilmes beer and a chat with the lovely bartender who was still on duty. Lola was only an hour away from the end of her shift, Tommy was quick to establish. She entertained him with her hotel gossip and they both predicted which divas would do well that night.

• •

There were at least half-a-dozen Belgian chocolate wrappers strewn along the carpet, as well as a single champagne cork on the floor of Tommy's room at 8 o'clock the next morning. A quiet knock and a room service waiter discreetly entered the suite, pushing a trolley gloriously laden with daintily prepared poached eggs with hollandaise sauce, honey-cured Virginia ham and tomatoes with tall glasses of freshly squeezed orange juice and Brazilian coffee for two. Lola hid her face under the sheets as the waiter secured Tommy's scratch on the bill and left. But not before he smugly took in the staff uniform draped over the sofa.

Lola quietly peeped from the sheets, looked around the room and across at the trolley. She shook her long dark hair free of the night and continued languishing in a room well beyond her own lifestyle. She saw her uniform over the chair and slid under the sheet again. Tommy slid out of bed to stand naked in front of the breakfast offering, popping a few tomatoes in his mouth. Lola peeped again, as he speed-read the front section of the newspaper in less than a few seconds. Then he sprang back into bed, a smile on his face.

'What time do you start work?' he asked.

'Not for a week. Things are slow in winter,' she said coyly.

There were more tasty morsels tempting Tommy than were on the breakfast tray that morning. He pulled back the sheets to reveal the stunningly beautiful Lola, who wriggled slowly as she gave an early morning stretch. He dropped a cherry tomato into her yawning mouth, which she eagerly accepted, and he watched her chew the tomato. The perfect invitation, he thought, as he gently eased his body over the top of hers and kissed down the side of her glorious neck. Lola's hands went exploring, finding Tommy at his most vulnerable. She held him softly, massaging ever so lightly as she parted her legs. Tommy's tongue glided slowly across her shoulder, and under her chin, stopping long enough to savour her previous night's scent. Then across her breast where he bit as gently as his urgent temptation would allow. Lola's wriggling stopped; he had her undivided attention.

She arched her back forward, in an attempt to push her nipple further into Tommy's mouth, further into the teasing zone. She enjoyed the delicious pleasure over and over, until the sensation ignited stronger triggers through her now glowing body. She grabbed both hands full of Tommy's hair, tugging at each clump before giving his head a gentle nudge, to send a message to her new lover and guide his head across her stomach and towards her expectant thighs. Tommy understood perfectly; his tongue tracked across her belly, playing momentarily with the gold-plated ring in her navel, before his whiskered chin found Lola's neat pubic hair. His eyes looked back at hers, which closed gently in anticipation.

She giggled nervously for a tiny second, more out of self-consciousness than anything else. Tommy's chin nudged into her, pressing firmly onto her. And there he would stay, softly devouring his beautiful new acquaintance. Teasing and playing with her as he savoured her captivating bouquet. When her ecstasy had almost reached a pinnacle, he lifted himself onto her. She wrapped her arms around him, kissing and nibbling at his well-defined shoulders as he gently entered her.

• •

A taint had hung over the team since news broke of the murder in New Zealand. That was always the way, Sandra thought; cops more often than not took the pessimistic approach in times of scandal. They'd rather hear a bad luck yarn than a sugar-and-spice story of heroics or good deeds. Not that the change in attitude necessarily devastated Sandra, it was just that she had enjoyed many years working on a crew that had never been associated with corruption or stories of dodgy behaviour. Now, knives were being sharpened. Looks were caught mid-flight. Conversations would stop when she stepped into a busy tearoom. She was worried.

She started on her emails; a few needed urgent attention. A few more dropped into her box as she was scrolling through. One was from the Prosecution office wanting her to collect paperwork left over after a court case. She pinged off a quick response. This was followed by a group email from the Police Association, drumming up support from the membership for the forthcoming AGM. The next email she deleted on first read—she didn't know a woman called Ingrid who had just gotten married.

The last email was from Jude to say that she was off to Sydney with her new crew, following up on some Lebanese targets importing firearms. She would be away for a few weeks, and asked Sandra to keep her in the loop if there were any developments or news on Cole. Sandra, knowing how emotional Jude had been when they last spoke, sent her back a sweet reply, telling her to be strong and that she'd stay in touch.

Time for a pot of Earl Grey tea, she reckoned. Something that she delighted in each afternoon shift, when the office would drop away to empty and she could enjoy a long cuppa and some peace and quiet. As she waited for the kettle to boil she made short work of the tin of biscuits lying open on the table-top.

Then it hit her. She sprinted back to her computer, reopening her deleted folder to find the Ingrid email. She clicked it open just as Spud walked into the office, sporting the uniform team look of misery.

Sandra read over the strange email, beckoning Spud to her desk.

'… please try to keep in touch, much love Ingrid,' she read aloud.

Spud glanced at the screen without interest and stood silently.

'It's him!' Sandra yelled, before realising she was doing so.

'It's him … Spud,' she whispered, her eyes darting around an otherwise near-empty office.

'Him, him, do you mean?' Spud queried, taking much more interest now as Sandra nodded excessively.

They printed two copies of the email and studied it, word by word. Midway through their appraisal, Sandra lashed out at her mate.

'I'm surprised you're making such fuckin' hard work of this, Spud. I don't know anyone called Ingrid and I haven't been to a wedding for three years. There isn't any family strife I know of, and yet it's addressed to me,' she stated firmly.

'It is odd.'

'What's the one thing Cole always says?' asked Sandra.

31ST MAY

'What's the bottom line. He always says that,' replied Spud.

'There's his bottom line ... "I had nothing to do with the family strife, please try and keep in touch",' she said, adding, 'Spud, he's saying he had nothing to do with the murder, the strife, and he wants us to reply.'

'You're right, dead right, good work,' offered Spud, a smile now spreading across his face.

The two of them spent the remainder of their shift reading and re-reading every word of the email: Cole was okay. They put their heads together to draft a lifeline to Cole.

∴

The corporate business centre's young attendant was pleased to see that nice Australian man who had said such nice things to him. He showed Tommy to a computer and handed him a note pad. Once the pleasantries had been dispensed, and the young fellow disappeared back to his own doodling, Tommy logged into his Yahoo account. He was delighted to find a message in the inbox.

Ingrid darling,

I don't know why you feel that you need to apologise. We have been friends for too long now to worry about silly wedding tiffs. I am more interested to hear all the gossip from the honeymoon. Don't worry about the argument at the reception. I know who really started it all.

Lots of love,
Your friend, Sandy

Tommy was elated. Sandra knew the true circumstances behind Lynette and Cary's fates. He would have to suffer these short snippets until he was safely tucked away, far enough from the ruthless thoroughness of the Calabrian punk, and Mack's connections.

He logged out of the Yahoo account. He acquired an envelope and stamps from the young attendant and returned his attention to the computer screen again. Tommy scrawled on the envelope the address he had been seeking out.

T. Paul,
Poste Restante,
Hoofdpostkantoor,
Amsterdam Central Post Office,
Singel 250 1016AB,
Amsterdam, Nederland.

He then retrieved the Cole Goodwin passport, credit cards and identification papers from his pocket, and placed them neatly into the envelope, sealing it. He affixed enough stamps to the front of the envelope before turning off the computer. With his Bees-Knees slung over his shoulder, Tommy walked back to the front counter and showed the envelope to the attendant, who read the address.

'Where do I post this, my friend?' he asked politely.

'It's quicker at the post box out the front of the hotel, it will be cleared in an hour,' the attendant stated, handing the envelope back to Tommy with a courteous smile.

Tommy thanked him as he walked out of the business centre. 'See you, my friend. I'm off home.'

'Goodbye, Mr Paul,' he replied cheerily.

Tommy strolled downstairs, past reception and headed for the main exit. He quietly slipped out the front door and posted the envelope, pleased with his productive start to the day. He thought he would travel up the Americas and then across to Amsterdam to pick up his envelope, in case he needed it, before hiding out somewhere in Europe.

31ST MAY

To carry a second set of identity papers would be foolish, especially when travelling through the United States. He would figure out the rest while he was on the road. He was no further than one hundred metres from the entrance of the hotel, heading towards the park, when he heard the sound of a motorcycle from behind. As it drew up beside him, his heart sank. The engine of the Chinese-made Tercel 175cc four-stroke engine idled as the passenger, wearing a tiny backpack, lifted her helmet, shaking a glorious dark mane of hair free. She smiled broadly.

'Do you want a lift?' Lola asked.

'I'm going to Australia. I told you,' replied Tommy.

'I know you're not, Tomas,' she said. 'You're going anywhere but.'

'Am I?' he stated with a curious smile on his face. He stared at the beautiful woman he had spent a perfect eleven hours with last night.

Lola pulled out a tabloid newspaper from inside her jacket and opened it to a small article accompanied by a cropped version of the fish photo showing Cole's face. She proceeded to translate the story as she read. Then she looked at him square in the eye, 'You're escaping from something, Tomas. Or is it Cole?'

Tommy/Cole stood frozen on the footpath.

'That wasn't in this morning's newspaper,' he said.

'We have ten newspapers in Buenos Aires, Tomas. The hotel uses the business broadsheet and international papers. This is the scandal paper,' she informed him.

'What are you going to do?' he asked.

'Be good to you. Like you were good to me.' Her smile held as she dropped her eyes to the footpath.

'How do I get out of this country?' he asked.

'Jump on,' Lola said with a delicious smile, 'we have a long ride. You can tell me your problems along the way.'

The pretty motorcyclist and her passenger headed off into the traffic on the undersized Tercel.

1st June

The desert town of Griffith basked the winter sun. The old Godfather walked between the rows of oranges, stopping every now and then to glance at the foliage and the ripening fruit. Walking towards him from the opposite direction was Massimo, who pulled a piece of fruit from the tree and crushed it in one hand to check the juice quality. He had been summoned by the old Godfather more than an hour ago, and he sensed the old man was somewhat anxious.

'Have you been with your girls again, Massimo?'

A smile ran across the younger man's face, but was quickly removed.

'I've been busy,' he replied.

'You have.'

'New Zealand was not good,' Massimo quipped.

'You have scared the detective to Argentina, the *Commissario* tells me,' said the old Godfather, handing him a torn-out section of a newspaper, with a photograph of the 'new'-look Cole Goodwin. 'Keep this with you, in case.'

'Shall I go after him?' Massimo offered.

'No. The water is too hot. You must go back to Calabria. You must help us with our next shipment.'

'In artichoke tins again?'

'Yes. You must prepare it for the boat.'

'I will miss Australia,' said Massimo.

'You will miss the girls, Massimo,' the old man said, as he looked Massimo up and down, secretly wishing he was thirty-five again. 'Say your goodbyes to the Juliets, you leave soon.'

And with that the old Godfather turned and walked back through the orchard, taking far more interest in his fruit than his Calabrian cousin's nephew.

• •

1ST JUNE

The young Alvear Palace Hotel attendant was in a lounge chair, a cigarette tucked behind his ear, wearing a five o'clock shadow, a plain white singlet and shorts. He sipped from a Coca-Cola can and continued reading his newspaper. While he was required to read the global newspapers and main national paper each day at work, it was his neighbourhood newspaper that he looked forward to. The football scores and gossip.

His mother walked into the loungeroom of their crowded high-rise public tenement and placed a meal in front of him. Then she went into the kitchen again. There were four other mouths to feed, all younger, all noisy. The attendant peered over the top of his newspaper at the plate of pan-fried liver with onions and mashed potato. He went back to his paper and Coca-Cola.

Once he had finished checking the scores of his team, disappointed at another loss for the season, he flicked the newspaper further to the front. On page ten he looked enviously at a photograph of Penelope Cruz and her new beau. She wore a long evening dress that was split down the middle and he imagined the shape of her breasts. He turned his paper ninety degrees to the right to further study the picture. He read on, glancing at the story of the New Zealand murder, initially not taking any notice of the grainy photograph of the wanted man. He was about to turn to the next page when he casually took another look, before bringing the photo closer to his nose.

That was the nice man from Australia, he thought.

• •

Seven hundred kilometres north of Buenos Aires lay the dishevelled concrete and plywood township of Paso de los Libres; a place famous for breeding magnificent Argentinian horses and far too many Aberdeen Angus cattle for the restaurants around Recoleta. The exhausted Chinese motorcycle was glad to find the end of its day as it pulled into the guest house by the side of the road, close on midnight. Tommy slowly removed his arms from Lola's waist. With just as much difficulty, he lifted his bright shiny new helmet from his head. Dropping his shoulder bag to the ground he manoeuvred his stiffened bowed legs comically in an attempt to straighten his very twisted torso.

Lola moved her younger body with considerably more ease. She led him through a rickety flywire screen door into a near-empty room that acted as a reception for the guest house. She signalled for Tommy to stay where he was. He offered no argument, preferring the comfort of an old easy chair in the corner of the blue lime-washed room. Lola walked further into the building, to the owner's quarters. The sound of her native tongue could be heard as she happily greeted someone Tommy could not see. Before long three gorgeous yet grubby little kids came running from the room giggling in excitement. They pulled up quickly when they first noticed Tommy and their smiles fell from their faces. Then, as if rehearsed, each of them turned around at the same time and ran back into the room, yelling a chorus of 'Gringo, gringo', before breaking into fits of laughter.

Five minutes later Lola and Tommy were ensconced in their near bare room, having shared the briefest of showers from a hot water system that had barely enough for a baby's bath. They walked from the shower, each with a less than luxurious small towel wrapped around their waist. Tommy combed his wet hair back and checked his bleary eyelids. As he turned to leave the bathroom he stood to gaze at Lola brushing her teeth. She flicked water in his face and he responded by trying to pull her towel away. Lola stepped into the bedroom and switched on a wall sconce as Tommy dealt a severe death to a large mosquito. They then flopped, letting the motorcycle vibrations seep from their tired bodies on the only furniture, a three-quarter-sized bed, and stared at a ceiling fan that whined as it turned. Lola snuggled into Tommy, placing her hand across his chest and easing her head onto his shoulder. It was a hot night, for winter.

• •

1ST JUNE

The same kids, with their same grubby faces, ran barefoot through the paddock, just a respectful enough distance away from a majestic chestnut stallion that pranced around the enclosure. Tommy leant on the railing and watched the combination of animal magnificence and child tomfoolery. The early morning sun glowed on Lola's face as she nudged into Tommy, placing both arms around his trunk and resting her face on his back.

'What a creature,' he said, watching the horse toss its head about.

'You have many horses in Australia, yes?' she asked.

'Many, and the countryside is similar. Lots of nothing.'

'But we have no kangaroos,' she laughed, breaking her hold.

Lola walked pensively away, back towards the guest house, head down, kicking dust with her boots. Tommy sensed it was time to walk together and he joined her, placing his arm around her shoulder. She looked up.

'You have been honest with me, Tomas, or whatever your name is. I worry your Inspector Mack will kill you.' She held her gaze on him, hoping for a comment.

'He hasn't so far,' he said, watching Lola, knowing there was at least one more hard question she needed to ask. He leaned into her and they kissed long and gently as his fingers ran through her hair. After the kiss she tackled her next question.

'Is there? Do you have? Is there, a wife?'

'No,' he answered, firmly, 'there was once but that was many years ago.'

'No one for *Señor* Tomas in Australia?' she pressed.

Tommy couldn't help but think of Jude. Someone who excited him, each time he found himself in her presence. The girl he had thought of each day since he had left Australia. He placed his arms around Lola, a woman who also excited him. One who was helping him to escape. He enjoyed her touch, her smell. Their love-making over the past two nights had been perfect. And she was beautiful. He thought again of Jude and how she was engaged to be married.

'There is someone in Australia. But she is with her man,' he said, 'so, no, there is no one.'

Lola responded by holding him close. For that moment, he felt that they were a couple. He stopped thinking of Jude altogether, closing his eyes as they held each other, as if not wanting to let go yet, knowing they soon would. Tommy looked over Lola's shoulder at the three energised kids in the paddock, who were now heading towards them. He turned and faced the guest house.

'How long to the border?' he said.

'We are halfway, Tomas. We'll be there late tonight.'

'Noooooo more motorbike … pleeeease,' he pleaded, as Lola broke into a laugh, along with the grubby kids who imitated Tommy's actions and words before giggling their way home.

• •

Inspector Mack sat opposite the stern-looking Deputy Commissioner, seated in his highrise office with views across to the Docklands and Melbourne skyline. This was the very same officer who had beaten Mack in the promotion stakes three years earlier. Mack despised him. In fact, he often wished to prise his two beady eyes out with a soup spoon and use them in a game of marbles.

But, this morning was not the time for thoughts of revenge—it was the moment for *his* grand performance. Mack had been summoned to discuss the actions of his wayward Detective Sergeant. Time to place a few nails into Goodwin's coffin.

'I just can't fathom that Goodwin could have done this,' the Deputy Commissioner began.

'Isn't it the most unbelievable turnaround? I mean, I always thought he was my finest team leader. A brilliant operative,' Mack said, shaking his head as if flabbergasted. 'But … there have been rumours of him smelling of late.'

'Really?' asked the Deputy Commissioner, not wanting to know details.

'Yes. I'm afraid the word was he was turning bad.'

'The media are having a field day with him being a cop. Will they find any shit?'

'How much more shit do they need, Sir? I mean, he is suspected of killing an old guy and cutting the wife's throat.'

The Deputy Commissioner lost himself in the newspaper article spread out on his desk. 'What's the condition of the poor woman?'

'Lucky if she pulls through, they say,' Mack offered, dropping his head down. He had high hopes that the old goat would snuff it at any moment.

The Deputy Commissioner's PA interrupted the solemn tone of the conversation with a tray carrying a pair of Wedgwood cups, alongside matching teapot and dish of fancy biscuits. She eased the tray onto the veneered oak desktop and excused herself graciously. Mack, who hadn't had time for breakfast, briefly forgot himself and reached for a jam fancy before realising his slight.

'What are our Argentinian friends saying?'

'Goodwin's arrival card was handed in at Buenos Aires three days ago,' Mack said.

'The Argentinians will get him. You know, Inspector, I read a fascinating book last year about their history after World War II, taking in Nazis and fascists to build the Perón regime.'

Inspector Mack looked dumbfounded at his superior, who had drifted off.

'Inspector, I want you to put your effort into tracking down your sergeant. Flush him out. Get the Argentinians working. This is embarrassing, don't you know?'

• •

Mack was alone in his office. He hadn't made any contact with Buenos Aires—he'd get to it, some day. Despite all the developments of late, he was a little busy with his very last annual report. At least he hoped it was his last. Hidden under the blotting board of his desk was a brochure for a Citroën 2CV. The quirky two-cylinder 'ugly duckling' car, as it was called in France. When in Provence the previous year, he and Dorothy had driven one belonging to a charming old Frenchman. The old geezer only wanted 3000 euros for it; a bargain, Mack thought. He might secretly buy the ugly duckling for his swan. The picture from the brochure could easily be wrapped in a birthday card and handed to his beloved for her birthday, in six weeks' time.

He was about to pick up the telephone to call the owner in France when it rang. It was his counterpart in the Argentinian Police department, Inspector Dias.

'Yes, of course, Inspector. I was going to call. Tomorrow, I think. I mean, yes, tomorrow,' Mack said. He was sure Dias would sense his run of nerves but Dias simply went on to explain that he had only just received fresh information that the Australian murder suspect was now travelling under the name of Tommy Paul, and that all borders had been alerted to watch for anyone by that name. Mr Paul had stayed at the Alvear Palace Hotel and his hotel account had been paid for with a National Bank MasterCard.

Mack scribbled the Interpol information onto the Citroen 2CV brochure, wincing as he did so. He now needed to print another.

He called Donny and asked him to drop by his office straightaway. His little mate was soon standing at his door, tapping his fingers annoyingly against the door jamb.

'Come in, come in and close the bloody door,' Mack insisted.

'I shouldn't come here, you know.'

'Okay ... okay, I know, but it's important,' Mack said.

'I won't ask,' said an inquisitive Donny as he looked at Mack's messy desk.

'Don't ... fucking annual reports! Look, take that,' Mack handed Donny the information about Tommy Paul. Donny studied it.

'That's the name Goodwin's travelling under and, as luck has it, he's using his MasterCard. Can you get your guy to tag it?' Mack asked.

1ST JUNE

Donny looked at the sixteen-digit number, then nervously through the partition at the other detectives.

'Sure, but keep it quiet. I've had that contact for years.'

'Good. Do you have a contact in Visa?' Mack asked.

'No, I'm fucked. My contact was sacked last year and all their shutters are down for me, but I might be able to ask around.'

'Any idea what's with the name Tommy Paul?' Mack asked.

'I was going to ask you.'

'Obviously one that has a passport and a MasterCard.'

'Spud would be able to tell us,' stated Donny, somewhat naïvely.

'That will never happen, him and his fucking secret laptop.'

Donny folded the brochure and slipped it into his back pocket before he disappeared out the door.

Alone again, Mack thought, truth be known, he didn't care too much about Goodwin. Goodwin, or Tommy Paul, or whoever he called himself, was a man running into a dead end. If the Mafia didn't kill him, then he'd be done by the New Zealand cops for murder and attempted murder in the long run. A perfect result.

• •

The following day Tommy and Lola found themselves at the northeast corner of Argentina, looking across at Brazil and Paraguay through a gasoline haze. The atmosphere suited the numbness of their bodies; their ride was almost complete. Before them, trees of exaggerated heights had created an enormous canopy over the lush undergrowth in jungle greens and emerald. The intimidating roar of Iguazu Falls could be heard in the immediate background.

Tommy pulled into a roadside eatery, scattering a flock of chickens in their wake. He smacked the dust from his T-shirt and dumped his helmet with disdain. Lola shook her head in her attempt to clear the past two days' ride. They straightened their backs. The open-walled bamboo-clad café was abuzz with slightly built, brown-skinned locals. Everyone was smoking. Lola ordered breakfast. The locals took a long hard look at Tommy, then spoke quickly to each other, glancing at the pair, waving their hand at Lola, as if in disapproval.

Lola, wearing dusty faded jeans and a loose-fitting pink singlet top, reached across the table and took Tommy's hands into her own. The watchful faces nodded, and the unwanted attention faded. Except for that of an Indian girl, no more than six years of age with a deep-brown complexion, chubby cheeks and eyes like coin slots. She sat at the end of a bench, wearing a brilliant multi-coloured Indian jacket and holding a string of beads in her tiny fingers. She flashed a smile and held up her trinket. A fat waitress served their coffee and plastic plate of fried eggs with beans with chilli. Lola was in a hurry; she had Tommy on a schedule. She planned for him to catch the midday flight from Alejo García Airport in Paraguay, but there was still harder road ahead.

'This is the Provincia de Misiones, the centre of South America. I was born only twenty minutes from here,' Lola said.

'Jungle people?'

'No. Traditional people. It's wild country, they don't like foreigners.'

Tommy nodded as he looked back at the little girl, still smiling at them with her beads. 'We're about to leave Argentina, eh?'

'Yes ... across to Brazil, then across the Friendship Bridge to Paraguay, all in ten minutes.'

'Passports needed?' asked Tommy, edging closer to Lola.

'Not usually. That's why we came. This region is full of smugglers.'

'What on earth for?' Tommy asked, looking around at squalor and mangy dogs doing surveillance on the tables.

'Once we cross the Friendship Bridge we'll be in the biggest duty-free town in the Americas. Full of bandits buying loads of goods to be sold for big profits in Brazil and Uruguay,' Lola added, as she finished her eggs and coffee.

'So what's the problem with buying duty free?'

1ST JUNE

'Nothing except they abuse the limit. And the border *Policia* accept kickbacks to turn a blind eye. It's bad country.'

'So why are we here?'

'Because the guards don't worry about tourists, just smugglers. We're just two on a bike,' Lola explained as she leaned across to kiss Tommy's lips.

The churning washing machine noise of the waterfalls competed with the racket from the herd of tiny motorcycle engines, let loose from the traffic light. Tommy watched a dozen or more bikes race into town, ahead of at least another dozen beat-up utes stacked with children off to school. The roads were potholed and debris blew into the air. A short stout Hispanic woman wearing an apron four sizes too large placed a scrap of paper onto the table, with '25' written on it. Tommy pulled a few coins from his pocket and handed them over. The woman flashed her mouthful of brilliant white teeth.

It was time to move. Tommy walked to the bike, pondering where he might have ended up if it hadn't been for Lola. They had come a long way together.

They fitted themselves onto their motorcycle for the last time. Tommy signalled to the smiling child to come forward. She obliged shyly. He reached deep into his jeans pocket to retrieve a fistful of coins and placed them into the chubby little hand, gaining another smile. Very dutifully the little girl offered up the delicate bracelet of polished river stones to Lola, who kissed Tommy and tapped the child playfully on the nose with her finger. The giggling girl ran back into the café as Lola hung on and the bike was kick-started.

'Just go easy on the bridge, the guards shoot first and ask questions later.'

Tommy eased forward, in sync with the next green light. Halfway through the lights he pulled back hard on the throttle and the bike raced forward.

..

Half-a-dozen turns left and right and a short stretch on a busy road and Tommy pulled the bike to a halt. The rear wheel slipped from under them but he managed to hold the bike upright as he stared at the Brazilian side of the Friendship Bridge. He pulled his helmet from his head. Up to twenty men and women walked from the Brazilian side of the border to Paraguay, each carrying empty baskets, no doubt heading over to buy duty-free goods. The National Guard boom gate was up and the occasional car approached, only to be waved through by the uninterested *Policia*.

'Easy. Just do it slow, Tomas.'

'Cool,' said Tommy as the helmet went back on. The bike moved forward. As they eased past the boom gate, five figures clad in khaki lazed about their guard box in the sun. Three were armed with old Russian army Kalashnikov .47 automatic assault weapons, the others with pistols, holstered at the hip. Tommy slowed to ten kilometres. One guard, sporting three stripes on his arm, took an interested look at Lola and threw out a smile. She reacted by turning her head and squeezing her arms firmly around Tommy. The bridge was almost empty. A gust of wind blew up and a mess of papers, dust and leaves spiralled through the air. They squinted to see the ugly township of Cuidad del Este, straight ahead. The river raged far below.

The shrill ringing of a telephone could be heard from the guard box. The pair continued steadfastly along their path, only one hundred metres to go to the other side. Tommy could see another bike approaching from the opposite direction, its lone rider also travelling slowly. The boom gate he headed away from was up, to allow free passage. Then a siren began to wail within the Paraguayan guard box. A red light flashed on its roof. The barrier dropped sharply and two uniformed men stepped forward, their Kalashnikovs pointed menacingly.

Lola gripped Tommy tightly; his back arched. He brought the bike to a halt and faced the guards, a pair of large armed dots in the dusty distance. He turned to look back at the Brazilian guard box. They too had closed their border. The five guards knelt on the road,

1ST JUNE

aiming their weapons towards the centre of the bridge. Tommy's heart sank.

The other motorbike also stopped, five metres away. The face of its lone rider, minus a helmet, was ripe with panic. A guard ran from the Paraguay sentry box yelling at him. The wailing from both sirens had become deafening. Pedestrians scattered and lay motionless on the roadway. The guard was now only twenty metres away. Tommy heard the other motorcyclist rev his bike. He noticed a massive fixed pannier attached to its rear seat. The rider dropped into gear, turned his bike around to face the direction he had come from and pulled hard on the throttle. He raced towards the boom gate. As quick as lightning, the guard shot him. The uncoordinated body fell heavily from the bike, which somersaulted twice before coming to a smoking rest against the bridge railing. Tens of thousands of dollars' worth of silver Gillette disposable razor blades spewed from the pannier bag onto the Friendship Bridge.

Tommy quickly clambered from his bike, his trembling hands raised high in the air. He used his body weight to force Lola to the ground. The guards from the Brazilian side raced at them, shouting *'Policia, Policia!'* as they pointed their rifles. Lola looked up and beckoned to the friendly sergeant. He leaned down as she whispered to him in her native dialect. The sergeant helped Lola to her feet and walked her to the bridge siding. She explained their tourist adventure and the sergeant smiled. She smiled nervously back, this time not turning her head away. He flirtatiously waved her on, while menacingly shooing Tommy away with his gun. The tiny Chinese Tercel motorcycle and its scared rider, passenger and their luggage moved off, passing the motionless body of the razor-blade smuggler.

• •

Lola's motorcycle was parked near the front door of the Alejo García Airport, fifteen minutes from the Friendship Bridge. Tommy was arguing at the desk counter with the ticket clerk, a heavy man wearing a once-white open-necked shirt. Tommy's Bees-Knees was at his feet. He had been trying his best to secure a seat on the midday flight to Nicaragua, yet the attendant didn't seem to want the fare. Lola, who was sitting and flicking through a magazine, stepped forward to lend her Spanish language skills.

'Tomas, give me your credit card and passport and go order two coffees,' she suggested. Tommy was glad to see the end of the waxy-skinned unhelpful man and handed over his documents. He strolled off, glancing for the last time at the dirt-covered Tercel, which stood, spent, at the front of the building. He spied a coffee machine at a kiosk that sold everything from American soft-porn magazines to dodgy cigarettes and ashtrays made from monkey feet. Ordering two coffees, he took a seat on a barstool. By the time Lola had joined him he had finished the second cup, and was looking frustrated.

She knew Tommy's stomach would be churning, as was hers. They had become so close in their three nights together, three different beds, and 1500 kilometres of bad road. She rubbed her hand across his back, then up into his hair and finally rested it on his neck, massaging gently.

'You're on the Nicaragua flight, leaving in thirty minutes,' she said, looking forlornly at him.

'Charming,' he replied.

'At least you're away. I've booked you a connection to the States from there, but you'll need to stay overnight in Nicaragua.'

'Want to come?' he asked, fixing the river-stone bracelet on her slim wrist.

'Don't ask, Tomas, you might be surprised by the answer. Now go over to the counter and sign your credit card and he'll give you the tickets.'

Tommy leaned across to Lola and placed a hand on each side of her face. He stared long and hard into her eyes, and then kissed her on the lips.

1ST JUNE

'Come,' was all he said as he turned slowly to walk towards the counter. Tears filled Lola's eyes as she watched him go.

As he watched the big man fuss over the fare at the counter, he considered abandoning the transaction and staying in the jungle, with Lola. A whole future rushed before him as he pictured himself with his new girlfriend selling trinkets to tourists, or opening a bed-and-breakfast.

But they were the dreams of a tired man who needed to keep moving.

Lola rejoined Tommy at the exit gate with an armful of motorcycle helmets and a heavy heart. Her new love wrapped his arms tightly around her.

'Remember, you might have two names, but you are alone. Nicaragua is dangerous, just stay in your hotel till your connection leaves,' urged Lola.

And with that, Tommy walked off.

• •

The one-time smiling sergeant from the guard box pulled up his boom gate to allow the deceased smuggler his final passage. Nervous locals, with heads bowed deeply, crossed themselves as they eased their way back onto the bridge. Some of them could only get part way over before their fear and superstition had them return, despite the sergeant's best efforts to wave them on. As he walked back into his guard box a fax was rolling out of the old machine, a security alert on a man wanted by the head of the Buenos Aires Criminal Investigation unit, Inspector Dias.

The sergeant looked closely at the bulletin. He then looked at the bridge. Then at his watch. He smiled slowly and screwed the bulletin into a neat little ball, throwing it basketball-style into the bin.

3rd June

The Taca Air twin engine DC9 aircraft with fewer than thirty passengers aboard landed unconvincingly at Managua. As Tommy climbed down the metal steps from the aircraft and strolled through the sweltering heat haze, a massive crack of lightning smacked him into reality. The skies opened and he was hit with a torrential downpour.

Tommy schlepped his bag through the sweaty, damp hordes. He watched in fascination as the locals abused any level of officialdom that slowed them down. Not once was he asked for his passport or any identification. Nor did he receive even a passing glance from the two national security guards on duty. It was lunchtime and they seemed far more content to gulp down their simple meals from stainless steel bowls than to waste any time on passengers.

He ventured onto the bus rank and into a foul mixture of humidity and heat. His shorts and sandals soon became saturated. The antiquated bus that he boarded bounced along the cobblestone road with Tommy and a cabin full of Hispanics. Some held cages with bantams; others had armfuls of vegetables and local trinkets: it was market day. An hour later they arrived in Granada, a neat grid of streets wrapped around a central park. Tommy found himself a room without a view at the Hotel Colonial.

He surrendered to a revitalising shower then made his way downstairs to the bar for a whisky sour. When that was met with a blank look from a moody bartender he settled instead for a beer.

A payphone in the corner of the lounge beckoned. Tommy dialled a telephone number he knew well: the telephone extension in the ACA tearoom, often used by the staff to take their private calls. He swigged the last of his warm beer as he listened to it ring.

'Hello ACA, Katherine speaking, can I help you?'

3RD JUNE

'Detective Butler, please,' he asked the administration officer in his best Italian-accented voice. He heard the sound of high heels tap-tapping along the tiled floor as his coins disappeared. By the time he heard approaching feet he was nearly out of silver.

'Hello, Detective Butler.'

Tommy struggled with a reply.

The voice said again, 'Hello, Detective Butler speaking.'

He finally managed to form the words. 'Hello, you.'

The line went silent for seconds. Sandra gave an awkward look at Katherine, who instinctively collected her coffee cup and biscuit and headed back to her office.

'Where are you?' Sandra asked, speaking very softly into the mouthpiece.

'Next dumb question? In hell actually.'

'Sorry. *How* are you?'

'Tired,' he replied honestly.

'Mack's stitched you into a dead end, hasn't he?' she said.

'Well put.'

'Did you see the punk in New Zealand?'

'Sort of,' he replied.

'Can we make mileage of it?' she queried.

'No, we've got jack shit,' came his response.

'What can we do?'

'Sweat it out, till Mack fucks up.'

'Do you want me to do anything?' she asked in a whisper.

'I'll let you know. I'm now the Sydney cocaine guy. I've got to go,' he said as his last coin vanished.

Tommy took his beer and moved to the front of the hotel, keeping a safe enough distance from the local Indian vendors who were busy fleecing tourists. He felt comfortable that neither of them had given away too much. He was also confident that the tearoom phone would not be bugged. If there was one location on the planet that would be untraceable, Granada was it.

• •

Spud was buried in a new investigation file; most of the copy he'd been supplied was pulled apart and strewn over his desk. He was busy linking electricity accounts with suspect names. It was the early hard-slog work, as boring as bat shit, he thought, as he looked up, pleased at Sandra's interruption. Her face was alive.

'Are you going to tell me?' he asked.

'Tell you what?'

'It's plastered all over your face.'

Sandra paused momentarily and fell heavily in the spare seat beside his desk, grabbing her friend's hands tightly.

'He just rang,' she told him.

Spud looked hard at her. 'Get the fuck outta here!'

'No … serious. On the tearoom phone, just now, Spud.' She kept hold of his hands and lightly banged them into the desktop in excitement.

'Slow down. What'd he say?' Spud was bursting with curiosity.

'Do you remember Cole doing that cocaine sting in Sydney maybe four years ago?'

He closed down the bat shit and attempted to open a highly secure file.

'Sure, the nightclubs'. He tapped away at the keyboard to open the file.

'Look away,' he demanded. His password had been accepted. Spud was now in the most sensitive program in the ACA—the highly confidential program that held the identities used by the covert operatives, a program that only Spud had access to. Sandra looked back at the screen. Spud opened an index in the name of Cole Goodwin. He scrolled down a list of seven identities and selected Tommy Paul.

'Great job that, but Tommy was killed off three and a half years ago.'

'The job was, but Tommy is still alive,' said Sandra. Spud raced from page to page on the electronic file, in an attempt to see when the identity papers, passport and credit cards had been surrendered by Cole to be subsequently destroyed. He soon gave up.

3RD JUNE

'The bugger's kept the ID.'

'For a rainy day.'

'For a rainy day.'

'We need to tag each piece of ID, Spud, so we can track him.'

'Easy. What's he got?' They scrolled down the list of identification issued. He then read them out. 'A passport, a MasterCard, a Visa card, driver's licence and a heap of business papers that won't mean much now.'

'The rest will though, he's obviously kept them active—tag them,' said Sandra.

'I'll be told if anyone is looking at the cards.'

'Brilliant, set up a 24/7 warning,' Sandra demanded as she watched the analyst play spooks with his system.

At that moment, Leigh came strolling into the office, having been out for a smart lunch with a sharp auntie. He placed an elbow on each side of the door jamb.

'Not much happening, guys?' he queried casually.

His question was met by intense looks from both Spud and Sandra.

'Time for a walk, Leigh,' said Sandra.

• •

Entry into the United States. The toughest gig around for drug smugglers, terrorists or honest cops on the run. His only relief was in knowing that he carried nothing on him of suspicion. First to Miami, then on to JFK Airport in New York City. Over and over Tommy had conditioned himself to accept the intrusive and belittling questions from the Customs Control officials, as well the ridiculously long queues.

Remarkably, his journey went smoothly. If anything it was anti-climactic. Tommy, most likely due to his 'nation friendly' Australian citizenship, seemed to move through the customs and security points with relative ease. Certainly, once the staff had assured themselves that he wasn't a native of Central America nor a cocaine smuggler, progress was remarkably quick and hassle-free.

He made the snap decision to investigate a fare to Amsterdam, to put an end to the endless travel. He picked up his Bees-Knees and walked back into the throng.

• •

Inspector Mack's pot of Cascade lager was half empty although he was glad to think it was half full these days, things were going so well for him. He had just met Donny at the Dogs Bar in St Kilda, to pass on the exciting news. Apparently the attendant in the business centre in the flash hotel where Cole had stayed had recalled extra information about Tommy Paul. He had told Inspector Dias that he had helped 'Tommy' post a letter to himself to the central post office in Amsterdam. The Argentinian inspector reckoned Goodwin was headed to Amsterdam to collect the envelope at the Poste Restante counter. Mack could only wonder what was in that envelope and why Goodwin was going to Amsterdam. Although, whatever it was, he was far more interested in the remainder of his $200 000 graft from the Mafia. He could almost smell the money now, the way his luck had turned. Mack handed a piece of paper, on which the words 'Poste Restante' were written, to Donny.

'Can you alert the old Godfather, mate?'

'Sure,' Donny replied, 'But who's Poste Restante?'

'Donny. Mate. Of course you wouldn't know, it's French. It means "hold for collection". You can have mail sent to the main post offices anywhere around the world, marked "Poste Restante" and they'll hold the letter for a few weeks.'

'Righty-ho. So he must be heading there.'

'Yes, Donny. Let the old man know.'

3RD JUNE

Donny placed the piece of paper in his wallet and left his half-full beer on the table to run across to the McDonald's opposite to use the payphone. He needed to ring the Calabrians.

By the time Donny had returned, a fresh pot awaited both of them.

'Done deal. I let them know,' said Donny.

'Was he happy?' asked Mack.

'I don't think Godfathers are ever happy, are they?' replied Donny.

They both laughed into their beers.

'He did tell me one interesting thing, though.'

'Mmmm,' said Mack.

'He'll double the fee to clear a shipment of tinned artichokes next month,' said Donny.

'Fuckin' artichokes?' the Inspector queried.

'Four tonnes of the stuff,' Donny continued.

'Four fuckin' tonnes!' Mack drained the last of the beer from his glass. After a quick exercise in mental arithmetic he looked back at Donny.

'Tell the fuck it will be a million bucks,' he said bluntly.

A smile spread across Donny's younger face.

'I already did, boss. They're happy with the mill.'

'That's a lot of fuckin' lovely.'

Mack, not believing his fortune, patted his little mate lightly across the cheek. 'You bloody little ripper,' he said, just before he yelled loudly to the waitress, 'Girly, we need a wine list over here!'

Yet Mack would never know Donny's cunning. Donny had already demanded one million dollars for a clear passage to the drug shipment. Should Mack have settled for less, Donny would have gladly and secretly pocketed the balance.

• •

ON THE RUN

A fresh-faced Massimo, toothpick in mouth, carried his powder-blue suitcase along the concourse at JFK Airport in New York City. He glanced at the departure board, looking for his flight to Milano. His mobile phone buzzed from within his suitcase. He dropped the case on the floor and bent down to rummage through the side pocket to catch the call.

'*Pronto, si, si,*' he answered.

He stood silently as the old Godfather explained the need for him to head immediately for Amsterdam. Massimo listened to the entire story and then hung up. He looked around the air terminal and found the ticket sales counter for Czech Airlines. The punk then moved to the queue, reaching for the wallet in his back trouser pocket at the same time.

• •

Several lines further along at the same terminal, unbeknown to Massimo, stood Tommy, looking haggard. He had edged his way to the front of his queue, a wait that had taken half a morning. One Virgin Atlantic one-way ticket to Amsterdam later, Tommy was reloading his wallet with credit cards and passport. He placed the ticket in his pocket as he headed towards departure gate B22, for a flight that was leaving in an hour and a half.

By the time he had proceeded to the long customs queue Massimo had begun his walk to departure gate B26. His flight was leaving in an hour.

• •

In Amsterdam, Massimo stood frustrated at customs, looking at his watch. He was a good half-hour behind schedule. No matter, he thought; he was merely checking into a hotel before heading to Dam Square the following day, where his work would seriously start.

3RD JUNE

Tommy, on the other hand, had landed on time. He and his Bees-Knees sailed towards customs to join the queue only a few bodies behind Massimo.

Mayhem reigned on the taxi rank mostly because it was a Friday afternoon and the EU diplomat flights had landed. The Dutch taxi spruiker did his best. It was almost theatrical to watch the stream of taxis filing along the curb-way; doors opening, cargo and fare in, and bulleting off along the freeway. Tommy was all but pushed into his car, happy to at least have a ride. From the rear window he noticed a couple of cabs behind, a driver struggling to lift a powder-blue suitcase into the boot of his little Audi cab. Tommy's senses prickled as he turned to get a closer look through the rear window of his taxi, at the traveller. His only glimpse was in silhouette, a male. At that point his own taxi saw an opening and catapulted from the curb. Tommy didn't see the cab again.

The taxi came to rest at the door of Tommy's chosen hotel, a short stroll from Dam Square. Tommy was quickly out of the stuffy vehicle and into the heat of the early summer evening, eager to check in and find a cool shower. He dropped his shoulder bag at reception and offered up his passport and MasterCard to the arrogant hotel clerk.

A few metres further up, Massimo's taxi also pulled into the kerb. He stepped out and through the front entry of his hotel. He too was eager for a shower. Unlike Tommy, Massimo had been to Amsterdam many times on business and he always stayed at the same hotel. If ever there was a problem with the drug shipments, particularly ecstasy, that needed to be sorted, Massimo was the Calabrians' go-to man. Hettie, the overly friendly receptionist, handed him his usual suite key with a smile that suggested she might just turn down his sheets a little later on. She often stayed overnight when Massimo was in town, a man with no shortage of cash and a generous disposition.

After his shower, Tommy headed out again in search of dinner. He walked to the Central Canal area and took a lone table at the famed Jim's Greek restaurant, ordering a whisky sour. Initially his waiter had ushered him to an outside table as it was a balmy night. Tommy politely refused the gesture, opting for the air conditioner inside the less crowded room. He was feeling melancholy and drifted into delicious memories of Lola as he played with his food.

Alongside Jim's was the competing Christo's Greek tavern. Seated at an outside table with chequered linen was Massimo, who asked a passing waiter for a glass of wine.

The adversaries had virtually identical meals. Plates of saganaki, the delicious fried cheese, followed by a Greek salad topped with Bulgarian fetta, then char-grilled octopus and lamb gyros with extra lemon. The only difference was that Massimo headed back to his hotel moments before Tommy. Both of them turned out the lights in their suites at near enough the same time.

6th June 9.30 a.m.

DONG, DONG! signalled half an hour to go before the post office would open. Tommy could hear the thunderous sound of the town hall clock as he stepped from his shower cubicle. Only 10 minutes into his early morning jog around the old town of Amsterdam and he was buggered, back at the hotel, undressed and enjoying the sensation of hot water on his traveller's back. He really hadn't done any exercise since his last run along the beach in New Zealand, 9 days ago. He hurried himself in getting dressed and pulled closed the door to Room 8. He had the strangest sensation of a countdown, to get to the post office and be front of the queue of the busiest travellers' Poste Restante section in Europe. He guessed that the parcel would have arrived by now, 7 days after being posted. If not he would call Amsterdam home until it did.

He headed off to a quaint outdoor breakfast bar on the medieval Dam Square in the centre of Amsterdam. He took his seat under an umbrella to indulge in an assortment of Dutch pastries and magnificent coffee. From his seat, he observed a beautiful woman parading over the cobblestones. The tall, dark-haired girl with the longest smoothly tanned legs sat down opposite his table, wearing a transparent fine white linen shirt with 6 buttons, the top half of which were deliciously undone. Her catwalk good looks and well-endowed cleavage captivated Tommy, who enjoyed a 5-minute game of hidden glimpses with her, as she pretended to read her magazine.

Massimo, on the other hand, had been up to more advanced pursuits in Room 4 of his hotel. He was too Italian to fuss over breakfast cakes, preferring strong coffee only, and a last-minute sexual frolic with his own treat of the morning, Hettie, who had just left, leaving Massimo time for a last-minute errand before the post office opened. He was in a stamp, coin and military memorabilia store

ON THE RUN

3 shops away from Tommy's café. He was negotiating with the stuffy old codger behind the counter but the man, with his ruddy face and pencil-thin grey moustache, was annoying Massimo, asking pesky questions.

A smiling Tommy casually paid his bill, leaving a 2-euro tip; well worth it, he thought, as he winked a goodbye to the pretty girl. He strolled across the Raadhuisstraat walkway to the central post office. One minute behind him strolled another tourist, Massimo, zero smile, having completed his transaction.

• •

DONG! DONG! DONG! DONG! DONG! DONG! DONG! DONG! DONG! DONG!

The town hall clock struck as the front doors were flung open and the milling crowd entered. Tommy's eyes searched around the room. He joined a few people at the Poste Restante counter and took up a position behind them. He hit his back pocket to ensure that his wallet and passport were there. Behind him was a pair of handsome blond Norwegians of university age. Both were Lycra-clad members of their national cycling team, obviously reliving the events of the night before as they laughed over stories. Behind them stood a stoic Massimo. Oddly enough, for such a warm morning, he was wearing a jacket.

Massimo glanced at the back of Tommy's head and then down at the crumpled newspaper clipping in his left hand. He returned the clipping to his pocket, and with his right hand, he tightened his grip on the handle of a Great War bayonet, now concealed under his jacket. The small band of travellers seeking mail all edged forward one pace.

Massimo eased the bayonet from beneath the cover of his black linen jacket, and held it beside his right leg. Coming through the front door of the post office, a little happier than she had been the morning before, swayed the curvy receptionist Hettie, wearing a close

6TH JUNE 9.30 A.M.

fitting floral dress and carrying the hotel mail. She moved briskly towards the counter with her arms full of guests' correspondence, pointless postcards in the main. She noticed Massimo as she teetered past the Poste Restante counter in her strappy heels, turned to him and said seductively, *'Massimo, ciao bello.'*

Tommy, a metre closer to Hettie than the man behind him, turned to face her.

For a split second, he assumed Hettie was looking at him, but then realised that she was in fact fixed on a man directly behind, apparently named Massimo, who by now had his knife arm pulled back ready to thrust into Tommy's liver.

The Norwegian cyclist saw it all, and screamed at the top of his lungs. His mate reacted instinctively, crashing his arm down onto Massimo's thrusting arm.

The next two seconds seemed like minutes to Tommy as the drama unfolded frame by frame. His body pivoted 180 degrees to his right with his left fist clenched and swinging. The Norwegian was screaming in pain, bone protruding through the flesh of his wounded arm.

Tommy's initial contact with Massimo was less effective than he would have hoped, only grazing the side of his face. Yet it was enough to cause the Calabrian punk to fall off balance, drop the bayonet and momentarily succumb to the weight of the Norwegian. The screams of at least a dozen petrified locals and travellers could be heard throughout the great hall of the post office and well into Dam Square. Tommy sprinted through the main door and back onto the Raadhuisstraat to stand facing the square and a maze of curious eyes.

• •

Tommy stood on the edge of the canal, unsure in which direction to run. He breathed heavily as he felt the perspiration dripping down his neck, soaking his clothes. The post office started emptying out onto the front steps. Fear had turned to panic, and panic had turned to a stampede. Tommy made a deliberate effort to breathe normally, to regain his composure. New Zealand flashed into mind, reminding him he was a wanted man. He couldn't yell for the assistance of the police. It was imperative that he get away without drawing any attention to himself. He needed to blend in, to stay with the crowd. He crossed Raadhuisstraat, walking briskly.

Tommy forced himself to move slowly and methodically with the small crowd of people, eager to escape the sounds of the screaming. As Tommy moved forward, he felt a sharp ache to his lower back in the kidney region. He kept walking, touching his back with his right hand. A throbbing pain kicked in. He looked down at his hand and saw the fresh warm blood staining his fingers. The bayonet had actually pierced him, not badly enough to cause a life-threatening injury, but he would certainly require some attention.

On the Dam Square side of Raadhuisstraat, Tommy looked back towards the door of the post office, relieved to find that Massimo had yet to run from the building. He knew that the now pooling blood on his waistband was becoming noticeable. He turned back to the horde of travellers in the square and worked his way forward and towards his hotel. As he passed a run of tables and chairs at a café he casually lifted a lightweight jacket from the back of an unoccupied seat, putting it on as he walked.

A lone police car was parked at the front door of the memorabilia shop as Tommy and the crowd moved on. Both lights flashed on its roof. A uniformed policeman ran from the door and towards his vehicle, almost colliding with Tommy. He moved off without an apology and leaned into the squad car, speaking urgently into the radio.

Behind the counter of the store lay an elderly gentleman with a pencil-thin moustache, a matching bayonet to the one that had pierced Tommy's kidney embedded in his right eye socket. He was dead. A trail of fruit and vegetables ran from the counter to the rear of the store where his overcome wife sat sobbing on a chair, the now empty shopping bag clutched tightly in her hands.

6TH JUNE 9.30 A.M.

• •

The third police car arrived out the front of the post office and parked alongside the other two, and the ambulance. Inside the post office, police busied themselves at the crime scene. An upturned empty cardboard postal pack lay at the centre of the floor. To one side of the post pack was a pool of blood in the exact position where the Norwegian had fallen. He was now in the safe hands of the ambulance medics on the other side of the hall, his arm encased in a splint and a mass of sterile cotton gauze. His friend sat nearby, troubled. Massimo was nowhere to be seen; Hettie's pointless postcards were scattered on the floor.

The police sergeant, obviously in charge of the crime scene, stepped from the third police car and entered. A younger officer, who had been first on the scene, walked him over to the upturned cardboard carton. They were both mindful of the congealing bloodstain nearby and crouched down carefully. The younger policeman lifted the box in the air. The bayonet lay discarded on the ground, its sharp tip bloodied. The sergeant looked at the eager young officer.

'We're missing one victim,' he said.

The young policeman's expression changed as he digested his sergeant's logic.

'Why would a victim run away, Sergeant?'

'Yes, why indeed?'

• •

The last number of the four-digit code was keyed into the hotel wall safe. Tommy opened it to expose a small wad of euros. He counted them out: 2000 in total. The exact amount he had withdrawn from his account at the Western Union office at JFK Airport thirty hours earlier. He then took the MasterCard from his wallet and stared at it, realising that it was the only credit card he had used thus far in the name of Tommy Paul. He wondered as he stared at the card how Massimo had found him at the Amsterdam post office. Dropping the card on the end of his bed, he picked up one of the hotel bath towels and pressed it firmly against the trickle of blood still oozing from his wound, before lying down. There was more that needed to be thought through.

Somebody had to be watching the MasterCard. He wasn't naïve enough to think that the answer to every one of the questions running through his mind was the Mafia. They, like any criminal organisation, could only flourish with the assistance of corrupt cops. The hunch that gnawed at him the last time he had dinner with his team in the Japanese restaurant in Melbourne surfaced again in his mind, as did the face of Inspector Mack.

Fifteen minutes later Tommy had checked out, happy to use his MasterCard once more. He had a plan. He walked to the front glass door of the hotel to take a taxi, his shoulder bag slung over his left shoulder, in an attempt to give some relief to his hastily bandaged right side. Tommy had borrowed a small guest towel as an impromptu first aid pad to protect his shirt from telltale signs of the morning's incident. He was about to push open the hotel front door when he noticed Massimo walk briskly along the footpath. Massimo was sporting a cut to the eye. Tommy's stomach sank when he saw Massimo disappear into the hotel three doors up. He quickly changed course and exited using the rear door that led him out onto a quiet alleyway adjacent to the canal.

He moved to the back of the hotel that Massimo had entered, and found its rear fire-escape stairs. He tucked his bag carefully under the bottom rung of the stair and then climbed the open metal treads to the first floor. He opened the fire-escape door just slightly, enough to see Massimo four doors down in the left side corridor emerge from his room as the cleaning lady and her trolley entered.

Massimo was in a hurry, and jogged down the staircase to talk with Hettie at the reception counter. Hettie, uncharacteristically, did

6TH JUNE 9.30 A.M.

her best to ignore Massimo, having realised that he was far too violent and unpredictable for her liking. She threatened to call the police.

Meanwhile, Tommy had entered Massimo's room to see a familiar object lying open on the end of the bed: the half-packed powder-blue suitcase. The cleaning lady appeared to be busy restacking fresh white towels in the bathroom. Tommy looked down to the surface of the credenza, beneath a large gilded vanity mirror, and observed a bottle of Hugo Boss In Motion aftershave, which he thought resembled a silver baseball of sorts, as well as an eyelash curler and shiny gold lipstick case, lying haphazardly nearby.

Downstairs Massimo was having no success in changing Hettie's attitude. He gave up, realising that she was more of a convenience than a necessity. Having sorted out his hotel account, he turned to walk back upstairs to his room. Once inside, he recommenced packing the suitcase. His work regarding Tommy was far from complete. Massimo grabbed his well-pressed T-shirts and slacks from the wardrobe and turned sharply to face the vanity mirror and what was scrawled boldly across the glass in vivid red lipstick: 'Get a new job!'

Massimo flicked his head back ever so slightly as he read the words. Their content and the messenger did not come to mind instantly. Then it dawned on him. He gritted his teeth. His hand reached down and grabbed the aftershave and hurled the bottle violently at the mirror, shattering it to pieces.

• •

The ATM on Damrak, the main street leading to the central station, spat out 500 euros in 100-euro notes, and then returned the MasterCard to Tommy, who hastily moved towards the station. He did his best to ignore the young, grungy beggars that plagued the street and the incessant number of Jamaicans offering everything from colourful beads to vouchers to hash cafés. As he walked, he scanned all directions, and occasionally stepped into the concealed doorways of the many shops to ensure that Massimo was not on his tail. He was determined, now that he knew that he had been followed, to lose the Calabrian punk—no, not punk, *assassin*. Things had become seriously dangerous and he needed to become seriously smart, before he ended up seriously dead.

In the front of the station, Tommy took advantage of another ATM, and withdrew another 500 euros, which he placed in his now bulging wallet, just as the 'Exceeded Daily Cash Allowance' warning flashed onto the screen. He moved forward to the ticket office and purchased a one-way sleeper, Amsterdam to Milano. He headed off to his platform to catch a train. As he sat tucked away among the crowd of waiting passengers, he afforded himself the faintest of smiles as he knew he had concocted a cunning plan and now had control of the game.

7th June

Eight o'clock the following morning saw the arrival of the Amsterdam train into Milano. Tommy spent the night sharing a twin cabin with an old lady from Scotland. They spent most of the night gazing at the passing scenery, which flashed by under a full moon. As they lay on their backs on their individual bunk beds watching out the window, Nellie recounted stories about her now deceased husband and herself, from earlier, happier years, when together they ran a typical tavern in the seaside town of Aberdeen. Tommy was glad to let her mind run from yarn to yarn, fascinated by her beautiful accent and her enthusiasm for life. The dear old soul had been forced to sell recently, and was now off to see the world.

Not once did she act at all suspicious about Tommy's injury, accepting at face value and with appropriate sympathy his explanation that he had been mugged the day before at the station. A grandmotherly type, she kindly offered to play nurse and refreshed his dressing before they went to dinner, exclaiming with a slap to his back, 'There, there now laddie, dinna' fash yersel'. It'll tak' mair than that tae see ye oot,' which Tommy roughly translated to mean that he would live, and that it would heal well. He felt a little sad to say goodbye to her. As he stepped down from the train, he looked back to give her a brief wave; she was going all the way through to Rome.

A short taxi ride later Tommy found himself walking through the Piazza del Duomo. The tourist within emerged just for a moment as he stood in admiration and awe before one of the great cathedrals of the world, beautiful still, despite a heavy draping of scaffold to cater for the current renovations. He wandered over to one of the few municipal rubbish bins in the piazza, opened up his bag and, apart from keeping a couple of favourite items of clothing, he upended the contents, then headed for the Grand Galleria as there was breakfast to be had and shopping to be done.

• •

Later that same morning, Tommy, sporting a new pair of sneakers and with a bag now brimming with new summer clothes, walked into a hole-in-the-wall travel shop located in a narrow cobbled laneway behind the Galleria. It was the one-way airfare to Kraków at 200 euros depicted in the front window that had grabbed his attention. Yet again that morning, he deliberately laid his MasterCard onto the counter. With his ticket in hand, he walked back into the Galleria and took a seat at a terrazzo table of the Ristorante Savini.

He had been to Italy many times over the years, often staying in Milano at each end of his trip. He knew the Ristorante Savini, Milano's finest eating establishment, had recently undergone a multi-million-dollar refurbishment. He and his palate were lost for two hours over a five-course lunch, his enjoyment intensified in the knowledge that he was about to throw Massimo completely off his scent.

He offered up his MasterCard for the last time. Tommy stood up from his seat, souveniring a knife from his table as he walked out of the Galleria.

He stopped in the piazza once more, tore up his airline ticket to Poland and disposed of it into one of the municipal rubbish bins. He then extracted the souvenired knife from his shoulder bag and cut the Tommy Paul MasterCard in half, dumping it and the knife as well.

With the purposefulness of a local, he walked swiftly through the side streets to the bus terminal. Paying cash for his ticket, he caught a bus to Bellagio and Lake Como, an hour's ride to the north.

• •

7TH JUNE

The in-tray on Donny's desk looked a little bit different from normal; there was paperwork in it. Donny had come into work on Monday morning having enjoyed yet another weekend away, skiing with his mates at Mount Buller. He had the keys to a dodgy Asian drug dealer's chalet these days, and availed himself and his mates of as much skiing and *après* socialising as he could in the five-star surroundings. He was annoyed that he was due back at work this morning but he had drawn the short straw on Friday. The initial sight of the paperwork in his tray made him more than a little despondent, until he picked up the half-dozen MasterCard alert sheets in the name of Tommy Paul. His contact at the MasterCard office had come through with the goods again. Donny hastily sorted the transaction chronology, following the movement of the card and its owner over the weekend: JFK Airport, to Amsterdam, to Milan. Donny clutched the alert sheets in his hand and headed out to find a payphone on the street.

• •

Leigh sat at his PC reading over a two-page report. It was an application to attend the covert investigation seminar hosted by the FBI in Quantico, Virginia in the USA. If he was lucky enough to be accepted, he would fly to the States, where he would be picked up at the airport, and quite literally disappear within the secret training facility for the duration. Short of a family death it would be impossible for contact to be made in or out until the course was over. Leigh desperately wanted to attend.

As he started to fax the application to police headquarters, he noticed Spud, seated at his desk, swearing loudly at his computer screen.

'What's the trouble, champer?' he asked.

'The fuckin' alert's gone mad. Look what's comin'.'

Leigh had no idea what he meant, despite the briefing Sandra had given him the week before.

'Look at this,' said Spud, who was studying a list of transactions by Tommy Paul on the MasterCard.

'Fuck. He's getting around, champer.'

'But why so quick, what's gone wrong?' said Spud, puzzled.

The next page of the MasterCard manager's email answered Spud's question. Spud's covert eye on anyone making enquiries on the passport or credit cards held in the name of Tommy Paul had spat out information he would rather not know, for he wasn't a Toe Cutter. Leigh and Spud looked at the line that said, 'Spudly, my old mate. Come and see me NOW!'

Spud picked up his coat and ran out of the building.

• •

Spud was panting by the time he got to the lift of the MasterCard building six blocks away. He hit the button to call the elevator and waited, pacing on the spot. A slim, well-dressed girl of no more than twenty stood next to him, also waiting for the lift, take-away coffee in hand. She glimpsed his impatience.

'Card overdrawn, eh?' she quipped.

'Something like that,' was all Spud offered as the lift doors opened and he pressed '14'. The woman stood back, happy that her button had been pressed. They rode in silence. Spud had too much racing through his mind to be concerned with making small talk to an attractive girl nearly half his age. The lift door opened and the girl glided out, turning left to face a security door and key her code into a contraption on the wall. Spud went straight for the reception counter and pressed the buzzer. In as much time as it would take to place her coffee on a desk the same dainty girl appeared to answer his call. She slid back the glass window and smiled.

'You really are overdrawn, eh?' she smiled.

'No, I need to see Jake Worthington,' he said.

'It's more serious than overdrawn, seeing the Head of Security.'

7TH JUNE

'No. Yes. I'm not overdrawn. Sorry, can I see Jake?'

The girl gifted him with another of her perfect receptionist smiles and she glided some more, across a busy office full of data entry workers, till she disappeared altogether. Five minutes passed before Jake opened a side door and welcomed Spud.

'Come in, Spudly.'

Spud followed behind Jake, as he criss-crossed past the many desks to a back glassed-in office. They took seats and got straight to the point. Jake nodded towards an ethnic-looking man, no more than thirty years of age who was seated at a desk several rows from Jake's office.

'The guy in the blue checked shirt.'

'Yeah, I think I know who you mean, with the head of hair?'

'Yep, a spy.'

'Go on,' asked Spud, wanting the full story. Jake handed him a copy of an email he had found that same morning, addressed from the MasterCard office to one Detective Donald Benjamin of the Drug Unit. Spud didn't have to read it in any great detail to know it was a list of transactions on the Tommy Paul MasterCard, the exact same list Jake had sent him only half an hour earlier.

Spud stated the obvious. 'He's supplying unauthorised information.'

'Seems.'

'Does he know you know?'

'No way. How do you want to play this thing?' asked Jake.

'Safe. Let's not let the rat know that the cats know about him.'

Jake nodded once or twice then offered Spud a cold drink from the kitchen.

. .

Pretty pleased with himself, Tommy sat on an antique chair that he'd relocated from the writing desk to the tiny balcony of Room 6 of the

ON THE RUN

Hotel Suisse on the waterfront at Bellagio. The French doors to his room were open and the wind from the lake whipped the delicate sheer curtains around his legs every now and then. So far he had spent two blissful nights in the rickety old bed, allowing his wounded side to heal. One of the things he always enjoyed about Italy was the free hospital and medical service, even extended to travellers. The little Aurelia surgery on the road to Bellagio had been more than obliging, as he stepped from the bus and explained his mugging again. Nine stitches later, a course of antibiotics and painkillers were prescribed and dispensed with the addition of a soothing smile from the nurse, and Tommy headed off to find his hotel.

It was the perfect retreat for him at this stage of his journey. It was only one-star rated, not that you'd notice. It was stunning. Perhaps the owners hadn't paid the payola to the local hotel inspector, he thought. Regardless, his trail so far had shown a man staying in superior hotels and eating in grand restaurants. He hoped Massimo would stay on that trail and look elsewhere. More so, he hoped that Massimo would surmise that, once Tommy had feasted at the Ristorante Savini, he had caught a direct flight to Poland.

• •

The door to the little hole-in-the-wall travel shop in Milano was reopened, this time by Massimo, who thought he had found gold. He sat down facing the only girl in the shop and smiled his best Latin Lothario smile. She returned his smile but hers was only half as confident. Northern Italians are often suspicious of their southern cousins. He placed the newspaper clipping of Cole Goodwin on the counter. She dropped her curious eyes onto the picture. It took the Italian charmer less than five minutes to ascertain that Tommy/Cole had purchased a ticket to Kraków. It took less than a second for Massimo's smile to disappear and for his hand to come down heavily on the counter as he mouthed, 'Fuck. He's in fuckin' Poland.'

7TH JUNE

• •

The phone behind the counter of the Café Azzurra in Griffith was picked up on the third ring by Penny. She had been madly cleaning, looking to knock off early for the night. At one table the old Godfather and two of his trusted lieutenants were on their last short blacks for the day. Otherwise, the café was deserted.

'Hello?' she answered without interest.

'Hello, hello,' she repeated. 'Massimo, *ciao*, how is Italy? You've been home a while?'

Penny laughed as she received a dose of Italian charm from her caller.

'You're a naughty man, Massimo.' She smiled as he spoke, and then placed the handset on the bench before turning to the old Godfather.

'Giovanni, Massimo is on the telephone. He is in Milan.'

She discreetly removed herself to reset her last table. The old Godfather moved more quickly than he normally would to the telephone, and placed the handset to his ear.

'*Buona sera*, Massimo.'

In no more than the time it took for Penny to lay a set of knives and forks, the old Godfather had ended the call. He looked annoyed and walked heavily back to his lieutenants.

All Penny overheard of the ensuing fifteen-minute whispered conversation was that somebody was in Poland, Massimo had fucked up and had been ordered back to Calabria to look after the tins of artichokes.

Penny felt troubled by what she'd just heard, especially as it had seemed to relate largely to Massimo. Her detective friend, Leigh, had asked her the previous week for news of anything that she may hear about him. She wasn't entirely sure what to make of these snippets of information, but she had given her word. So, once the old Godfather and his entourage had left, and she had locked up the café, Penny made a quick call to Leigh from her darkened office.

• •

The modest kitchen at Sandra's house had no room for the cat at this meeting. Once Leigh had reported back his conversation with Penny, Sandra called them together. They were even more worried about Cole since Spud had found out about Donny. The team also felt a little uneasy about sitting around the office discussing their secrets; hence they found themselves squeezed into a huddle at Sandra's. They hadn't been going long before she plonked a large plate of nachos down in the only small space left between them. Of course to keep Spud happy, there was extra guacamole, sour cream and melted cheese. Sandra chipped in between mouthfuls, 'Don't get too cosy with my gourmet talents, boys. We need to work out what we've got.'

'Let's start with the Mafia,' suggested Leigh.

'Okay. Let's see, Griffith was linked to a container out of Reggio Calabria to Sydney eighteen months ago, but customs fucked up and it left the dock never to be seen again,' said Spud, as he pulled at the corn chips, lassoing one with elastic cheese.

'Why do you think that container was tied in to what Penny told me about tins of artichokes, champer?'

'Because the copy of the manifest from the missing container, which was at the stevedoring office, listed the goods in Italian as *prodotti alimentari*,' said Spud.

'Which is?' asked Sandra curiously.

'Delicatessen food,' explained Spud.

'And Giovanni's gang aren't grocers, they're supposed to be citrus growers,' Sandra caught on. 'But what about Cole? He's now in Poland,' she continued.

'Yeah, and Massimo's got the big smack and has been sent home to look after the artichokes,' Leigh added.

'Method of smuggling a massive shipment of ecstasy,' said Spud.

'And Donny?' asked Sandra.

'He was always an arse-wipe,' Leigh replied. 'Interesting that he's wandered into our lives. He's been suspected of selling out jobs for

7TH JUNE

ages. Even the Toe Cutters have got an interest in him. His mouth came up on a listening device a year or two ago. He stinks.'

'Well, if the Toe Cutters are interested, and they know he stinks, there's our opening at last. Who's handling his file?' asked Sandra. The three of them looked at each other and none of them had the answer.

'I'll see their analyst and get a referral,' offered Spud.

'And I'll get an email to Cole and let him know he's not alone,' said Sandra.

'Let's do it,' Leigh said with a newfound enthusiasm.

Sandra thought for a moment as her two close mates tucked into the last of the nachos. She then offered up a comment that was perhaps more in line with something Cole might have said had he been there.

'Look, if we're going to do this—get in bed with the Toeys, I mean—then let's do it properly. Keep our mouths fuckin' shut and get on with it and bring Cole home safely.'

She pushed the now empty plate aside, and placed her open fingered hand on the bench top, as Leigh and then Spud placed their hands one on top of the other.

11th June

While the tiny village of Plati, nestled on the edge of the Aspromonte Mountains, offered some magnificent views of the Mediterranean coastline below, it was not a town visited by tourists. But back in the summer of 1972 the region had been put on the map, in a moment that gave one of the poorest regions of Italy a lustre that shone for many years.

A group of local fishermen, from the seaside village of Locri, overlooked by Plati, waded with their old wooden-hulled vessel, *Judas*, out into the magnificent blue of the Mediterranean Ocean. They had done this every morning of their lives, as had done their fathers, chasing the plentiful runs of swordfish and deep-sea marlin. On this particular morning, as they urged forward in the warm, shallow water, the half-dozen men stopped dead and stood in utter astonishment. Lying supine on the water's edge was a pair of perfectly preserved, two-metre-tall, solid bronze statues. The two elegantly bearded warriors of Riace proved to be one of the most remarkable representations of the Hellenic period dating back to the fifth century BC. Despite the smarts of all the world experts, no one was ever able to say how they arrived at that particular location, how they could be so wonderfully preserved and, more intriguingly, why they had never been discovered previously. Both warriors, when found, seemed to be looking towards the Aspromonte Mountains.

Plati had one other claim to fame: it was the headquarters of the N'Drangheta, the local name for the worst criminals in Calabria: the Mafia.

The three most infamous regions of Italy each had its own name for the 'Mafia'. The Cosa Nostra were the mobsters of Sicily; the Camorra were the gangs in and around Naples. While each organisation was in the main content to busy itself with its own

11TH JUNE

rackets, standovers, murders and demands for payola, every now and again, when it suited them, they would join forces. Such a union usually only came about to further a complicated drug importation or solve a distribution need. Otherwise, the neighbours kept pretty much to themselves, taking care of business as their corrupt conglomerates thrived and spread throughout the world.

Each of the regional Mafia organisations had become specialists in specific crimes, which to some degree helped them co-exist harmoniously. The Cosa Nostra had long been the experts at payola, tickling every till in Sicily for a monthly or weekly kickback. They also had large shareholdings in the passenger ferries and car rentals on their island, as well as contacts at most customs offices throughout Italy. The Camorra were slightly more commercial than the Sicilians, specialising in the illegal disposal of hazardous waste materials, as well as taking control of the construction industry down south. Their biggest money-spinner, however, was running the multitude of illegal sweatshops, which produced the highly profitable 'made in Italy' fashions sold to tourists everywhere. Business was booming.

The N'Drangheta were far more down-to-earth in their crimes and were also considered the most violent. Their specialities were the kidnapping of the wealthy—hiding them in the caves surrounding the Aspromonte Mountains until distraught loved ones coughed up the ransom—and global drug trafficking.

∴

The black Alfa Romeo 156 sedan cruised effortlessly up the hill towards Plati. Massimo, in the passenger seat, glanced back along the road towards the ocean. He and his driver, his cousin, Pino, were only one bend away from entering the town. At no more than five feet in height, Pino had to be propped up on three folded sheepskins to allow him a proper view through his putrid windscreen. The texture of his face resembled dry, cracked soil and his greasy black hair appeared never to have seen a comb in its forty years.

Pino couldn't resist throttling the engine and hurling gravel into the air before coming to an awkward stop in the piazza. He killed the engine and stepped from the vehicle, his head only just above the roof of his pride and joy. Massimo took a more worldly approach to getting out of the car. He stepped effortlessly onto the piazza and strolled in a classic *bella figura* manner over to the dull little Café La Vista. Before he had taken more than a half-a-dozen steps, a feisty teenage girl sprinted from a nearby doorway. She waved both arms madly in the air.

'Uncle Massimo! *Benvenuto!*' She leapt excitedly towards him from almost a metre away. His strong arms caught her in mid-flight. She proceeded to cover every inch of his forehead and cheeks with sloppy kisses.

'Did you bring me a present, a koala bear, Uncle?' she pestered. Massimo eased her feet gently back onto the ground.

'No, little Lydia. I didn't bring any koalas, no kangaroos and no crocodiles either,' Massimo replied. He looked her carefully up and down.

'I'm not little any more, Uncle,' Lydia said defiantly.

'Off home, little miss movie star. I have business with the Godfather. I will see you later for dinner with your mamma and papà.'

As Lydia sulked seductively back home as instructed, she called out '*Ciao, Papà*' to her father, seated near the entrance to the café. Massimo shot her a final cheeky-uncle wink, then redirected his attention and shot a friendly smile at his three mates, including her father, his cousin Giuseppe, who sat lounging in the sun with three identical espressos. He flicked an offhand nod towards Pino, to the boot of the car and the powder-blue suitcase.

'*Ciao, Massimo!*' the mini chorus broke out. Each man stood in turn to shake Massimo's hand and to kiss both cheeks. They were pleased to see him.

'*Ciao, amici,*' returned Massimo as his gaze drifted around his home village. He signalled to the peasant-faced old waiter for a coffee and dropped his weary body into a seat, splaying his legs in the sun.

11TH JUNE

'So, the kangaroo's come home?'

His friend Illario's question brought a raucous laugh from all seated, which became louder with his cousin's enquiry, 'What about the women?'

Massimo stood tall, made the shape of a large hourglass and pumped his right arm vigorously as he answered. '*Bellissima, Giuseppe.*'

The laughter was joined by a short round of applause. The old waiter brought Massimo's espresso.

The conversation turned to the old Australian Godfather. 'A good man, with a great world' was Massimo's assessment.

His three partners broke into another chorus, this time '*Bravo, bravo*', elated at the good fortune of their Australian connection.

Pino walked towards them, leaving the boot lid up. He was carrying a modified Kalashnikov assault weapon, the AK 74 Polish Army–issue automatic rifle. He struggled with the powder-blue suitcase in the other hand. The little man also had a Browning MKI 9mm semi-automatic pistol tucked inside his belt. He dropped the rifle to the ground near the table and let the suitcase fall over the top of it, hiding it. He heard the '*Bravo*' compliments and took them as meant for him, which brought yet another round of guffawing from the four *amici*. Pino pulled up a chair to join them at the table.

'Are you home to stay now, Massimo, or running from the *Polizia?*'

The still-laughing Massimo explained that everything he did was now another man's problem.

Illario was the one to ask the question on all their lips, 'But Massimo—are you here to help with the artichokes?'

'*Si, si.* We have much work to do. Australia is waiting.'

Massimo went on to explain that the Australian Godfather had requested the delivery of another shipment of ecstasy tablets. He added that the old Don had enlisted the special services of the head of the police to help with the safe delivery.

A blue-and-white coloured police car cruised into the piazza, stopping a few metres away from the café table. The lone driver took his time stepping from the vehicle. Pino pulled his soiled white shirt from inside his trousers to cover the Browning pistol. Massimo observed Pino's attempt to hide the pistol and nodded, then checked that the AK 74 was still covered by his suitcase. It was. He placed his left boot firmly on top of the case and looked out in the direction of the sea. Pino broke the silence, whispering to Massimo, 'Kill him.' Massimo ignored the comment, and remained staring steadfastly towards the sea.

The policeman, a cop for ten years, was a handsome young local man, Mario Messina. He lived with Lina, his wife, and their baby daughter in Gerace, a neighbouring hilltop town. Almost every night for the past six years, he had burnt the midnight oil studying for his law degree. Mario had one more term until completion, when he could apply for promotion to *Commissario*: detective in charge of a region. Law enforcement and honour ran in his family and, like his father and grandfather, Mario despised the *Mafiosi* that festered in his region. Equally he despised the likes of Massimo and the gangs ruining the southern seaside villages in Calabria, frightening tourists away from the big cities and hilltop towns. His hatred extended to many of the local policemen who took to payola or outright bribery to turn a blind eye.

Mario had known Massimo since their schooldays, 14-year-olds on the same football team. While they were never close friends, they had been aware of each other's strengths and weaknesses even then. Almost overnight Massimo and Mario ceased communication on almost every level. Mario's father, who had been on patrol in the capital city of Reggio, Calabria, was shot dead. No one was ever brought to justice for the murder but the entire region knew that the elders in the Plati gang were behind the death. Massimo's uncles had been forcing their way into the rear of a shoe factory on the outskirts of the industrial zone when the lone patrol officer had stumbled across them, only to be cut down in a spray of bullets as the bandits fled the scene. Not long after, Massimo stopped going to school altogether; he was taken under the wing of his uncles for a very different

11TH JUNE

education. Mario, on the other hand, put his head down, spending almost all his free time in his schoolbooks. He secretly took to wearing his father's old police shirts while he sat alone in his upstairs room, studying earnestly.

An accident on the main highway, midway through his patrol, involving a Spanish tourist in a rental car and a local moped rider, meant that Mario was now more than an hour late for his visit to Plati. Accident or not, he would always ensure that he drove the fifteen minutes from the main highway into Plati and out again. As he also did in San Luca, another wretched N'Drangheta-controlled town on the hillside. Mario reckoned he had more than family honour on his side; he had the weight of the Anti-Mafia unit in Naples. They would come in truck-loads, with machine guns and tanks, to avenge any pre-meditated death of a Magistrate, *Commissario* or even a lowly *Carabinieri* officer doing his job. This had been the case with his father, some twenty years earlier when the N'Drangheta had been sent scurrying into their caves for many weeks as the tanks rolled into town. Massimo and his crumby little gang were aware of the boundaries, so they tolerated the *Carabinieri* asking their questions and patrolling the piazza. They knew that the real action was hidden well away, and that the chance of a lowly local officer making any impact on their criminal enterprises was next to zero.

Mario closed the driver's door of his patrol car and walked into the *Tabac* shop immediately next door to the café. He came out to stand to one side of his car and pull a smoke free, tapping it firmly on the side of the pack, making an exaggerated action to smell the cigarette before he lit it. Mario too looked out at the ocean in the same direction as Massimo. He drew back again on his cigarette and slowly exhaled.

'*Benvenuto, Massimo,*' he said, without breaking his stare.

'*Grazie,*' was all that Massimo would return and he too kept his gaze.

Ten more puffs and the butt was stubbed out by the toe of Mario's cheap yet sturdy boot. He walked to the car door and got back into the patrol vehicle, driving away from the café and out of the piazza. He'd be back tomorrow, when the sun was high again. In the meantime, he would gain a degree of pleasure by sending an intelligence report to his contact, *Commissario* D'Alfonso, at the Anti-Mafia unit in Naples. D'Alfonso was a good man who had already promised Mario a recommendation for the role as regional *Commissario*. Mario would advise him of the latest movement of their main suspect in this region for major drug trafficking and unsolved murders: Massimo.

As Mario's squad car disappeared along the Via Roma, as if beckoned by the siren call of the startlingly blue coastline again, Pino hurriedly moved across the piazza. He carried the AK 74, while Giuseppe and Illario followed behind with the powder-blue suitcase. All three quickly disappeared behind the carved wooden door of the finest palazzo in town.

The town's most respected and feared elder, Don Carbone, shuffled from the back of the coffee shop. The 78-year-old was the Godfather of the Plati clan, cousin to the old Australian Godfather—they shared the same surname—and uncle to Massimo, heir apparent. The Don, wearing lightweight navy gabardine slacks held up by black braces over a white collarless shirt, the sleeves of which were rolled to the elbows, stood alongside his nephew. Massimo fussed over him, accepting the Don's welcome back to the town after his six-week absence. Massimo could see the age in the old man's face; he was near his end.

'Uncle, please, my seat,' he insisted as the Godfather eased his old frame onto the chair and rested his simple wooden walking cane next to it.

'He has gone?' he asked.

'Yes, the pimple has gone for another day.'

'Remember this, Massimo. An annoying little pimple one day, a niggling fester the next and soon an unbearable rash.'

'Yes, Uncle,' replied Massimo humbly.

'Forget him, that one. He lives in a dream of his father. Worry only about the shipment to Australia,' instructed the Godfather,

11TH JUNE

pushing Massimo's empty coffee cup aside to accept a strong fresh espresso from the quiet waiter. Massimo sat diligently listening to Don Carbone as he continued.

'Tell me, Massimo, what went wrong with the Australian in Amsterdam?'

The nephew inhaled sharply and attempted to provide answers.

• •

A few peaceful minutes in Sandra's otherwise busy day were presented to her, with Spud and Leigh out of the office, forced to do a minimal amount of investigative work on a new job that they had on the books. A good deal of their time these days was spent in their collective worry over Cole, but there was still routine police work to do. And to ensure that Inspector Mack remained unaware of their suspicions, they made sure that they knocked on a crook's door, interviewed a suspect or followed up a lead. It was important to look busy. The boys had drawn the short straw today and Sandra was left alone. She began to compose a message to her dear friend Ingrid. She had to let Cole know that everybody was watching his MasterCard.

Ingrid,

I'm so glad we're talking again. It was good to hear your voice the other day, but I am concerned that you sound like you have been run ragged. Honeymoons are for relaxing, sweetie. Your parents are so concerned for your health. Get that man of yours to take better care of you. All eyes will be watching how you master this. Oh, and thanks for your card.

Lots of love, Sandy

• •

As the message pinged through cyberspace to the other side of the world, Tommy walked along the *corso* at Bellagio. Every now and again he looked down at the local old men in search of freshwater mussels on the rocks. He liked the synergy between old men and fishing. He enjoyed the slowness of the peaceful and traditional pursuit, set against the gentle lapping sounds of the lake's tiny waves. By now he was sporting the start of a fairly reasonable beard. During the mornings, Tommy was enjoying the company of Rossanna, the young receptionist from his Hotel Suisse.

Rossanna was a cute girl, he thought. Just twenty-three, and looking forward to marrying her man, the son of the town mayor. More small town stuff, he thought. Tommy learnt much about Rossanna during those strolls as his beard became thicker and more dishevelled, including the fact that she was an ex-hairdresser. He thought her desire to assist in this area might just be handy one day.

She worked each afternoon at the Hotel Suisse throughout the summer, the busy times. Her near-perfect English welcomed guests hospitably. She was lucky with her constant afternoon work, in so far as her handsome intended was a sometime waiter at the downstairs restaurant and they could steal a few moments together between courses and check-ins. Rossanna and Tommy had taken to these late morning walks each day before her shift commenced. Rossanna jumped at the opportunity of broadening her English with Australian colloquialisms, and Tommy delighted in teaching her. This morning he and Rossanna were joined by her beau, Paolo, as they practised their Ocker slang.

Every now and again as Tommy tried to explain a phrase like 'fair dinkum' or 'bonza, mate', Rossanna and Paolo would fall about on the *corso* in fits of laughter, completely unable to comprehend the strange words. Their thirst was insatiable for anything Australian. An uncle of Rossanna's had migrated to Perth some twenty years earlier, and she was curious to visit her never-seen cousins. They all hatched a plan that, once the lovers were married, they could honeymoon in Australia, and stay a week or so with Tommy in East Melbourne.

11TH JUNE

Although he did secretly wonder how the hell he would tell two wide-eyed Italian honeymooners upon their arrival that his name wasn't Tommy and he had been hiding out from the Mafia as well as several police forces.

The trio had soon gathered a small following of local Italian tourists, all fascinated to overhear the colloquialism lesson. Tommy would offer a saying and sit back enjoying the wait for one of his young friends to repeat it.

'Try this one,' he suggested to Paolo. 'G'day, blue, how they hangin'?'

Paolo was at a loss, as was the audience. He looked at Rossanna but she too shook her head, totally bemused. Tommy translated the meaning and the raucous laughter from his lively crowd increased.

'Tomasso, Tomasso, give me one to try?' Rossanna pleaded.

Tommy stopped deep in thought for a moment and then looked up at the expectant group, apologising first to Rossanna as he said, 'Bugger me dead, digger, it's a stinker of a day.' Rossanna blushed profusely as she attempted to translate with the assistance of a near-obscene mime. Her crowd mimicked her gyrations all the way down to the sweaty brow.

Amid the heightened laughter, Tommy snuck away for a walk, still smiling broadly. Initially he dawdled along the wharf to give thought to his next move, where he would next travel. Daily, he would catch the ferry to a neighbouring town on the lake for a lazy fish and salad lunch and a read of the novel he had purchased at the local *libreria*. He had become a great fan of the famed Italian author Andrea Camilleri and had devoured three books in recent days. On this particular morning, though, he hadn't felt like a ferry ride, not just because the water was a little choppy, but also because he had visited most of the towns by now. Menaggio, Lenno and Verenna had proved to be his favourites, particularly the last one, which he thought was pure postcard material.

He decided instead to head back to the little doctor's surgery and have his stitches removed; his wound had healed beautifully. His thoughts, as the nurse carefully snipped away at the surgical thread, returned to home and he felt the need to check Ingrid's email, which he had set aside since the week before with all the panic in Amsterdam. He was acutely conscious that by now Inspector Mack would have his corrupt tentacles spread far and wide in search of any information on his foe. Tommy could only imagine the catalytic effect of a joint effort by Mack and the Calabrian punk, in an attempt to flush him out.

During his undercover days in Griffith, Tommy had virtually lived with his Italian criminal targets for extended periods, toughing it out. He had often been forced to rely on no more than his own wits until he could make his way back to the lawful fold and file his report. He had fallen back into that self-reliant way now, for, it seemed to Tommy that this whole affair was beginning to resemble some sort of covert nightmare, without any back up or anyone to report to.

He went in search of an internet café. Tucked away in the upstairs mezzanine of the trendy enoteca were a couple of PCs for hire at 6 euros an hour. Tommy pulled up a stool at the bar for a wine or two first. He enjoyed the esoteric stories of the eccentric proprietor. His favourite yarn involved his supplying a dozen bottles of the same Primativo 2006 vintage red to George Clooney each month, as well as a selection of his personal premium wine recommendations. Clooney lived, at times, in an opulent villa across the water from Bellagio, in the little village of Laglio. If the wine shop proprietor was to be believed, George only ever purchased wine from him. Or so he said to Tommy, on his second glass of Negroamaro wine. At the end of the tale, Tommy took the remains of his drink upstairs to enjoy as he tapped away on the computer.

He was glad of the single item in Ingrid's inbox, from Sandra. It made him feel less alone. He skipped through the body of the message, to the bottom line. He read it over and over,

> All eyes will be watching how you master this. Oh, and thanks for your card.

11TH JUNE

Here it was at last, absolute confirmation on two fronts of what he had long suspected after fleeing Amsterdam. First, that everyone was aware of him travelling under the name of Tommy Paul and, second, that the Mafia had tapped into his MasterCard. He was convinced that Inspector Mack must have had an alert on that card, somehow. Thankfully, there was nothing said about his Visa card. It must be safe.

Tommy was elated. The trail he had laid through Milano had credible legs. Massimo must have taken the bait or he would be dead by now.

He reached into his back pocket, pulled out his wallet and rested it on the keypad. He emptied the contents and counted out just over 1400 euros in cash remaining.

He prayed that no one was aware of his Visa. The only person who lawfully knew that he had the Visa was Spud … and maybe now Sandra. He would know soon enough should corrupt elements be onto the card, but knowing might come too late for him.

His mind went over the 1400 euros. And his expenses. The Hotel Suisse bill was paid up for another three days, and most of his downstairs restaurant tabs had already been covered. He might just be alright.

..

Five hundred metres above the township of Plati were the thickest regions of the Aspromonte, the start of tens of thousands of hectares of pine forest. It was also the start of an infinite network of caves, many of which were no bigger than a domestic kitchen in size. Just volcanic holes in the mountain side really, ideal for animals in hiding or the occasional hunter in need of cover during a sudden downpour. But every now and again, a tiny crevice would lead to a run of honeycomb-like underground openings linked by a fault line in the rocks. Only a century ago the poorest of all Italians, the hilltop Calabrians, had lived in these caves, along with their chickens and the occasional goat or sheep. Such a lifestyle was now relegated to the stuff of folklore rather than the reality of day-to-day life. The caves these days were the property of the gangsters who used them to stash weapons, contraband or drug shipments until they could be routed to their destination, and, more notoriously, to hide kidnap victims.

Massimo sat inside the coolness of one such cave, a crevice that he had fashioned into an office of sorts a few years earlier. It was easily accessible, to those in the know, only a short stroll from the end of Via Guiseppe Carbone, a backstreet of the village that petered out at the lower reaches of the slope of the mountain. The entrance to Massimo's hidden mountain den was partly concealed by a large boulder that itself was covered by an overgrown saltbush. It contained a couple of old timber desks and a few simple wicker chairs. Massimo opened the top drawer to the desk and pushed aside a Smith & Wesson .38 six-shot revolver, in favour of a solitary pencil. He placed the simple writing implement on the desk alongside a bundle of blank notepaper. A small kerosene lantern was his only light source.

He blew away a fine layer of silt that had fallen from the roof of the cave since the desk was last in use, and prepared to make some notations. Deeper in his stone room were a dozen or so cases of wine and a multitude of jars of preserves maturing perfectly in the cool conditions. Further towards the back was a network of galvanised metal rods just below the roofline that stretched from wall to wall. Each rod held several salamis of varying sizes tied with string, also taking advantage of the ideal climate to air dry. The most modern piece of equipment in Massimo's retreat was a touch-pad telephone/fax, which sat somewhat incongruously on his desk. Its electrical cable could be traced from the back of the phone, under the dirt floor, out of the small entrance and into the forest below. Eventually the cable could be seen to run up the side of the closest telephone pole, about one hundred metres away. Massimo's cousin, Giuseppe, had cleverly wired the telephone into a junction box and then into the main cable for the district. No one would dare tamper with the illegal

11TH JUNE

phone connection, allowing Massimo free and untraceable telephone calls around the world.

Half an hour earlier he had ended the last of a string of calls to his criminal contact in Poland, who had spent the better part of the last week trying to trace one Tommy Paul. His final communication on the subject made it very clear to Massimo that Tommy Paul had never landed at any airport in Poland, and certainly there was no one by that name registered in any of the hotels in Kraków. Once he had ended the final call he sat thinking, wondering where the Australian detective had run to. Massimo felt certain he hadn't yet left Italy; all he needed to do was find out where he laid his head at night. Massimo was determined to kill the detective, to avenge his Australian cousins and improve his status with the Australian Godfather in Griffith. As the number two in the Plati clan, it was paramount that he succeed. He sat chewing his pencil end, waiting for Pino to return from his latest errand.

Pino shuffled in, wearing dust-covered loafers, and placed a *Regione Milano e Como* phone directory on the desk. Milano was the last place Massimo knew for certain that Tommy Paul had visited. Without a word, he flicked to the accommodation and hotel section, guessing that he had hundreds of calls to make. He picked up the handset and began to dial. Pino went directly to the back of the cave, slipped a small effective pocket-knife from his waistband and placed it between his teeth as he pulled a cured salami from a roof rod and a single plate from the top of the other desk.

• •

The annual gathering of the Association of Crime Analysts was held each June in the same conference room in the tired old building that once housed the Melbourne casino. Detectives jokingly referred to the conference as 'the geeks' get together'. Twenty or more specialists in their field from across the country collected in one space for a keyboard fest of all the latest computer gadgetry, software programs and whizz-bang analytical paraphernalia. Just the sort of stuff to send hardened detectives running, yet just the sort of stuff that helped solve crimes.

Spud was seated front and centre in one of those fold-down cluster rows of mobile function seating. Before him was a weighty table stacked with pamphlets and the odd giveaway, to encourage commercial relations. The talk of the conference this year was a USB drive in the shape of an oversized bullet. Such comics these analysts could be, all together in one room.

Morning tea could be just as stimulating with all the geeks huddled around the urn dunking tea-bags and roaring into the free banana cake. Spud didn't mind helping himself to a second slice in among the jocularity and camaraderie of the group. One of the analysts was sitting alone. No one passed him a hedgehog or offered him a top-up of his Darjeeling. Spud had noted that for the past two days everyone seemed to deliberately ignore him; it was as if he had leprosy. Ironically, this was the one man Spud wanted to speak to, when the time was right; it was the Toe Cutters analyst.

'Any good ideas for you guys at the conference?' Spud asked in his best attempt at an opening line.

'Yeah, I don't mind that software we were told about at the start of today. I could see us using that on asset disclosure,' the man replied, delighted that he finally had someone to talk to. He proceeded to ramble on endlessly about a list of purchases he wanted to make.

Spud, who had nothing much to offer in that regard, thought he would cut straight to the chase. His analyst colleague seemed up for a chat.

'Listen, Henri,' he began, 'we reckon we've got a real stink in our office.'

Henri moved his chair in a little closer.

'The life of one of our members might be at risk.'

Henri was now all ears and big eyes. 'Talk to me,' he said.

11TH JUNE

'Confidence?'

'Confidence,' came the reply.

'Donny Benjamin. He stinks,' said Spud. He had thrown out his best bait.

Henri was a little slow to reply, but he knew that Spud was squeaky clean. He batted back. 'We've suspected that for months.'

'Well, he's watching the credit card of someone important to us, and passing on information to the Mafia,' Spud continued in a hushed tone.

'And what's the flow-on potential?'

'That someone special to us could be killed.'

'Cole Goodwin,' Henri stated, sure of the correctness of his statement.

'He never killed the old codger in New Zealand,' said Spud.

'We thought that,' Henri replied, 'but we're not the Homicide Squad. Who did the old guy?'

'The Mafia.'

'And who's driving it?'

'Inspector Mack.'

Henri smiled broadly, as if a secret tucked away at the back of his mind had been touched. He pulled his calling card from his shirt pocket and handed it to Spud. He said firmly, but with a wink, 'You get your people to contact my people.'

Spud took the card, placed it into his own pocket, and with an equal smile said, 'I'll get my people to contact your people.'

They both laughed as the conference was called back to order.

• •

Rossanna had Tommy looking utterly ridiculous. He sat on the small stool on the balcony of his room with a bath towel draped around his shoulders and a waterproof gown over the top. His look was completed by the addition of a heavily stained, thick, plastic skullcap that fitted snugly over his head and concealed all of his hair beneath. Rossanna plucked at Tommy's head with what appeared to him to be an oversized crochet hook. Each time she prised out a tuft, he screamed and she laughed. The bottle of white wine that sat on the old parquetry floor beside the stool was all but empty. Both of them held a glass to toast Tommy's successful travels. He had just told Rossanna that he planned to leave Bellagio the following morning. She in turn had insisted that he allow her to tidy up his wayward facial growth and he had found himself as he was now, enduring the addition of a few blond tips to his otherwise brown locks. Rossanna worked away, conjuring a sticky paste of bleach in her plastic beaker. She applied it liberally to Tommy's cap; too late now, he thought, as he sat with the cold mauve mass on his head.

'Are you going back home, Tomasso?' she asked as she worked.

'I can't.'

'But why not?' Rossanna asked just as the incoming ferry master blasted his horn. They both looked across at another near-full load of tourists. Tommy had to think of an answer to Rossanna's question apart from the obvious, so he focused on Jude, whom he had often mentioned to Rossanna during their morning walks, as he had also mentioned Lola. They had become more than good friends, Tommy and Rossanna. He saw her as a confidante.

'I'm still uncertain about Jude,' he offered, 'I don't know if it's time to go home yet.'

'Are you sure you are uncertain? You speak of such love for her.'

'Yes there is a strong attraction, I'll admit, but she may be married by now, Rossanna. She has a fiancé, remember.'

'But maybe she's not. You men are so strange,' Rossanna placed down the bowl of bleach and took another mouthful of wine.

'If I cared for her so much, why did I get involved with Lola?' he said.

'Because something sad was on your mind and she was there. Simple.'

11TH JUNE

Although Rossanna didn't know anywhere near all there was to understand about the circumstances that caused Tommy to leave Australia, she was right about Lola, he thought. She appeared at a difficult time for Tommy, and it was easy for him to lose himself in her arms. She was beautiful, very hard to resist.

'Could you live in Argentina, Tomasso?' Rossanna enquired further.

He didn't answer that question straightaway. Instead he drifted off to Buenos Aires and the little he had seen of it, the long motorcycle ride through the jungle regions, the Iguazu Falls and Paraguay.

'You're right,' he said, returning to the present, 'I couldn't live there.'

'But you could live with Jude in your *bellissimo appartamento?*'

He didn't answer that question either. He knew the answer, and he knew that he desperately wanted to see Jude again.

20th June

The rattly second-hand royal blue Fiat Uno travelled easily along the Bellagio–Como road, Como bound. It had done that twenty-minute drive hundreds of times over the years, when Rossanna attended university in the town. Today her passenger was Tommy, who, since his hairstyling appointment, now resembled a Miami drug dealer. He was delivering up a last-minute string of Australian colloquialisms to keep Rossanna in fits of laughter as she drove him to the bus stop.

'It's true. It means, that's amazing!' Tommy said.

Rossanna laughed and repeated the unusual phrase, 'Stone the crows.'

'How do they happen, your funny Australian words?' she said.

'I don't know,' he answered. 'Maybe it's 'cos we were all convicts once?'

'Really, Cole? I will miss your talk,' she said as the car turned the bend at Torno. Lost in memories, it took a little while for Tommy to realise that Rossanna had called him Cole.

'What did you say, Rossanna?' he enquired, puzzled and momentarily unsure of his hearing.

Rossanna realised her mistake and tried to brush it off as insignificant. A now very worried Tommy demanded that she stop the car. She pulled in nervously to the tourist wayside stop that overlooked the beautiful Moltrasio village across the lake.

'Tomasso, what's wrong? You are angry?'

'Tell me!' he almost yelled. He mentally rechecked the possibilities. He knew that there was nothing in his room, his luggage or even in his wallet that would associate him with the name Cole. What else did Rossanna know? How had she discovered his real name?

Rossanna attempted to explain.

'Well, last night during dinner service, a Calabrian guy rang and asked a strange question.' She took a breath and swallowed deeply. 'He said, is there a Tommy staying there?'

'And?' encouraged a very anxious Tommy.

'Well, I get calls every day for people, but it's always like, can you put me through to Tommy, or has Tommy arrived yet, never do you have a Tommy staying there? It was odd, and we are suspicious of the motives of southerners. His dialect was Calabrese, the worst of them all. And then he asked do I have a Cole staying there, an Australian?'

'What did you tell him, Rossanna?'

'I told him nothing. I said no. Then he tried to sweet-talk me like a Casanova. I asked him why he was so interested in an Australian. He wouldn't tell me but, Tomasso, I really tried to find out. All I could get from him was that he was ringing all the hotels in Como and Milano.'

He couldn't really imagine little Rossanna as a spy and her flustered explanation sounded believable; someone else had found him. Tommy sat in the car and looked out across the water to the village. He wondered what a mess Rossanna may have made of her attempt at being a 'Rossanna Hari' to a world-savvy Massimo.

Neither of them spoke as they drove on.

The silence hung over the little car for the next forty minutes except on one occasion when Rossanna offered and Tommy accepted a lift straight through to Milano Railway Station. On the way there, in the convenient silence, Tommy formulated a plan: he would head for Greece.

In the awkward few moments that the car idled illegally in front of the railway station, Tommy attempted to make amends with his young friend. He reassured her that no harm had been done, and also that his name wasn't Cole, and that he had no idea why anyone would be searching for someone called Tommy. The strained and far-fetched explanations sat heavily on both their minds as Tommy collected his Bees-Knees from the back seat and placed a kiss on the cheek of the very troubled Rossanna before uttering his last goodbye. He walked away briskly, heading into the train station and towards the ticket office as Rossanna's car pulled slowly from the kerb.

• •

Taking up the vacant car space left by the royal blue Fiat Uno was Pino's 156 black Alfa Romeo, completely covered in dust from its ten-hour overnight drive from Calabria. Massimo was behind the wheel and Pino sat jittering on the passenger seat, his dirty shirt covering his stomach, belt and waistline.

'*Stupida*,' said Massimo tersely.

Pino opened the door and stood on the roadway, leaning in.

'*Buona fortuna, Pino*. Good luck. Kill him good.'

'*Nessun problema, capo*.'

The Alfa Romeo left the kerb as Pino also disappeared into the railway station crowd.

• •

There's a first time for everything, Sandra thought. She was ushered sheepishly into the Toe Cutters office, to a strategically arranged meeting with the second-in-command, Superintendent Willy Fountain. They walked together through the main muster room, and surprisingly she saw that it was not dissimilar to every other detectives' muster room she had been in. Pinboards, dozens of photos, headshots and happy snaps, paraphernalia, cluttered mess, empty coffee cups with fungus growing in the bottom, and even a few girlie calendars with darts embedded in their breasts gracing the walls. Most of the time she focused on the back of the superintendent's balding head.

Just before they reached the interview room where they planned to spend the next half-hour, she stopped and stood firm in her tracks. She glanced back into the muster room, and more particularly at the

20TH JUNE

photos she had just walked past. All cops, she realised, all serving policemen and women, mostly young, mostly less than her own age. Suddenly she felt very unwell. No high-ranking officers. She thought of Inspector Mack, and wondered whether Cole's affair would change that.

Sandra took her seat opposite Fountain, and her first impression as the coffees were placed between them was that this was a thoroughly decent man. They made small talk for a while. It was Fountain who took the first serious serve.

'Henri's briefed me on the chats he's had with your analyst, and you have to know, Sandra, we're on your side.'

Sandra let that ball go through, and then served up her own. 'There's little value in fucking around, Boss. I'll be honest from the start. Until the other day we had no evidence to give you. Now we do. But first you have to know one thing. We did an illegal phone tap on Inspector Mack's mobile.'

Fountain momentarily lost most of his composure as he replied, 'Maybe we should be working on you, Detective?'

The mood shifted.

'Maybe I should just go,' said Sandra. She edged herself cautiously out of her chair, only to be stopped by Fountain who had moved around from behind his desk towards her. He sensed the need for an olive branch if his unit was going to move any closer to arresting Donny and Inspector Mack, and he reached his strong arm out to gently guide her back into her seat.

'Okay. Okay, Sandra, let's start over again, full disclosure. No problems for you or your team. Let's do this properly.'

An hour later, Fountain escorted Sandra out of the interview room. Both looked exhausted but they walked closely together. Clearly they had formed a trusting relationship of sorts as they passed conspiratorially through the muster room. Half-a-dozen bent heads looked up. Fountain gave a silent 'thumbs up' and a smile. Sandra broke from her position alongside the officer, went over to the pinboard and pulled a dart from a calendar. She took deliberate aim and bullseyed the head-shot of Donny pinned to the board. She was gone within the minute. Fountain then returned to the muster room and clapped both hands together loudly to corner the attention of his crew.

'Grab a coffee, and get ready for a briefing,' he said.

• •

The TGV train to Venice had long ago left the station of Padova, travelling rapidly due east. A blur of farmhouses, paddocks, crops and the autostrada that paralleled his journey was visible from Tommy's carriage window, which was mostly shaded by the blind that the two female backpackers had pulled down. Tommy had sat beside one of them. Since the start of their trip nearly three hours earlier, he had been pretending to read his Andrea Camilleri novel, *Scent of the Night*, when what he was in fact doing was constantly going over the words Rossanna had spoken, as she had nervously described her conversation with the mysterious caller. A southern Italian who could be none other than Massimo, he thought. These thoughts of danger and Italians led him back to the previous year, when he had lived undercover buying cocaine, kilos at any one time …

Having arrived, as usual, at an otherwise normal-looking house, he found his Mafia mates in the back shed offering pure blocks of the stuff for sale. Packaged up into the size and shape of footballs, these large pure white rocks would each fetch up to a million dollars on the nightclub scene. Cole's mind's eye almost surreally saw his own figure blend familiarly among the group as he weighed each block on the minute scales and watched the electronic weight indicator register 1000 grams. He'd barter the price down to wholesale rates, drug-dealer mate's rates, and, once it was over and the deal was done, they'd all sip wine and enjoy some friendly southern Italian hospitality, before agreeing on a time to meet and do it all again. In, out and gone, quick business for all, profits to be shared, such was his relationship with the Mafia. At least until the arrests

20TH JUNE

came, that is, until the giggle was over, and everyone was locked up, everyone except him.

With the information from Rossanna, Massimo was now searching the Milano area, and Tommy's plan had to change. His revised plan was simple. After an overnight stop on the outskirts of Venice, he intended to be on the very first ferry of the morning to Corfu. From there he would ferry on to Igoumenitsa, where he would find a local boat to take him to Lefkata Island, off the Greek coastline. There he'd bang on the door of an old and trusted friend, a mate from his early childhood. He'd left Australia years earlier to marry his Greek girlfriend and had taken to driving a Holden Commodore around the island as a taxi. Tommy couldn't wait for the sanctuary of their home and the sight of a couple of friendly faces.

Intermittently he chatted with the two young backpackers, a pair of 20-something New Zealanders who were in the middle of a gap year from Wellington University to see the world. He told a couple of white lies initially, claiming he had never been to New Zealand, but otherwise they freely swapped travel talk and playful verbal sparring over cricket and rugby. The only thing they agreed on was the music of Crowded House, although there was a short dispute over the origin of the group. When they weren't chatting they were reading their respective books. At least Tommy was pretending to.

As thoughts of New Zealand took their natural progression to those New Zealanders of his personal acquaintance, he sunk into a valley of gloom recollecting Cary and Lynette. His mind kept imagining with the death of Cary, and his worry escalated, wondering whether Lynette had died. The only information he had been able to glean on her state was from the newspaper stories that he had read a couple of weeks earlier.

Tommy decided to stretch his legs and clear his head. He shuffled past an elderly couple in search of the rest rooms and went looking for the buffet car, which was situated one carriage back. His young

Kiwi friends were happy to keep watch over his Bees-Knees, which he had tucked away safely on the overhead luggage rack.

Sitting immediately behind Tommy was Pino, who had hardly moved in the three hours. He kept his sweaty hands clasped tightly over a slight bulge on his waistline. When Tommy stood, he too stood and headed for the buffet car, following just a few steps behind. Always courteous, Tommy held the door open for him.

Twenty minutes later and Tommy was at the froth end of his beer when an announcement came over the public address system, first in Italian and then repeated in English. 'We will arrive at Venezia Station in fifteen minutes.'

As he stood from his bar stool, he noted that the train had reduced its speed drastically. It was no longer rocketing along; it was crawling. He paid for the overpriced Peroni beer, realising as he did that the train had continued to reduce speed. It was now merely trickling along. The peasant-looking bar-girl with the makings of a faint moustache handed Tommy his change, then stopped midway to look out of her carriage window to the train tracks. There appeared to be a handful of workers gathered together every fifty metres or so, wearing fluorescent orange safety vests and caps, fastening loose sleepers on the tracks.

'Work-a-man,' she said as she turned back to face Tommy.

'Workmen,' Tommy corrected.

'*Si, grazie, Signore,*' she nodded.

'*Prego,*' he smiled.

She smiled back, nodding as he walked off.

As Tommy returned to his own carriage via the transit door, he noticed the same horrible little man behind him again. No 'thank you', '*grazie*' or '*va bene*' offered as he held the door for him, he thought. Rude little bugger.

Four carriages up in the locomotive, the driver cautiously looked left and right as he eased the train through the gang of spasmodically placed workmen. Ten metres away was the next quartet of workers, each of whom was walking a little too close to the tracks. At the sound of the engine's whistle, one of them slipped in the loose bluestone chips and fell, his leg finishing on top of the outside rail. His closest workmate instinctively leaned over to grab him, also exposing a good deal of his body to the oncoming locomotive. The train driver pulled hard on the brake, jolting the train to a violent stop.

Tommy sailed down the aisle and past three rows of seats. His right knee collided heavily with the armrest of one of the chairs and he buckled at the impact. Coming over the top of him was the lighter weight of the horrible little man for whom he had twice opened the door. He too was out of control. His 9mm Browning automatic pistol had been prised loose and had flown along the vinyl-covered floor just ahead of them both, spinning in a clockwise fashion as it travelled the remaining length of the carriage and came to rest near the far transit door.

Nobody in the carriage escaped the hard shunt of the brakes. A few screams were heard; some people lost their seats altogether and half-a-dozen bags and suitcases toppled from the overhead luggage racks. There was genuine chaos for a split second. Tommy's knee was as sore as hell and he instinctively moved to push away the little man on top of him. His nostrils filled with the smell of his putrid body odour. To Tommy's utter amazement, the mangy individual started thrashing into him and delivered several strong blows to his head. Something was wrong here, he thought. The pain in his knee was soon forgotten as Tommy returned the blows in defence. At least three of his punches landed to the face of the tough little guy before Tommy could push himself free.

By now the old lady who was sitting in the chair, the arm of which had nearly destroyed his knee, was screaming. Tommy got to his feet and, with his left hand holding a fist of shirt and jacket, he yelled at his aggressor, 'What the fuck are you on about?'

Tommy received two heavy fists in reply from the little guy, straight to the side of his head. He was dazed, but still held tightly to a fist of clothing. A small Italian boy sitting two seats away was yelling as he pointed towards the far transit door. It was then that Tommy saw the gun for the first time. He understood instantly why the little man had been behind him on his way to and from the bar.

The fighter's arms began thrashing again. Tommy could see his stained, gritted teeth. His breath stank. Tommy pushed him with all his might. The little man bent backwards over the offending armrest and onto the lap of the screaming old lady, which only increased the volume of her screams. Tommy then hit him twice in his yellowed teeth with as much force as he could, before he let go of him to run towards the gun. Exactly one pace later his injured knee had him sink in pain to the floor of the carriage. The aggressor had a second to recover. He clambered over Tommy and ran towards the gun. The entire carriage had now erupted in a chorus of screams.

The little man picked up the firearm and spun around to face his foe. Tommy seemed to come from nowhere with his 180-centimetre, 85-kilo frame and collided full on with the little man, who in turn had nowhere to move as his back was slammed firmly against the door. His head smashed brutally against the heavy safety glass of the transit door. The impact was so intense that it caused the pane to shatter. Blood tricked from the gunman's nose. The pistol dropped heavily from his hand and the little fighter slumped from the door to the floor, dead.

Tommy too slumped to the floor of the carriage; the impact had winded him and his shoulder muscles burned from the struggle that had unfolded with the tough midget. He looked back along the aisle, frantically searching for the face of Massimo in the crowd. He was nowhere to be seen in the flow of terrified passengers evacuating the carriage via the opposite transit door. None of them had thought to stay long enough to gather up luggage or possessions. Among those fleeing were the two New Zealand backpackers. All Tommy could think of was to flee the train himself, but in the opposite direction. He leaped gingerly across to his seat to grab his shoulder bag and, after negotiating his path over the body of his aggressor, he jumped from the train and hobbled as fast as he could across the railway tracks towards some warehouses, bag over one shoulder and pistol in one hand. A milling mix of railway workers watched dumbfounded as the carriage completely emptied with crazed passengers scattering in all directions.

• •

Tommy peered around the corner of a building no more than 600 metres from the trainline. He leaned his back against the wall of the rust-stained building before slumping slowly to the ground. He desperately needed to rest his knee. His gasps for air were so audible that he covered his mouth with his left hand, praying that no one would hear. His right hand still held tight to the 9mm Browning pistol as he unbuttoned his shirt in an attempt to cool down. He looked again around the corner, along a laneway to an estate of postwar saw-tooth warehouses. He was in the industrial zone of the town of Mestre, the edge of the thin strip of water, Laguna Veneta, just before the long bridge across to Venice. The storage rooms were all locked up, except one.

A tiny teal and bright yellow forklift was loading the back end of a small refrigerated truck, two factories from where he stood. Having caught his breath and regained his composure, he stepped forward on his leg. He stopped. The rush of adrenalin required for flight had all but drained from his body. He felt the soreness to his limb increase but he was so used to firearms that he had completely forgotten about the handgun he was carrying. Tommy unclipped the straps to his shoulder bag and stuffed the Browning inside his clothing before he recommenced his attempt at walking normally towards the truck. The sign above its parked position read *Trimbole Pesce Prodotti*: a wholesale fish supplier, he reckoned, by the smell. All he could think of was ice for his knee. Relief was only steps away. So far the forklift driver hadn't noticed him as he methodically loaded his vehicle and then disappeared once more inside the wholesaler's.

Tommy eased his way between the side of the truck and the warehouse wall, to the unlocked driver's door, which he quietly opened. He figured by now that if the local *Carabinieri* were any good, they would be racing along the train tracks to hear the thirty-odd versions of the events that had just taken place. Knowing witnesses, the one thing Tommy was sure would be consistent to all was that 'a big man killed a little man, and the big man ran away with the gun'. It would be a long time before the *Carabinieri* would find the true identity of the little man, if they bothered at all. He was sure that their focus would be on the armed Australian heading to Venice.

He reached over and grabbed a fist full of invoice dockets fastened to a clipboard on the driver's seat, and tried desperately to decipher where the load of fish was headed. Anywhere but Venice, he hoped, as this would undoubtedly be the course of the *Polizia*, after not finding their suspect amongst the warehouses. The only name on the delivery docket he could read was *Quadri*, which meant nothing to him. His investigative work was interrupted at that moment by the sound of the driver approaching, speaking in rapid Italian and gesturing goodbye to the forklift operator. Tommy hobbled to the rear of the truck, threw his shoulder bag forward onto the platform, and heaved his sore body up and on to the apron. He slid along the floor of the vehicle and secreted himself behind several polystyrene cartons of lobsters and oysters, pleased at the chunks of ice on top of the lobster bins. He heard the freezer van's door being locked tight and settled in for a chilly ride.

An hour later, after a journey in heavy traffic, Tommy sensed that they had come to a final stop. The overweight driver finished off a handful of pistachio nuts and walked to the back of his small truck. He threw most of his not-insignificant weight on to the lever and snapped open the seal on the door. He spat a few broken shells from his mouth as he slowly prised the door ajar. He reeled backwards suddenly into a crowd of passing tourists with a look of utter shock at the sight of an upright Tommy positioned as close to the rear of the door as had been possible. His now near-empty Bees-Knees draped over his shoulder, he was wearing virtually every piece of clothing he owned and still shivered noticeably. Without a sound he stepped from

20TH JUNE

the truck as fast as his frozen limbs would allow and vanished into the crowd. The still open-mouthed driver gaped as he watched him fade away before he hit his palm to the top of his forehead and exclaimed loudly in his native tongue.

Twenty paces further on Tommy broke free of the crowd and out of view of the truck driver, to find himself standing dead centre in the Piazza San Marco, the heart of Venice. He spun 360 degrees, taking in the seemingly hundreds of arched stone columns and dozens of shades of grey. Behind the truck, which the driver had already begun to unload, he read *Caffe Quadri* on the ornate façade of one of the finest restaurants in northern Italy. His shoulders slumped as he fell in line with a group of Chinese travellers hovering in an orderly fashion behind their native guide, who was holding a peach parasol high in the air. They looked Tommy up and down, in his layers of clothes and laughed raucously, causing a couple of hundred pigeons to take to the perfect blue sky.

∙ ∙

The early evening tourists on the pretty outside boardwalk at Harry's Bar sipped Bellini cocktails, Campari and soda and the occasional martini, no doubt reliving their favourite James Bond moment. Tommy, now thawed in the late afternoon sun, and back to a single pair of jeans and an Armani shirt, could see himself being squeezed out of his comfy position. He had settled up with the waiter for his whisky sour and was in no doubt that he had to find somewhere to hide, if only for one night. He couldn't help wondering where Massimo might be. He would certainly be aware that his little assassin was no longer on this planet. Tommy's only consolation was that Massimo too would be surely trying to stay shy of the *Carabinieri*, who would be on high alert in Venice.

His knee felt slightly better, no doubt the enforced and prolonged 'icing' had helped. He took the side lane along Harry's Bar and worked his way back to the Piazza San Marco, through the wafting scent of steamed mussels and coffee beans. A short cut through the five-star Luna Hotel Baglioni, Venice's most ancient and exclusive, had him exit at the other side of their restaurant, to face a labyrinth of tiny lanes, just proud of the main piazza. Only a short stroll along the eastern porticos and Tommy dropped himself into a chair and table for one, hard up against a pillar at the Florian, the famed tearoom in Venice since 1720. This beautiful relic of a bygone era was an emblem of impeccable service and offered a selection of gourmet finger food and an impressive list of teas and coffees at absurdly inflated prices. The tearoom guests swelled onto a goodly portion of the square as an orchestra played Puccini soothingly in the background. Not the sort of location that one would expect a lunatic gun-wielding Australian evading arrest to sit, was Tommy's whisky-induced rationale. He ordered a round of salmon and artichoke cream sandwiches and a pot of chamomile tea and practised his best Pommy accent. He turned the collar up on his shirt and disappeared into the *Times*.

Tommy sat mulling over the economic problems facing Britain for the next three hours, and watched the tables fill and empty a few times over. The occasional pair of *Carabinieri* fussed through the laneways on the opposite side of the piazza. At closing time he took his bill into the reception area at the Florian under the guise of wanting to purchase a gift. Once the bill had been settled, he politely requested the toilet and was directed to the upstairs bathrooms. At the door, he quietly took instead the stairs up to the private level, past the staff change rooms, down a short corridor and into a storeroom that to his delight housed the table linen for the restaurant. An hour later, when the final light had been turned out in the early closing establishment, he bedded down for the night.

• •

A far-too-cocky Donny stepped into a backwater pub in North Melbourne. He was alone and he wore his coolest gear: patent black

20TH JUNE

snake-skin pointy-toed shoes, black drainpipe denims, black T-shirt and black leather coat. Inside, at the 'tough guys' bar, Donny gave a nod to the barman, who instinctively pulled him a pot of beer. He headed for a pair of Asian toughs leaning on the far end of the bar. The pot of beer was placed in front of him at the same time that Donny took his bar stool. The Asian pair both shook Donny's hand, one smiled broadly while the other, the boss no doubt, just nodded. They then chatted away quietly among themselves.

Not far away, standing next to a tall pedestal table, was a frumpy-looking piece, her huge arse squeezed into a pair of tired jeans. She sipped from a glass of rough red wine and spoke flirtatiously to her male companion, who needed a darn good shower and a packet of razor blades. A worn-out Nike sports bag was slung casually over his shoulder, the hidden covert camera trained perfectly on the two Asians and Donny. It was textbook surveillance. The videotape captured the serious Asian handing Donny a wad of money, which must have totalled at least $10 000.

Donny seemed to look everywhere around the bar except at the two Toe Cutters, who discreetly and expertly filmed his every move. Donny secured the wad of money in his back pocket. He straightened himself up and walked quickly from the bar.

• •

Wearing the same clothes, Donny jogged up the steps of the Bar 99% strip joint in Melbourne. It was five in the afternoon, and the after-work office crowd had yet to appear. Donny stepped into the nightclub unchecked by the security guards, and weaved his way through stacked tables and chairs towards a room at the back. The inside security guy flicked his head towards one of the private lap-dance rooms.

The instant the door was opened, Barry White's 'Shaft' could be heard pumping through the speakers. A gorgeous redhead was hard at it, one hand resting on each of her client's knees as her amply endowed body gyrated to the rhythm. She looked up and smiled her russet lips as Donny entered. He was acknowledged less warmly with an off-handed wave by the otherwise engrossed client. Donny sat and watched the routine. The stripper leaned back against the wall and raised both arms into the air to clasp her hands around a huge pole. Each hip moved up and down in alternate timing as if her butt was kissing the pole. A blue chiffon sarong lay on the floor to one side of the tiny room, leaving her dressed in nothing more than the briefest turquoise G-string and tiny rhinestone studded bra that failed to cover her oversized silicon-enhanced breasts. Her hands left the pole to seductively unclip the back of her bra and she leaned forward to her client. He reached out with both hands, grabbing a breast in each as she nuzzled into him. The sound of the world's best fake orgasm moaned from her pouting mouth. The track ended and she ever so lightly messed her hands through his hair and slipped her miniscule panties down just a fraction to reveal that she was indeed a genuine redhead. As she walked out, a crisp $100 bill was wedged between the sparkling sequins of her tiny g-string.

Once the door was closed Donny got straight down to business. He pulled a clear plastic bag from his inside coat pocket and threw it on his mate's lap; his mate was slowly coming back to earth. The bag contained 200 ecstasy tablets.

'Fix us up next week,' said Donny, 'It's on the tick.'

'*Muchas gracias*,' replied the non-Spanish drug dealer. 'How's supply?'

'Drying up,' said Donny. 'But good news, the wogs have got a shit-load coming through in a couple of months.'

'There's always wild stories like that about, Donny.'

'This story's not wild, Kemosabe. I'm connected to it and we'll have enough eccies to flood Australia. Just you wait.'

The drug dealer smiled in return.

'Gotta get back to work to knock off,' was Donny's closing comment as they hit a high five. He left the room and headed out of

20TH JUNE

the nightclub. As he jogged down the main steps and out onto the street, the digital movie camera stashed in the observation van parked across the road filmed his departure and the operative tapped away on his surveillance log, which was transmitted instantly back to the Toe Cutters office via wireless.

• •

'Yes, I'm the same detective from Melbourne who rang yesterday—and the day before,' replied a frustrated Sandra, waiting on the telephone line for an update on Lynette Peterson's progress. Every day since the tragedy she had called, and every day she had been faced with the same animosity from the hospital staff, and the same sterile comment, 'The patient is still critical, still in a coma.' Sandra guessed that she couldn't entirely blame the nursing staff for their bland one-liner on the health of their most newsworthy patient. After all, the key suspect was another Melbourne detective. She dropped the phone despondently. It was time to knock off, she thought, as she gathered up her handbag and waved lazily to Spud and Leigh on the way out.

21st June

A faint metal-to-metal noise broke Tommy's silent slumber. He lay snuggled in only his briefs, among a dozen tablecloths, head resting on his shoulder bag. The cold touch of the Browning automatic reminded him rapidly of yesterday. He listened for just a minute before he adjusted the serviette that bandaged his swollen knee. The smell of liniment recalled his midnight raid on the staff first aid kit. His knee had felt considerably better as a result. He also recalled his less-than-successful attempt, sometime after midnight, at using the Florian office telephone. He had dialled the tearoom of the ACA office, hoping to catch Sandra. The call had rung out unanswered. He needed to tell her of the attempts on his life.

Tommy's mind raced. Could Inspector Mack have been involved in the play? Was he now aware of the death of the little tough guy? Would he be using Interpol to track him down? So many questions. Tommy was sinking deeper and deeper into a very dark hole, walled with the unexplainable, hideous crimes that were being attributed to him. He could see no way clear of the mess, and had become aware for the first time that paranoia was gripping him. He saw an image of himself, locked away in an Italian gaol cell for half a lifetime, pleading his case to indifferent Italian prosecutors. It was imperative to talk it through with Sandra. His paranoia set him wondering if she or indeed anyone would believe him.

Dressing quickly in his jeans, shirt and sneakers, he kicked aside the dozen or so after-dinner mint wrappers on the floor. The metal-to-metal noise screeched again as his ears strained for the source of the sound. Very slowly he opened the storeroom door and listened again. All was quiet outside. Tommy tiptoed along the corridor to the staff change room and peeked in. A lone girl, no more than twenty years of age, he thought, was standing facing a tall narrow metal locker. She had removed her T-shirt and stood momentarily in nothing more than a pair of black briefs before she donned her chef uniform. Tommy glanced at his watch: just before 8 a.m. He descended the two flights of stairs, crept through the empty kitchen, picking up a small water bottle from the fridge, and left through the delivery door to a back laneway.

With a knee that now troubled him less, he zigzagged through a dozen weathered lime-wash alleys past two full dump-masters and the occasional rat, until he happened on the Grand Canal. He found himself standing at the water taxi wharf adjacent to a deserted Harry's Bar where he jumped a 20-euro cab to the tiny island of San Michele. Here he joined a short queue of early morning travellers with their heavy suitcases and backpacks as they waited impatiently for the ferry ticket office to open. The sign on the window advertised ships to the southern regions of Italy, Greece, Istanbul, and Alexandria in Egypt.

The window was flung open at 8.30 a.m. Tommy watched a typically loud American family wrestle with the purchase of their two adult and three minor tickets on the Istanbul ferry. The ticket seller had demanded their passports and the father was ratting around in his backpack, while juggling a gelato belonging to one of his screaming children. Tommy stepped aside, vacating his position in the queue. Instead he took a long espresso with milk and a pastry and watched the queue slowly whittle down. Each traveller, it seemed, was asked for a passport. He knew that he was unable to put his own document down on any desk in Italy.

Massimo's response to the death of the angry little man would almost certainly involve the Calabrian Mafia tapping into their corrupt customs and border police. Not to mention what dots the *Carabinieri* of Mestre would have joined believing that an armed foreigner had killed a national. Any thoughts of risking it were thwarted when Tommy heard a horn from an approaching craft, then turned to notice a police launch carrying six armed officers approaching San Michele wharf from the tiny island of Murano. An obvious police alert blanketing the entire town scared him back into his water taxi. His talkative driver raced ahead.

As Tommy's taxi approached the bank of the Grand Canal at Piazza San Marco, he racked his brain for ideas. As he sat low on the bow of the cab, he watched the tribe of street vendors pushing their carts of wares and setting up for the day. He did his best to ignore the incessant chatter, in near-perfect English, of his driver, who persistently tried to accommodate him with a hotel room, or perhaps a tour to the Murano glass factory or a seat in a good restaurant. His eyes scanned the dock for police uniforms. Tommy feared seeing Massimo in the growing crowd. The romance of Venice was lost on him; he stood motionless, alongside the lion column, looking up at the grandeur of the San Marco Basilica, realising that he was completely trapped on a network of islands that, apart from a single six-kilometre-long bridge and train station, held no other route back to the mainland.

He made a snap decision and headed for a nearby payphone, slipping a pre-paid phonecard into the slot and calling the ACA tea-room number again. The connection was clean and swift and he listened impatiently to the ringing. 'Come on Sandra, pick up, pick up.' After fifteen unanswered rings, the line automatically disconnected. He glanced at his watch. In Melbourne it was after 7 p.m.; the office was certainly closed. He dare not call Sandra at her home; Mack or the Homicide Squad would almost certainly have her phone tapped. Or was he being too paranoid? He needed to eat. His mind was fuzzy, his belly was empty and his judgement was starting to fail him. Defeated, he retrieved his phonecard.

With half an idea, he walked straight for the breakfast café of the opulent hotel he had snuck through the previous night. On the way, he purchased a cheap but suave-looking Panama hat from a street vendor and plonked it on his head. He took a seat and ordered the best breakfast available, at 25 euros. As he waited for it to arrive, he tucked his shoulder bag out of sight beneath the linen-covered table, and stepped over to the concierge's desk. He made a deliberate fuss and bother to a busy concierge about needing a newspaper with his

21ST JUNE

breakfast. He mentioned in passing that he had forgotten to order his hotel shuttle to the Aeroporto Marco Polo the previous night when he had checked in. The occupied concierge nodded once or twice without interest before he handed Tommy a newspaper. Tommy tipped 10 euros to the suddenly delighted and accommodating concierge. An offer of a seat on the next hotel shuttle, leaving in less than fifteen minutes, was promptly forthcoming. Tommy explained that he had checked out earlier and would be waiting for a nod from the breakfast room.

..

The church bell rang twice from St Christopher Cathedral in the centre of Mestre, indicating 9.30 a.m. Tommy was seated comfortably in the back of the courtesy bus to the airport. He was safely off the island of Venice, having cleared the road block at the end of the *lido*, away from the scurry of *Carabinieri*, well fed, and hopeful of a domestic airline ticket to the western side of Italy, near the French border.

The feeling of euphoria at his escape was short-lived as Tommy's coach approached the airport terminal and he saw the pairs of officials stationed at every entrance, inspecting the passports of all foreigners arriving. He stood lost as the well-attired hotel driver carefully unloaded the guests' assorted pieces of luggage. He was handed his shoulder bag and remembered the weapon it now housed. To the left he observed the directional arrows to the bus depot. From there he deciphered with the assistance of the universal pictorial symbols that there was a connection to a trainline twelve kilometres away. Tommy picked up his Bees-Knees and headed rapidly that way. A hire car was not an option; passport identification would be required. He moved briskly with the cover of a small crowd towards the bus terminal but his journey soon came to an abrupt halt, his crowd becoming a queue fronting a team of *Carabinieri* demanding passports at the entrance to the bus station. Tommy stepped casually from the line and dropped to one knee as if to do up his shoelace, looking furtively behind him. There were two other *Carabinieri* approaching on foot, not twenty metres away. His view of the two guards was hindered somewhat by the trolley of a van driver, who was unloading three large tubs of flavoured syrup to the adjacent gelataria. He spied the keys inside the van's ignition and quickly stepped inside the shop to purchase a cone.

• •

Three hours later, Tommy was on the A1 autostrada, approaching the ring road to Florence. Determined to stay on the main thoroughfare towards Rome, he jolted along, ignoring the last exit ramp to the capital of Tuscany. His newly acquired gelato van was bound for Rome. He seemed destined to travel in a direction that he didn't want to go: towards southern Italy.

22nd June

The brilliant early morning southern sun broke through the window of Tommy's hotel room, a no-star dive opposite the Napoli Central Railway Station. The faded chenille bedspread that was strewn haphazardly across the thin mattress of the single bed would not normally have looked inviting but Tommy had drifted into the deepest of sleeps after arriving late the afternoon before. He had dumped the gelato van on the outskirts of Rome and caught the metro into the city. Three attempts to book a room in a series of cheap hotels had resulted in the repeated demand for his passport. Tommy was now certain that he would never get a bed in Italy's capital without proper credentials; he was far more confident, however, of lucking in to a room without questions in Naples, the most corrupt city in the world. With some degree of trepidation, he finally shuffled back into the train *termini* and headed south towards the lions' den.

The receptionist at the dodgy Naples hotel soon forgot about asking for his passport when a crisp 20-euro note was placed on the counter. In exchange, Tommy was presented with the dirty key to an untidy single room on the second level overlooking the main entrance, the taxi rank adjacent to the station and a multitude of African street vendors. It was the week of the Italian Formula One Grand Prix and the street vendors were busy selling a myriad of junk. By the end of his first beer, as he sat in only his shorts and Panama hat on his miniscule balcony, Tommy had latched onto a lucrative street scam. He had long heard that the Mafia no longer picked the pockets of passing tourists, or fleeced the travellers at the train station. They had far bigger fish to fry. This allowed room for ruthless gangs of Albanians and Romanians—hard men, mostly illegal immigrants with nothing but spit and time on their hands—to lighten the wallets of the unsuspecting public. He watched as one such well-dressed and clean-shaven Albanian approached a couple who were walking from the station to the street. They were travel-weary and laden down with designer luggage, the perfect bait for a sting.

Feigning an accidental bump, the gentlemanly and highly obliging con man offered his assistance, summoning a private car as he professed the untrustworthiness of the taxis and repeating his profuse apologies for knocking over the poor lady. The now charmed and relieved travellers were elated by the assistance, and in no time a private car had appeared. The boot was opened carefully to receive their luggage and handbags by a smartly dressed driver. The Good Samaritan gangster then requested 30 euros to cover the expenses of the car, as he exclaimed generously, 'Half the price for my new friends, sir'. The gullible couple quickly parted with their money and the leader of the sting just as quickly jumped his own cab, whereupon he, the driver and the luggage disappeared into the massive Piazza Garibaldi, leaving the bewildered travellers standing shocked on the footpath with nothing more than the clothes they were wearing. Their wallets had been lifted as well.

Every ten minutes a different con man would appear out the front of the station to repeat the performance with a different car arriving as ordered for a new set of travellers. And so it went on, hour after hour. Tommy watched, powerless, as the scams continued; he ached for a badge and his crew and the chance to exact some revenge. Streams of heartbroken holiday-makers circled the streets frantically searching out the uninterested *Carabinieri*. Before too long, Tommy spied the ringleader—a middle-aged guy with his arms covered in gaol-house tattoos. He sat quite still behind the grubby window of a coffee shop. The front table was his office nook for the day and a row of empty espresso cups sat lined up like soldiers in front of him. Apparently business was booming. From there, Tommy surmised, he oversaw the movements of his entire gang, watching their victories between the gaps in the flashing iridescent signs affixed to the window advertising panini and gelato. A pattern very rapidly developed, as

22ND JUNE

each driver would return to him shortly after a sting and present him with a wad of cash.

By 10 p.m. Tommy had stepped from the balcony and back into the bleakness of his room. Under the glow of the lone light bulb, he counted his own stash of sadly depleted lovely. Just under 900 euros remained, although the Visa card was as yet unused. Although Sandra had hinted through her 'bottom line' that the Visa card was safe, Tommy realised that the message was now many days old, and he couldn't take any chances—at least not in Mafia country. He changed into jeans, shirt and shoes, and with his Browning tucked into the small of his back, he went in search of the fire exit to the rear of the hotel.

Once on the main street, he purchased a McLaren Formula One cap from one of the many vendors without the slightest effort to bargain the price down, and placed it firmly on his head. Mingling with the night crowd that was spilling out to enjoy the perfect summer's evening, he strolled casually past the café window. The gang *capo* was still seated alone, his now bulging briefcase by his heels and a coffee cup at his lips. Tommy took a covert position, not dissimilar to a drunk, in the doorway next to the café, and watched the traffic, an unopened bottle of Peroni beer in his hand.

A garbage truck crawled along the right side of the street, and before long it was immediately in front of the café attending to a nest of bins. With the lip of his cap now pulled down, Tommy surreptitiously walked behind the truck and onto the blind side of the café. As the garbage men busied themselves raising bins to the back of the truck, Tommy raised his own arm and hurled the full beer bottle at the window of the café. The entire window broke free and fell in thousands of pieces to the pavement. Tommy walked casually through the mayhem straight to the door of the café, his timing perfect to see the *capo* scuttle urgently towards the rear door.

Through the confused and panicked patrons, Tommy followed his target to the corridor leading to the gents' toilet. The tough looked back momentarily, just fast enough to glimpse the Grand Prix cap and to see the butt of Tommy's Browning come crashing down on the back of his head. Before the Albanian leader of bad men had even hit the piss-stained tiled floor, Tommy had relieved him of his satchel and had continued out towards the laneway. This left an unconscious gangster lying outstretched on his back with a McLaren cap lying on his chest. An even trade, Tommy thought, as he disappeared into the dark network of Naples.

Two hours later, having allowed the dust to settle on his recent adventure, Tommy returned to the fire escape. His booty was stashed safe and sound inside a newly purchased Vietnamese 'Louis Vuitton' carry bag. He made his way slowly up the two flights of stairs to his room, bolted down tightly and settled in for the night. It had been a long, hard day.

• •

Tommy stepped from his bed, stretched his body and ambled over to close the heat-twisted shutters on the brilliant sunshine and the noise of the street below. He attempted to kick-start the 20-year-old television with its disobedient remote control without much success, and so opted for a quiet start to the morning instead. Tommy left the hotel, the Bees-Knees over his shoulder and the new addition to the luggage family tucked under his arm. He had four jobs on his mental list for the morning. He set off through the Mercato district to tick off number one.

The old-world market district was alive with produce stalls, offering daily fresh fruit, vegetables and an odd assortment of meat, all to the constant hollers of the vendors, attempting to out-do each other. It was also awash with busy little barber shops; a candy-striped pole beckoned and Tommy soon sat proudly on a cream-enamelled barber's chair. The barber worked his shaving brush into an intense foaming lather and then stopped to expertly sharpen his cut-throat razor, smiling as he did at the Bombe Alaska he had created on his client's face. One long sharp stroke after another and Tommy's face returned to a boyish youthfulness. A luxury of five minutes under a steaming hot face towel left just enough time for Tommy to say a silent goodbye to Rossanna's creation as his blond tips fell to the barber's parquetry floor. He was new yet again, he thought. He walked from the barber shop, gifting his Panama to the oldest in the row of waiting men. An impressive array of gold fillings flashed from the whiskered Italian in return.

Tommy's next task took him to the Via De Gasperi in the docklands, where he took a plastic moulded chair at an internet café to draft a message to Sandra. Before he did, he read a message waiting for him.

Dear Ingrid,

I have been pondering what to do, so you can feel better, well again. I have talked to some of our old friends and they are working hard to think of ways to help. I'm sure a fountain of ideas will soon flow.

Stay well, darling. Love, Sandy.

Tommy sat dumbfounded for a moment, trying to decipher the bottom line. Over and over he read the message, coming up with the same result. It could only mean that Sandra had gone to the Toeys and the head of the unit, Superintendent Fountain, was working on his case. While he naturally worried about the Toe Cutters hunting him, as any detective would, this time around he felt the message was a great positive. After all, he trusted Sandra's judgement. If only the Toeys could prove Massimo was in the Bay of Islands at the time of the horrific stabbings. He wondered how that could be achieved as he typed a response to Sandra.

Dear Sandy,

Tried to call you a few times, honey. I really wish I was home with you. I've had another miscarriage, Sandy. Yes, I am unwell, hope there are some ideas forthcoming. This is my third miscarriage and it's putting so much pressure on me, and on the marriage.

Otherwise I'm fine, Ingrid.

Satisfied with the contents of the bottom line, Tommy clicked 'send'. He moved past the teenage attendant at the front counter and dropped a single euro coin into the tray as he hit the street again, mentally ticking off item two and wondering how to prove Massimo had been in the Bay of Islands.

His third job for the morning was a mere hop, skip and a jump around the corner to the Piazza Municipio, the legal precinct of the city of Naples. He had been mulling over this chore since he first stepped off the little balcony the previous night. Tommy walked up to the office of the Anti-Mafia Unit at the northern end of the piazza. The massive fortified building was surrounded by squad cars. Uniforms and suits ran purposefully in and out of the grand archway of the main entrance. It was all a bit too busy for Tommy who carried with him not just, as always, the Bees-Knees with its secret compartment, the new home of the Browning, but also the Albanian's satchel, hidden in the Vietnamese Vuitton. He turned promptly on the ball of his foot and headed in the opposite direction.

Diagonally opposite the police headquarters was a McDonald's. Tommy ordered a long black coffee of questionable quality and found a booth near the front window. He dropped his phonecard into a phone adjacent to his pedestal seat and placed a call to the police headquarters across the road. Once answered he asked to be transferred to an English-speaking investigator.

'Hello, *Commissario* D'Alfonso.'

Tommy hesitated for a moment, realising he knew that name. This was Spud's trusted contact.

'Hello, *Commissario* D'Alfonso,' the Italian repeated.

Without offering his own name, Tommy launched into his tale of the central railway scam that he had observed the night before. The

Italian guessed from the way his caller spoke that he was talking to a traveller who was also a detective; they spoke the same jargon. He listened intently as Tommy further explained that the black satchel that now sat inside the Vietnamese Vuitton bag at the bottom of the garbage bin at the centre of the piazza was full of almost all of the money stolen. Just before he had closed his eyes the previous night, Tommy had counted out more than 6000 euros, of which 5000 remained in the bag. He went on to inform the Italian investigator of the passports, credit cards and the other items of identification of the many victims that the garbage bin now held, as well as the wallet belonging to the leader of the gang. There was a slight pause on the end of the phone before Tommy heard a burst of raucous laughter.

'*Magnifico, Signore, magnifico, Signore Robin Hood,*' came enthusiastically from the Italian's end. Tommy hung up the phone immediately and with a trace of a smile himself, ordered another bad coffee, before returning to his booth and settling in to watch police swarm into the piazza.

Tommy left the McDonald's, glancing back occasionally at the half-dozen uniforms squatted over the now up-ended satchel. A tall, lean and handsome Italian investigator stood confidently overseeing them in a beautifully tailored suit. He was still laughing as he glanced below the trees in the garden and around the rim of the piazza for his anonymous caller. He guessed his fellow detective was out there, watching.

On the opposite side of Via Acton, Tommy stood facing the largest ferry terminal in Italy, the Stazione Marittima, his best way off the mainland. If he were to stand any chance of survival he couldn't venture any further south by road or train, as the next region was Calabria. He surveyed the dozens of ferries before him, and the many destinations. Corsica, Sicily, Tunisia, Malta, and on the list went, each destination requiring a passport. Tommy read over the names several times and his eyes settled on one location he knew well; it had become a great curiosity to him only months earlier. Chances were that it was remote enough not to have a customs desk or a vigilant police department, having only 400 residents. He confidently stepped forward to the ticket office with the word 'Stromboli' on a card in the window, and placed 85 euros in front of the collector. A gift from his Albanian friend.

The attendant in his well-starched white maritime shirt with its shiny brass epaulettes handed Tommy his one-way ticket.

It was a different world, southern Italy, he thought, as he stood beside the gangway and surrendered his bag to the luggage trolley. No armed security in sight, no passport checks, no customs dogs, an easy state of travel that was rarely seen after 9/11.

Tommy sighed as the tension dropped from his shoulders along with the Bees-Knees. He took his seat alongside a couple of Italian fashion icons on holidays to the Aeolian Islands, off the coast of Sicily. They were both his age and beautifully dressed. He ordered three beers.

Four hours later, on the scheduled three-hour journey, the hovercraft eased into its lone dock at San Vincenzo, the only town on Stromboli. Tommy couldn't help but be overawed by the magnitude of the volcano, which comprised almost the entire island.

Tommy hurriedly collected his Bees-Knees, not giving too much thought to the illegal firearm stowed within. He took a seat at the Ossidiana Hotel coffee shop and bade his fun-loving friends, *Signori* Dolce and Gabbana, farewell; they went off to find a cart ride to their holiday house. As he waited for his brew and the accompanying *cornetto*, he fingered through the postcard stand and selected one, much like all the others, an aerial shot of an angry volcano with the word 'Stromboli' beneath. He paid for the card and postage and sipped his coffee as he racked his brain to remember Sandra's home address. He had only shared a BBQ there once or twice before.

In the text section he scrawled nothing more than the number '467' before taking the final mouthful of his beverage and strolling back onto the wharf. He slipped the card into the waiting post bag on the dock's edge to ensure that it would commence its journey with

22ND JUNE

the return of his ferry to the mainland in a couple of minutes' time. He turned to face a landscape that would be home for a while.

• •

Tommy walked the entire town of San Vincenzo, exploring his new environs. Even at dawdling tourist pace, it took no longer than an hour. He surmised that it would now be 8 a.m. in Melbourne. He checked his wallet for the pre-paid phonecard and went to one of the two phones on the main causeway, dialling police headquarters in Melbourne and asking for Superintendent Fountain. As he waited for the connection he rehearsed his brief lines. The Toeys had the capability to trace calls if the caller stayed on the phone long enough. Tommy needed to be brief and succinct. The phonecard had almost run out of credit when Fountain finally picked up.

Tommy began, 'I hear you're making a fair attempt to investigate my role in the Bay of Islands mess?' No name, no pack drill.

'Is this ... ?' the Superintendent was about to ask confirmation of Tommy's identity.

'You've got half a minute left,' Tommy broke in.

'And you're running out of time yourself. Help me.'

'You need to prove Massimo was in the Bay.'

'So, where's the help in that?' asked Fountain.

Tommy checked his watch. If he held the connection for much longer a trace would be a sure thing.

'The dago went to the Marlborough Hotel, on the waterfront, and spoke to staff before going to Inn the Black. Go find yourself a good witness there.' He hung up, not daring to wait for the reply. He breathed slowly, thinking that he wouldn't be pulling that little trick again any time soon and went in search of a room so he could rest for a while.

27th June

Superintendent Fountain stood proudly at the lift of police squad headquarters. He wasn't one to be intimidated by the rank and file of other detectives in the more glamorous squads like Armed Offenders or Homicide. He liked his job, rooting out corrupt cops. In return he gave a sort of dignity to a career that had owned him for more than twenty years. As always, he noticed a few sideways glances as he waited for the lift door to open. And the odd snicker, a small price to pay, he thought, for a guaranteed crack at a commissionership in a year's time. The lift opened and he and his cheap suit took it to the eleventh floor, the Homicide Squad. Not surprisingly, Mick, the sergeant whose job it was to liaise with the New Zealand police department on the death of Cary Peterson, was waiting for him. They shook hands in a manner that could best be described as professional. Mick ushered him quickly into a private room. They took their seats and both opened their folders at the same moment.

'I'm not too sure what I can give you, Superintendent,' began Mick.

'It's probably more what I can give you, young Michael,' answered the Superintendent.

'How do you mean?'

'Well, I'm assuming that you have fuck all to prove that Cole did the murder, other than that he was known to have stayed at the house.'

'But everything points to him,' said Mick.

'Sure, but take away your pointy stick for a second, Mick, for Christ's sake!'

'Until Lynette Peterson regains consciousness, we only have what we have. Fingerprints, circumstantial evidence, a credit card,' said Mick.

27TH JUNE

The Superintendent tapped his pen anxiously on the table and asked, 'But there are no witnesses to the Peterson murder, are there, Mick?'

'No. Dead men tell no tales.'

'No witnesses to the attempted murder of his wife?'

'Not unless she comes out of the coma.'

'We can now prove the real killer was in the Bay of Islands that day.'

Mick, impressed, closed his notebook to let the internal investigator speak his mind. 'You've got the floor, Boss. Tell me what you know.'

'This is what we've confirmed. Cole sent the Mafia to gaol, after being undercover for two years buying pure coke and grass, right? Then, a couple of days after the court case, a *Mafiosi* hitman arrived in Australia to bump him off. We've tracked his movements in and out of Australia and New Zealand.'

'Aahhh,' said Mick, startled, and remembering Sandra's earlier comments. 'Is that why he was on the run?'

'Maybe,' said the Superintendent. 'What we do know is that Detective Donny Benjamin from the drug unit is giving the old Godfather in Griffith a lot of attention these days.'

'A go-between?' asked Mick.

'Undoubtedly,' said the Superintendent. 'Plus, he's running drugs around the nightclubs.'

'Have you got him, Boss?'

'Yeah, he's fucked. We're just playing with him now. He's not smart enough to be doing this on his own. We've just got a 28-day warrant for a camera in his apartment.'

'So you want us to have a sleep too, for a month?'

'Please, Mick. We'll have it wrapped up by then. We think there's a bigger fish involved than Donny.' The Superintendent closed his file, having offered up more information than he initially intended.

'Besides, I don't reckon Cole did it,' he finished.

'Neither did we. But you've got one problem, Boss.'

'What's that?'

'You need real fucking evidence. Or else I'll have to charge him.'

'I know. If you can find him.'

• •

Mario, not in uniform but a grey suit ensemble, stood to one side of the village piazza, alone. He took a mental note of all the proceedings as he observed, head bowed, the entrance of the old stone church. A single white-robed server reached the bottom steps of the church entry, gently waving an ornate thurible, incense wafting in his wake. He was followed closely by another server, this one holding aloft a two-metre-high gold-plated crucifix. Their pace was slow, allowing the ageing priest who was close on their heels, his missal held ceremoniously in both hands, time to adjust his eyes from the candlelit darkness of the narthex to the brightness of the sunny Plati morning. As he too began to descend the short stone staircase, six pallbearers, each dressed in an ill-fitting black suit, emerged through the archway behind him to continue the solemn procession. They carried, at waist height, a simple timber casket bestrewn with garlands and wreaths of white fragrant flowers. The family fell in behind, sobbing into their hand-embroidered handkerchiefs, among them an appropriately dressed, tearful Lydia. Watching from the wings, their fidgeting backs against the stone church wall were the township's nervous schoolchildren, filed in by their quietly observant teacher to pay their respects. There was no chorus, no choir boys or ear-piercing organ tones. After all, it was Plati, in the wretched hills of southern Italy. The procession stood in a reverent silence as the casket was gently lifted into the waiting hearse.

Apart from a minor adjustment or two, the coffin slid easily into place; it was not as weighty as some. Pino's body had been released two days earlier, after the family's frequent requests to allow a burial.

27TH JUNE

A baffled Mestre *Commissario* had struggled unsuccessfully for leads on the crime, and the Venetians had long ago given up arguing with the rabble from the south. As the hearse moved slowly towards Via Roma, the town swelled out from the church. A respectful silence remained, broken only by two soft voices, those of the head pallbearer, Massimo, and the Godfather, Don Carbone. Massimo had broken away from his five soldiers to place a consoling kiss on Lydia's forehead as he moved to assist the old Godfather, who was so stricken with grief at the death of his nephew that he had given up his cane and taken to a wheelchair. The Don waved his tired right hand in a gesture to Massimo to wheel him away from the crowd, which was fading away, along the exit to the town.

'Massimo, are you sure the Australian is responsible?'

'I know it, as I know my own hand,' replied Massimo.

'Then you must avenge our Pino.'

Massimo remained silent as he slowly pushed the wheelchair. He fussed over a light summer scarf around his uncle's neck. There were tears in his eyes.

The old man pulled on the younger man's hand. The heir apparent knelt before him. He knew full well that his time was only months away, maybe weeks. The old man squeezed Massimo's hand more tightly. 'Go to Germania, and organise the shipment first.'

Massimo nodded as his uncle finished his final instruction.

'Then return and use this hand to destroy the Australian and his blonde undercover slut.'

Massimo lifted his bowed head and stared solemnly into his uncle's eyes. 'For Pino,' he said.

'For me,' the Godfather commanded.

• •

The noise of the sturdy industrial vacuum cleaner broke the otherwise tranquil silence in the corridor on the twenty-first floor of the trendy

ON THE RUN

Establishment apartment block in the Docklands. The small bespectacled cleaner shuffled from door to door, passing a busy lift mechanic. It appeared that both lifts had jammed and were out of order. The technician in his logoed blue overalls looked impressive as he played with the various wires and terminals that led from the junction box; a quick manoeuvre or two and the lift lights were also out, temporarily. With the coast now well and truly clear, he winked to his mate, Superintendent Fountain, who was also sporting the blue technician's overalls. The head man then walked briskly to Apartment 2103, home for the previous two years of Detective Donny Benjamin. In less than two minutes the front door lock had been picked and Henri the analyst switched off his vacuum cleaner and disappeared into the apartment along with the Superintendent. They each stopped at the entry long enough to don a pair of the thinnest white cotton gloves.

On first viewing Henri was very impressed with the décor. Black leather lounges, Bang & Olufsen audiovisual system, a CD and DVD collection that could almost stock a retail outlet and a collection of Giaconda wines. And the views were just as impressive. With rent of $800 a week, and on a gross salary of $1300 a week, the drug unit detective was doing alright for himself.

After the initial sweep of the vista, Henri moved on to Donny's laptop computer, which sat proudly on an antique executive blackwood desk. He found the Toshiba in sleep mode, for which the analyst was more than grateful. He pulled the thinnest business briefcase from inside the chest area of his overalls, unzipped it and laid it out on the desk, careful not to interfere with the assorted paraphernalia that Donny had left cluttered there. Henri then went about the task of reviewing the directory and copying as many files as possible onto the memory sticks he had brought with him.

'Is he on any chat sites?' whispered the Superintendent, peering eagerly over his shoulder.

'Facebook and Skype are all I can find,' replied the analyst as he pulled out two miniature screwdrivers from his briefcase and began

27TH JUNE

to carefully remove the casing from the superstructure of the laptop, allowing him access to the workings beneath, and in particular the inbuilt camera. In the meantime, Fountain completed his drawer-to-drawer inventory of the kitchen, photographing everything he considered relevant. He discovered two nice fat rolls of cash, which he counted out at $20 000 apiece. He placed them neatly back in their hidey-hole inside the rangehood's air filter. He then moved on to the hall closet and bedroom, admiring for a moment the collection of at least half-a-dozen leather coats in the walk-in robe, Max Mara and Ben Sherman among them.

Donny's top dresser drawer revealed yet more designer gear tucked under a clump of socks and jocks—and five watches. The Breitling and the Rolex looked genuine to the Superintendent. Moving back to the study where Henri was still busy with the laptop, the Superintendent extracted the mobile scanner housed in his own briefcase and started copying much of the documentation including eBay accounts and bills in Donny's haphazard personal filing system. It was the single sheet of paper filed under 'C' that worried the internal investigator most of all. He was uncertain as to whether the 'C' was a direct reference to Cole or to a Citroën 2CV. It was the A4 brochure printed out by Inspector Mack, with details in the Inspector's own scrawl of the whereabouts of Tommy Paul in Argentina and details of his MasterCard. He scanned it twice, and tucked it safely back into the file.

Through the corridor walked an exhausted tenant from the next-door apartment, who had tired of waiting for the lift and had just climbed the twenty-one flights to practically crawl into 2105 and close the door behind her. This prompted the pseudo lift-repairman to tap softly on 2103 to allow Henri and Fountain a quick unobserved exit. A flick of a switch and the lift groaned to life, transporting them all to the depths of the basement carpark.

∙ ∙

The steely sounds of an unracking Winchester pump-action shotgun sent shivers through the ACA office. Heads turned to gawk in the direction of the noise, at Leigh, who was clearing the shells from his weapon. He noticed the stares and apologised.

'Sorry, guys,' he said, 'just back from a raid.'

He strutted past the desks, past Inspector Mack's office, catching his loud comment as he drew closer.

'There's mail for you,' said the Inspector. His right hand flung out from his desk towards the corridor, holding an official-looking letter. 'Have fun,' were the only two other words he offered. He didn't so much as raise his eyes from his daughter Chloe, who sat pensively in front of him, as Leigh reached in and accepted the envelope. Leigh couldn't help but notice in that brief moment before he made a hasty retreat to the corridor that her face bore the tell-tale puffy redness of one who had been crying for hours. She dabbed at the end of her damp nose with a tissue from a box on her father's desk.

'We never see you any more, Dad,' she sniffed.

'Of course you do, honey puff,' Mack continued his attempt to console.

'When, Dad? Christmas? Birthdays? That doesn't count.' Both Chloe's hands began to tremble uncontrollably. The girl was clearly troubled emotionally and physically.

'Are you going to Paris again with that … that … Dorothy?' She looked down, fascinated with the lines of her ribbed pantyhose and began to pull at her knees to straighten the stockings.

'She's my wife now, Chloe.'

'Yeah, and we're your ex-kids,' she sulked. Chloe's fidgeting progressed upwards to her hair as she ran her fingers through her matted hair.

'Honey puff, you look a mess. Are you still going to those nightclubs?'

'What do you care, anyway?' Chloe bit down hard on her lip and drew a little blood, which she wiped with one of her soggy tissues.

27TH JUNE

Inspector Mack sat heavily in his large leather desk chair and looked cautiously through the glass partition wall of his office at the occasional raised head. Chloe pulled another wad of tissues from the box and continued sobbing.

∙ ∙

Leigh had walked to his own desk, frowning at the official-looking envelope in his hand. Sandra came in after Leigh. She cleared her revolver and handed it to Leigh, who stowed both firearms safely in the locker as well as the shells and his jacket. Jude strolled out of the tearoom, mug in hand, and beamed at her friends.

'Well, now. Welcome back, Missy,' said Leigh as he closed the firearm cupboard.

'Why, thank you, kind sir. I've missed you all so,' said a smiling, happy Jude.

'I heard you made a big splash, babe. How many crooks?' enquired Sandra.

'Seven all up, and one that got away. Jumped a plane to Lebanon, last heard.'

'Ooh, that's what we like, a nice extradition for Jude sometime next year. Hey?'

Sandra picked up her folder and pen and walked into the tearoom. She took a seat at the makeshift desk she had set up four or five days earlier beneath the tearoom phone. A curious Jude left Leigh to open his letter, opting to follow Sandra instead. Puzzled as to why she had given up the best-placed desk in the office, she cornered Sandra with the question.

'No reason, babe,' said Sandra.

'Like the biscuits that much, do you, Sandra?' an unbelieving Jude replied.

A pregnant pause followed. Sandra pretended to fuss around her new desk, doing her best to avoid the forthcoming question. She lifted her eyes to meet Jude's.

'No news?' asked Jude.

Sandra pondered the question, knowing all she could really offer was a white lie. She stopped making pretend entries into her diary concerning the previous raid.

'I wish there were something I could tell you,' was all she said as she dropped her eyes from Jude's questioning face and back to the diary page.

Jude took the hint and wandered out, muttering 'I wish' under her breath as she left.

Sandra put down her pen and sat in silence, her loyalties torn. She knew she shouldn't tell Jude of the communications between herself and Cole. Jude would take that information hard. She quickly logged on to the server, opened her email file and drafted an overdue reply.

Dearest Ingrid,

I was so shocked to receive your tragic news. You can't imagine how I feel for you in this dreadful situation. I'm waiting by the phone day and night for your call, girlfriend; whatever help or support you need, just ask.
Always in my thoughts,

Sandra

Satisfied, she clicked 'send' and went back to her diary entry, only to be interrupted by a shout from the outer office.

'You bloody little ripper!' bellowed Leigh. He had opened the official-looking envelope from FBI headquarters in Quantico, Virginia, to find an acceptance letter to his application; he was on their course. Better still, he was on a plane to America next week.

• •

27TH JUNE

Henri sat at his pigeon-hole desk in analytical heaven. He had never had a job quite as fascinating as the one that had been presented to him with the Detective Benjamin case. While Donny had proved to be a very clever drug dealer, able to move with ease among the shady underworld, he was a fool to himself. He seemed to enjoy, if not splash about, every ill-gotten dollar that he had made. He was, in the area of cunning, Inspector Mack's antithesis. Donny squandered his lovely at a rate almost greater than which he acquired it. The statistical spreadsheet on Henri's computer was filling quickly, thanks to the information, account codes and data obtained during the covert search of Detective Benjamin's plush apartment.

As Henri tapped away at his keyboard he was interrupted momentarily by Spud, who was personally delivering photocopies of Inspector Mack's diary, for handwriting comparisons against the Citroën 2CV brochure. Spud looked around the simple office and was a little taken aback; he had somehow expected that the Toe Cutters would have state-of-the-art paraphernalia: ultra-modern, chic-tinted, blue glass-walled panels, whizz-bang techno equipment with huge flashing banks of monitors beaming images and data from around Australia. Instead he was looking at the same cheap, poorly assembled office furniture that was found in every other department. Nothing like the popular television cop shows. Henri was squeezed at his overstretched desk between monitors stacked on boxes and books and folders encircling his chair on the floor.

Spud threw the envelope into the only space he could see—on top of Henri's busy fingers.

'Don't say I don't ever do anything for you.'

Before Henri had time to look up or reply, Spud corrected himself. 'Better still don't say anything, you're a Toey.'

He looked slightly nervous, standing as he was in foreign territory. He leaned over to take a more probative interest in the spreadsheet in front of Henri.

'Donny?'

'Sure is.'

'Well, now, he's doing alright.'

'What with rent, seventeen eBay purchases for leather coats, watches and even a motorbike. Take living expenses and lifestyle, he only needs to earn about $200 000 a year to keep this up.'

'Not a bad salary for a detective, eh?'

Spud noticed a second screen with a live camera image eyeballing a rather plush lounge room with a spectacular vista across Port Phillip Bay.

'Who lives there?' he enquired, his nose almost meeting the screen as he peered into the room, curious to ascertain the height and placement of the apartment.

Henri placed a finger across his lips.

'Keep it to yourself. That's Donny's apartment.'

'Very nice,' said Spud. 'But where's the camera?'

'It's in his laptop, through his internet connection.'

'Cool.' Spud was suitably impressed. 'But can't he tell that the camera is on?'

'No. I killed the solenoid.'

'So you can only watch when Donny's online?' asked Spud.

'Yep, but lucky or unlucky for us, he never seems to bother turning it off. It's not pretty sometimes.'

'Huh?'

'When he checks out the hard-core porn sites.'

'Well, what about Mack?' Spud enquired, still with a fair level of anxiety.

Henri merely shook his head. 'So far, stuff all. He's much cleverer.'

'There's his share portfolio,' offered Spud.

'We know all about that, and his bank accounts. But his wife's business can cover all that,' replied Henri.

A dejected Spud turned to walk from the office. Henri rose from his desk and joined him.

'Give it time,' urged Henri. 'There's lots of stuff happening. Just give it a bit more time.'

27TH JUNE

'But what about Cole? He's stuck out there, somewhere,' said Spud, frustrated.

'Give it time,' Henri urged again as he escorted Spud from the office.

• •

It was mid-morning and just like every other morning on Stromboli Island—as hot as blazes with the perfect holiday pace: slow. The past eight or nine days had been much the same for Tommy, since he had checked into Casa Greco, a cash-only bed and breakfast. He had received Sandra's email reply on day six, and had felt comforted.

His room was on the ground floor of the 100-year-old whitewashed building that was Casa Greco. Very little of the craftsmanship that had gone into its construction was now visible through the masses of wisteria that adorned all the façades and trailed elegantly over the rich bottle-green balconies. Tommy could stand on his balcony and take in a view of an orchard full of ripening nectarines and peaches; on occasion he would see a stray goose wander through to sample the produce. Below that, the panorama spread to take in the dotted terracotta rooftops of the village, which were bordered by a thick ribbon of black sand that drew his eye out to the ocean, some 400 metres below. Blue-hulled fishing boats with matching white sails bobbed in the waves.

On his first day, Tommy had ambled along Via Vittorio Emmanuelle, the main street of San Vincenzo, taking in the aromas of freshly baked biscuits, strong coffee and *arancini*, the superb savoury rice balls filled with eggplant and tomato. The eclectic mix of food shops wound along with the laneway, up the tiny hill that sat alongside the mother volcano. There were no cars on Stromboli, just the occasional moped. The only other traffic, Tommy discovered, was foot traffic. There was no electricity and the population survived with the use of generators. The proprietor of his B&B had allocated Tommy his own hand-torch. By 10 p.m. of a night, the two streets and few laneways on the island were illuminated only by the tourists' torches flickering as they wandered in search of a candle-lit restaurant for an evening meal.

It was just the pace that Tommy needed after the calamity of the previous weeks. He rose by mid-morning to face a breakfast of duck-egg frittata with garden tomatoes and Greek coffee, prepared by his hosts, Nick the Greek and his wife, Aggie, two runaway Athenians who had found the whitewashed buildings of Stromboli more home than home. With his red towel, sunscreen and bag of stone fruit, Tommy would then amble down the gravel footpaths to the beach and hire a royal blue deckchair and matching umbrella for the day. Most days he had the company of Cinzia, a tiny, almost bird-like Sicilian schoolteacher on holidays, another guest at the B&B.

For hours the two swapped stories of their many travels throughout Europe, and their mutual passion for the music of Italy. Artists Tommy enjoyed, like Pino Danielle and Fabio Concato, were heroes to Cinzia also. He was ever mindful to avoid any conversation that included Australia. The interesting and somewhat shy schoolteacher believed that while Tommy may have been born an Australian, he had lived most of his life in London—a premise he encouraged. Indeed, he revelled in the opportunity to totally relax for the first time in months.

30th June

Inspector Mack was having some trouble getting to his Sidchrome toolbox. It was now literally buried in a collection of snail bait, pesticides and other less attractive gardener's needs. All designed to deter a prying detective, should he ever suffer the misfortune of a raid by the Toe Cutters. He eventually dug it out and laid it down on the timber workbench. There was the almost 100000 euros that he and Dorothy had squirrelled away over the past twelve months. He liked the rewards of the twilight of his career, and had virtually forgotten all the disappointment that he had carried in recent years. Now, he was happy to be retiring with just the rank of a Detective Inspector, and a prince's ransom.

Dorothy was rugged up in her winter woollies and wearing a pair of black gumboots and heavy green canvas gardening gloves as she prodded in the daffodil bed on all fours with her butt facing the garden shed. Inspector Mack leant over the workbench and turned the CD player on. The sound of Edith Piaf, '*Non, je ne regrette rien*', wafted melodically through the garden speakers, catching Dorothy's attention. She looked up at her man; he was now approaching her with a glint in his eye.

'How much, my love?' he enquired contentedly.

Dorothy had just pulled up the last of four Vegemite jars, filled to the brim with rolls of Australian currency.

'At least $100 000, handsome,' she purred.

She discarded the soiled garden gloves and walked into the shed with an armful of jars. Inspector Mack had recently purchased a large metal-clad and pop-riveted shipping chest. Just the sort of thing immigrants would use to send precious items home. The sturdy travelling box was lined with three-ply sidings and base. For the previous week, Mack had come home each night after work to remove, very methodically and patiently, the pop rivets from the casing to allow the three-ply panelling to be removed.

Dorothy and Mack placed their booty on the workbench and spent the next hour carefully lining the travel case with the now large pile of European and Australian currency. Over this they secured a layer of dry handkerchiefs that had been previously doused in dissolved mothballs; just the sort of thing to deter a curious customs dog. Once this was completed, Dorothy stepped back inside the house, leaving Mack to reaffix the lining to the sides and pop rivet the steel facing. There was only an hour before the DHL courier would arrive to collect the chest.

Dorothy emerged from the kitchen carrying two long-stemmed glasses and a bottle of Moet & Chandon. The Inspector finished his task by wiping all the surfaces of the packing case to ensure that it was free from fingerprints, Australian soil and grime. The pop of the champagne cork ceremoniously signalled the end of their joint task. It had been a long afternoon in the garden.

'To us, and Beaucaire,' announced Dorothy as she raised her glass in the air. The Inspector too raised his glass and clinked the side of hers as they both sampled the champagne.

'Non-vintage, my princess?' Mack questioned with a frown, the instant he had swallowed the wine. 'Only vintage for us in a month's time back in France, my petal.'

'When do you get the million, my darling?' Dorothy whispered into his ear.

'The moment the dagos put the container on the ship in Italy, princess, just after we arrive in Beaucaire.'

'Can I help you come and collect the lovely?' Dorothy giggled as Mack emptied his glass and placed it on the bench. His hands found a new task in unfastening the buttons of Dorothy's cashmere cardigan and helping her out of her woollens.

• •

30TH JUNE

A grin from ear to ear was permanently plastered on Leigh's face as he strutted around the office. He made sure that his journey was stopping all stations. At every desk he paused to spread the news of his acceptance to the FBI course. Of course, no one could be told where the training facility actually was, not even Leigh, such was the secrecy associated with the covert course. He had planned to head out early tonight to have drinks with the crew before he packed his suitcase for the great unknown. Having finished his round of gloating with the immediate cast of characters, he went off in search of the team, hoping to find another ear to hear the tale for the fifteenth time.

He found Sandra at her desk.

'Leigh, if you've come in here to tell me about that fuckin' trip of yours again, I'll throw something at you!'

Truth be known, Sandra liked Leigh; in fact, she thought he was quite cute. Tall, a few years older than her, broad shouldered with a body as hard as armour, and a libido that never went to sleep. Sandra had a golden rule with friends and workmates. 'Don't fuck your friends or sooner or later you'll have no fuckin' friends,' she told herself.

But every now and again she would look at Leigh and think, 'Just once. I wonder what it would be like, just once'.

'An all-expenses-paid trip to the States, champer, for fuck's sake.'

'Yeah, Leigh, I'm over the moon for you,' she said with a generous lashing of insincerity.

'Let's grab a drink. Time to get away from this desk, and this phone, champer.' He lowered his voice to a whisper. 'He's not going to ring.'

She wasn't too sure whether Leigh was being flippant or in fact realistic with this comment. She pulled her weary self upright, grabbed her handbag and locked her arm onto her friend's arm as together they walked down the corridor to Spud's office.

'Come on, champer, let's see if the other champer is up for a drink,' she said. Leigh laughed good-heartedly.

Inside Spud's office an analyst talked on the phone and scrawled on a notepad simultaneously. *Commissario* D'Alfonso was providing a crucial update into the investigation on Massimo and the Plati Mafia. Spud waved his pen frantically in the air to silence the still-laughing Sandra and Leigh. Their mouths closed.

Spud finished the call to his Neapolitan comrade, '*Ciao, ciao, si Signore, Bongiorno, prego amici,*' and hung up, realising what a silly concoction of Italian he had just put together.

'D'Alfonso has just invited us in on the Australian end of a huge importation,' began Spud.

'Naples to Melbourne, Spud?' queried Sandra.

'No, pretty much like I mentioned a couple of months ago. The container's going to start somewhere in Plati. They have no idea where. Then from Calabria to Melbourne.'

'Container!' exclaimed Leigh.

'Yeah, seems our dear Massimo is the key to it all. And the Anti-Mafia unit are following him around Germany right now. He's organising a shit-load of ecstasy tablets.'

'When does it leave Calabria?'

'Next month sometime,' answered Spud.

'Fuck. Six weeks on the water, and she'll be comin' in after I'm back, champer.'

'You and your bloody trip again,' said Sandra. 'Grab your coat, Spudly, we're drinking tonight. He's leaving in three days.'

'Yo, we're drinkin' tonight, champers!' declared an exuberant Leigh.

• •

A mop of dyed blonde hair fell over the side of a very disorganised bed. It belonged to a very hungover and very tired Sandra. Her naked body protruded in way too many places from beneath the crumpled doona, exposing all but a miniscule section of her backside to the morning light. Her arm was draped forward and the fingers of her hand had found the shag-pile carpet. Her cat, Cecil, had found her fingers and was licking them with its rough little tongue, just enough to rouse her consciousness to a day she would rather not have faced.

'Bugger off, cat,' she said sleepily. Her eyes remained closed and her head down. Cecil took the hint and moved to the other side of the bed.

No more than ten seconds had passed when she heard an echo that was not her voice.

'Bugger off, cat.'

She sprung upright from her slumber and pulled the doona up to her chin.

'Who's that?'

Leigh too shouted, 'Who's that?'

The confused and startled cat sprang like a pogo stick a metre into the air before landing on its feet and scampering off into the kitchen.

Leigh and Sandra turned to face each other, filled with anything but a romantic afterglow, and yelled in unison, 'Nooo!'

All of five minutes later and Leigh and Sandra were still coming to terms with the romantic tryst of the night before. Or perhaps it was the morning before, only a few hours earlier; a few drinks had turned into a few too many. Sandra, fuelled by gin and tonic, had apparently decided that the time was right to test Leigh's armour.

As she fussed around the kitchen gathering cereal and crockery, Sandra stared smugly, almost girlishly at her workmate, now lover, propped on one of her bar stools dressed only in her pink fluffy dressing gown. She placed two empty mugs and the pot of brew on the small counter.

'You're the man of the house, at least this morning, darling. Pour the coffee, champer. Milk's in the fridge, oh and Cecil might like a saucer too.'

She winked and walked with a spring in her step to her front door and the letterbox.

When she returned, two white coffees lay in wait. The now very preoccupied Sandra ignored her guest, head bowed as she read over and again a postcard that she held tightly in her hand. She dropped the assortment of other correspondence on the bench top, and paced around the small kitchen. Leigh slunk across to peer over her shoulder.

'What's wrong?' he asked as he sipped the soothing brew.

Sandra, still deep in thought at the card with seemingly no message, fanned herself with it momentarily, before handing it over.

'Guess who?' she asked.

Leigh too studied the postcard. 'What makes you think it's him?'

'Come on Leigh, you know his handwriting. You work with him.'

Leigh did know his handwriting.

'But what's the 467?' he asked as Sandra began to speed dial Spud's home phone number.

'Spud, yeah, yeah, yeah, sure it was a great night. Enough. Spudly, please. Straight to the office now, something important,' Sandra said. She hung up, careful not to say too much, just on the off chance that her phone was bugged. She headed towards the shower followed closely by Leigh, as if it was a race to see who could get there first.

• •

There is nothing better for a detective than a puzzle. It is a professional need, to want to solve the most difficult of all puzzles. Two seasoned detectives aided by one fine sharp analyst sat in their ACA office for an urgently convened meeting that Saturday afternoon, to solve one such puzzle. The office was otherwise empty and their hangovers were fading; they'd drunk plenty of coffee since Sandra placed the Stromboli Island postcard on Leigh's desk. Each of them had in turn picked the card up a few times, read it, stared at it. Spud even smelled it.

Spud would occasionally tap into Google and Bing as an idea spun through his analytical mind.

'Stromboli Island, in the Tyrrhenian Sea, a massive volcano, a tiny village, hardly anyone lives there ... ancient, ferries from Calabria, Naples, Sicily. What can it mean?' Spud asked, sharing his thoughts as he paraphrased.

30TH JUNE

'Could the island mean all hell's breaking loose?' asked Leigh.

'Duh,' said Sandra. She glared at Leigh, failing to see any significance in the comment.

'What's it famous for, apart from the volcano?' asked Leigh.

'And what's Cole doing there, more importantly?' said Spud as he continued his search through Wikipedia.

Sandra glanced up from an atlas with a worried look on her face.

'It's only a bee's dick away from Calabria. He's crazy going there.'

'There's nothing I can find,' interrupted Spud. 'A couple of old movie farts made a film there in 1950. Other than that, it's got no electricity ... '

Sandra's hand thumped down hard on the table. She literally jumped across to Cole's disused desk and began to ferret through the drawers. Impatient, she pulled the top drawer out and completely upended it on the surface of the desk, scattering pens and papers everywhere.

'It's here, I know it's here,' she said as she ratted through all the paraphernalia, tossing pieces of paper onto the floor as she discarded them in her quest for the movie magazine.

'Got it, it must be in here.' She flicked to the dog-eared article. Her eyes darted across the text of the page she had meant to read weeks earlier. The page Cole told her to read. She began half aloud and half in silence.

'The movie of the island of Stromboli ... Staring Ingrid Bergman ... Roberto Rossellini ... fell in love ... and lived on the island happily during the making of the movie ... Ingrid got pregnant ... a love story.'

She sat down relieved in Cole's office chair. She dropped the magazine and stared at Spud, a smile from ear to ear.

Sandra had the key. Spud knew that, or at least one of the two keys. He waited for her to explain.

'Perhaps he was always going there. Perhaps he just kept the idea up his sleeve, once he shot through from Melbourne ... Stromboli Island. Guess we won't know.'

She had their undivided attention. 'What we do know was that he told me not to forget the name Ingrid Rossellini. That's his email name. Ingrid Bergman fell in love with Roberto Rossellini.'

'And now he's there,' said Leigh.

'And now he's there,' echoed Spud. 'And he couldn't tell any of us?'

'Nor should he have, Spud. Three times they've tried to kill him.'

'But he has now, darling ... sorry, champer. Sorry.'

Spud looked across at Leigh and then at Sandra, who both tried to hide their smiles.

'My God!' exclaimed Spud, 'Don't tell me youse two ... No ... I don't want to know about it.' His head shook in amused mock disbelief.

'Change of subject,' said Sandra. 'There's still one more puzzle to go ... "467", what's it mean?'

'What's it for?' asked Spud,

'Who's it for?' said Leigh.

'467,' said Sandra.

This time it was Leigh's hand that came thumping down on the table.

'It's "for 67".'

'What's for 67?'

'The card is for 67 ... covert operative 67 ... Spudly, who's 67?'

'Well, Sandra, let's see ... Covert operative 55 is Cole Goodwin, but 67? Hmm. It's familiar. The undercover infiltration of the Mafia ... that was covert operative 67. His partner. Leigh, it's Jude.'

'The card's meant for Jude,' said Sandra

'He must want her to go to him, in Stromboli,' said Spud.

'Bullseye!' exclaimed Leigh.

'I don't know what this all means but we've got some serious work to do—now! Cole's obviously under enormous pressure. He needs help,' Sandra said. She picked up her phone and dialled Jude's home number.

30TH JUNE

Upon answer, all she said was, 'Can you come around tonight, babe? We've got secret women's business to discuss, hon.' Jude didn't need to be persuaded; she could tell by the tone in Sandra's voice that something important had finally happened, important enough to need her input. She confirmed the time and spent the remainder of the afternoon pacing nervously around her apartment.

• •

The doorbell chime sounded at exactly 7 p.m. Jude waited on Sandra's bluestone porch with a chilled bottle of chardonnay, her anxiety evident as she shifted her weight awkwardly from one foot to the other. Sandra opened the door and greeted her with a huge grin. Words weren't necessary. They hugged and Jude followed her through to the kitchen where Sandra popped the cork on the bottle and placed two glasses down on the counter. As she was pouring the wine, she handed the Stromboli postcard to Jude. Through Jude's silent musing, she explained the events of the day, and how the three investigators had deciphered the message. Jude sat on the little bar stool without speaking, holding the card and reading its simple message over and over.

'I'll take leave. I know I can take leave. I'll see Katherine tomorrow.'

'Just make sure you have a good excuse ready, sweetie. Katherine's an easy touch. But Mack may get nosy.'

'I could be there in a couple of days.'

'And not a word …'

The conversation was interrupted by the sound of slow heavy footsteps, obviously of a man, and Sandra's back screen-door opening. Jude reached instinctively for her handbag and rummaged for her .32 pistol. Sandra moved quietly to one side, out of sight from the approaching intruder. The handle of Sandra's back door turned slowly and the door creaked open; the shadow of a man with something in his right hand fell across the tiles. Jude raised her weapon and crouched slightly, steadying herself against the kitchen bench, and holding her breath as she watched the large figure step softly into the room.

Leigh stepped from the dark, holding a vintage bottle of shiraz. Seeing the pistol pointed at his chest, his bottle fell straight to the floor and his hands raised in stunned surrender.

'Whoa, whoa, champer.'

A relieved Jude lowered her weapon and stared at Leigh with a perplexed look.

'Leigh, what are you doing coming in the back? You scared us half to death!'

Sandra eased from her posie behind the fridge and collected the bottle of wine from the floor.

'Better get another glass then,' she said as she grinned at Leigh. 'That's something else we have to talk about, Jude,' she added as she poured a third drink.

'More secret women's business?' asked Jude, her gaze flashing from the embarrassed Leigh, to Sandra, who looked quite at home in her new role as *femme fatale*. The cat nudged familiarly between Leigh's legs, curling its tail around his calf and purring softly.

• •

The small town of Leverkusen was not dissimilar to many of the postwar towns of Germany, blanketed with factories and foundries, most initiating from the war efforts. In its heyday, at the crossover between the nineteenth and twentieth centuries, the little town had been alive and thriving with commercial activity. It was the industrial hub of many large companies, including the world's largest pharmaceutical company, Bayer. It was Bayer who, in the industrial age, invented aspirin. And even heroin: a drug that was outlawed in 1913, due to its addictive qualities. Now, almost a century later, under the extended glow of the 1712 light bulb 'Bayer' sign, an abandoned

30TH JUNE

factory was tinkering with today's most illicit drug: ecstacy. The local population had witnessed a rapid decline in industry and the younger generations had begun to drift in greater numbers to the big cities of Düsseldorf and Cologne in search of university degrees rather than the simple blue-collar occupations of their home town. It became easy to find empty factory space in Leverkusen, particularly in the outer regions, and just as comfortable were the rents on offer. Commercial agents were more than willing to turn a blind eye here and there, anything to sign the deal and fill the floor space.

The same abandoned factory had begun its life spitting out tractor parts and producing the metal casings used to house Bayer's mustard gas. It was now the home to another 'Bayer' relic; a massive lone pill-press controlled by the Plati Godfather and under the watchful stewardship of Massimo and his gang. The 50-year-old contraption was extraordinary, capable of stamping 880 pills per minute. A grand old machine, back geographically in its rightful place, albeit to manufacture the wrong type of drug. In an ironic twist, the technology that Bayer had developed to produce its revolutionary medicines—such as aspirin and its equally remarkable cough medicine: heroin—had now been adopted for the production of some of the world's most harmful illicit substances.

The only problem Massimo saw with the press was the noise it produced along with the pills.

Although the pre-production of the glutinous chemical paste used to form the ecstacy pill would not stir a mouse, the final step in the clandestine manufacture was not a process that could be carried out in a library. Clanking and clunking, over and over, the press would hiss as the damp sticky mess was skimmed onto the mould. The cap plate would make even more racket as it clamped down and fashioned the pills. The process stopped only to be repeated, as each batch was made and gently tipped onto a drying belt to allow the next damp batch its turn.

A shipping container full of ecstasy pills, bagged, sealed and hidden inside large cans of artichokes, allowed for approximately

15 million tablets. A $300 million haul: enough to keep every dance party, nightclub and rave spinning in the southern hemisphere for months. Although the tractor factory was a good half-kilometre away from the nearest public housing, to produce the racket it did twenty-four hours a day, seven days a week, would certainly give rise to complaints from the apartment building on the outskirts of the estate. So it had long been established that a five-day working week, with eight-hour days and weekends off, was a necessary precaution. The operating noise of the press was intermittently muffled by the sounds of a few tractors scattered around the front of the factory under repair, engines sometimes running, sometimes not. Allowing for imperfections with the pills, breakages and other reject runs, the black market press could achieve 2 million tablets a week. It had been operating on this schedule for almost eight weeks now, and thus far, not a murmur from the neighbours. Such was the efficiency of the Mafia.

Five metres above the heavily reinforced concrete floor of the factory was an original mezzanine level, once used to store the generators and alternators used during the production of the tractors. Now it housed, tucked out of sight, under a tarpaulin, many thousands of sealed one-kilogram bags of ecstasy pills, awaiting the final run to complete the order. Also behind the tarpaulin sat two armed guards, engrossed in a game of cards.

A black 7 series BMW drove along the weed-infested but otherwise empty laneway that led to the factory door and loading dock. It was just before 5 p.m. as Giuseppe pulled the car to a stop and allowed an eager Massimo to step from the passenger door. Carrying a black twelve-shot Glock pistol in his right hand, he looked around cautiously and then moved swiftly up the half-dozen steps to the dock, meeting one of the two guards at the heavy metal sliding door to the loading bay. Both men were dressed appropriately in greasy blue overalls, although better armed than the average mechanic, each with an Uzi sub-machine gun.

30TH JUNE

Their only communication was a wink and a nod as the door was slid open to allow entry to Massimo, closely followed by Giuseppe. They both squinted and frowned at the almost-deafening noise of the press. Massimo approached a tractor with its bonnet up and engine running. He turned the ignition key to off, which reduced the noise by half. To his left, a team of half-a-dozen white-coated chemists were busy tending their clanking diva's every need. Each of them wore a breathing mask and goggles; it was the end of another long day. The leader of the crew, a failed fourth-year chemist from Frankfurt University, nodded a welcome to Massimo. Another ten stamps from the machine and he hit the red safety button, killing the remaining racket. He approached his two Calabrian partners, removing his mask and breathing apparatus, and then his coat. He began to fidget incessantly, rubbing both hands through his hair, across his forehead and behind his neck. He was suffering the effects of prolonged exposure to amphetamine dust, which had seeped through the protective gear and into the pores of his skin.

'Massimo, Giuseppe, *ciao*, we're finished for another day.'

Massimo nervously tapped his watch.

'Yeah, yeah, sure, tomorrow. Tomorrow we will be finished for sure,' the chemist said.

'Fantastico, Otto,' Massimo beamed in reply. 'Giuseppe will have the truck here at this time tomorrow.'

'OK. *Alles in Ordnung*—we will have our people ready to help carry the bags down from the mezzanine.'

'*Nessun problema*,' said Massimo.

'*Nessun problema?* There's four tonnes—it will take you all day, Massimo! Of course, there are problems. *Mein Gott!*' Otto shifted on the balls of his feet and jittered as he spoke.

'I will have six more men here tomorrow morning for you,' replied Massimo flatly.

'And six more guns, please,' requested the chemist.

'*Si, si,*' said Giuseppe.

Massimo placed the palm of his right hand on the white dusty chin of the chemist and said very fondly, 'You have done well for us again, Otto, my friend. Your Swiss bank account will feel our appreciation tomorrow night.'

The chemist smiled greedily and shook both men's hands firmly before he walked away, turning to impart a final message: 'I need a shower, guys—this stuff is getting into my skin.'

• •

Katherine took a firm hold of the leave certificate that a nervous Jude had handed across to her. She glanced at her cynically over the top of her glasses.

'Four weeks, girl? We've got a few others on leave at the moment. I'll have to check.' She opened her leave folder, licked her index finger and paged through the file to Jude's record.

'You want to start leave today?' she asked, somewhat surprised as she studied Jude's request slip more closely.

'I have to, Katherine. I'm sorry. I would have given you more notice if I could.'

'Well, I don't know, Jude. I'll have to run it by the boss. It being such short notice and all. You understand?'

Jude leaned in to the business manager.

'I'm so sorry, Katherine. I need to take you into my confidence. You see, there's something very important I need to do.'

Jude knew that Katherine was the confirmed office gossip and that any attempt at confidentiality would be betrayed within nanoseconds of her leaving the office. Katherine leaned forward, a little too eagerly.

'You can tell me anything, Jude dear.'

'Well, Katherine, you see, it's just that, well … ' Jude began very softly, struggling to get to the point, 'Katherine, you see I'm … well, you know … I'm pregnant. I need to get it fixed. I need my leave immediately.' A tear dropped from her eyes and fell to the top of Katherine's desk.

The glasses fell from Katherine's face and she looked back at Jude in shock, her eyebrows raised.

'Oh dear, Jude, oh dear, you poor dear,' was all she could offer. She instantly stamped the leave application approved and handed it back.

Less than a minute later, Jude walked from Katherine's office, mission accomplished. She headed out of the ACA building for four weeks. In that same minute, Katherine was at the door to Inspector Mack's office with a sordid slice of gossip.

By the time Jude had made it to the bottom of the final flight of stairs and into the basement carpark of the ACA building she was beaming. Sandra stood waiting for her next to Jude's little white diesel Golf.

'Easy work,' she boasted. Sandra greeted her with open arms and enveloped her in an enormous hug.

'Good luck, girl,' she whispered. 'Tell him thanks for all the worry.' She let go, and handed Jude a sealed yellow envelope, 'I hope you know I can't take you to the airport, in case someone sees us.'

'Of course not. I've got my suitcase all packed and ready in the boot with the ticket. I'll go straight there now, hide my car in the long-term carpark and have a few lattes till the flight. No one will know.'

'Good luck, babe. Report back—you know where my desk is.'

5th July

The simple suburban Trattoria al Forno on the outskirts of Leverkusen, five blocks from the industrial estate, was known for two reasons. First, it offered probably the finest and most authentic Italian cuisine in that part of Germany, what with its real Calabrian owners, genuine Calabrian chef, and meticulous attention to authentic produce. Second, although only a 30-seat establishment, it had found itself splashed across the front pages of every newspaper in Europe only two years earlier. A Mafia feud between the Plati clan and the neighbouring San Luca clan had festered to the point where it was resolved in the trattoria.

Both clans had earlier invested in the Bayer pill press, and had installed it in the factory. Production ran swimmingly for a year or two until, one day, the San Luca clan decided they would move the press to a different location, and not take the advice of the Plati clan, who preferred to leave it where it was and to continue to share the spoils. No amount of negotiation could shift the San Lucans. On the eve of their attempted coup of the massive machine, six of them were gunned down in the trattoria. The pill press remained where it was, temporarily immersed in tonnes of tractor parts, hidden until the heat died down and the investigation faded.

A year later, Massimo, Giuseppe, Illario and little Pino decided that all was well again. They sent the electricity back into their valuable contraption. There hadn't been a peep from the San Lucans since. Well, not until a few months earlier when, mysteriously, a white flag was dropped in the centre of the piazza at Plati. Any wonder, with the massive fortunes to be made in Leverkusen.

Massimo sat at the head of the table with Illario to his left and his cousin Giuseppe to his right—a spot that until recent times had been for Pino. The remnants of a four-course meal lay before them;

5TH JULY

the last of the *linguini al forno* with the discarded prawn shells and tails, the leftover quail bones and a sprinkling of *spinaci con aglio*. The near-empty carafe of *vino rosso* sat among their plates. They clinked their final glass together. Massimo struggled with quail meat between his teeth.

'*Buona fortuna,* Giuseppe. *Buon viaggio.*'

'*Grazie,* Massimo. I'll be home in three days.'

'Slowly, slowly, cousin. Don't break any records.'

'*Si, si,* hold a gun to the driver's head. No speeding,' Illario quipped.

'*Si,*' said Giuseppe smiling broadly.

The door to the trattoria was pulled open and a recently bathed chemist, without his white coat, walked briskly to the spare chair at the table. His hair was still dripping wet but combed back. As he sat, he clicked his fingers towards a timid waiter.

'We are done, again, Massimo,' said Otto.

Massimo glanced at his watch. It was 7 p.m. 'A good time. The highway police will be having their dinner.'

The comment brought a mild laugh from the four. A stein of beer with a massive head of froth was placed before the thirsty Otto. The three Italians watched in amazement as the chemist consumed the entire litre in one long gulp. He banged it down hard on the table, and demanded another.

'Will you stay for dinner, Otto?' asked Massimo courteously.

His German friend looked around at a table that appeared far from appetising.

'I think dinner is finished. A couple more steins and I'll go home to my computer. I have a bank balance to check.'

'You're a hard man, Otto,' said Massimo.

'I've learnt that with the Calabrians, business is business. Isn't that what you taught me?'

'And business awaits,' Giuseppe interrupted. He got up from the table and dropped his napkin awkwardly onto his seat. He kissed both cheeks of his two *amici* and rubbed his hands through the chemist's wet hair as they said their goodbyes. Giuseppe left the trattoria with his overnight bag and walked the hundred metres to a waiting small Mercedes truck, sporting French licence plates, and its Italian driver. He climbed on board. Behind it was a diversion car, a nondescript white Opel sedan, rented the same day by one of Massimo's men using a false driver's licence and credit card. The car, its driver and two passengers were armed with Uzi sub-machine guns and would tailgate the truck for the entire journey, thereby ensuring a clear passage all the way back to Calabria.

• •

At the back table of his usual Lygon Street restaurant sat the Griffith Godfather, with his arms folded and a fixed stare; he was silent. Opposite was a more upbeat Inspector Mack, alongside Donny, who also looked pleased with himself. They had just finished explaining that their corrupt customs official had agreed to ensure the safe passage of the Mafia's container into Australia. Inspector Mack had enjoyed a long lunch with his customs contact, promising him $100 000 for his involvement. Friends of more than twenty years standing didn't need more than a handshake on such a deal. The old Godfather was impressed and promised a similar alliance in the future.

'You have done well, *Commissario*,' the old Godfather said. He unfolded his arms for the first time since the explanation had commenced fifteen minutes earlier.

'As long as the lovely comes through,' replied a confident Inspector Mack. He tore the tops off four sugar satchels to sweeten his espresso.

An uncertain Godfather looked across at Donny.

'He means money,' said Donny.

The old man smiled. 'You Australians have funny words.'

'We have funny ways too,' Mack said. He was about to make a non-negotiable condition. 'Your payment must be in cash, and not into my bank account. I will collect it myself in Calabria the day the shipment leaves.'

5TH JULY

The old Godfather sat silently for a moment or two. His mental arithmetic complete, he finally nodded, happy with the condition.

'Make no mistake, Giovanni,' a finger-waving Mack continued, 'no mistake at all. Or else your shipment is doomed.'

The old Godfather for the first time in his life placed his Italian hand out to shake that of a policeman. 'No mistake,' he said, 'no mistake, *Commissario*. And your Australian detective? Have we heard?'

'No. But he will be home soon. His girlfriend has just had an abortion and will call him back.'

'Oh, yes, the undercover slut. I asked for a photograph.'

Inspector Mack reached into his inside jacket pocket and produced the missing photograph of Cole and Jude.

'*Perfetto, perfetto*,' the old Godfather said.

• •

For such an old industrial estate, the plumbing was in fine condition, Otto thought. In fact the entire structure was soundly built, typical of German engineering. He stood beside his fortune-making pill press; the water pressure emanating from his hose was magnificent. The machine was now well doused with all telltale signs washed away. He turned the tap off, as his two most trusted assistants used a ragbag full of cloths to mop up the excess fluid before applying a fine coating of oil to the polished steel surfaces. It had been a busy day but, as with all successful operations, it was just as important to clean up as to do the exercise in the first place. Last of all was the draping of the heavy green tarp, which had been dragged down the steps from the mezzanine, to cover the clandestine press. The machine would be rested for a few months before Massimo would again set the wheels in motion. It was midnight before Otto finally locked the steel door; his assistants had long gone. He glanced back as he turned off the last of the lights, at his mountain of tractor parts and the disengaged forklift that sat parked beside it. He flicked the final light switch and snapped the padlock shut. He reckoned he had seven hours to go before his flight to the Caribbean and then a summer on an island with a pretty *Fräulein* and a case of rum before he needed to think of Leverkusen again.

As the engine of Otto's Audi A4 Cabriolet roared into the distance, a small clang could be heard on the concrete floor of the warehouse's mezzanine. High up in the apex of the roof, in the cavity between the asbestos roof tiles and internal sheet lining, crawled a surveillance operative, covered in dust. With as much strength as he could muster, he pulled himself clear of the space. He attached his guide rope to a metal truss and dropped the rope to the ground. His mate at the opposite end of the roof apex executed the same manoeuvre. He too was covered in grey dust. They simultaneously shimmied down their four-metre-long ropes and flicked their hooks free of the overhead truss. Both carried a tiny bum-bag with a digital video camera that, like the day before and the day before that, had filmed the largest shipment of ecstasy tablets ever watched by a police department. As always, they meticulously cleared away the small amount of dust on the floor, before quietly sneaking down to the sliding factory door. Two raps from their knuckles and it was swiftly opened by *Commissario* D'Alfonso. He stood proudly and immaculately dressed alongside his German equivalent, who held up a master key to the padlock.

'*Bravo, bravo Signori.*' He patted the dusty men on their backs, as the lock was snapped to its original position.

• •

A busy Leigh was attempting to clear his desk. It was a shambles. He clipped pins to papers, read over a handful of reports and generally tidied in preparation for a month away from the office. He could see Sandra through his glass partition wall, still sitting at the desk in the tearoom. He shook his head, silently mouthing 'blind faith'. Spud, who happened to pass by at that moment, caught the end of the gesture, and turned towards him.

5TH JULY

'What?' he queried.

Leigh stopped his cataloguing and looked up at the analyst, now firmly planted in front of his desk.

'Oh, nothing,' he began with a sigh. 'It's just that the poor darling'—he indicated towards Sandra who, as if on cue, looked up from her own work to stare at the silent telephone—'just sits around all day long with that pathetic look on her face waiting for that damn phone to ring.'

Spud, too, turned to look at Sandra. He shrugged his shoulders as he said, 'The rest of the office think she's just lost the plot.'

'If only they knew … '

At that moment Leigh's phone rang. He picked it up and was duly informed that he had a visitor downstairs at the security office. He excused himself to Spud and, taking his folder and pen, he walked down to reception, where he found himself standing face to face with the prettier of the security officers.

'Detective,' she greeted him sweetly.

'Champer,' came the professionally delivered reply, accompanied by a polite nod of the head.

The security officer looked at him, puzzled.

'You haven't sweet-talked me for a few days, why not?' Her face was cocked quizzically waiting for a flirtatious response. 'Is your mind elsewhere, Detective?'

He stood thoughtfully, uncomfortable with the question. He settled on another polite smile, which resulted in the raising of two arched eyebrows.

'How romantic,' she replied, a little miffed. 'Anybody I know?'

'You've got a curvy young brunette waiting to see you, Detective. Looks like it's your lucky week all round. Wouldn't give her name,' she said, still looking at him expectantly. 'She looks awfully nervous. I sat her in the waiting room.'

Leigh smiled, offered her his thanks and turned to walk into the waiting room, where he found Penny, the waitress from Café Azzurra. Her head was bowed as she flicked through a magazine.

'Hello, gorgeous. What a nice surprise,' Leigh said with a genuine warmth in his voice. 'What brings you down here?'

It was obvious by the look on her face that she was troubled.

'What's happened?' he asked, pulling up a plastic chair and leaning in to her.

'I just wanted to let you know ... well, I've resigned from the café, Leigh. I'm going to work with my sister in the Whitsundays.'

Leigh was secretly pleased and more than a little impressed, but there had to be more to the change of employment than Penny had offered.

'What's she do at the Whitsundays, gorgeous?' he asked her.

'She works at the Proserpine Pub. They're looking for bar staff. I start tomorrow. There's something I need to tell you before I go, Leigh.'

'I'm all ears, gorgeous.'

'A couple of nights ago, I heard the old man ... He was talking his usual gangster rubbish with his mates, you know the sort ...'

'And?' probed Leigh.

'They were talking about "ending" someone, "a blonde slut". It had something to do with that undercover couple who used to come to the café. They had me fax their photo ...'

'You're sure of this?'

'Positive. The old man, he's getting information from somebody in the cops. On the inside, definitely.'

'Good girl.'

'Dumb girl, Leigh. It's been too long. Time for me to get out ... to move on.'

She looked up to Leigh's face and then past his head to the entrance of the waiting room half-a-dozen paces away. She could see the back of someone's head. It was poised as if listening to their conversation. She tapped Leigh lightly on the knee and threw her eyes towards the door. Leigh turned and jumped quickly from his seat, inadvertently dragging the plastic moulded chair squeaking along the floor. As he untangled his trouser leg from the chair, he caught a

5TH JULY

glimpse of Inspector Mack walking briskly up the stairs. The Inspector keyed his PIN to break the seal on the door, turning back momentarily to the reception area below to see Leigh standing alone, staring up at him.

∙∙

The cunning Inspector, a man who prided himself on his ability to outsmart the system and just about everybody in it, felt somewhat rattled by the time he had reached the sanctuary of his desk. He loosened his necktie and wiped the sweat from his nose with a tissue. He was absolutely livid that Leigh had caught him eavesdropping. As far as a lifetime of work was concerned, he was only five minutes away from securing a million dollars from the dago connection. He couldn't afford any suspicion right now. There was only one loose end in the police department, only one thread that could unravel him and his corrupt ways, and he had great plans for young Donny once he got hold of the lovely. There would be no 20 per cent commission for that useless excuse for a junior detective. No way would he be giving $200 000 of his hard-earned dollars to that pathetic little weasel. Once he had his hands on all the cash, Mack would offer $50 000 back to Massimo to kill Donny. So simple—after all, Massimo was planning to bump off Cole and Jude and, for an extra $50 000, why not the trifecta, he thought.

He admired his beautiful princess and her clever strategy. He had never seen the possibility himself, until the other night when he and Dorothy had snuggled cosily together to plan their retirement—plans that had inevitably led them to lust. From the lounge room sofa, to the kitchen bench adjacent to the fridge, where they had stopped briefly to collect another bottle of champagne, and finally to the bedroom. They tumbled together like a couple of puppies with more and more passionate sex until the wee hours. While the delicious thoughts of their acrobatic love-making and financial management had rolled around his head often in recent days, he now found himself tormented at his downstairs waiting room blunder. He walked thoughtfully from his office into the tearoom for a jam fancy and coffee. To be taken with a slice of peace and quiet.

He cursed to himself as he entered the room. He had forgotten about Sandra sitting underneath that silly phone, waiting for her ex-sergeant to ring. The whole office knew that, he mulled. Didn't she ever go home? Couldn't he even have a cup of coffee without being reminded of Cole? He collected his empty mug. As always, not so much as a hello passed between them. His mood change of a few minutes earlier got the better of him.

'No calls from invisible sergeants, Sandra?' he asked tersely as he stared at the phone.

She glanced up with her best fake smile and then dropped her head back to her work without uttering a word.

'He won't ring. And it's high time you went back to your normal seat, thank you, Detective!' he snapped.

Sandra dropped her pen, wondering what words she could use other than 'get fucked'.

'I don't know what you are talking about, Boss,' she replied innocently instead. 'I've just been sitting here waiting for my informers to call.'

The tearoom phone was occasionally used by informers to reach detectives with information on sensitive investigations. Inspector Mack knew that, but also knew that Sandra was not involved with any such investigation at present. Mack took a few too many jam fancies and his coffee cup and walked out. He tapped loudly on the door frame before giving her his final word on the subject. 'Return to your normal desk instantly, Detective. That's an order.'

He felt a little easier as he walked back to his own office, the authority he had just exerted in part making up for his error of judgement in the waiting room below. A loud crashing noise could be heard coming from the tearoom down the hall as he bit into a jam fancy.

• •

5TH JULY

By the time Sandra had marched, disgruntled, back to her original desk, carrying a full 'in' and 'out' tray, stacked with a pen jar and teledex, Leigh had wandered back upstairs, having said his 'goodbyes' and 'good lucks' to Penny. It was the sheer decency and honesty of informers like Penny, he reflected, that made the efforts in law enforcement so much easier, and he let her know that in no uncertain terms as she prepared to leave for good.

Another woman he thought was quite delicious, although somewhat older, yet a lot more fascinating, was now standing in front of him throwing office equipment around the room. Despite their sexual tryst, he wasn't stupid enough to go anywhere near her right now. Instead, he tiptoed lightly to his PC; there was an urgent short report he needed to compile. A top-secret report, to the course director of the FBI, Quantico, Virginia, USA. Half an hour later, he looked up from the proof of his printed report and noticed that Sandra seemed to have calmed to an automatic pilot mode and sat working through a pile of documents. He dropped his report in front of her. She read through to the second paragraph, the bottom line.

> … and as I am therefore required to take on the investigation of a terrorist threat in our own country by Al Qaeda, which will involve many months of secret inquiries in Melbourne, I must regrettably withdraw from your covert training course.
>
> This report is top secret and I respectfully request that you speak to nobody, other than my superior, Detective Inspector Sandra Butler, on the above-mentioned telephone numbers.

Sandra noticed that Leigh had signed the report. She looked up. 'Thanks for the promotion. What are you doing?' she demanded.

'I'm not going, obviously.'

'*What?* And what's this crap about a terrorist threat in Australia? There isn't any such thing.'

'The FBI doesn't know that, and they won't ring back here if it's top secret, will they? That way I can fuck off.'

ON THE RUN

'You're on drugs, Leigh. Where the hell are you planning to fuck off to?' she said as she looked over the report a second time.

'Stromboli. Penny from Griffith just left. They're planning to kill Jude as well.'

Sandra dropped the report and dropped her head into her hands.

• •

Drug dealers didn't tend to receive their orders by fax. But a couple of days previous Massimo waited impatiently in his cave for one such document, which served in some small way to break up the long hours as he hovered anxiously by his secret phone. Just in case Giuseppe got into any trouble transporting the precious freight from Germany. The Australian Godfather was to fax a photograph from the Café Azzurra. At least the old man would have the cute Penny transmit the picture to the long-winded Italian number. And so she did.

The happy-snap of Cole and Jude at their engagement dinner found its way into Massimo's back pocket. He had a long drive ahead of him. Destination: Corleone, Sicily. Almost five hours away, with a ferry trip in the middle. By dusk, his car rolled into the tiny town in the Sicilian hills. He needed an important favour from his equivalent in the Corleone clan, the Cosa Nostra. It was they who had the corrupt connection to many of the customs officers throughout Italy. If his adversary was still on the mainland, he wanted him found. Jude was a bonus.

As a gesture of goodwill, Massimo took with him, as a gift, a five-kilo bag of recently manufactured ecstasy tablets, just to stir the pot.

• •

Tommy had put away his joggers and Bees-Knees, well and truly. The Browning automatic had taken up semi-permanent residence, wrapped in plastic and buried in the back of the duck pen behind the B&B. He had done very little in the past couple of weeks other than improve his suntan and his appreciation for Sicilian food. He and Cinzia had also become great confidantes. She confided in Tommy about her fractured love in Palermo, which she hoped to repair upon her return the following day. Her holiday in the sun was nearing its end.

Cinzia, Tommy, Nick the Greek and Aggie had planned a dinner together that evening, as they did most evenings. But tonight they were to dine at the salubrious La Locanda del Barbablu, which just happened to be immediately across the laneway from Casa Greco. Cinzia and Tommy had dined virtually everywhere on the island, but they had saved La Locanda for their final night. The menu was so highly thought of with its nightly changing five-course *degustazione* and superb wine list that the chef was spoken of in places as far away as Rome.

Tommy had given much thought to what he might do once Cinzia had left the scene. The other guests who had come and gone during his time were mostly couples. Not company for a lone lodger. On the way down to the beach that afternoon, they dropped in to the tiny *pasticceria* for their usual bag of warm biscuits and a couple of bottles of water. He had quickly checked his email at *La Libreria sull'isola,* a button-sized bookshop he had frequented. There were two terminals in the back corner that operated a couple of times a day for a few hours apiece. They were painfully slow but no more painful than the feeling that had enveloped Tommy this morning when he had found no email from Sandra. He was starting to wonder whether she had received the postcard, whether the address he had used was correct or, if it was, whether the team had understood the code and the significance of the card. He knew it was only a matter of time before he would have to move on again, perhaps picking another island, before his money ran out.

Once he logged off, he and Cinzia took to the beach. His friend was rested and tanned but anxious about her return to Palermo, and she was feeling mischievous. As they walked she playfully flicked

Tommy with her beach towel and teased him with the bag of biscuits.

Later, sitting on their deckchairs, he and Cinzia discussed the other islands of the Aeolian Archipelago.

'Lipari is a big island, Tomasso, with many people. Maybe if you want something little then you should go to Panarea; it's like Stromboli, very Greek, very tiny, very expensive, and very good biscuits.'

Tommy laughed, but didn't bother responding to her recommendation as soon as he heard the word expensive. He gazed at the shallow water, at the crowds that had slowly increased day by day. Mostly couples sharing suntan lotion, water bottles and blissful harmony. He spied a solitary bikini-clad girl up to her thighs in the tiny waves. She was looking out to sea. He admired her figure, albeit in need of a tanning. Her black bikini clung snugly with its traditional two-strap top and hip-hugging bottoms with a tiny white belt threaded through.

He and Cinzia sat up together, in the shade of their umbrella, to take a break from the sun and make short work of a pair of nectarines. It was now well past lunchtime. The bikini girl had turned to face the beach and surveyed the crowd and the beautiful bodies in the glaring sun. She glanced momentarily at Cinzia, with her deep ochre colour and her tiny figure, then at Tommy, equally bronzed and looking fit. She thought they made a good couple. Her eyes continued scanning the deckchairs, getting familiar with her territory; she had only been on the island a couple of days, and was very, very alone. She looked back across the water towards the line of Calabria. Tommy had been casually eyeing her figure, then, when he saw her profile, his heart jumped.

He wiped the juice from his lips and, using a splash of water from the bottle, he washed his hands and stood up quickly. Cinzia watched in surprise. Tommy walked gingerly over the wet stones towards the bikini girl, who was now facing away from him. He waded through the shallows to stand immediately behind the blonde. He crossed his arms firmly and said in his best Sean Connery accent, 'Goodwin, Cole Goodwin.'

5TH JULY

The girl froze for a second before she spun around. Jude then faced Cole straight on. Her eyes desperately took in his change of appearance. No more moustache, no more long hair, clean shaven, tanned. She threw both hands ecstatically into the air and leapt on him yelling 'You idiot! You complete idiot!' They kissed in the water with a somewhat bemused Cinzia staring on, half a nectarine still in her hand.

• •

Jude stood under the cooling shower, the water trickling down her body. Her eyes focused on the black sand between her toes pooling as it spiralled down the drain. It washed away, as did the two months of utter worry, tension and stress. Her body tingled with the expectation of what lay ahead at the end of the evening. She gently massaged suds over her shoulders, across her breasts and under her chin as she closed her eyes and drifted back to the sexual tension that had teased her and Cole. But, no longer; she was certain that she was now gloriously in love and lust, pleased to be finally stuck on a magnificent island with the man of her dreams.

As she put on her make-up and fussed over her hair, she felt her hands shaking with anticipation. She stepped from her marbled bathroom into a magnificent oversized bedroom. Tommy had booked them a room at the house that the locals called Casa Rosso; the red house, the most famous building on the island. It was the house that had been rented by Ingrid Bergman and Roberto Rossellini when they too were stuck on the deserted island, filming their movie. They had stayed six months in that same room. The house was now owned by two brothers who squabbled occasionally, and spent a good deal of the rest of the time keeping tourists at bay. It too was on Via Vittoria Emmanuelle, the next house up from Casa Greco. The only thing between the two homes was the tiny orchard.

Tommy stepped in through the french doors off the ornate little garden full of fruit trees. He had cut across the orchard from Nick the Greek's, having made a convenient diversion as Jude showered, to explain to his three friends that Jude was an ex-girlfriend who lived in Australia. Their meeting had been completely accidental, but he hoped they would indulge him and allow her to join them for dinner that evening. Nick was unfussed with the explanation; he was pleased to know that Tommy would have company once Cinzia departed.

Tommy had whispered to Jude in the water, before he had introduced her to Cinzia, about his alias and supposed background. A covert operative of her experience would adjust rapidly.

And now she stood before him, wrapped in an oversized thick white bath towel, holding a sealed yellow envelope. He lay on the bed admiring her and thinking of ways to cancel dinner, before he accepted the envelope from her damp, shaking hand.

'What is it?' he asked.

'She told me. But you open it.'

And he did, tearing a neat break along the seal of the lip. He tipped the contents onto the white linen sheets. A brand-new passport, Visa card, MasterCard and driver's licence in the name of Robert Bergman lay before him, along with 3000 euros in large denominations.

'Spud arranged it in an hour,' Jude said as he stared down at his new self on the bed.

His face lit up; he thought of Spud and Leigh. Of his dear friend Sandra and her support since he had been in this mess.

'You know Sandra sits by the phone every day, waiting for you to call, worrying about you?'

He looked up at Jude.

'I've been selfish, haven't I? Not making more contact.'

'No, you haven't. Whatever you did worked. You're alive and that's the most important thing. Email Sandra tomorrow and give her a good bottom line. In the meantime we have a performance to put on and dinner to eat.'

• •

5TH JULY

Given that Nick and Aggie were the restaurant's most immediate neighbours, and were also kind enough to frequently pass on bookings from their own guests, the Casa Greco crowd of five enjoyed the best table in the house. An ornate dinner service of fine silver cutlery and crisp starched napkins graced their grand old mahogany table in the centre of the lush Mediterranean courtyard. '*Piccola Trattoria*', a beautiful ballad by Fabio Concato, was playing; it reminded Tommy of the many meals he had endured, alone, in the occasional little trattoria, thinking of Jude.

Tommy, at the head of the table, under a leafy peppercorn tree, led the way with the conversation during the night. After all, he was the nexus between each of the dining guests. The delicately flavoured *zuppa di pesce* was cleared away and Tommy poured them all another splash of the chosen Cantina de Bartoli 2005 inzolia white wine to enjoy while they waited for their second course, carpaccio of smoked Aeolian swordfish with the zest of limes. The conversation flowed easily; it was clear that each of these five people could have been friends anytime, anywhere.

'So, Tomasso, how long has it been since you and Jude saw each other?' Nick enquired, with a sly wink in Tommy's direction.

A cautious Tommy looked across at Jude. She reassured him with a cheeky glance. He had a déjà vu moment of the many times he and Jude had dined with the Mafia and faced similar questions about their relationship. They were so close back then and for that reason he enjoyed Nick's question.

'Well now, Nick,' he began, as if seriously racking his brain for the date of some non-existent distant rendezvous. 'I think it would be at least a year or more. What do you think, Jude?'

She too presented a realistically studious face before offering her own version of the events, 'Maybe a year and a half, I think, Tommy. Didn't we celebrate my thirty-third birthday together in London?'

'Of course, you're right, tenth of March last year, wasn't it? We went to that new Terrance Conran restaurant?' Tommy answered. 'And I drove you out to the airport next morning.'

'Back to Australia and you flew on to Edinburgh.'

'Yes, that's right,' he feigned.

'You were going to Sotheby's to buy three Michael McCartney oil paintings,' said Jude.

'I bought them, you know. Quite a good price, too. They're hanging in the flat in London—flew back down with them only a few days after.'

Tommy raised his glass and four others followed.

'So, how long do you plan to stay in Stromboli, Jude?' enquired Cinzia.

'I hadn't planned on staying long at all,' she replied as she turned to take in Tommy's reaction. 'I was just passing through. I'd read a romantic story once about Ingrid Bergman and I always wanted to stay at the house.'

'And Tomasso,' Cinzia's gaze too drifted to the man at the end of the table. 'You will go on to Panarea?'

'I'm not too sure any more,' he replied, as he stared lustfully across at Jude.

Nick, who saw the pairs of locked eyes, added, 'I think the red house will be occupied for a while.'

Two hours later, after the tagliatelle, char-grilled squab and pomegranate panna cotta, Tommy was quick to take the cheque across to the cashier and settle the entire account privately with his new Visa card and pseudonym. He had spent too long eating quick frugal meals and managing his palate on house wine and local beer. Robert Bergman was relishing the chance to splurge, just this once.

• •

Jude walked in front with the aid of her torch, through the side gate, weaving past the nectarine trees to the open french doors, one hand holding Tommy's. She hardly needed the torch with the glow from the full moon over the distant hills of Calabria. The fine lace curtains

5TH JULY

fluttered softly in the light warm breeze. She casually pushed them to one side, to allow them entry to the luxurious room. The romantic glow from the outside continued in their boudoir; the owners had thoughtfully lit the bedside candles.

'What was that rubbish about Edinburgh?' she asked Tommy playfully, as she ran her fingers through his short locks.

'The same rubbish you put out about Michael McCartney—who's he?' Tommy placed his arms around Jude's waist and drew her to him.

'Probably Paul's little brother. Who knows? I don't.' She giggled as she stepped in even closer.

They laughed together at their ability to work a table under pressure. They truly were a pigeon pair. Not just as operatives, but in their feelings towards each other. The breeze continued to play with the doorway curtains. Tommy broke away momentarily and pushed down on the CD button. He had borrowed the restaurant's Fabio Concato CD and played the romantic '*Buonanotte amore*' as he took Jude in his arms once more. They moved together in a near-motionless dance. Her hand moved up to caress his clean-shaven chin, then traced across the smoothness of his top lip to rest on his mouth. He reached up, held her fingers and kissed them gently. His head lowered to meet hers and he placed his lips firmly on hers. Tommy reached for the thin straps of her black silk dress and eased them gently from her soft white shoulders. The gown fell to the terracotta tiles in one fluid movement. She stepped back two paces to find the softness of the feather down. Tommy unbuttoned his shirt and partnered it with the dress as he slowly eased his eager body onto hers. Jude blew out her bedside candle.

• •

Under that same full moon sat Massimo with his cousin Giuseppe and Illario. They were at their usual table, just a little forward from the door of the café in the main piazza in Plati, sharing a bottle of Averna Digestivo with a small tumbler of ice and three heavy-bottomed glasses. Giuseppe had not been back long, after four days on the road, and they were enjoying a quiet time of reflection on their enterprise thus far. Massimo had always said there were four acts to his play. First, the manufacturing of the huge quantities of amphetamine in Germany. Second, the pill-pressing process, which they said goodbye to in Leverkusen. Act Three was the risky movement of the ecstasy pills from Germany to their secret cave in the Aspromonte Mountains. The stash would stay hidden for a week or so to let the dust settle before being packed among the artichokes and, as the final act, being shipped to Australia. Then the rest was up to the Australian Godfather, who had eager buyers waiting for the booty.

Massimo was three-quarters through his play and three-quarters through the bottle of Averna. His pretty niece, Lydia, was on the other side of the piazza flirting with a couple of the local boys. She was the princess of the otherwise miserable little piazza.

'She is growing too fast,' said Giuseppe, riddled with fatherly worry as he watched his teenage daughter cavort.

'She will not embarrass you, Giuseppe, she respects the family. She is just playing with the boys,' Massimo replied as he smiled at Lydia's antics.

'She wants to go to a dance next week in Costanza, Massimo.'

'Her first dance?'

'Her second. She went to one when you were in Australia. She didn't come home till 3 a.m.'

'Will you let her go to this one then, cousin?'

'If she leaves those silly boys in the piazza alone, I have told her I might think about it,' said Giuseppe, laughing a little as he reached for the bottle of Averna and poured his *amici* another round of drinks.

It was Giuseppe who was feeling more tired than anyone else, for it was he who had jockeyed the amphetamine-laden truck all the way from Germany. Initially they had taken the network of national roads

5TH JULY

to Strasbourg, crossing into Switzerland. He had navigated along the E36 autobahn before he had insisted on a few hours' sleep in a wayside hotel in the village of Luzern. His escort car with the three Plati underlings suffered the long watch on the truck; they put up with each other's salami-induced belching and rancid cabin air, while Giuseppe and his driver got whatever value could be gained from a tiny bed and a hot shower. The next day the convoy of contraband had driven into northern Italy, along Lago Maggiore then around the Milano ring road to Genoa, where they camped another night in much the same circumstances. This night was somewhat easier, with their contraband hidden away in a backwater warehouse, thanks to the assistance of the local *Mafiosi* who were glad to help, and even more glad to accept their allotment of drugs.

It was the early-morning ferry ride from Genoa to Reggio Calabria that they were all waiting for, a far easier proposition, eleven hours by boat instead of the risk of eleven hours by highway, especially with the aggravating ways of the Anti-Mafia units in Rome and Naples. Giuseppe had worked this route out three or four trips ago after a previous shipment had been stopped just out of Rome. He and his men had jumped four metres below, clear of the autostrada and then escaped into the foothills, but lost their entire load in the process, as well as the driver, who was shot in the back by overly zealous *Carabinieri*. Once aboard the ferry, it was easy-going with the drugs locked away in the hull, and a revolving shift of watchmen. The whole process was aided by the merchant navy crew on the ferry, which was owned by the Cosa Nostra in Sicily. A 1000-euro gratuity to the head seaman ensured that nobody touched the truck or its hire-car escort.

Once the ferry docked in Reggio Calabria it was a mere thirty-minute drive along the A3 autostrada to the turn-off to the Aspromonte Mountains at Bagnara Calabra. The last hour was the most difficult part of the route, taking the seven-tonne truck with its four-tonne load through the treacherous thirty kilometres of winding roads to the turn-off to the tiny town of Piminoro, just on dusk. It was there that Giuseppe would always wave to his friend, who sat dutifully by the roadway, waiting, watching. Six kilometres more, hiking along a fire track that formed the roof of the mountains, and he would finally weave a short distance under the tall pine trees to the heavily camouflaged entrance to their cave. The passage through this final six kilometres had been aided by the Mafia, who had, many years earlier, smashed the asphalt of the road, rendering it unlikely that anyone would venture along it.

Giuseppe ran to his own rule once the truck arrived at the cave; he threw his kitbag onto his dusty trail bike and headed back to Plati, a mere two kilometres away, to say hello to a bottle of Averna and his lovely daughter, leaving his soldiers to safely stow the fortune in nightclub pills. Sometime after midnight, they would then take the Mercedes truck and the Opel rental car and motor through the night towards Naples, where both vehicles would share a bath with a twenty-litre drum of kerosene and burn to a crisp.

• •

By the time the last of the Averna had been poured from the bottle, Mario had given up his mountain trek in search of the final resting place of the ecstasy pills. As instructed by his Anti-Mafia colleague, *Commissario* D'Alfonso, he had secreted himself just before dusk in the dense undergrowth near the Piminoro turn-off to lay in wait for the Mercedes truck. It was here that the Anti-Mafia unit had lost the previous shipments, unable to track them under the massive canopy of dense forest, a terrain that was a *Commissario*'s investigative nightmare.

This time around, the Mercedes truck's headlights had flashed as it had drawn closer to the turn-off road. Mario had even seen Giuseppe wave to the nit-keeper, who sat on an old stool keeping watch and had signalled with a 'thumbs up' that the 'coast was clear'. A network of nit-keepers had been installed by the Plati clan in the surrounding hills, and Mario was aware of the location of almost all of them.

5TH JULY

The truck bounced, struggled and pig-rooted along the broken asphalt. As it had rounded a bend just past his covert hideaway, Mario had cut through the bush and jogged along, following at a safe distance behind. D'Alfonso had recently brought him in on the Anti-Mafia sting to report the final location of the stash. Surveillance operatives had tracked the container all the way from Leverkusen with a GPS tracking device that they had secretly installed in the vehicle before it had left the factory. This had allowed easy surveillance all the way through to Reggio Calabria, their obvious destination. The shortfall to the investigators' plan was in the Aspromonte Mountains themselves, and that is where Mario came in. With the dense coverage of the sixty-metre-tall pines, no signal could be picked up from the tracking device. Mario, himself living only a hilltop town away from Plati, knew the region better than any of D'Alfonso's regular operatives. The *Commissario* knew Mario to be a good policeman and had accepted graciously when Mario had enthusiastically volunteered his local knowledge.

Two kilometres along that precious final route, the Opel came to an abrupt stop. It was no more than a hundred metres away from where a panting Mario dived suddenly to the ground behind a large, moss-covered log. His overconfidence may have allowed one of the Uzi-toting gangsters to catch a glimpse of his movement in the forest. The thug had stepped out onto the roadway and, without taking any direct aim, he had showered the immediate forest area with thirty or more rounds of deadly bullets. Mario lay petrified and motionless in the dark until his weary, undisciplined, would-be assassin climbed back into the Opel and drove away. It was enough to completely deflate the shaken Mario. He gave up his task in preference to survival, and hobbled home, begrudging the phone call that he would have to make later to the *Commissario;* another load was lost to the Mafia.

9th July

Two pairs of arms and a few shoulder muscles were being stretched on a glorious new morning. Tommy brought his hand down to the firm belly of his partner and slowly traced his fingers up to her chin. She responded by turning towards him. To kiss him 'hello' for the day. The sound of feet padding on the terracotta tiles could be heard at the foot of the bed. Unconcerned, they both looked up to see a large white goose that had entered the room through the still-open french doors. They dressed and followed the goose out the doors and into the orchard. Tommy pulled a fresh nectarine from one of the trees and ate playfully, as the sweet sticky juice ran down his forearm. Tommy was completely happy for the first time in months.

'So that's the famous Calabria,' Jude said.

'You betcha,' came Tommy's reply.

'You wouldn't know about Massimo and the drug importation?'

'No ... Is he involved in one?' enquired Tommy.

'Apparently. And your team are supposed to be helping out on the Melbourne end when it gets there.'

The common walkway used by other travellers was a mere stone's throw away, so the two spoke softly, careful not to be overheard. They noticed a thin stream of travellers walking up towards the red house, each of them laden with a backpack or suitcase. The 8.20 a.m. ferry from Sicily had obviously just arrived. Tommy moved slowly in to kiss Jude once more and as he did so he heard a roaring shout from somebody in the passing foot traffic, wearing a bright orange Hawaiian shirt: *'Champer!'*

• •

9TH JULY

Some time after the welcomes, backslapping and general greetings had been done and done again, Leigh put three small wicker chairs in the middle of the orchard for a meeting. Beneath the late-morning shade of the nectarine groves the trio came together for a briefing, with a real-life rather than pinned-up vista of the hills of Calabria across the strait. The perfect stimulus, as was the percolator of freshly brewed coffee delivered by Nick the Greek. Leigh went into detail about the drug investigation involving Massimo. As they sat together for the first time in ages, the coffee long consumed, the impact of the news of the death threat on Jude loomed heaviest on their picturesque horizon. Tommy found himself drifting from his recently claimed comfort zone and Jude fell into a quiet, reflective state. It was the ideal time for Leigh to offer up a BlackBerry Bold, one of a matching pair, handed to him by Spud, who had driven him out to the airport. The master phone remained with Sandra; the analyst promised that the account and the messages transmitted or received were untraceable, certainly out of the range of infiltration by the prying Inspector Mack and Donny. For the first time in three months Tommy had instant communications. Spud had set up the directory index of both phones with a safe a link to the other phone, eliminating the need for any future covert emails or bottom lines. Also eliminating any paranoia of whose personal lines may or may not be tapped.

Jude continued to sit in silence, looking far out over the waves, lost in her own thoughts. Leigh, meanwhile, offered Tommy a quick tutorial on the email retrieval capabilities of the BlackBerry. As a test, they checked the Ingrid site for any new messages from Sandra. When the new mail message lit up all three pairs of eyes, without focusing at all on the preamble, went straight to the bottom line of the note.

Our dearest girlfriend from school is facing similar problems.

The message made it abundantly clear to Tommy what he had already heard in person from Leigh. Jude was now a target also.

ON THE RUN

With the brief technology lesson over, the ominous silence fell once again over the reunited team. Nobody seemed to have any smart ideas. Leigh attempted to draw them together.

'So, how are we going to get rid of these threats?'

Tommy didn't reply. His head was down. He was intently watching the sticky juice seeping between his toes from the errant apricot that he had taken to rolling along the surface of the drying soil with his foot.

'The threat will never go away,' Jude said, frustrated. She lifted her body wearily from her chair and, without turning back, drifted over to the red house and her elegant suite.

Leigh's eyes moved from the retreating Jude to Tommy, still lost in preserving fruit. He got up from his seat and followed Jude.

• •

The heavy-handed fist of the neighbour next door pounded on the sculpted brass knocker of Inspector Mack's carved-oak front door. The knocking was closely followed by the shout of 'Turn it down, for Christ's sake!' Inside the house, in the centre of the lounge room with the coffee table pushed randomly to one side, were Inspector Mack and Dorothy. They were clutched tightly together in an embrace. The extraordinarily loud music that accompanied their waltz was a recording of Maurice Chevalier's 'Thank Heaven for Little Girls'. They reacted in a good neighbourly fashion by gliding over to the CD player, where Mack lowered the volume with one hand as he lowered Dorothy in a dip with the other.

It was after midnight and the couple were taking a short break from an evening of packing. Beaucaire was a mere day or two away. Tonight's packing had been particularly arduous as they prepared their exodus from Australia. Upon receipt of their million-dollar bounty from the Mafia, Mack would return to Australia briefly. To resign and cash in his superannuation. Rent out their palatial Malvern home on a long-term lease and jet back, first class.

9TH JULY

And he would busy himself as a consultant, taking the Calabrian Mafia as his sole client. He would go on arranging safe passage through customs for his Mafia mates a couple of times a year. For a fee, of course. The perfect retirement for a talented ex-police inspector who should have been a deputy commissioner.

• •

Tommy was still sitting on the same chair three hours later. It was as if time had stopped in the Aeolian sunshine. He devised a plan to get rid of the threat that hung heavily over him and Jude. They needed to be rid of Massimo and his lieutenants so they could get on with their lives. He picked up his new fan-dangled contraption, the shiny BlackBerry, and summoned up the only number in its index and selected 'call'.

In six short rings it was answered by a sleepy Sandra who seemed rather alert, considering the time difference.

'Mr Bergman?' she asked gleefully.

'Hello, you, talk to me. Sorry it's late.'

'You're the one with all the news, Mr Bergman.' She couldn't stop the smile that practically crept through the phone.

'Mr Paul, still.'

'Okay, got it.'

'Well, I was having the time of my life, until the prophet of doom arrived on my doorstep.'

'You mean the threat on Jude?'

'Yep … it's sitting pretty heavy here. We really need to do something. How long before Massimo's locked up?'

'Unsure, Boss. He's behind 15 million eccies, destined for Australia.'

'Leigh's briefed me about the artichoke scam. Any idea where it is now?'

'No idea, the Anti-Mafia unit lost it in the Calabrian hills.'

'Fuck, this could go on forever.'

'Any plans?'

'Not yet, I need more time … I need Spud to contact his mate in the Anti-Mafia unit in Naples … now.'

'Right now?'

'Right now.'

'Ask him to meet me in the piazza in front of his office at one o'clock tomorrow.'

'Sure. How will he know you? What name will you use?'

'Robin Hood.'

Sandra laughed, wondering whether she had heard right. Tommy reiterated his previous comment before indulging in small talk and a long-winded tale of his Italian adventures. Within half an hour he turned off his impressive new gadget.

As he pocketed his BlackBerry, Tommy looked up at the approaching Nick, who carried a bottle of Nero D'Avola Sicilian red wine and two glasses. He took a chair next to Tommy and poured two generous glasses. Nick handed Tommy the customer copy of the 400-euro MasterCard restaurant receipt from the previous night, when Tommy had so generously covered the bill. Trouble was, it was billed and signed in the name of Robert Bergman. Tommy was livid at his error; his mind processed the significance of the slip of paper and his eyes looked up at Nick. He was pleased to accept the accompanying smile on Nick's face as he handed him a fortifying glass of red.

'You left your copy at the restaurant desk. But you don't have to explain, Tomasso. Something tells me you are busy enough.'

'It's not what it seems, Nick.'

'It seems nothing, Tomasso. You come to Stromboli, then a woman, then a man, a different MasterCard. It's not for me to ask.'

Tommy was momentarily lost for words as he studied the face of a man who was clearly showing all the signs of being a great man, a good friend.

'We all have secrets, Tomasso,' Nick continued. 'You never ask me why I live here with Aggie, why we run from Greece, with no papers, no residency.'

9TH JULY

'No. It's not my business.'

'And yours is not mine.'

Tommy took the wine bottle from his host's hand and topped up his now near-empty glass. There was more to be said.

Nick began, 'During the Athens Olympics, Aggie and I were running a bus company. A small business, with tours of Athens.' Nick was struggling with his story, and he took another sip of wine.

'We were driving American tourists to the stadium when a truck crashed into us. There were three dead, two children and one old woman.'

The story had now gotten the better of the teller as tears welled in Nick's eyes. His spare hand rubbed through his jet-black wiry hair. Nick composed himself by taking one large breath.

'Did they blame you?'

'The newspapers ruin us. The police charge the driver. His truck was bald tyres and no brakes. But the deaths kill me too ... I no longer hold my head up. My people turn against me.'

'But it wasn't your fault?'

'No. But the insurance bill was ... how you say, the last straw.'

'And you and Aggie are now here, living quietly on a tiny island, minding your own business.'

'Yes. We too have new names. So the insurance company doesn't find us.'

Both men raised their glasses.

'Is the ferry running tomorrow morning to Naples, Nick?'

'Every morning, from 8.30, my good Australian friend.'

Tommy got up stiffly from a chair that was not designed for so many hours of sitting.

'I have someone special I have to talk to,' he said as he walked towards the bedroom of the red house.

'If you need my help, just ask,' offered Nick.

• •

ON THE RUN

'True to form,' Tommy thought as the Stromboli to Naples ferry docked at the wharf on the Bay of Naples; the scheduled three-hour journey had taken four. Continuing with happenings identical to his first trip across the water was a reunion with his Italian designer acquaintances, both deeply tanned and still full of jolly. In case the need arose, Tommy had slipped his new Robert Bergman passport into the pocket of his shorts.

He took shade under a magnificent plane tree in the centre of the piazza that threw its wide shadow over his familiar rubbish bin. It was a scorchingly hot day. *Commissario* D'Alfonso didn't approach from the impressive front door of the Anti-Mafia headquarters as Tommy had expected. Instead he weaved his way suavely through the string of taxis at the nearby rank, striding proud in his royal blue shirt, contrasting tie and cream slacks. He greeted Tommy with an exuberant belly laugh and offered up his big hand. A smile sat on his handsome face.

'*Allora*, Detective Robin Hood, *si*.'

'At your service,' Tommy replied, as the two detectives walked slowly together. They had both been too long at the wheel, albeit at opposite ends of the investigative world, to care too much for small talk. Their main preoccupation was the problem now before them. The *Commissario* had made it abundantly clear through his conversations with Spud that he would offer full disclosure, and full assistance. But first Tommy needed to explain the incident involving the little punk with the handgun on the Venice train. Tommy took his time telling his story and the *Commissario* nodded. Once Tommy's explanation ended, the Italian offered an impressed look. 'You've been giving our criminals a hard time, Robin Hood.'

With a smile, the big man assured Tommy that his men would follow up the incident and fill in all the right forms. Such was the life of detectives, sometimes slaves to officialdom, even in Italy. Tommy, pleased with the response, pushed the real business to the forefront.

'I hear it's over four tonne.'

'It gets bigger each shipment. We have to stop them.'

9TH JULY

'You know Massimo killed an old man in New Zealand, and the wife hangs by a thread?'

'And he needs to kill you and your female operative before taking over from the Plati Godfather.' The *Commissario*'s comment, and the thought of losing Jude, almost riveted Tommy to the spot.

'How good is your evidence now that you have lost the drugs?'

'Italian courts don't like conspiracies.'

'Then you need to find the cave.'

'We might have only three days before it disappears onto a container ship.'

'The ship is leaving in a few days?'

'There is one in three days, and another in five days. We need to find the cave with Massimo inside.'

'So, what's the bottom line?' asked Tommy.

'The hills are full of Massimo's spies. There are more than a hundred caves. The forest is huge. My men would be sighted as soon as we entered the Aspromonte.'

'Even undercover?'

'Italians look like Italians.'

'What about a couple of tourists going for a picnic in the mountains?'

'Massimo knows you.'

'I'll work on that.'

'Does he know your female operative?'

'He's never seen her.'

The proposition appealed to the *Commissario*.

• •

The *Commissario*'s briefing to Tommy and their joint plans were completed well before the departure of the last afternoon ferry back to Stromboli, ensuring the Australian's arrival on the Scari dock at 7 p.m. Tommy's weary body stepped onto the concrete jetty. His spirits lifted with the sight of Jude standing alone, waving. A perfect homecoming for a man searching desperately for a solution to his problem. Jude had lain on a deckchair at the beach all day with Leigh, worrying and praying that an answer could be found. She was now blissfully happy, except for the interfering news of Massimo's need for revenge.

She kissed Tommy tenderly on the lips and he wrapped his arms around her waist, scooping her up momentarily. They then turned and wandered slowly along the only other road on the island, the coast road, returning to Casa Greco by dusk.

Their arrival was met by a very sombre Leigh. He sat in his lone deckchair, staring out to sea. A dozen fruit flies buzzed around above his head as he worked through problems that Tommy guessed were mostly identical to his own concerns.

'How did you go, champer?' asked Leigh.

'We need a clever plan, Leigh. Are you in?'

'Of course I'm in.'

'And so am I,' Jude added.

'I'm not too sure about you, Jude,' replied Tommy.

'Then get sure. If I was good enough for the Mafia in Griffith, I'm good enough for the Mafia in Calabria … What's the difference?'

Truth be known, Tommy saw no other way of achieving the desired result without involving Jude to some degree. It was time for surveillance, time to find a cave, time to create a happy couple and a picnic setting in the mountains. Jude was the perfect asset for such a plan. He pulled up a chair, as did Jude, and sat down to detail his plan, one that he'd discussed with the *Commissario* during their meeting.

• •

In the other hemisphere, seated in a far more formal version of an office was Sandra, not long into work. As per her daily routine, one of the first telephone calls she made was to the Auckland Base

9TH JULY

Hospital. She had been waiting for a good five minutes, while the less-than-interested nursing sister toddled off to enquire as to the progress of the patient Lynette Peterson. Sandra, expecting a version of the usual pro forma answer and fed up with a longer than average wait to boot, almost hung up in frustration. Just as she moved to take the handset from her ear, she heard a faint young female voice on the other end ask whether she was still there.

'Yes, of course I'm still here,' she replied tersely, making a simultaneous note of the call in her diary.

'Doctor told me that I'm allowed to say to you that Mrs Peterson is recovering and is progressing well.'

'Simply ... wonderful ... Nurse, what does that mean?'

'There's no need to be short, Detective. I'm just telling you what Doctor said. She's drifting in and out of consciousness. She spoke for the first time to the night nurse.'

'You ... she ... *what?*' exclaimed a stunned Sandra. She straightened her back and her posture from its slouched position.

'Are you deaf, Detective?' enquired the nurse tersely.

There was no answer to the question or the sarcasm. Sandra simply dropped the phone and sprinted for Spud's office.

∴

Their plan was a good one, the three of them thought: simple, innocent and highly feasible. Leigh and Jude would fill the back seat of a hire car with breadsticks, wine, picnic rug, plus prosciutto, cheeses and fruit. They would take with them two torches and a map supplied by Mario, which would highlight the ten caves closest to Plati—the immediate area where Mario lost sight of the shipment, the night he was shot at. The *Commissario* felt that ten would be sufficient for the first day; some were a kilometre apart, and the next most probable ten would feature on the second day, and so on. A distinctly different car would be arranged each day to fool the nit-keepers. They would drive into the region like a pair of lovers and amble hand in hand with their picnic basket, covertly ticking off the caves. Should they locate the right cave, the happy couple would return immediately to a pre-arranged rendezvous, where Tommy and the *Commissario* would be waiting. Tommy was aware that his own face was too well known to Massimo; he had to lie low. Should Jude and Leigh find the cave, the investigation would be handed over to the *Commissario*, and the Australian contingent would disappear back to Stromboli.

The success of the operation depended on a quiet and subtle approach, making sure that Leigh and Jude weren't seen before they spotted the Mafia. With this in mind, Leigh had suggested that they both wear dark clothing to facilitate a casual, camouflaged approach in the forest. Jude thought she would make good use of her new digital camera with its powerful zoom lens and try to take a couple of photographs of the cave entrance. They would be very much the loving couple out for a stroll in search of a picnic location. The team gave considerable thought to their contingency plan should they be confronted. It was decided that the best response would be to adopt the personas of honeymooning English tourists, no links to Australia.

With the final details of their plan down, Tommy required nothing more than a few minutes with Nick the Greek, who had, only the night before, given his assurance of help. Leigh spied him as he walked across the orchard, and nudged Tommy, who turned and yelled loudly in the direction of their friendly host, who was disappearing in through his front door: 'Nick, I need a boat!'

• •

The ACA squad car screeched to a halt outside the departure section of Melbourne International Airport. Sandra had said everything she needed to say to Spud on the journey out. In fact she had become so anxious that she had said it several times and had started to babble slightly, repeating herself. 'My visit to Lynette's bedside must be kept secret until such time as she can positively state who was responsible

9TH JULY

for the atrocity. Then pass on the details to Superintendent Fountain, who will take over and, hopefully, clear Cole's name.'

'I've got it, Sandra,' said Spud. 'Just go, your flight is about to leave.'

'Wish me luck,' was all that Sandra said as she leaned over and kissed her friend on the cheek. She grabbed her briefcase and overnight bag so hastily that she was out of the car and into the crowd before Spud could wish her good luck. She checked her watch and confirmed that there was a mere half-hour remaining. She looked up at the departure board. The final-call green lights flashed intermittently as she squeezed her way through the milling crowds. It was all push and shove.

She brushed against Dorothy, who stood pouting impatiently at the check-in counter. There was no tracksuit, joggers or sloppy joe for Dorothy this time around. She wore a brand-new pastel-pink Chanel suit with matching pumps and her fair share of bling. She, like Sandra, was full of anxiety, but of a different strain. Her nose was raised more than usual from the floor; she had at last found her station in life.

Her husband was busy at the first-class ticket counter, upgrading their economy seats. He looked a spiv in his navy blue Hugo Boss blazer adorned with gold buttons, matching a pair of white cuffed slacks and cream patent-leather loafers. A white silk handkerchief, blossoming from the chest pocket of his jacket, accompanied his boarding passes. They were off to the south of France.

He glanced back at Dorothy and gave her a charming smile. As he did so, his eyes moved momentarily from her to the rushed figure of Sandra, who had all but hurled a fellow passenger to one side as she fought the crowd. His delighted face turned sour. Mack, with fresh boarding passes in hand and luggage disposed of, stepped away from the counter and paced hastily in the direction in which Sandra had disappeared, looking up at the board to the only final flashing call: to Auckland. Dorothy clomped along behind him, somewhat perturbed at his change of demeanour. Her ruby-painted fingernails grabbed his arm, causing him to turn sharply and face her.

'Have you seen the Grim Reaper, darling? Not a good way to start a holiday,' she commented as Mack sank heavily onto a nearby seat. He looked around for some water and took his silk handkerchief from his pocket.

• •

Sandra stepped smartly from her double-parked taxi in front of the Auckland Base Hospital. She bounded through the hospital's automatic doors, ignored the reception staff and headed straight for Lynette Peterson's ward.

Half-a-dozen corridors later, she reached Room 7B on the ground floor of the East Wing. The timber door was slightly ajar and the single-bed private room was in relative darkness. Sandra walked gingerly through the door and leaned into the unknown. Lynette lay motionless on her back in a room devoid of any radio or television noise. The only sound that broke the stillness was the constant beep of the heart-rate monitor. Sandra was surprised at the serene look on Lynette's face. Her hands were clasped together on her lap, her neck bare of any bandages. Clearly the work of her surgeons had been exemplary.

'Lynette,' she whispered. There was no hint of a response. She pulled up a mustard-coloured vinyl seat and made herself comfortable. She surveyed the prettily framed photographs of Lynette and Cary in what were more idyllic times, and settled in for the night.

11th July

With a few hours of night sky left, Tommy and Jude stood huddled together on the Scari wharf. A distant band of tiny fairy lights from across the bay twinkled under a near-starless night. Jude's overnight bag sat cosily alongside the faithful old Bees-Knees, near the mooring post at the end of the pier. A pair of seagulls glided through the inky blackness and settled on a mooring post next to the bags, in search of scraps. Leigh strolled along the far end of the pier, gathering his thoughts, sucking in the coolness of the night air as well as the smoke from his cigarette. The glow from his cigarette tip traced a path as he smoked. Jude shone her torch to illuminate a shiny circle of glassy water. At that moment, the sound of a small motorboat could be heard in the distance, a distinctive *put put put put* coming from a well-worn engine.

Tommy flicked his torch on and the two lights danced across the otherwise dark sheet of water. Leigh stubbed his cigarette butt under his foot and turned his attention to the increasingly noisy approach of the water craft. A single, stronger light shone in their dazzled eyes as a small blue-hulled fishing boat came into sight. As the boat drew nearer to the trio, the seagulls took flight with a screech and a flutter of wings. All three torches now shone on the edge of the dock as Nick expertly steered his craft into perfect alignment.

'Tomasso, be quick, before the tide shifts,' the Greek said. Aggie, seated alongside, gently planted a farewell kiss on the side of his face. 'Don't go running away on me now, Nico,' she said.

'Never,' her husband replied. 'You and me ... forever.'

Nick helped Aggie ashore before he reached out and took Jude's hand, guiding her into the boat. Likewise, the two men and their bags. Tommy's shoulder bag was somewhat heavier than would be expected for a simple change of clothes and toiletries. He had retrieved his

Browning automatic from below the duck pen. Once settled, the four turned to wave a goodbye to Aggie as she disappeared along the pier and back into the darkness of San Vincenzo.

'You must tell me now, Tomasso, where are we going?' the Greek captain enquired. Tommy looked across at the man before him and without a word pointed across the bay to the cluster of tiny lights at the foothills of the Aspromonte Mountains.

• •

As dawn broke, Nick the Greek's blue-hulled fishing boat settled in to a makeshift mooring. They had reached the tiny port at Santa Domenica, below the cliffs of the hauntingly beautiful medieval town of Tropea, to the waiting wet feet of their Italian entourage. *Commissario* D'Alfonso stood a head above the next tallest man, Mario, and a band of surly plain-clothed *Poliziotti*, who were doing a less-than-impressive job of pretending to look like fishermen. There was a sweet, pungent smell in the air. Nick could see Tommy's nostrils flaring as he stepped from the boat.

'It's the red onions, Tomasso. Tropea is the home of the red onion. The hills are covered in them,' said Nick. Leigh, too, snorted the intoxicating aroma.

The now dozen or more gathered men, and one woman, shook hands as the morning sun made its first impression. The *Commissario* stepped towards Nick, who seemed to be the only outsider among the police, and handed him his calling card.

'Tomasso said you are to be trusted. If you need me for any reason in the future, ring my office: I will help you.'

The Greek captain of the now-empty vessel looked down at the card quizzically. Tommy stepped in to explain.

'It's what's called a "get out of gaol free card", Nick—keep it.' And with a wink and a 'See you back in Stromboli in a few days', he left the Greek to stash the card in the pocket of his shirt and head

11TH JULY

home across his empty sea. Leigh pushed the small boat into deeper water as Jude cleared the slippery stones.

The others scrambled over the large wet stones towards a gathering of nondescript hire cars in the bayside carpark. They all left in a convoy as invisibly as they had arrived.

In less than an hour, the big Italian in charge of the investigation and the three Australians pulled their car into the driveway of Mario's modest villa on the edge of the village of Gerace. Gerace was only ten kilometres as the crow flies from Plati, yet thirty-five kilometres along the winding laneways. As with all the villages on the mountain, it overlooked the fishing village of Locri, immediately below. The *Commissario* had scattered carloads of twitching, adrenalin-riddled investigators to one side of the national park. They would lie in wait, hidden well away, ready to act in an emergency.

The cosy little kitchen of Mario's home welcomed the strangers with the smell and taste of strong coffee and the cries of a cheeky toddler. Lina, Mario's dutiful wife, commenced the preparations for a hearty cooked breakfast for all. It was a proud moment for Mario and Lina, having the finest anti-Mafia investigator south of Rome sitting at their well-worn kitchen table. The pride on Lina's face was evident as she poured second cups of coffee and glanced at the five heads poring over the large topographical forestry map spread across the table. By the end of their breakfast, Leigh and Jude were comfortable in their roleplay as wayward picnicking travellers. The *Commissario*, too, was pleased with the plan, having assessed their exemplary level of undercover experience. He used the house phone to call his assistant to collect the two picnickers and take them to their task.

All of a sudden, silence fell over the kitchen; the game was on. Tommy reached for Jude's hand and took the liberty of finding a quiet space in their hosts' backyard. They sat alongside each other on a wrought-iron seat under an arbour covered with sprays of wisteria flowers.

'No hero shit, sweetheart,' he said to a clearly worried Jude, who was getting her mind set for her role.

'Leigh will have a six-shot .32 down his pants in case there's trouble.'

Jude nodded, needing the instruction, the jolt into the world of covert reality.

'Your only role is to try to find a cave. It's going to be a long day. Watch each other's back and, if anyone sees you, go into lover mode.'

She continued to nod; she was ready.

'Once you've ticked off the list get straight back to your hire car and back to the rendezvous. I'll be waiting at the RV for you. Be back by 7 p.m. at the absolute latest.'

'Easy-peasy. I've been doing it for years.' Jude reached over and gave Tommy a peck on the lips, running her hands through his hair.

'And you've got years more to go, babe,' he said directing her back to serious matters. 'With me.'

Jude liked what she heard and wrapped her arms around him. They kissed tenderly for a moment before being disturbed by a loud cough from the *Commissario*, who handed Jude the neatly folded map with a smile.

• •

Daybreak in a hospital was a strange occurrence. Lynette Peterson's room was perhaps the quietest in the hospital. It had become the place where tired, caring nurses would come to sit, to take a break from the maddening hustle and bustle of the wards and ponder Lynette's serenity and struggle for life. Sandra's head lay on the open-weave cotton blanket at the foot of the bed; she had been asleep for hours. The rest of her was wedged awkwardly into the forced curvature of the moulded chair. The person she was most interested in slept peacefully close by. The door of the room slowly opened more fully and the Charge Sister stepped inside. At first she was startled by the sight of Sandra's uncomfortably draped body, unused to visitors in 7B. She picked up the patient's notes on her clipboard.

11TH JULY

Pinned inside was a note: 'A detective from Melbourne is waiting to speak with the patient'. The Charge Sister looked at the sleeping pair and quietly retreated, closing the door behind her.

• •

That same winter daybreak reflected off the mirrored glass of the massive unclad windows of Donny's apartment. Henri was at the very end of his night shift and, thankfully, running to rule, Donny had left his internet connection on. Every ten minutes or so, in between a whole mess of unrelated analytical duties, Henri would glance up at the screen, just in case Donny was visible. There was a log book beside him on the desk, where he would note his observations along with a time and date for each occurrence. Long-winded and boring work to some, Henri relished it; it was the type of detail that juries loved to see, especially if the audio-visual evidence was damning enough.

It had been a quiet night shift on that front, Donny having grabbed his house keys and headed out for the evening many hours earlier. Henri looked up from his musings at the sound of rustling; his quarry was returning, from an obviously very, very long night out. Quickly, Henri swivelled his chair across for a better view. The target cast his valuable leather coat onto the floor and unclipped his Rolex, placing it down on the credenza next to the computer. He tapped a few keys to check incoming messages as he peered closely into his screen. Henri felt sure that Donny was looking up at his nose hair. He edged his seat back just a tad. It was the next sound that made him realise that his observations were going to be a little more interesting this morning. He was certain that he could hear the flushing of a toilet, even though his view didn't encompass the bathroom.

On cue, a young girl with somewhat disarrayed, matted hair strolled in front of the monitor and embraced Donny. She flopped her tired, drug-wasted body onto his, draped both arms around his neck and they kissed unromantically. Henri felt sure he recognised her face, as he rummaged through a stack of assorted photographs on his desk. Donny's hands groped her tight jeans and loose-fitting blouse just for a moment or two before the spent pair slumped themselves onto chairs at the dining table. Henri's chair swivelled urgently across to his main desk, where he opened a manila folder, still searching for the image of a girl he felt sure he knew. He watched the corrupt detective pull a small plastic bag of white powder from his trouser pocket and, using a Visa card, chop and cut at a small hill of it on the table surface, producing four neat parallel lines. As soon as that small task was completed, the detective and his lady friend each snorted two lines. Most probably cocaine, Henri thought, trying to keep up with his photo search while he scrawled notes on the changing images in Donny's apartment in his increasingly fat log. At about the same time as the drug hit the brains of the two users, the identity of the girl hit Henri, as he found the photograph he had been searching for. It was a happy-snap, a family photo, stolen on a midnight covert entry into the office of the co-suspect in this case, Inspector Mack. It was his daughter Chloe.

It had been a long shift the day before for Donny. He'd been suckered into helping out another crew, who were closing down a job. A handful of South Americans were to be raided and there was much work ahead. Begrudgingly, Donny joined the search crew for one of the raids. As luck would have it, a drawer he happened to open in one of the dealer's bedrooms was home to six one-ounce bags of cocaine. Donny declared three of them and squirrelled the other three down his Y-fronts. Later that night, during his traipsing of the nightclubs, he rid himself of two of the three bags for a tidy $10 000 profit. While he had no idea of the purity, Donny had made his own private professional assessment that, given the Colombians were at the very bottom of the drug-trafficking ladder, the bags were most likely to be cut sufficiently for immediate use. That was certainly the yarn he told his buyer at Bar 99%, the same bar in which he happened to bump into Chloe. She was having difficulty walking with a tumbler of gin and tonic between the bar and her booth full of spaced-out girlfriends.

11TH JULY

Henri's next observation would cause him to react in a way not familiar to an analyst. He watched the two drug users slump slowly back into their individual chairs, both pairs of eyes closed, as if their minds were travelling to another world somewhere. At least that's what he thought until his eyes fixed more closely on Chloe, who, without warning, began to convulse. Her back and shoulders surged violently forwards, and she was jittering frantically as she attempted to stand. Having fallen back into her chair, she attempted again to get to her feet with more exaggerated convulsions before projectile-vomiting across the table and finally collapsing, motionless, to the floor. Donny remained still, lost in his own personal heaven, oblivious to the tortured Chloe. He was also oblivious to the fact that the cocaine he had stolen from the drug-dealers was in fact 96 per cent pure, strong enough to stop a herd of elephants. Henri, too, was somewhat in a mess. He frantically tried to recall the police emergency number to call for an ambulance, a procedure he hadn't had to bring to mind since his graduation from the academy fifteen years earlier.

∴

Spud was first in the office, bright and early that morning, for one very good reason: there was no one else left in his crew—they were all overseas. No sooner had he placed his lunchbox, with its two neatly cut and cling-wrapped sandwiches, two pieces of fruit and snack box of biscuits, on his desk than his phone rang. It was his Henri, spouting the news of the day Henri was no different from anyone else. He hit the speed dial to a dozen different people before he got to Spud. His description of what happened seemed to floor his new analyst friend.

'She's dead. They tried everything but couldn't revive her,' explained Henri.

'And Donny?' enquired Spud.

'He came good halfway through the ambos trying to revive Chloe. Just as Fountain arrived.'

• •

Tommy had hardly sat down all day, constantly pacing—initially in the backyard of Mario's home and later that afternoon with the *Commissario,* as they waited together at the RV. They were well secreted in the dense undergrowth between the tall timbers. Tommy held his left wrist firmly and observed anxiously as the second hand of his watch ticked over to exactly 7.00 p.m. Although the *Commissario* hadn't said as much to his Australian equivalent, he had sensed since breakfast that Tommy and Jude were more than mere co-workers; it was clear that they held a great affection for each other.

A mere four kilometres away in the thick of the forest hiked the exhausted Leigh and Jude. They'd had a big day, ticking off far more caves than they had originally planned, as well as several others that weren't even registered. The sun had taken its piercing rays to the other side of a high ridge, and with less than an hour left before complete darkness, they welcomed the soothing coolness of the early night air. Jude was attempting to gain her bearings for the last cave of the day as she studied her map by torch light. She was overly conscious that she and Leigh were now officially running late but she felt certain that they were only metres away from the entrance of the last cave. Leigh handed her the picnic basket, which was now completely empty.

'Hold that, champer. I'll just climb down here,' Leigh offered.

'It should be just about ten metres away, Leigh,' Jude said, pointing towards where she reckoned the cave entrance would be.

Within a dozen short steps, Leigh disappeared from her sight, so dark was it becoming under the canopy. All of a sudden, she felt an extraordinary sense of aloneness, total vulnerability. For the first time that day, Jude felt scared. She listened painfully for Leigh's steps, hoping to keep hearing them. Then from the opposite direction,

11TH JULY

somewhere behind her, she thought she heard another set of steps. At least it sounded like shuffling among the dead foliage of the forest floor. She dropped to the ground instantly and crawled behind the trunk of a large moss-covered pine tree. The noise that she was now certain was footfalls increased in volume as it approached her. A man appeared from the shadows and stood beside her, looking down upon her huddled form. She clung as tightly as she possibly could to the handle of the picnic basket and rose to meet the gaze of the heavily whiskered peasant face. The man's full height was no greater than hers, and he was dressed in a putrid pair of dark trousers, an equally dirty shirt with a seriously frayed collar and a sports jacket. He was at least sixty-five years of age. There was nothing friendly about him and he grimaced at her, revealing rotten teeth.

'*Signorina?*' he enquired.

Jude returned the comment, 'No. *Signora, scusa. Signora. Mio* husband *Inglese*,' she said firmly but nervously as she pointed towards the last location she had seen Leigh.

'*Toilette, toilette, mio* husband,' she repeated as she continued to point to the now dark side of the hill.

The old man looked just as Leigh appeared, fumbling as if doing up the fly of his trousers.

'Sorry I took so long, darling. Who's your friend?' he said, smiling broadly.

The elderly man stood with both hands clasped behind his back, watching the two of them. He didn't utter another word, looked long and hard at Leigh, then turned around and simply walked back in the direction he'd come from. Leigh took a deep breath, released the grip on the firearm in his pocket and wrapped both arms around Jude. He felt the adrenalin dissipate.

'You okay?' he asked, lifting the face of Jude.

'Sure, just a scare,' she said somewhat unconvincingly. 'What about the cave?'

'Hasn't been used since the Bronze Age. Let's get to the car. Our day is over.'

ON THE RUN

• •

The very fast train pulled to an abrupt stop at the Avignon Railway Station, a short drive from Beaucaire. A slightly more relaxed Inspector Mack helped his wife from the train before returning to the carriage for the four fat suitcases and various pieces of hand luggage. He was glad to almost see the end of his long journey. It had been a difficult trip despite the comfort of first class, what with the worry of second-guessing his detective's jaunt to New Zealand. As tempted as he was in Singapore, and then later in Paris, to telephone the Auckland Hospital, he bothered not. Once or twice before, when he had attempted to source information on that near-dead pesky bed-and-breakfast woman, the snooty Charge Sister had insisted on knowing his name and rank, details he didn't care to pass on.

Dorothy knew that her husband had something significant on his mind. She'd seen that look a number of times in recent years, a look of uncertainty, of trouble looming. Just as she'd seen that same look on the face of her first husband, the bank robber. She'd suffered his moods until after the armed robberies when smiles returned to faces and good times rolled. And now her Mack too often had that same look; she didn't like it.

As Mack neatly stacked the suitcases on the railway platform, Dorothy rummaged up a porter's trolley to lend a hand. They were the last out of the side gate of the railway station, out to the carpark and into the dark. Standing alone, and waving for the Inspector, was Pierre, the local man Mack had been dealing with for many weeks; the man who had received 3000 euros in payment, via the Western Union office, for the 1990 model Citroën 2CV. It was still a secret from Dorothy, who was expecting a taxi to be waiting.

Pierre, in a strange and peculiar way, was standing to attention beside the driver's door of the 2CV as Mack approached, recognising the car, not the man. A confused Dorothy followed. She watched as Pierre stepped forward and handed over a set of keys. Mack, clasping

11TH JULY

the keys and offering his best version of *merci beaucoup* turned to his wife and handed her the keys along with the birthday card he had printed out weeks earlier. Dorothy instantly comprehended the surprise and squealed with delight.

As Mack stared longer at his new purchase, his mind drifted to a more imminent troublesome equation: how to fit so many suitcases and people into one tiny vehicle?

• •

The old oak tree growing in the grounds of the Base Hospital had the most perfect seat underneath. One of those old-fashioned timber-slatted park benches, each slat painted a different colour, just to brighten up the day. It was midday and Sandra was well into her novel, borrowed from a patient across the hallway. She lay on her back under the spreading branches, taking up the entire bench, flicking her eyes up from the book every now and then to watch the patterns made between leaves and sky. She had made her calls for the day, and fielded a few as well, none more important than that from Spud. His news, she was certain, would find its way onto every media broadcast in Australia: 'Cop's daughter dead from overdose'. Sandra had never met Chloe, although she'd seen her once or twice in her father's office, looking like death. As sad as the news was for any father, Sandra couldn't help but hope that she too could deliver a little more bad news to her boss, but of a different type. If only Lynette would drift into consciousness again.

She could hear herself being called from the distance. 'Detective!'

She recognised the voice of the Charge Sister, and she turned to see her frantically waving her back into the hospital. Sandra hurried across the lawn.

'She's been conscious about half an hour. We think it's probably safe for you to have a short conversation with her.'

They walked together to the ward.

Just as they reached Lynette's room, Sandra retrieved a large blow-up copy of Massimo's passport photograph from her briefcase, ready to show to Lynette. The sister, quick to decipher the purpose of the snapshot, blocked her way into the room.

'You are not to show her that photograph,' she instructed.

'Of course I am,' returned Sandra, whose patience was starting to wear thin with a woman who had been difficult every time they had spoken. The sister stood her ground and, almost nose to nose, issued the sternest of warnings in a loud whisper.

'This patient has spent weeks in a coma and has just drifted back into consciousness. If you dare to show her a photograph of her attacker she is very likely to return to that state. You will not show her any photograph. If you attempt to do so I will have you escorted from my ward.'

Sandra snapped back, 'How am I supposed to clear my sergeant's name then?'

'You're the detective. You work it out. Just keep your photographs in your briefcase.'

The sister marched away from the room towards her nursing station. Sandra quietly opened the door and tiptoed inside.

The bedside lamp to the far side was switched on, and Lynette sat partially up, illuminated by its soft glow. A young nurse sat with her and encouraged the intake of fluids. She smiled towards the detective and introduced the two women. A few moments earlier the young nurse had explained the visit of Detective Sandra Butler and had gained Lynette's consent for a brief conversation. She was lucid and more than willing to greet her Australian visitor.

'You've come a long way, Detective.'

'And so have you, Lynette.'

'The nurse said you've been here a couple of days, sleeping by my bed?'

'We've been worried for you, and are just so pleased that you're recovering.'

11TH JULY

'And you're a friend of Cole's, they said?' Lynette seemed somewhat confused by the association of the man she knew as an art dealer, and the detective.

'Yes,' was all Sandra could reply, and all she should have offered, bearing in mind the independence of the investigation.

'Cary will be pleased to meet you, and to know that you are Cole's friend,' she said.

Sandra looked across at the nurse who gave her a surreptitious wink. Sandra wasn't to know but, on doctor's orders, the nursing staff had informed a very worried Lynette that her husband was still alive and in another ward of the hospital. They hoped to reduce the shock for the patient, until she was well enough to deal with the truth.

'How is Cole? He's such a nice young man. How is he?'

Tears found their way to Sandra's cheeks at that point as she struggled with the tragedy of the situation that lay before Lynette in the next day or so. She desperately wanted to tell her that Cole had been framed for murder, that three attempts had been made on his life and that he was stuck somewhere in southern Italy, but the issue that choked her the most stared back at her from the other bedside table. In an ornate silver frame sat a photo of Cary, arm in arm with his beloved wife.

'He's fine, Lynette. He's home in Melbourne and sends his love.'

'I was worried, Detective, that that Italian man might have killed Cole.'

'What man, Lynette?'

'The man that did this to me, the man with the knife. The man that stayed at the Marlborough Hotel.'

Sandra opened her briefcase again to a frown from the young nurse, but this time she reached for a tissue. She'd heard enough to both know and prove that her friend was innocent of all allegations.

• •

ON THE RUN

The office of the Toe Cutters was hushed in silence only rarely present in a detectives' muster room. A respectful quiet, usually reserved for the most important of occasions: a big arrest at the end of a taskforce, the eclipse of an investigation. Such was the level of importance that the Toe Cutters had placed onto their probe into the activities of the corrupt Detective Donny Benjamin. It was Donny, they believed, who could lead them to a satisfying conclusion to the even more corrupt pastimes of his superior, the wily Inspector Mack. Donny's evidence would solve the New Zealand tragedy and unravel the corrupt connection between law enforcement and the Griffith Mafia.

There was an air of anticipation in the muster room as the detectives looked up expectantly at their leader, Superintendent Fountain. He had deliberately stepped out for a coffee to kill some time, knowing that the real killing would be felt by Donny, who even now was sitting alone in the locked interview room, awaiting his fate. He had spent a good portion of that day under guard in the police wing of the Royal Melbourne Hospital, the doctors and nursing staff there giving him the once-over for his cocaine ingestion, monitoring his progress until he was given the all clear. The Superintendent had then had him frogmarched down to the interview room, where he'd sat nervously now for the past couple of hours.

Apart from consuming half-a-dozen coffees and taking as many anxious toilet breaks, Detective Benjamin hadn't said a word. His choice of silence suited the Superintendent, as he himself was on stand-by, waiting for a call from Sandra. The last thing he needed to do was interview the catch of the year without being fully armed with all the facts. His mobile rang, just as he opened the interview room door. He continued in, answering the call.

'Detective Butler, how's New Zealand?' he asked, somewhat louder than necessary for Sandra's audibility, more for the convenience of his suspect.

Donny sat with his elbows on his knees, giving his best impression of total indifference, when in reality he was listening to every word

11TH JULY

of the conversation unfolding before him on the Superintendent's phone. He was desperately trying to work out a way through his mess.

'Well done ... fantastic ... wonderful. When can she return home? ... The Italian ... Massimo ... positive identification ... Griffith ... That's fabulous news, Detective Butler, and we're so pleased that Sergeant Goodwin has been cleared ... Yes, now Homicide Squad will take over ...' Fountain was privately pleased with the news about Cole but refrained from saying anything more than Donny needed to hear. He disconnected his call, turned his mobile off and dropped it on the desk in a deliberately aggressive manner. He pushed one of the two lattes he had purchased from the take-away café towards Donny, whose head was still bowed.

'I think we can probably start the interview now, Detective Benjamin.'

Donny remained true to his position, completely silent. The Superintendent switched on the audio tape. Once he had been through the mandatory procedure of time and date and letting the suspect know his rights, Superintendent Fountain got straight to the point.

'We can do this formally a little later on, Donny, for now let's just have a casual chat about it.'

Donny's 'no comment' attitude continued.

'You're fucked, Donny. And this is how our case will unfold. You've been under surveillance for weeks, in and out of every shit hole in Melbourne, selling drugs, taking cash, knocking off gear from raids, making telephone calls to the old Godfather in Griffith.'

The Superintendent noticed the first movement from Donny at the mention of the word 'Godfather'. Donny's head rose slightly until their eyes met.

'We've even got you photographed coming and going with Inspector Mack and the Godfather, in Lygon Street, Carlton, late one night.'

Donny casually, and almost arrogantly, remained silent, preferring to remove the plastic lid from the take-away cup, gulping at its contents.

'We've had the bag of powder found on your dining-room table analysed. Pure cocaine, Donny.'

Still silence from the chair opposite.

'We'll be charging you with the death of the Inspector's daughter.'

The Superintendent's comment found the chink in the armour of the corrupt police officer.

'She brought the bag of powder into my joint, and she told me to take some.'

'That's great, Donny, you just stick with that answer, that's absolutely fabulous—a naïve 21-year-old telling a 30-year-old detective what to do.'

'In the absence of anything else, that's the truth,' Donny replied with a smarmy little smirk.

'And you came home this morning at 5.55 a.m., took your jacket off and then your watch. Checked your emails, Chloe took a piss; you took the bag of powder out of your right trouser pocket, chopped it up with your Visa card and snorted two lines each. In the absence of anything else, that's the truth.'

For the first time since his arrest, Donny showed signs of losing the plot. He realised there must have been a camera inside his apartment. He knew he was fucked and began to nibble manically on his fingernails.

'And the Mafia, over the last few months, have had a hitman running around Australia and the rest of the fuckin' world, trying to kill an honest detective from the ACA … On the instructions of you and Inspector Mack, and in the absence of anything else, Donny, that's the truth also.'

This latest revelation by the Superintendent caused Donny's face to turn a sickly shade of grey. His eyes began to search frantically for a hole in the wall that he could crawl out of. It was now time for the Superintendent to drop a few trump cards on the table.

'And we've tracked the Mafia hitman from Calabria to Melbourne to Griffith to New Zealand, where he murdered the old-timer and attempted to murder his wife. Who, I might add, has now positively identified him. And we've got your phone taps talking your cocky head off to the Godfather in Griffith, including helping with the importation of a container-load of drugs.'

He then dropped into Donny's lap the brochure of the Citroën 2CV with the notations in Inspector Mack's handwriting.

Fountain eased back in his chair and waited for the full reaction, knowing, of course, that everything he'd said was correct—except for the taped phone conversations, which were a bluff. He also knew it would be the bluff card that worked hardest on Donny. He only hoped Donny really had made a few mobile telephone calls to the Godfather, and that the calls were damaging.

Fountain sat and watched a man in strife, a man pondering his next ten years in ten seconds. Donny's nervous system reacted so adversely to the shock revelations that he, like Chloe, attempted to stand from his seated position. Fountain shifted in his own chair and braced the table. Then, as had Chloe, Donny's shoulders and chest started to convulse, and he vomited all seven coffees over his shirt front.

The Superintendent pressed 'stop' on the recorder.

12th July

Tommy's BlackBerry rang for the first time in its short life. It sat on the beautiful marble surface of the bedside table of his suite at the Hotel la Casa di Giama in the centre of Gerace. The hotel, chosen by Mario, was completely free of any associations with the N'Drangheta. He leaned across Jude to grab it. She stirred but then buried her head back under the covers.

'Yo,' was the only response he offered as he answered. It was Sandra, finishing up her long day. She was halfway between the Melbourne airport and home, and couldn't resist passing on the news, the same news that the Superintendent had passed on to her only moments earlier. News of the complete and unequivocal admissions of Detective Benjamin, relating to more than three years of corruption and conspiracy with Inspector Mack as well as the many meetings and arrangements with the Griffith Mafia, who had imported Massimo to kill Cole ... on and on Donny had apparently babbled, interrupted only by the occasional coffee belch or request for toilet breaks.

'So you can come back home now, Cole. And stop calling yourself Tommy or Robert, or anyone else you have been hiding behind.'

By now Cole was well awake. He was delighted he was no longer a wanted man but he had no intention of returning home immediately.

'We have to find the cave, Sandra. Then we'll come straight back.'

'Leave it to your Italian mates, Cole. Just come home. It's over.'

'It's not over till Massimo's locked up, Sandra. For Jude or me.'

'The New Zealand detectives will have Massimo identified for Cary's murder in a couple of weeks, once Lynette is strong enough to view his photo. Just come home, please.'

12TH JULY

'Jude and I would always be looking over our shoulders. We will be home in a few days, promise. Too much can happen in a couple of weeks, Sandra.'

'Crazy man.'

'Good woman, you. And thanks for New Zealand.'

'You're welcome. Say hello to Jude.'

'And I'll say hello to Leigh,' said Cole with a smile. 'I heard a little story the other day, about you and him.'

'Good night, Boss.'

'Good morning, Detective.' Cole leant across Jude again to replace the phone on the bedside table. She stirred again, rubbing her shoulders in to the pillow, and accepting Cole into her arms.

'Sounded like good news, handsome.'

'It's official. I can be Cole again.' He nuzzled into her.

• •

The owner of Café La Vista on the Plati piazza was a little surprised as she opened the door that morning to a crowded set of outside tables and chairs. She hadn't even turned on the coffee machine and already she had a notepad full of espressos. Massimo sat at the head with his lieutenants, Illario and Giuseppe, to each side of him and a few underling thugs kitted out in overalls ready for a heavy day's work completed the table. There was a violent wind ripping through the township, uncharacteristic for that time of year and enough to raise goosebumps on even the toughest of Calabrian punks.

Around the corner wandered Lydia. She too was up bright and early, as she had to be at school in less than an hour for her final exam.

'Uncle Massimo. You have never been up so early in all your life!' she joked as she kissed her father 'hello' and then walked over to her favourite uncle.

'Go to school and get smart,' Massimo instructed with a smile.

'Yes, Uncle; *ciao, Papà*,' she said as she again kissed her father.

'Lydia, please do me one quick favour,' Massimo requested.

'*Si, si*, Uncle.'

'It's cold and I have to wait for my coffee. Can you run over to my apartment and get me a jacket?'

With more enthusiasm than would normally be expected from a teenager on an errand, she seized upon his keys, calling out 'Of course, Uncle' as she skipped across the piazza to the door of Massimo's dwelling.

The espressos were placed in the centre of the table.

Massimo requested an additional coffee as he looked across to the other end of the piazza and an approaching, somewhat dishevelled, older man.

• •

Lydia bounded up the flight of stairs and into the main room of the aged building. She looked around for a likely place for a jacket in the middle of summer. Taking herself into Massimo's bedroom, she opened an ornate antique wardrobe and grabbed the first jacket she found. As she started to walk from the room, she stopped and glanced to her left through the window that overlooked the café and the now seven seated men, all busy in conversation. The seventh and older man was the poorly dressed peasant nit-keeper who had scared Jude the previous evening in the forest. He'd come to explain his sighting of a girl with long blonde hair and a tall, strapping man, looking into a cave. Lydia felt sure that the group would stay seated for a moment.

She carefully opened the top drawer of the bedside credenza, as she had done once or twice previously. She pocketed a couple of loose packaged condoms and moved on to the back of the drawer. She knew exactly where to look. The old Cuban cigar box sat temptingly beneath a neat stack of underwear. Lydia opened it. Quickly snatching one of a few clear plastic bags, with ten ecstasy tablets

12TH JULY

within, and placing the items securely in her skirt pocket, she walked briskly back down the stairs with Massimo's jacket.

By the time she had delivered it and the apartment's keys to their owner, the old man had finished his tale. Six men sat around a table, all frowning.

'*Grazie, Lydia,*' Massimo said, still deep in thought and thousands of miles away from the conversation. He realised his niece was saying goodbye.

'*Ciao, ciao*, Lydia, and be good at that dance party tonight.'

• •

The wind that was whipping through the Aspromonte Mountains didn't reach across the Mediterranean to Provence. The morning was sheer heaven. At least that's how Dorothy summed it up as she padded barefoot across the marble-tiled floor of their large bedroom with a tray of coffee and croissants. Her lemon chiffon gown with its matching feather-boa collar shimmered as she walked. Her husband sat proudly up in bed. Their smiles met, as did their coffee cups, as Dorothy snuggled back into bed.

'Are you confident that nothing from New Zealand can come back to you?' she asked, having extracted his worries from him the night before, halfway through a bottle of vintage Moet & Chandon.

Mack was decidedly more comfortable with the New Zealand problem this morning, having slept on it now for more than two days. He was certain that his worst-case scenario was that the wretched bed-and-breakfast woman might identify Massimo, but nothing could lead back to him directly. And he would warn Massimo when he saw him in Calabria the following morning to collect the balance of the million dollars.

'When are you going to turn your phone back on, darling?'

'It stays off until after we've got the money.'

'But won't that dago Mafia man want to talk to you?'

'No, darling. It's all locked in, all arranged. Nothing to worry about, my pet. From the moment we left home, till the moment we've hidden the money, that phone will stay off. No interruptions for us, my sweet, and no way any prying cops can track my phone.'

'What time's your ferry leaving, handsome?' Dorothy asked as she wriggled closer to her husband.

'Four o'clock, petal. Plenty of time for us, don't you think?' Mack answered as he placed his hands gently on the nape of Dorothy's neck and let his fingers wander down to the delicate lace-covered buttons at the top of her negligee.

• •

The big Italian *Commissario*'s hands skimmed across the surface of his topographical map, an identical copy to the one carried by Jude and Leigh, who were in the forest on their second and last day of searching. The *Commissario*, Cole and Mario were finishing up a meeting before heading off to the RV to wait for the afternoon.

'They won't be late back this time, I can promise,' Cole said.

'No problem, Robin Hood,' grinned the big man.

'So what happens if they don't find a cave by tonight?'

'We bring in the Assault Team and the tanks, and scour Plati and San Luca,' said the *Commissario*. 'We have a hundred men who will re-do the mountain; we'll block the port so no ships can leave, and spend the next week searching for the drugs.'

'We'll find them,' vowed Mario. 'In the meantime we have to get to the RV.'

As they rose from their table and rolled up the map, the wind hit the courtyard, throwing leaves and debris against the back windows and door.

• •

12TH JULY

Mid-afternoon found Cole sitting impatiently in the rear seat of a nondescript car parked in dense brush at the RV. Alongside him, the ever-serene *Commissario* flicked quietly through pages of reports. Even Mario, calmly ensconced in the driver's seat, listening intently to the low hum of a police radio, was devoid of conversation. The silence of his companions, broken only by the constant whistling of the wind and the regular smack of leaves as they peppered the side of the car, had Cole on edge. Their covert hidey-hole was becoming claustrophobic. Just then the *Commissario* asked to inspect the 9mm Browning that Cole had taken from Pino during their fight on the Venice train; he needed to log the make and serial number for later investigation. Cole gladly handed the weapon across and decided to take a walk. He quietly closed the passenger door and let loose the build-up of nervous energy in his legs. Pushing through the wind, head down, hands deep in his jacket pockets, his thoughts drifted back to the audacious sting that he and Jude had pulled off against the N'Drangheta, and now here he was wandering aimlessly through the rugged forest of the Aspromonte, looking for something that no other investigator could find, a booty of drugs. Madness, he thought.

A crack under foot startled him. He looked up and spun a full circle, squinting through the semi-darkness of the woods. A leaf hit his face; he pulled it away and looked again. The *Commissario*'s car was well behind him now, far in the distance. Another crack. He focused well off towards a clump of oak trees, skirted by wild thistle bushes. Something moved—Cole saw an image, a silhouette, easing back behind a tree, a male figure. He sprinted ahead a dozen paces and took cover behind a similar oak tree, then peered out. The male figure was also looking at him, face on. Cole and Massimo stared at each other, only twenty metres apart, fallen leaves blowing in the air. Cole pulled his head back and rested, breathing heavily, back against the bark. Instinctively he reached for a firearm that wasn't there. He thought of racing back to the car, yelling to Mario and the *Commissario*, but held back. He feared for Jude and Leigh, who were still out there, somewhere. He slowly peered back but Massimo was gone.

ON THE RUN

• •

The wind buffeted Jude's map, turning it inside out and creating a lengthy tear down the centre. Her hair had blown into her face and she was struggling to focus as she found a tree to shelter behind. She looked up momentarily, and it appeared as if the whole floor of the forest had been blown up into the air, spinning crazily in the lower stratosphere before it settled, completely blanketing their car. From high above she heard the loud crack of a branch as it crashed from the topmost reaches of the canopy to the ground, perilously close to where she stood. She looked around anxiously for Leigh, who had planned to check a small cave nearby, just as she too was to tick off one only metres from where she now huddled against the trunk of an old pine. With her map folded awkwardly into a squarish pad, she pushed it down the back of her jeans and under her blouse. She gathered her bearings as best she could and crab-stepped tentatively down a few metres to the entrance of her cave, taking one last glance for Leigh who was obviously still busy elsewhere.

The howling wind hit her once more, the cold sending shivers through her core. She attempted several times unsuccessfully to sweep her thick straight hair from her face while shielding her eyes with both hands; otherwise, she may well have noticed the excessive number of footprints and the half-dozen cigarette butts at the cave's small entrance. She ducked her head slightly to clear the threshold of the well-camouflaged opening and shone her torch inside. To her amazement, the cave was massive—and empty. She decided to step in and shelter out of the wind, and perhaps have one quick look towards the rear, an area beyond the shine of a torch. Four paces in and she could see the back end of the cave fifteen metres away, a vast cavernous vault. It felt unusually warm; she had expected it, like all the other caves, to be chilly and eerie. A little confused at this peculiarity, she dropped the light of her torch down towards her feet. There, lying in the dirt, were a dozen loose, pearly white ecstasy tablets. Jude turned around quickly to leave and find Leigh. She faced instead a smiling Massimo.

• •

'*Juuuude!*' echoed through the forest. An exhausted Leigh ran, yelling, first in one direction then another. The best he could do was run short distances in different directions, yelling her name as loudly as he could. Most of his calls were lost to the wind, and Leigh was lost to his search. He had been scouring the area for more than an hour now, becoming disoriented at the noise of the wind. He turned a full 360 degrees, stress ripping across his face. He had lost sight of the car. He pulled the .32 pistol from the front of his trousers and yelled again: '*Juuuuude!*' A massive crack of thunder broke over the dark forest floor.

• •

The *Commissario* had changed tack in his investigation many hours earlier, throwing every man, motorcycle, four-wheel drive and powerful floodlight into the forest. The need for being covert in the massive N'Drangheta investigation had been abandoned. A visiting international detective was missing. The wild storm continued to play havoc, making D'Alfonso's work much more difficult than he would have liked. He, Mario and Cole had found Leigh some hours earlier, slumped against the grille of the rental car, exactly where the picnicking couple had originally parked it. Leigh's lone fruitless search had left him totally fatigued, dehydrated and depleted of any of his considerable reserves of strength.

The car was now isolated and surrounded by crime-scene tape, and Leigh, having been checked over by paramedics, had joined Cole in the wait for information on their partner. The big Italian

Commissario stood over the bonnet of a four-wheel drive issuing instructions to an army of well-equipped *Carabinieri* who had just arrived. Like giant fire flies, dozens of torches danced and flickered between the trunks of the tall trees on his horizon as an earlier group searched for clues. After setting the tasks for the newest arrivals, he regained some valuable solitude to enable him to consider his next move. He privately feared that he knew exactly what had happened to Jude. He couldn't bring himself to discuss his suspicions with his two Australian detective friends, least of all Cole, who leant, hunched and gutted, against the trunk of a nearby oak tree. Had it really been Massimo, or had it just been the stress, manifested in the form of the face of his adversary, in a darkening forest? He asked himself this question over and over, and got no answers.

The *Commissario* was walking towards him as he heard the frantic calls of Mario: '*Commissario, Commissario!*' He turned and bolted in the direction of Mario's torch, not fifty metres away. It became a scramble as to which of the three men would arrive first at the cave entrance, to stand alongside Mario who was shining his torch towards the well-camouflaged opening and onto the many footprints and cigarette butts outside. The first thing Leigh could think of was of how absurdly close the cave entrance was to the parked vehicle. Strangely, the head of the Anti-Mafia unit didn't concern himself with that particular detail. He was more fascinated at the perfect choice of cave by the N'Drangheta, so inconspicuous in the thick of the forest. The thing that struck Mario was that at that exact moment the storm, the wind and the thunder stopped completely. There was an eerie silence as the four stood looking at the entrance and also at each other.

Mindful to preserve any footprint evidence, Cole, overdosing on anxiety, snatched the torch from Mario, stepped clear of the still-preserved imprints in the dirt surface, and bent down onto his knees to push the dense brush aside. He shone the powerful light into the cave and four heads lowered simultaneously to peer in. Still lying dry on the cave floor were a dozen ecstasy tablets but next to them was a

12TH JULY

sight that sent shivers through the four men. In the dead centre of the cave lay Jude's map, opened fully, corner to corner, with a knife fastening it to the dirt floor.

13th July

It was extraordinarily busy for a Friday. No one was winding down; in fact the entire southern peninsula of Calabria was seeing more law enforcement activity than it had since the day Mario's father had been murdered. Carload after carload of *Poliziotti* converged on the area to help in what was now being broadcast as an international incident. Lina's kitchen, in fact Mario's whole modest villa, had become the command post, with *Commissario* D'Alfonso moving from house phone to mobile to radio transmitter as he directed the search, primarily for Jude but also for the 15 million ecstasy tablets. Mario passed him Cole's BlackBerry for the umpteenth time.

'*Pronto*,' he answered.

It was Spud on the other end. They had been talking for most of the morning.

'Did you get the fax?' asked Spud.

The *Commissario* turned to the portable fax machine plugged in on top of the washing machine. He walked across and pulled the pages free, numerous sheets of colour photographs of Inspector Mack.

'*Si, si*, Spud.'

'His corrupt mate Donny, in Melbourne, has coughed up some more information. Apparently Inspector Mack is due to arrive in Reggio this morning to collect nearly a million dollars from Massimo.'

The *Commissario* handed the photographs onto Mario, whispering an instruction in his ear and pointing to Leigh, who was assisting other Anti-Mafia investigators, crossing off the searched caves on a new map. D'Alfonso continued his conversation with Spud as Mario grabbed Leigh's arm and pulled him towards the front door.

'We must go. Your boss is coming to Reggio,' he told the rejuvenated Leigh. The *Commissario* removed the coffee cup from his lips, the BlackBerry Bold from his ear, and called out to the two men as they walked through the door, 'Mario, shut down Porto Gioia Tauro—nothing leaves!'

The pair left the house and fought their way through the media to a squad car.

• •

As Mario's squad car raced from Gerace to Reggio, Cole trudged exhaustedly over the same territory he'd walked since last night in the Aspromonte Mountains. Over and over, he paced the earth. Around him, scattered loosely in pairs, were support search teams of the uniformed *Carabinieri*. Yet nothing had stirred in the forest since the wind had fallen away at midnight. Cole rested briefly and leant his right shoulder against a tree, pushing his left hand deep into his trouser pocket. He pulled his fist free and opened his hand to once again stare at the twelve pearly white ecstasy tablets and a smattering of dirt from the cave floor. He shoved them back into his pocket and resumed his search.

• •

The *Neptune* overnight ferry from Marseille to Reggio, via Palermo in Sicily, had now docked. Inspector Mack had slept like a baby, all things considered. He'd paid for a double cabin, ensuring that he would be alone and comfortable on this most important of journeys. As he had said to Dorothy, whom he had left after lunch, this would be 'the beginning of the end' of his long career. Once he had returned home, they would set about hiding their money in a false wall they intended to build between the bedroom and the dining room. The building materials needed for the construction had arrived only a few hours before he left their Beaucaire haven. Dorothy would oversee the local carpenter complete the task, until Mack returned in a few days' time with the lovely. It was around that time that the DHL international freight courier had delivered their packing chest with the clothing that would see them through the winter months to come—and with the secreted stash of money.

It was all running so smoothly, Mack had thought, as he struggled with the chest, heaving it up the stairs to the apartment to be locked away until his return. The false wall had kept his mind ticking overnight on that ferry ride, in between sips from his half-bottle of Gordon's gin.

The ferry's huge, rusted, metal crossover-cum-drawbridge winched downwards onto terra firma. Mack kicked life into the tiny Citroën 2CV, rolling it over the metal and into Italy. With a brief flash of his passport to an uninterested customs official, he was waved on to the streets of San Giovanni, and pushed on into the traffic to Reggio, a few kilometres away, the capital of Calabria.

• •

Complete silence hung in the muster room of the ACA office in Melbourne; not a single investigator had gone home. Every member of the team was hunched over a desk staring at the various TV monitors, catching the late news. The lead item showed a photograph of Jude in better times. Information concerning the suspected importation of ecstasy had been fed through an otherwise impenetrable united front to the hungry journalists. Solidarity and camaraderie kept the hard-working officers of the Australian Crime Authority glued to their seats.

It was the next occurrence that took everyone's eyes from the TV monitors, yet surprised none. Spud and Sandra were at each end of Inspector Mack's office desk, midway through lifting it into the common office area. They struggled through the doorway. As they reached the main security door, the other investigators seemed to cotton on to their endeavour, and lent a hand. The whole squad either helped in carrying the desk and its chair and coat rack or opened the various doors, all the way through the building to the street level. Without a word, they plonked the desk unceremoniously onto the footpath, as well as its accompaniments, and quietly filed back into the building, to pick up the news stories again.

• •

An empathetic Superintendent Fountain sat in his car at the front of the building, having just come to a stop. He watched the furniture removal escapade. It was obvious that the squad was hurting in more ways than one. Once the detectives had all re-entered the building, Fountain quietly stepped from his vehicle and, circumnavigating the office ensemble, continued up the steps to sign himself in. He completely understood the anguish of the crew. Apart from the corrupt behaviour of one inspector, he had great admiration for an exemplary body of people. Besides, he had a late-night meeting with the director to seek a provisional extradition warrant for Inspector Mack—once he was located.

• •

The roller door to the dispatch depot of the La Cucina canning company in the industrial zone of San Gregorio had been slammed shut since the Anti-Mafia unit arrived. Two machine gun–wielding *Carabinieri* stood out the front as their investigative team scoured the factory. With no contraband located, they walked back to their squad cars, dejected. Four blocks away at La Nova canning company, a similar raid was underway. The drama on this occasion was not drug-related; rather, it centred on the otherwise honest proprietors. A small brawl had developed inside the factory, their reaction to the insult of being raided. After a short time, however, the Anti-Mafia unit again moved on, disappointed that it had located nothing sinister.

Simultaneously, the eight food canning companies in Reggio Calabria were hit, locked down and searched. The production of cannellini beans, *pomodoro sugo*, peeled tomatoes and artichokes had come to an abrupt halt in town. The industrial streets now swelled with angry workers, mostly women, annoyed at the heavy-handed ways of the Napoli and Roma Anti-Mafia units. Hundreds of disgruntled employees, an army of blue-uniformed, white-capped peasant labour, moved through the streets, spitting vitriol at the truck-loads of *Carabinieri* who stood sentry on every corner. On the horizon hung container cranes, frozen, as armed police ringed off the entrance and exit and every gangway on the massive port. All manifests were seized and had been safely transported to the hands of the investigating magistrate. By afternoon, the women were joined by husbands and sons as they marched on to the Piazza Grande. Still, the shipment of ecstasy remained missing. A now very tired *Commissario* D'Alfonso stood on the top step of the *Municipio* building and discreetly watched a new storm brewing.

• •

Inspector Mack, like a few other brave—or possibly stupid—motorists, pressed on through the midst of the army of protestors in the tiny Citroën. He'd advance a metre or two, then stop, and then another couple of metres and stop again, edging his way painfully, slowly, through the melee. He had taken a risk with the crowd—and occasionally the flimsy little car was rocked from side to side as hands banged on the pristine duco—but he'd taken a lot of risks in recent weeks. Every now and again a tough and angry Calabrian would break into laughter at the odd shape and look of the ugly duckling car. Mack worried most about the couple of attempts the crowd made

13TH JULY

to open the doors, for it was what he had stashed behind the rear seat that was his greatest concern.

He'd spent a good part of his visit to the capital city parked illegally down a back laneway in the industrial estate in San Leo. Massimo had made him sweat it out. He seemed to enjoy delaying the Inspector's receipt of his million dollars, disappearing as he did for a couple of hours to put together the money before returning to help secrete the tennis sports bag behind the back seat of the small car. It was a last-minute conversion of Australian dollars to euros that slowed the Inspector down most. He had come to the meeting with an up-to-date conversion rate, and felt that the Mafia had undercut him by $10 000 or thereabouts. A bewildered Massimo, not one for figures unless they were female, baulked at the attitude of the Australian as he argued his end of the bargain. Massimo just ached to cut the throat of the ageing imbecile, and would have—save for the fact that he was absolutely necessary to the export of the ecstasy and its subsequent safe arrival in Australia, now and in the future. Eventually, he agreed to the Inspector's demand, paid out a few euros more, and handed him a full copy of the manifest for the shipment to Australia.

The Inspector felt uneasy with the way in which Massimo had conducted the affair and didn't bother with the request for him to do away with Donny Benjamin at a later date, nor did he bother warning Massimo of his impending arrest for the murder of the New Zealander. He was now more concerned with fleeing with his lovely. And after all, he thought, Donny wasn't a bad sort of bloke, and he hadn't done him any harm.

• •

Mario and Leigh had just finished checking the last of the arriving ferries, a hydrofoil from Lipari Island, full of sunburnt tourists who whined at their slow egress from the vessel. It would be the last inspection for the day, as none of the ferries were returning to their points of origin to bring additional passengers; they were all tied up on the dock. Mario fielded a mobile call from his *Commissario*, who was still overseeing the near riot in the piazza.

'*Pronto.*'

'Mario, we need to speak to your informer again.'

'*Si, si, Commissario.*'

'We're going backwards here. He has to help us again.'

'*Si, si.* I'll pick you up and take you there.'

'*Bravo.* But go around the town and beware of the piazza.'

'*Grazie.*'

Mario turned to Leigh and explained that it was time to leave. They both handed their photographs of Inspector Mack to the team of *Carabinieri* guarding the wharf, before stepping back into their squad car. Mario took to the relatively empty, narrow laneways. He dropped the gear box of the Alfa Romeo down a cog or two and roared through the familiar network at breakneck speed, giving Leigh a white-knuckle ride.

Mario stopped once only before they gathered up the *Commissario*, for a run of traffic consisting of four cars heading out of town in the opposite direction. A route that wove past the port on the A3 autostrada on the road that goes directly to Naples, Rome and further north. Unbeknown to them both, the second car in this run was driven by Inspector Mack, the fully laden Citroën 2CV, heading in the direction that would eventually take him around to France, and then home in twelve or so hours. Mario sped on through the southern end of town, to the coastal road running along the Mediterranean, in the opposite direction.

The Alfa roared up the ten kilometres of road off the beach highway, coming to a halt on the top of the hill at the other Mafia stronghold, San Luca. As had been the case in Plati, it had been surrounded by police all day. D'Alfonso's vehicle was given immediate clear passage and it sprung to life again, heading straight to the centre of town, braking sharply in the tiny piazza, beside a small basilica. The three men strode from the car down three or four lanes towards the edge of town to face the aged and weathered façade of the finest villa in the region. They banged softly on the 200-year-old timber door with the heavy knocker. A quaint, almost delicate *Signora* pulled open the door. Oddly, the woman of the house bowed at the sight of the big man and his friends. She seemed to recognise Mario, and motioned them in before closing the door behind them.

They were led, without comment, through the grand old palazzo, past unpolished antiques and tired paintings, alongside heavy drapes, across the rippled surface of terrazzo to a rear courtyard where the aged man of the house sat under a wisteria that was almost as old as he. He was halfway through devouring a peach, taking thin slices with a finely sharpened small knife. He watched with affection as his brindle-coated whippet, with its long narrow snout, licked the inner surface of an empty can of Chow Ciao dog food, nudging it noisily across the terracotta-tiled surface. The Godfather of the San Luca clan offered his three guests a seat, as his wife followed with a jug of home-made lemon granita and a set of glasses.

'Young Mario,' began the Godfather. 'You have closed my town.' He shifted his eyes to Leigh. 'And this must be the Australian we have heard of?'

'One of them, *Signore*,' replied Mario.

'Why have you lost sight of the shipment?' the old man asked as he rose and walked over to the ornate wrought-iron aviary, stocked with illegal North African birdlife. He fed a slice of peach to a red-crested parakeet that had shoved its beak expectantly through the bars.

'We are searching everywhere, *Signore*. The mountains, the canneries, the ships, Plati.'

'And you haven't found it?' He turned and sat back down heavily on his chair.

'No. That's why we've come to see you.'

'I have helped you many times now, Mario. You forget ... I helped you find the laboratory in Germania.' The Godfather looked at the big man. 'Do you not remember, *Commissario*, I helped you to get rid of the Plati gang who killed our six sons?'

'And we are very grateful for your help, *Signore*,' said the humble but still proud D'Alfonso. 'We couldn't have come this far without your valued assistance. But you have enjoyed your revenge, now let us finish the job.'

'And so you've come back to the well, *Commissario*.'

'I've come back to the hand that works with me just this once,' said D'Alfonso.

The *Commissario* watched the tired yet supremely relaxed old man skilfully take another sliver from his peach; spearing it with his knife, he offered it to the policeman.

'Answer me one question, *Commissario*. Is it because you have lost the shipment or is it because you have lost a pretty blonde girl? Think hard,' he said. 'All rests on whether I help you even more.'

The *Commissario* thought as he watched the whippet, which had now given up on the pristine can and nestled in for a nap at his owner's feet.

'It's for Mario and the memory of his father, that's why I ask.'

The old man looked across at Mario, whose head was bowed.

'You know, young Mario, that the Plati clan killed your father?'

Mario nodded without speaking.

'Then your answer is a good answer, *Commissario*. Massimo came to see me yesterday. He asked to use my own cannery to pack his drugs. He pleaded with me, after killing our six sons.' The old Godfather shook his head slowly in disbelief before continuing, 'Because he knows you are watching the other canneries.'

'Do you have a cannery, *Signore*?' asked Mario.

The Godfather cast his eyes down at the beloved whippet and then across at the empty tin. His last words on the subject were, 'You must hurry. He was packing it this morning. Now take your men from my town.'

Mario bent down and picked up the dog food tin. The packaging address was printed clearly on the back of the label: San Leo, in Reggio, one suburb away from San Gregorio.

13TH JULY

• •

The Supervisor of the *Carabinieri* search team had just finished addressing his men. He was standing in the centre of the only clearing in the area. The men had worked consistently on east to west grids and then repeated their effort north to south, convinced they had searched every cave in the Aspromonte Mountains. The supervisor fully intended to take the search on to the docks and each vessel that was tied to the moorings. There was a solid couple of days' work ahead of them, and he began to dispatch his instructions. Midway through, a police helicopter eased from the sky onto the clearing, causing the team to dissipate. It had come to collect Cole, under advice from D'Alfonso, to take him to the port, where he might like to assist in the unfolding search. In no time Cole had said his goodbyes and was in the air. He would be in Reggio in minutes.

• •

Mario hurtled down the San Luca road to the coast, drifting his vehicle onto the siding at every turn until he finally braked at the T-intersection at Porto Bonamico. The highway traffic was full of holiday-makers. They allowed a large royal blue transport to pass before swinging onto the highway in the opposite direction. Mario gunned it as fast as he could towards Reggio. His *Commissario* was in the front, holding tight to the seat with one hand and, with the other hand, clutching a tin of dog food. Leigh was in the back seat looking through the rear-view mirror at the royal blue truck that had just gone past them in the opposite direction. He placed both his hands onto the rear of the *Commissario*'s headrest and pulled himself forward, leaning in to the free space between the two front occupants. The car was now travelling at 160 kilometres per hour.

Leigh stared at the tin in the *Commissario*'s hand and the royal blue label that spelt out Chow Ciao, the same name as on the tarpaulin on the passing truck.

ON THE RUN

He looked up with a tinge of renewed excitement and said to the big man, 'The truck carrying the drugs has just gone past us.'

'What, Leigh?' queried the big man in disbelief.

'The arse-wipe's just gone past.'

Mario brought the Alfa Romeo to a screeching halt in a cloud of white smoke, before executing a near-perfect 180-degree turn in the oncoming traffic. He worked some heat into the gear box as it raced forwards. It was now Massimo who was on the run.

• •

Inspector Mack was starting to lose patience with his wife's quirky little car, with the two-cylinder engine that didn't seem to want to go fast enough. Although he was now a hundred or more kilometres north of Reggio, halfway to the border of Campagna en route to Naples, he wondered when in the hell he would get home at this 80-kilometres-per-hour crawl. He pulled in to the wayside stop on the freeway at Falerna. It was certainly a beautiful part of the road, raised above the ground on forty-metre pylons at the gulf of Santa Eufemia. It afforded stunning views across the water to the seven Aeolian islands, the most prominent of which was Stromboli. As the Inspector alighted from his vehicle to stretch his cramped legs and allow the tiny engine of his getaway car to cool down for a spell, he mused on the possibility of turning on his mobile phone for the first time in four days. He was, he thought, safe—and very fucking wealthy.

The telecommunication network's mobile roaming system sprang to life. He was confused, however, by the constant pinging of his phone once it switched on. One message, two, three, four: on and on it beeped in an extraordinarily quick fashion, forty-eight new messages in total. He stared at the screen filled with foreboding. He leant on the bonnet of the car to collect his thoughts. He sighed and looked back at the incessantly flashing blue light on his phone and did what he had to do. He listened to the first message.

13TH JULY

∴

Mario knew the slow corners and the fast bends. The Alfa was immediately behind the fully laden semi-trailer. The *Commissario* was busy on the police radio, calling for assistance. He had ordered that the freeway be blocked at the Roccella bypass, the newest section of the highway. At this speed it was less than ten minutes away and the perfect location to pull up a truck, as the road surface was elevated ten metres. No escape.

The first response, in fact the only response thus far, was from the helicopter transporting Cole. It had only been airborne a couple of minutes. The pilot banked to the left. Leigh heard the adrenalin in the captain's voice.

'We'll be at the Roccella bypass in three minutes, *Commissario*.'

'Then land on the Roccella bypass,' came the instruction from the chief of operations.

The pilot demanded a repeat of the order, normal procedure in such a potentially dangerous manoeuvre. The big man had no hesitation in reiterating his demand.

'Land ON Roccella bypass!'

Mario held his position immediately behind the truck. There were two potential turn-offs ahead, one after the other in quick succession, both towards Marina, a seaside village riddled with cheap and nasty hotels and Russian prostitutes. To their relief, the last turn-off disappeared; they were on the right track.

The helicopter with the *Carabinieri* livery appeared in the sky about one kilometre ahead of them. Cole looked both left and right and helped guide the helicopter in, as he reached for his handgun. There was no turning back now.

'Down, down,' commanded Cole as he looked up to see the truck fast approaching. The pilot hesitated momentarily.

'Down, now!' Cole ordered, watching, face on, the cabin of the prime mover get larger.

The pilot eased the helicopter expertly into the centre of the autostrada as the brake lights on the transport flashed on brightly and its screeching wheels began to lock. Mario struggled with his steering wheel to keep the Alfa Romeo immediately behind the truck and hidden from the view of the driver, who was reducing the speed of his semi-trailer at an alarming rate. Cole and the pilot waited a few seconds for the blades to lose some velocity before opening their doors and jumping onto the roadway. Cole stood his ground for few seconds, gun raised, before he turned and ran after the pilot.

The rear tarpaulin, now only five metres away from the windscreen of the Alfa, was flung open, to reveal Massimo, Illario and Giuseppe all standing in front of forty tonnes of tin cans, the intended contents of which had been largely replaced at the cannery during the long previous night. Each of them was holding an Uzi submachine gun. Mario braked instantly, broad-siding the vehicle at right angles to the road. The Alfa's tyres were peppered with rounds.

They watched as the truck suddenly accelerated forwards and the three men each emptied a clip of rounds just short of the Alfa. At the opposite end of the highway, Cole and his pilot were sprinting, and glancing back at the truck, grinding its gears and racing forward towards them. It was evident that both men needed to be clear of the elevated freeway to avoid the collision. But they were trapped ten metres above the ground; a jump would surely cripple if not kill them. Foreseeing such an outcome, the *Commissario*, Leigh and Mario ran towards the rear of the truck, each with a handgun aimed and ready to fire. At a speed of 150 kilometres an hour and with a gross weight of 52 tonnes, the semi-trailer, its driver, passenger and the three *Mafiosi* from the hills of Calabria hit the recently refuelled chopper with its nearly full tank, and exploded in a massive ball of orange and yellow flames.

One week later

The only thing shared by the trio of hilltop towns of San Luca, Plati and Gerace was their perfect views to the marina below, and out across the Mediterranean. On a clear day Africa was visible, or so the locals bragged. Otherwise, the towns kept to themselves.

It had been a busy week.

Jude was still missing.

The small Citroën 2CV still sat unobtrusively at the wayside lookout at Falerna, covered in freeway dust. A gang of highway bandits had gotten to it, removing the quirky hood-badge, grille and even the two front tyres. Otherwise, it was just as Inspector Mack had parked it before attending to his string of messages. The doors were locked, the pristine interior was still neat and tidy, although free of any luggage and, of course, free of the lovely. A cursory vehicle registration check by passing *Carabinieri* the night before, upon observing the missing front wheels, traced the ownership to a Pierre Leblanc in Provence. It was just another dumped vehicle littering the autostrada.

On the Roccella freeway on the opposite coastal peninsula, the municipal traffic police had only just reopened the carriageway, having finally cleared the burnt remains of the semi-trailer, its illicit contents and the helicopter. The only evidence of the world-shattering news event that remained was the charred surface of the road and a half-dozen mangy dogs that scoured the area for the few remaining broken tins on the roadway.

In the main piazza of San Luca was gathered a great portion of the town, sitting happy and united again; a feast was underway. The aged Don of the *Mafioso* clan wandered contentedly through his domain, with his whippet close at his heels. It had been a quiet week for the old man; no one had connected the dots and he was confident no one ever would. He thought, as he looked out across the waterfront towards Locri, of renewing telephone contact with Otto, just to see how his suntan was faring, and when he might be thinking of returning.

In the piazza in Plati sat the sole figure of a melancholy teenage girl, on the chair at the Café La Vista normally occupied by her uncle. The town was empty and the church bells had gone silent long ago. Lydia had lost her virginity and her innocence. More tragically, she had lost her father, her uncle, three other town friends, and the town's Godfather, who had died from grief almost before the dirt had hit the lids of the other coffins. She had also lost her desire to live, for even another day, in Plati.

The disappointment. The waste.

There was no reason to stay. But she could see a life to be made elsewhere, perhaps university in Torino in northern Italy, away from the drugs, the anger and the vendetta.

Seated in the beautiful and idyllic medieval piazza of Gerace were Cole and Leigh. Cole was focused on an image of Massimo that had hung in his memory for a week, next to another indelible image: Jude. They had just been joined by Nick the Greek, who, having watched the awful news unfold, had come to help in the search for Jude. He had always known that the Australians were more than just reunited travellers; their bond was too strong.

The men had just returned from another round of cave searching. Leigh was certain they had been inside each and every cave at least three or four times. But he would continue searching until Cole chose to go home.

Cole's BlackBerry Bold rang and was ignored, as was the accepted practice since the *Commissario* had gone back to Naples. The pesky ringtone continued chirping, until Leigh gave in and took the call.

He walked into the centre of the piazza as he listened, and looked down onto the coastline six kilometres below, down to the village of Locri where the famed bronze warriors of Riace had been found, mysterious, serene, in the shallow water, gazing towards the mountains. He could see the faintest signs of flashing red, blue and white

ONE WEEK LATER

emergency lights on the foreshore beyond the brush and the dotted terracotta rooftops.

The caller was brief. Leigh clicked the BlackBerry off, and stood staring at his feet and the weathered white marble blocks that made up the surface of the piazza. He didn't move. Nick had watched the conversation take place and walked over to Leigh. He, too, could see the flashing lights. He turned to look at Leigh, who nodded slowly without a word.

Cole read the play. He reached into his left trouser pocket, into the jeans he had worn for a week. Pulling his fist free, he glanced again at the ecstasy pills still covered in the cave soil. He looked back at the men who had stood so loyally by him and limply tossed the pills onto the well-worn marbled piazza.

Ten minutes later, the three men stepped out from their Alfa Romeo. They walked in single file towards the water's edge and the wall of Calabrian uniforms. Leigh and Nick dropped back to allow Cole lone passage.

He walked slowly and solemnly forward, then stopped and knelt down beside the supine body. Jude looked peaceful, he thought, as he reached his fingertips out to caress the ends of her long blonde hair, which floated gently in the still waters. She was dressed in the same clothes in which she had gone picnicking with Leigh. There was no evidence that she had been in the water for a very long time, and she bore no obvious injuries. Her face was tilted upwards and slightly towards the Aspromonte. In a state that would never fully be understood, she alone held her secret, and a haunting look of serenity.

Mario was standing nearby, his uniform replaced by a suit. The new *Commissario* of the district turned and walked from the scene, taking a few uniforms with him to shield Cole from the media throng. Mario then stepped aside from the flurry, to stand alone for a moment to raise his hand to the sun and look towards his mountain. His past, and his future.

To be continued ...

Acknowledgements

The difference between a writer and a hack is an editor, and I'm blessed with the best. Thanks Alison and Susan.

Colin McLaren
cm@scuttlebuttmedia.net